# HΣX

a novel

Sarah Blackman

FC2

TUSCALOOSA

*P*
*Bla*

FC2 is an imprint of The University of Alabama Press

Inquiries about reproducing material from this work should be addressed to
the University of Alabama Press

Book Design: Publications Unit, Department of English, Illinois State
Univeristy, Director: Steve Halle, Production Assistants: Erica Young,
Caitlin Backus
Cover Design: Lou Robinson
Typeface: Garamond
⊗
The paper on which this book is printed meets the minimum requirements
of American National Standard for Information Sciences—Permanence of
Paper for Printed Library Materials, ANSI Z39.48–1984

Library of Congress Cataloging-in-Publication Data

Names: Blackman, Sarah, 1980- author.
Title: Hex : a novel / Sarah Blackman.
Description: Tuscaloosa, Alabama : FC2, 2016.
Identifiers: LCCN 2015047549 (print) | LCCN 2016000365 (ebook) | ISBN
  9781573660563 (softcover : acid-free paper) | ISBN 9781573668675 ()
Subjects: LCSH: Cherokee Indians--North Carolina, Western--Fiction. |
  Folklore--North Carolina, Western--Fiction. | Tales--North Carolina,
  Western--Fiction. | Storytelling--Fiction. | BISAC: FICTION / General. |
  GSAFD: Fantasy fiction. | Ghost stories.
Classification: LCC PS3602.L325298 H49 2016 (print) | LCC PS3602.
L325298
  (ebook) | DDC 813/.6--dc23
LC record available at http://lccn.loc.gov/2015047549

# HEX

a novel

To Helen and Louisa

To John

# Table of Contents

"I have been loved," she said, "by something strange and it has forgotten me."
—Djuna Barnes


"The Future has an ancient heart."
—Carlo Levi

# HEX

a novel

## The Before

I HAVE KNOWN Thingy since before we were born. This is not hyperbole. The womb is patterns of light and heat. Rose light, black light; a wave of heat that is the sun or a heating pad shifting as the mother rolls in bed. The fetus doesn't know the mother's body because it doesn't yet know its own body, but it knows light and heat and Thingy was like a searchlight beaming from the guntower. She was intermittent, penetrating. As her mother turned to face mine, she beamed to me through the old walls of her father's house and the walls built around those originals, over the gullies of her father's orchard and up the increasing hill, past the stone border which somebody's great-grandfather (not

1

mine) had stacked and through the flapping sheets and sodden jeans of my mother's clothesline to my mother, stretching with her hands on the small of her back, clothespins clipped to the hem of her dress. My mother stooped over the basket and rose with a paisley patterned sheet, a garland of my father's dripping boxer shorts to hang like Christmas lights along the line.

In my neonatal life, Thingy was a dazzling code: Darkness, Brilliance, Darkness, Brilliance. This could also be described as solitude and awareness. At first I was alone, a pulse, the convulsive absorption of nutrient and oxygen. Then there was another, something that came from Outside, which contained within its shape—like mine, our bodies unconsciously mimicking each other's tuck and slow gillessness—an awareness of Outside and thus, inversely, an awareness of Inside, of Self, of Me. It is to Thingy, who did nothing but latch to her mother's womb and stick around, that I owe what has been described as my almost supernatural composure. It is also to Thingy that I owe my greed.

And now, as if by accident, I have begun my story. There will be consequences to this telling. Perhaps to me, more likely to Ingrid the Second who even now, asleep in the basket tucked in the corner next to my table, kicks a prescient leg as if warning me away. She is so new she still can slip effortlessly into the no-space of before; she is effortlessly alone. She yawns and I can see the jutting berms from which, in a few months time, her teeth will erupt. Surely it is a mother's heart that wishes them sharp—fish-killing teeth cut to strip the fine bones. She yawns again, fisting a hand near her mouth, her palate receding in pale ridges like the gullet of a minute whale. She is enormous in her infancy, her fingernails so sharp I have to keep her hands snapped inside terry-cloth mittens or she will scratch her cheeks open. She is growing and growing. Every day she appreciably grows.

The men are on the porch—one as always talking and the other present only in the slow creak of his chair. The sun slips past the edge of the tallest ridge, another early dusk. Soon, Ingrid the Second's father will come into the room, as he does, to marvel over her basket and Jacob will lean in the doorway watching me; I will get up and begin again the work of being a woman in this strict house. But for now the table before me is strewn with papers and the light from the lamp I've switched on mellows the mountain shadows that begin with the dusk to wick through my window. A bee, disoriented, attracted by the flowered dash of my curtains, beats herself against the glass. Her body makes a tiny sound, a patter that reflects nothing of the terrible bruising she must feel and when she finally reels away, stuttering back to the hives, Ingrid the Second relaxes a tension I hadn't recognized and lets loose a trilling, liquid fart as if she had struggled along with the bee, battering the panes of an inexplicably hindering world.

From the porch the men are seeing the last of the day flash out exuberant in the summer ridges, but from my window it is already dark—our yard filled with shadow, the henhouse quiet, the hives settling by the creek, the forest pressing closer, testing its borders. I hear the screen door creak, Ingrid's father's voice draw closer. "But you agree it's a philosophical problem," he is saying to Jacob, "not a social one, not a practical one. A problem of misplaced will." Jacob's answer isn't audible, but I hear his particular footsteps coming down the hall and in these last moments, seconds as he rounds the corner, I begin, I begin, I begin.

~

This is my story. I am sorry for nothing. Should Thingy appear now, tapping on the window, I would say, "Dear Love: Remember, now you are nameless, but I am still here."

"I am here," I would say, "and my name is Alice Small."

# The Dragon's Tale

My mother was the daughter of a family of some small renown; my father was infamous. They were raised in adjacent towns, but where we are from that may as well have been different kingdoms—the geography of the mountains is jealous and indifferent to the human need for a hive. So the story of their meeting is like a fairy tale in which there is a King and a Queen, a Princess, a Knight, a Dragon. I used to tell it to my brother Luke in quiet hours when Thingy was away at her flute lesson or her tap-dancing class—her tap-dancing costume was a red tulle skirt and a black leotard armored with sequins; I coveted it and picked sequins from its hem at every opportunity—but it was never clear, even to me, which of my family members filled which roles.

My mother, I have been told, was a good student, pretty in her way with long brown hair that was slick at the tips from her habit of sucking it as she read. She had very small teeth, some sharp, which were spaced far apart from each other. When she smiled she gave the impression of jumble and roominess all at once. This made her self-conscious, as it might any girl, so she rarely smiled, or when she did she raised a hand to her mouth as if her smile were a private thing, self-referential and treasured.

It might have been that mannerism that so attracted my father. Or it might have been her hair-sucking habit, her tendency to keep place in her book with a hawk's feather, or the way her skirt slipped up over her round knees. It might simply have been the fact that my father, then as now, is a roving cock, as helpless to contain himself as he is to constrain the desires of the many women who see him as a once-in-a-lifetime lay. The kind of fuck they will learn from and bring home to their husbands as a gift to the marriage.

However it came about, my mother and my father met.

My mother's father owned the longest running business in the town of Elevation: the Taut County Feed & Seed which he had inherited from his father who had founded it with his father as a dam to stem the tide of money flowing out of the mountains and down into the Piedmont where, every spring, mountain farmers were forced to make the winding trek to buy their seeds and supplies for the short growing season up in our old, thin-soiled hills. The Feed Store began as a typical farmer's co-op selling sweet alfalfa hay, turnip and beet seed, various equipments, cracked corn for the hens, sorghum grain, lengths of calico cloth, calipers and rolls of cattle wire, post-hole diggers, crackers and hunks of waxy cheese, multiple poisons, dark bulbs for the ladies to bury in rings around the well.

By the time my grandfather inherited the store the times had begun to change, if not the mountains. For one thing, there weren't as many farmers around. These had been old families— the McClountrys, the Rourkes, the Talberschmidts—who had washed up in the ports of South Carolina and found the low country too stagnant and bloated for their tastes. I imagine them as evolutionary tangents, covered with a coarse, russet hair and many-jointed, spidering their way up into the hills where they found some semblance of the lands they had left. For the McClountrys and Rourkes perhaps it was the air, thin and sinewy; for the Talberschmidts perhaps the fauna—squirrels like those in the vast Bavarian forests, boars truffeling the loam, black bears as beetle-eyed and innocent as the witch's many victims transformed from boys and girls into ignorant, powerful brutes.

In my grandfather's time, there was also less water. Some of the creeks had dried up entirely, leaving what Thingy and I recognized as roads from the other world—smooth-rocked paths with high banks twisting up the ridge. Others had thinned to a trickle, hemmed with a thick yellow foam which Rosellen's breeding pugs snapped at when it piled at the edge of their run and Thingy's mother warned us never to touch, and if we did touch to wash our hands instantly, and never, in any event, to put our hands into our mouths, and to come inside anyway, it was getting dark, the both of us she supposed if it wasn't time already for me to go home.

The foam and the waterlessness and the way the skunks and possums and raccoons came up to trashcans during the day and rooted there, grunting in the backs of their throats, were a product of the modern mining concerns which moved into our mountains in the eighties. This was after the old concerns had guttered through the ancient rock beds, leaving some mountains almost honeycombed by caverns and tunnels; sinkholes green and fathomless with their unnatural birth then abandonment. In short, along with their greed and hope, their foolishness, their luck, leaving behind the opportunity for magic.

As for our town, prosaic Elevation with its synchronic roads—Top Road and High Street and even an Up-Side which meanders a little way along the flint ridge above the high school before dead-ending into the quarry—it behaves as if everyone who ever lived there mumbled the answers to a census all at once. *Where do you live?* Up. *Where are you going?* Up. *Where did you come from?* And so on...

The old concerns were memorialized in sepia-toned photographs on the walls of the Feed Store. These were pictures of men—singular at first with their pick-axes and thick leather boots, then groups, then committees, then coal-faced working parties in Dickies, the foreman smoking a cigarette, the piping of their machinery glinting in the frosty light behind them. Aunt Thalia once said these photographs were not history, but nostalgia. At the time, still mired in my pupae form—I think of myself then as featureless, my true self a shifting gather of shape taking place behind a veil—I had never heard the term. The way she intoned the word made me think of the way my father said 'management,' or Rosellen, then only my father's friend, said 'ladies' rotary,' so I asked for a definition from the Nina, one of the three girls my father employed to tend the house in the years before Rosellen became my father's wife.

The other was the Pinta, a sad amalgam of her parent's genetics, and the third the Sainte Maria, dark and fast and scornful, a furious shadow stitching the edges of our childhood. Their real names were Nina, Pauline, Marie, easy targets for Thingy and I who had nicknames for everyone in almost every occasion. They were just three girls, at first in high school and later not in high school but still hanging around as so many girls in Elevation did, working cheap jobs, going on cheap dates, everything about them provisional and spare.

First they all three worked for my Aunt Thalia, running the register at the store or running dishes from the kitchen she had tar-papered onto the side of the building, down the long corridor and into the high windowed back room which my great-grandfather had built as a tack room, my grandfather used for storage, and Thalia, always a restless innovator, had reimagined as a dining room serving up blue plate specials in shifting dust-gilded light. Later, with my mother gone and my brother clearly incapable of improvement, the girls formed a shifting phalanx of wholly unqualified home caregivers: preparing meals for Luke and I, scrubbing us down in the tub, bunking at night in a cot at the foot of Luke's bed because he could not be left alone, not even in his sleep, for fear of the damage he might inflict on himself.

Of all of them, the Nina was the most approachable, and when I had questions Thingy and I could not work out the answer to between us, I went to her. In this particular instance, she seemed hardly to be aware I was there and went on scooping coins out of their individual wooden slots in the Feed Store's antique register and sifting them through her fingers, keeping a tally on a stenograph tablet as she counted. Thalia kept the register polished to a high shine and its many long-levered buttons seemed to reach out toward the Nina's face like the spines of some loving but poisonous animal. The Nina could only have been about nineteen at the time, her face lengthening into a caustic horsiness accentuated by her stiffly teased bangs and the generally dusty color of her hair. I stood at her side looking up at her as the coins spilled from her fingers and back into the drawers.

"Nostalgia," I repeated for the third time, resisting the urge to slip my hand between hers and the drawer and snatch nickels out of the air. "Aunt Thalia said it and I don't know what it means."

"Stop whining," said the Nina without looking at me. She closed her eyes as if catching up with something in her head and referred back to the steno pad, moving her lips as she counted. "It means knowing better, but thinking you can make a profit," she finally said and then fluttered a hand in front of my face. "Go away now, Alice," she said. "You're a pest."

At the time, overheated and dirty inside the hot-dog casing of my brother's used down jacket, I was disappointed in this answer. First of all, I knew I was a pest. I could feel my pestiness, my mean-toothed smallness, in all my actions. Secondly, I have always resisted riddles. *I am taken from a mine and shut up in a wooden case…I go around and around the wood and do not enter…I live in a golden house with no doors or windows…Scarcely was my father in the world before I could be found sitting on the roof…*I don't want there to be answers to their litany; certainly not ones as simple as lead, as bark, as egg, fire, smoke. If there is an answer, I want it to be me: Alice Small dug from a mountain burrow, skimming the undergrowth, locked in a golden bower, escaping up the chimney.

I wouldn't leave the Nina's side and sat instead on a vegetable crate beside the counter scuffing black streaks into the floor with my cheap rubber soles and counting out loud in random order. From my vantage, I could see the back wall, those framed photographs hanging at dusty angles, and across the hallway into the kitchen. The Pinta was there, bowed over the deep stainless steel sinks with a pad of matted steel wool in one hand. So was the Sainte Maria, who was supposed to be at our house but had been called in by Thalia to help with a particularly busy lunch crowd.

Where was Luke? He must have been in the store somewhere. He couldn't be left at home alone, and there was no one else to sit with him. My father was working. At that time of year he was probably on the crew charged with clearing and leveling land in anticipation of the summer pool installation season; or perhaps, the timing is right, finally tearing down the town bandstand whose rotting, bunting-draped pillars had framed everything from church revivals to the annual grade-school food pyramid pageant (Thingy was a lemon, firm and resplendent; I was a shoulder of lamb).

Minus my father and Thingy, who was undoubtedly at one of her many extracurricular accomplishments, everyone in the world who knew me was in that building. I have interrogated my memory, but I still can't find Luke in it. Not a noise from him or a dark corner where we might have parked his chair out of the way of both the girls and the customers, pulled a blanket over his shoulders and let him sleep, or stare, whichever.

If I ask my memory in some other way, I still return the same basic results. The smells: old wood, floor polish, bacon fat and the synthetic flower scent the Nina wore mixed with the warm fug of her feet inside her pantyhose. The sounds: the regular clunk of metal against wood, the hiss of pressurized water hitting the sides of the sink, rasp of dishes, clitter-clat of the

Sainte Maria's guava-pink kitten heels, which she was wearing with two sets of ankle socks, as she trotted up the hall with loaded plates, trotted down the hall with empty ones.

Further away, I could hear the hum and grumble of the diners and the soaring tones of my Aunt Thalia, her voice carrying like a bell that had been hammered flat on one side. Every luncheon, no matter how many or how few customers there were, she made it her practice to go from table to table catching up. Rosellen would have called this a sound business tactic. "Butter them up," I can hear her saying, "No one's more likely to spend some money than a man who thinks you give a shit about his mother's corns." Thalia was an equal opportunity judge. She reacted to the news that a neighbor had committed some obvious farming gaff—raising pigs on the side of a notoriously flood-prone branch, or planting tobacco too many years in the same plot—with the same tone of incredulous superiority as she would the news that his child had been born with a brain tumor, his house struck by lightning and burned to the ground. For her, there was no such thing as luck—only planning, only work. She understood opposition, but had no time for pity. The girls, even the Sainte Maria, were terrified of her.

When Jacob and I were first married we lived with Thalia in the house on Newfound Mountain where she and my mother grew up. It was only for a short while, four months during which we three battered around the house like dazzled moths. Or, I suppose that's what it felt like at the time. So many years have passed since then and it is possible I am remembering the gustiness of that time, the sense of being individually pulled toward something only to find we had, all three, simultaneously ended up in the kitchen staring at each other over the empty expanse of the butcher block table, in light of the events which came after. Which makes the image of Thalia as a moth—a great white moth with scarlet dots at the tips of her wings, false eyes rising in peacock fringes from her antenna—a terrible sort of joke given what came next. I might as well tell you now, Ingrid: it was death by fire.

I don't think I'm spoiling the suspense. Surely, by whatever age you come to read this manuscript you'll have already heard the story of your Great-Aunt Thalia. No matter how gently we tried to expunge her, there are clunky artifacts left all over the house. Just this morning, you in my arms, both of us in white and the white pine boards of the stairs airy under my feet in the cool, clear light, I came across Jacob in the hall turning a pair of Thalia's work boots over in his hands. He'd fished them out of the cedar chest we use to store things that can't be left behind. Some of my mother's schoolbooks are in there. One of Thingy's raincoats, primrose pink with a wide, soft belt and used tissue still wadded stiff in the pockets.

Jacob knocked the boots together. A little sift of red dirt drifted down from their treads and Jacob brushed it into a wide seam in the floor. Then he tucked the boots under his arm and strode into the dining room and through that into the kitchen and so out the back door. We hadn't yet seen each other that morning and, as he passed us at the foot of the stairs, Jacob pressed your head into my chest and held it there, his hand square and economical over your ear. He grazed the back of my nightgown with the other hand, not touching, just ruffling the cloth. He and I are not moths but a man and a woman who have known each other for a long time now and have learned how to share a space. Whether or not we could have come to this understanding if Thalia had stayed in the house—her house, after all, her boots and stairs and butcher block and sideboard decorated with a frieze of humming bees—is a part of the timeline we have not had to consider. Closed to us forever. Consumed by flames.

Later in the day I came out to feed the chickens and saw Thalia's boots jutting from staves on either end of the garden, laces undone and tongues flapping. To scare the birds, I suppose. What else would find a pair of boots so dreadful that, even empty, they would frighten them away?

Aunt Thalia came down the hallway toward the kitchen. She was a tall, square woman, packed with meat and muscle the way an ox or a cow is packed, not fat so much as filled. Her hair had gone white at a very young age and she wore it long, white as rope woven from a horse's tail. If she had been born only slightly earlier in the century, she would have come kicking at the hem of a boiled green wool skirt and rattling a ring of keys at her stout, matronly waist. As it was, she came wearing jeans, a man's leather belt buckled high over the unflattering pouch the pants made of her underbelly, a thin red T-shirt she had picked up somewhere which strained across her breasts so the swooping white script stretched and warped like a reflection seen in the blade of a saw. *The Lucky Bunny Bar and Grill*, the shirt said. I still remember; it was one of her favorites.

Someone came in the front door of the shop, letting a gust of chill air in with them, and crossed heavily behind me to the trowels and gardening forks, but the noise seemed far away. Even the Nina's counting, the Sainte Maria's little jog as she maneuvered past Thalia, careful not to touch her or brush up against any of her clothes, seemed to dim and retreat. Thalia's head was bowed, her arms canted behind her at an awkward angle like wings about to downbeat into flight. She was fixing

her hair, concentrating on the action her hands were taking beyond her sight, and had not yet seen me. For a long moment I
watched my aunt as she stood bisected in the shaft of light that
drifted down the hallway, her head in darkness, her hair falling
one panel at a time across her hot, square face.

It must be understood: I was a motherless child. I always
had been. I didn't know how to yearn or mourn, how to soften
my face so it could be filled with whatever the person I faced
had to offer. Thingy could tilt her head and peep until whatever
it was she wanted was offered to her of the adult's own accord.
She was marvelous at letting people believe they were giving her
a gift rather than fulfilling a demand. I, however, was a clumsy,
blatting thing: the kind of child who will stand at the refreshment table all through the magic act and the pony rides eating
and eating, stuffing herself past the point of illness because she
is incapable of understanding that all this will come again.

I imagine I was disgusting. Thalia certainly looked disgusted
when she finally looked up and saw me there. Slowly she stuck
the pin between her lips, the last twist of hair tumbling to her
waist with a shifting whisper. We stayed like that for a while,
regarding each other. I hunched on the crate so my belly pressed
against my thighs, craned my neck. My posture was awkward
and abject. Thalia stood, pins bristling her lips, hands on her
hips, hair crackling around her as if offering advice. Then she
decided something and beckoned me over to her side.

"I'm not asking you, Alice," she said when I hesitated. She
turned away from me without waiting for a response and began
to rummage in the pockets of the flannel shirt hanging from a
peg on the wall.

I crossed the hall reluctantly. Thalia, still without turning
back to me, reached out and hooked my shirt collar. Her fingers

where they rubbed against my neck were so rough it was almost as if the skin had curled up into scales and she smelled like the split-pea soup and ham hock she had tasted and retasted as it simmered on the stove.

"You keep forgetting we're related," Thalia said, finding what she was looking for and bending forward slightly to peer into my face. This close to her I could see the sweat beaded under her eyes and at her brow line. Her hair was damp at her temples and droplets of sweat hung in the fine blond hairs above her upper lip.

"You forget we share blood and that that means something," Thalia said, shaking my collar slightly. "There's really no excuse for it. Give me your hand." By this point, I was in a trance created by her smell, her odd clanging voice, the precise detail of her sweat, her color, her waxy complexion and the hectic blots of red that rose high in each cheek. She had to reach down and unfurl my fingers for me in order to drop whatever she had pulled out of her shirt pocket into the palm of my hand. Then, she rose to her full height, which seemed even more geological than normal. I could hear the Nina finish her count and bang shut the register drawer behind me. In the dining room, a man raised his voice as if shouting after the Sainte Maria's retreating back and said, "With extra gravy, please. Make sure. I don't want it dry."

"Look at it," Thalia said. "We haven't got all day."

At first it seemed to me that what Thalia had put in my hand was nothing more remarkable or interesting than a ball of wax. It was red, pliant; the sort of wax that covered the round white cheese the Pinta put into my lunch sacks and which Thingy and I often used as casts to compare the growing discrepancy between our bite marks. For once, I was the winner here. I had my mother's teeth, small but even, and though the problem would soon be corrected by braces, Thingy's mouth was rapidly filling with an off-kilter snaggle of which she seemed very proud. I brought the ball up to my nose and sniffed at it carefully, keeping my eyes on Aunt Thalia's face. The ball still smelled like cheese, probably even the same brand, and I shrugged and dug my thumbnail into the wax, disappointed.

"Go on, you stupid girl," Thalia said, looking over her shoulder toward the dining room where the Sainte Maria could be heard repeating an order. "Do I have to spell out everything? Open it."

Obediently, but with no great expectations, I dug my thumbnail deeper into the ball, prising it with my other nails until it suddenly split and fell into almost even halves. Nestled inside a cavity in the wax was a nasty thing. It was like a broken tooth, the shape bulbing into a jagged crown with two long roots forking downward. It was deep maroon in color and when I jiggled the ball I could see it wasn't quite a solid, but rather something like jelly. It seemed to be oozing, a slick of tea-colored liquid coated the wax where it had rested, and it was bound at the top and bottom by what was surely just a thread, though one the same dead white color as Thalia's hair. It smelled as well, a sharp copper tang that reminded me both of blood and the smoke from my father's soldering iron. I reached to touch it and Thalia tapped my fingers away and fit the other half of the ball carefully back onto its seam.

"It's a root," she said, "a rare one. One of these days, I'll show you how to find it for yourself, but until then pick one of these pockets." She gestured to the wall in front of me. A couple of Thalia's extra shirts hung there, a black, deep-pocketed kitchen apron, Luke's new parka (evidence! he was there after all, behind me somewhere in the long gray building) and the coats the Nina, the Pinta and the Sainte Maria had shrugged off and hung, each on her particular knob, at the beginning of their shifts. Somehow I knew it was the latter three to which Thalia was referring.

"Go on," Thalia said again, "It's okay." It was not okay, that was something a deep, shifting part of me unequivocally knew, but before I could stop myself—without wanting to stop myself, with a wild glee like one gets from breaking a window—I shot out my hand and dropped the tiny ball in the pocket of the Sainte Maria's tatty fake leopard fur coat.

"So," said Thalia, nodding, laying her heavy hand on my shoulder. "That's the kind of girl you are, is it? I can't say I'm too surprised, though I might not have made the same decision."

Thalia bent down again, swooping very close to my face as if she wanted to kiss me. "Still," she said, scanning me from chin to forehead and back again, each time managing to avoid looking into my eyes, "now at least you know what you are, don't you, Alice?"

"No," I said, "I don't," but it was a lie. It was clear to me something had changed. I felt flushed all over, an ache in my armpits and at my groin as if I suddenly had a fever. In the back of my throat I could feel a hot plug as if something in my body had surfaced and was bobbing just behind my teeth. I felt as if I was still touching the tiny ball of wax where it caught in the lint of the Santa Maria's pocket, or could feel without touching it's dead, plastic surface, could sense somehow the particular, nasty quiver of the root.

"Mmm-hmm," said Thalia. She straightened up and backed away. Just then the Nina came into the hallway and yanked me back by the arm.

"I'm so sorry, Ms. Lutrell," she said, her voice high. "I was doing the cash drawer. Is she bothering you?"

"Yes," said my aunt. "Yes, she is," to which the Nina responded by giving me a hard shake and pulling me back into the darkening store. A storm was blowing in, the clouds tinted green as they streamed past the windows. Thalia stood in the hallway a moment longer, twisting the last sheet of her hair up with slow, thoughtful motions, and watched us. Her niece and her shopkeep. Two sullen girls surrounded by relics for sale from another century, ugly and stooped in the sudden dottering glare of lightning over the mountain. She paused after the last pin, patting the top of her bun reflexively, and smiled before turning into the kitchen already shouting at the Pinta for letting the soup bubble over onto the stove.

I don't remember what happened the rest of that day. I suppose the Sainte Maria gathered Luke and I up as soon as the lunch shift was over and took us home. She probably packed the kitchen leftovers into Styrofoam take-home boxes, as the girls often did at the end of the week when my father hadn't yet given them money for groceries. At home, around our kitchen table, she fed us the gritty soup and fatty ham, cutting Luke's meat into small bites while a cigarette burned in the ashtray next to her. Later that evening, just before the Pinta came on to take the night shift, she gave us both our baths and, as was her habit even though she was the one who ran the washcloth over my body and wrung it out over my head, shut the door to my bedroom quietly behind me to give me privacy as I changed.

Probably, the Sainte Maria took her jacket home with her that night and hung it in her own front hallway. The ball was so small and her pockets so cluttered with thread and coins and stones and all the usual detritus of a girl with busy hands that I doubt she even noticed the thing was there until much later when she may have drawn it out, examined it with brief curiosity and tossed it away. One more inexplicable object that had been drawn to her. One more tiny satellite at orbit around her fickle moon.

I still don't quite know what the object meant, but I know that I marked her and I know that Thalia—moth white, moth red—watched and made note of the marking. That I was a child is no excuse. A child can smell smoke on the wind, after all. Even today, with so few people left in the world who can do me any harm, I am cold when I think of Thalia's smile, mean as a cut, opening across her face.

# Queen Of The Tie-Snakes

But wait… I've confused myself. I began intending to write about my mother—little Alice Luttrell, who grew up on a mountain and should have stayed there—and ended up at Thalia. I can't say I'm too surprised. If Thalia was anything, she was an omega. A stocky vanishing point standing spraddle-legged in heavy brown boots. It is Thalia who I miss the way I imagine a daughter might miss her mother: with a mixture of melancholy, indignation and relief. My own mother is harder to quantify.

What is more, in between where I began and where I find myself now, several days have come and gone. It was a rainy spring, Ingrid—your first—and the season has passed into a rainy summer. Our house is high on the southern slope of the mountain, parallel to a gap where millions of years ago some geologic schism thrust one fold of rock deeper into the mantle and levered another to crooked angles above the valley. It leaves us exposed, which is to say when a storm rolls up from the south it finds the house unprotected on its bald and levels us.

When you are older, Ingrid, you will be able to stand with me on the creek bank and watch the storm come. The house will be behind us, its windows catching the sunlight and flashing it back as if they were shields, and before us: the creek, swift and busy, the lower field frosted with bluet and the edge of the forest where the solomon seal and jack-in-the-pulpit grow. Then there will be nothing but trees, miles and miles of them rolling variously green up and down the sides of the ridges. And the storm, of course. Always the same storm coming back around. You'll find it feels a little like being on a boat. We here, the family, with our hens and bees, our piles of wood and stone, all together hanging as if tossed from the crest of an enormous wave. Frozen in the whistling space between the foam and the green depths, watching the ocean come rushing up.

I have laid you on a quilt on the floor where you can see the birds as they squabble at the feeder, but you are unusually intolerant, thrusting your arms and legs into the air and grunting in the way you do just before you lose all patience and begin to cry. A spell of bad weather unsettles everyone. It brings the men into the house, brings us all too close together for comfort. Daniel claims to be fond of this.

"Nature's vacation," he says gaily, leaning back in his chair with his hands laced behind his head. The perfect conscientious picture of a man at ease, but he is faking it. I can tell by the way he watches Jacob as he paces the rooms, pausing to consult the windows as if he feels the evidence of his hearing—rain pounding the tin roof, roaring in the gutters, tocking the windowsills with the hollow rap of a geologist's hammer—cannot be wholly trusted. When the men are in the house there is very little time left for anything else. There are the usual meals to prepare and serve and then the cleaning up to do. The usual chores: beating the rugs, changing the linens, washing the laundry, darning or mending or cutting clothing into strips, blacking the belly of the coal-black stove…all made infinitely more tedious by the presence of an audience.

When the storm comes and stays to swell the creek in its banks and devil the hens until they are uniformly beleaguered and peevish, I get up at night and creep down the hallways on the hard edges of my feet just to remember myself as I am without someone watching. Sometimes, if I am very tired, I do this in my nightclothes: a moth-white woman haunting the halls of her cold house. More often I get up from whichever bed I have lain down in and re-dress in a dark corner of the room. Then I walk about the house like a fairy tale child who has gone to sleep in the familiar world and woken up in its mirror twin—the dolls and jacks, cups and boots and brushes, needles and pearls that surround her all the more sinister for their insistence that nothing has changed.

Thingy's father, Mr. Clawson, had a collection of steins in his basement entertainment room. He arranged them seasonally in the niches behind his half-bar with the two mahogany vinyl-padded bar stools which always squeaked when we came down the stairs as if a party of somber drinkers, already elbow-deep in their beers, were turning to observe us, not particularly impressed. The steins were lidded and fanciful. Some were ceramic, some pewter. There was even a wooden one, the belly lined with lead, a motif of berry-laded vines massing up its sides; one stein even glass, soldered into panels, the glass old and wavering toward its bottom, the lid tinted an optimistic pink. Do I need to say how much I loved them? They were forbidden; they were jealously tended. Sometimes Thingy would take them from their niches and we would consider them closely. Thingy insisted on holding them. I constrained myself to reaching out one finger to mark the dust in the pursed mouth of a rosebud or brush a cobweb from the brim of the mountaineer's cap. Sometimes, I fit my thumb into the groove at the top of a handle and pressed the lid slowly open and shut.

The mountaineer stein was a particular favorite of Mr. Clawson's. This was another ceramic mug, the base thick and imprinted with the name of its Swiss manufacturer. The lid was shaped like a mountain top—austere and alpine, its glacial peak bearing no resemblance to our own worn, tree-furred ridges—and the handle was an oversized, rosy-cheeked, loden-capped yodeler, lips puckered, head flung back, pheasant feather unfurling brilliantly down his spine. It was a beautiful, foolish thing. Mr. Clawson was proud of it.

"Purchased from a store on Mount Blanc," he told Thingy and I as we sat uneasily on the barstools. He was drinking clear liquor from a tiny glass into which he would sometimes allow us to dip the tips of our tongues. "Little place, untouched by time, the glacier melt turning a water wheel outside." Mr. Clawson considered the stein ruminatively, turning it to its best advantage. "It made a little scooping noise. That's the only way to describe it. That water wheel I mean, and the glacier water like milk, I mean milky like what is that liquor? Ouzo? The one the Greeks drink. Right away I knew I had to have it, and what's the name for a glacial valley, Ingrid? Morass, that's right."

Then us alone, Thingy with the stein cradled in her lap, her corduroy skirt pulled over her knees to form a sling for it, and I with my rough finger pressing the hinge that would make the mountain open and the mountaineer's head tip back still further, unperturbed, whistling now in idiot surprise to see the wall of rock suspended above his face. But of course it never fell. The mountain opened and shut, hollow, disgorging no treasures. When one day we filled it with water from the bar sink and each took prim, sacrosanct sips, the only prophecy the stein reflected was the sad fate of a spider, washed from her web, drowning peevishly in the water's dusty ripples. "Yodelehee-hoo," I instructed Thingy, but she was listening to the sound of her mother's footsteps in the kitchen above our heads and she would only titter. "Hee Hoo, Hee Hoo," she said while clapping the lid of the stein roughly shut.

In the other real world that was going on all around us it wasn't as simple as clapping the top of the mountain back on, but this was the general idea. The new mining concerns understood the pace of the century better than the old loners. Certainly, better than the gaunt, blackened pickmen with their company issued work pants and their 1930's collectivism who were so saturated with coal dust that when cut they bled first black and only later a reluctant red. What I'm trying to explain is how it was to be a child then. Thingy and I can be imagined in any number of topical scenarios—picture the legwarmers and Thingy's flaxen perm—and that would be true, but what we were also like was two small, densely furred creatures crouched in a burrow, listening to the sound of a huge, inexplicable purpose going on over our heads. We grew up. Time can't really be stopped; only paused, vibrating along its edges like a bee trapped in a glass jar.

The new mining concerns drove through mountain towns in phalanxes of white vans, pick-ups and belching diesel trucks. When they came to a mountain that seemed likely they arranged the ranks of eager machines and sheered the top of the mountain off. Then they went to work rooting out what they found there: copper and lead, zinc, gold, silver, olivine and feldspar, mica, quartz, emerald and kyanite, apatite, tourmaline, saltpeter, marble, slate, quartz and porcelain clay, beryl, amethyst, ruby and sapphire, limestone and even uranium, innocuous and deadly.

When I was a child, the days of discovery seemed to have ended. Off came the mountaintop, out came the treasure, dumped with the fill dirt for later sorting. It was business, progress. What the mining concerns really wanted were the iron and the coal. Jacob tells me that some mountains still show to the south or east their ancient faces thick with deadfalls, but from the north or west they reveal themselves to be hollowed entirely. A mask. Scooped so only their expressions remain.

When they were finished, to tidy things up I suppose, the mining concerns gathered all that had been sorted and discarded, all that was left, and tumbled it back into the mountain's empty core. Imagine that: bears and panthers, long needle pine, the massy trunks of tulip poplar, eagles, moss, river trout, old leather shoes, gold panning plates, brick foundations, lakes, bones and older bones, wood burning stoves, hickory ghosts, balding tires, skins, fish-rib hooks, boulders, flint arrow heads, generational beds of bluebells, church spires, snakes, chicken wire, sulfur-bellied newts all jumbled together, slick with muck. And their voices…a torrent of voices, unintelligible, meaningless as the shadow of the mountain top crests over their pit, as the lid claps shut.

These were not our mountains, Ingrid. This happened further up the chain, and what rimmed the edges of the creek beds was just an echo. When the mining trucks came through Elevation—traveling north, skirting the parklands, heading upstream—Thingy and I would stand on the corner and wave. Sometimes we clasped each other's hands and held them up over our heads and the men in the trucks and vans waved to us. They were mostly young, hair held back in practical fashion from their eyes with blue bandanas. Thingy and I thought they were handsome, and we looked winsomely after the trucks though we were too old to chase them as some of the boys in the neighborhood did. Later, we lingered in the hollow heart of Mrs. Clawson's forsythia bush and gloated over our future. Thingy would marry the one sitting high in the cab of the Bobcat and I would marry the man driving the truck. We never saw them again, or if we did we didn't recognize them. The next week or month there would be a new batch winding through. Thingy would marry the man who blew her a kiss from the jostling cab window; I, she chose for me, the one in the bed of the pick-up truck, eating a banana, blinking the wind out of his eyes.

Maybe she was right. I've never asked Jacob and I doubt he would remember. Did you see two girls? One silver blond, hair like a spent dandelion drifting up from her head; one small, ill-favored, looking behind her to the window in the ranch house that was always left open to the street? Did you see me? I would have to say.

But back to the story at hand: Alice and Dax and how they met. Really, I have no idea.

There wasn't much left of my mother in the house I grew up in. A photo of her holding my brother Luke just after he was born. The color is super saturated. My mother's hair looks like varnish, a slick cherry, and her T-shirt is almost ultraviolet. She is very young and she holds her baby like she might a book, away from her body. She is not smiling and Luke is already looking nowhere in particular. They are standing together in the driveway of the house I would be born into, pocked brick, the azalea beside the front door blooming so white in the oversaturated corner it has lost all definition.

It seems like a lethargic photo, perhaps one that confirms a general suspicion about our poverty or emotional sloth. The azalea appears to stalk my mother and her son, a ravenous void descending, and to get this angle my father must have stood in the steep road where often the logging trucks would pop their brakes only at the bend and squeal in barely contained slides down to the sand ramp 100 feet past our drive. That was Top Road, named because it went on all the way to the top of the mountain, and that was Alice, named because her older sister Thalia had already taken their mother's name and she was born a little more free.

Other than this photo, which I keep tucked as a place mark inside various books, there was little in my childhood to remember my mother by. A set of garish plates, turquoise glaze patterned with elephants outlined in rose. Each elephant gripped the tail of the one before so they went around and around the inner face of the plate, around and around the yellow corn, the sliced hot dog, the smear of ketchup. As a young child I understood they were all mother elephants, though there was not a baby among them. As an older child, Rosellen gave them back to Thalia to keep for my adulthood. They were too nice for me now, she said. She said I was the kind of girl who might be inclined to thoughtlessly, willfully, break.

The rest was detritus, much of it anonymous: an egg timer, a red, bell-sleeved wool coat. A clock carved from a slab of wood in which an owl swooped and seemed about to snatch a frozen rabbit, though Thingy and I once plotted its trajectory and concluded that each time it would narrowly miss. And Luke, of course. And me.

Once, Alice Luttrell left her house by the back door, but not before packing a little red backpack with a hunk of bread wrapped in foil, a sweating piece of white cheese, a yellow thermos filled to the brim with coffee. She also packed a book—any old thing, *Reader's Digest Condensed* about a mountaineer and his Sherpa, his yak, his perilous victory—and left the door unlatched. The house, which was spare but grand, sat alone at the head of a bald on the mountainside. From behind her now, growing further away as the forest pressed together in her wake. By this point, Alice Luttrell was a motherless child as are so many of us. It had happened quite recently, a lingering illness, one of those events that seemed to belong to a previous century. She did not know what to make of her recovery.

"O mother, my mother," she said at night in her bed, the quilt pulled over her head for a tent, the room dark around her, spreading low under the roof beams. No one answered. No star detached itself from the sky and floated through her window, no green light unfurled from between the floorboards. No response but the old wood popping and once the muted thud of an owl landing on the roof. It seemed many stories she had once believed in were false, or at least exaggerated. Alice recognized within herself a sort of relief that this was so. Every day her father went alone from the house to tend to the store, and every day Alice came alone to the house and went out again, with a pack and a book, to a certain clearing she knew of around the side of the mountain.

Here is Alice and her red backpack. And here is Alice with her small meal, unfolding the tinfoil, unscrewing the mug.

Alice with her book at the boulder she uses for her table. The girl is so still two titmice flutter into a nearby puddle and scoop water onto their wings. The foil catches the sunlight and attracts a crow which lands breasty in the near grass and examines her over the top of its heavy beak. The girl is so still the rock under the mountain yearns for her, reaches toward her, caresses the sole of her little white shoe.

But what is this? A girl alone in the forest? So many place settings at which she could be joined and so little left of her meal. The book's pages turn steadily, hawk's feather ruffling in the index. The sun, too, beginning to turn. Time failing her as time will always fail her. Shadows stretching their long legs out from the forest. What is the use of a book? Alice was trying to remember. What is the use of an empty space? She was thinking when she heard an unusual noise.

You know, let's not overdo it. Alice was a curious girl and the noise was an attractive one. It sounded like suffering, but of a small sort. An animal suffering which can be comforted or, at the last extremity, humanely exterminated by a brave girl with nature in mind. A wise girl who knows the pressing impetus all nature has toward death—red in tooth, the saying goes, displaying its beautiful ruby red claws. In other words, a very young girl.

In any event, she followed the noise, her book forgotten, feather blown away, and found at the base of the rock a hole, perfectly round, very deep, such as the one a snake might make. Needless to say, down she went.

~

After a long and varied time, much travail, some confusion, some tears, Alice came to large lake in the world that was under her world at the other end of the very deep hole. In the center of that lake was an island, tiered like a pyramid of petit fours and as variously colored. It rose to a jeweled height above the lake's still, black waters, ascending in steps which sucked at the light that was in that place as if they were made from slabs of sponge and the light itself a thin, blue milk being sopped. From that island, clearly from the pyramid, clearly from the pinnacle—a murky box barely visible atop the fantasy steps of madder rose, curded lemon, stale, ladyfinger green—continued to come such gentle, sorrowful moans that Alice's heart was mostly wrung from her. She spotted a little boat, folded tight as an oak leaf, bobbing at the edge of a splintered green dock. Without any more thought than that, she was rowing for the further shore.

As Alice drew closer to its source, the sound changed its timber. Now it was reedy and granular—like sand gritting against the sides of a tumbler, like sugar soaking up an egg in the slurry of the whisk. "This whole dream has the sound of a dessert coming together," thought Alice even as she looked for toeholds in the sides of the lowest level, the rose one, its fondant shell crumbling away in her hands to reveal the core which was indeed a cake, though one brittle with age.

Up, Alice went, up and up. She climbed a coralline layer rubbled with candied violets. She climbed a sulfurous layer of frangipane studded here and there with ancient, dolorous pralines. Up Alice went, punching determined fists through layers of gingerbread, red velvet, lemon curd, devil's food.

"In a way," Alice thought, "it's lucky I don't have a sweet tooth." Her paltry meal in the meadow far above was a long time ago and as she climbed the layers grew fresher—an airy tuft of angel's food that was almost appealing, a moist wedge of Lady Baltimore delicately scented with orange instead of mold. She was very hungry. Indeed, Alice had seen all along evidence of the appetites come before her scalloping the edges of the fondant. The climbers, children it seemed by the size of their leavings, had burrowed a series of tunnels that turned past her sight as if the mountaineer himself, pushed past extremity, abandoned by both Sherpa and yak, had used his frozen mitts to fashion a last shelter. In fact, she believed it was getting colder. And wasn't that she saw misted before her the ragged vestments of her breath?

Again she heard the sound, a sob at the end of human anguish, and up Alice climbed to the top of the last level.

Before her stood what she took, with a pang of disappointment, to be a hut of some sort, blear and squat. Then, squinting through the strange air—which had grown thicker as she climbed, milky as glacial water—she determined it was a hive, conical and many-layered. Finally, scrubbing a rind of sugar from her wrists and adjusting the little red backpack on her shoulders, she realized she was looking at a bundt cake: perfectly fluted, dusted on top with a drift of powdered sugar as fine as new-fallen snow.

Alice looked about, but there was nothing else to see. She walked to the edge of the pyramid and looked over. Below her the white air swirled. Here and there, immense firs pierced the cloud layer. The air ebbed around their bristling, dark crowns as if the trees rose from water. As if they and their brethren grew below the waters of the lake that floated still and black in the world underneath the world along the edges of whose own streams Alice had lain to consider the blonde murk of pebble and sand, translucent fry and the nymphs, dark against the dark weeds, lazily extending their jaws.

"A little much," said Alice, but behind her came again the sound—faint now, ragged—and, as there was nowhere left to go, Alice turned and entered the bundt cake through its single arched door.

She found herself in a round room paved with closely laid slabs of slate. The walls were waxy, fashioned of ascending cells that rose above her head to a much greater height than seemed possible from the outside. In the middle of the room a sullen fire and beyond the fire—how to describe it?...a cane chair upon which coiled the largest snake Alice had ever dreamed, and beside the snake a roiling shape, a ball, so hard to see as its parts lifted and seethed, separated into here a tail tip, tensile ribs, here a wedge head, eyes glittering, another lifting to rap the first below the chin—a battle then? A slow luxury?...the dry shift of their scales rubbing, the cream bellies and white throats turned to the firelight, and then again the moan—so low it is now just a whisper—and again the compacting shift, here a tail tip, there the arch of a foot, a wet mouth, a rolling eye, the head of a man.

"Hello, Alice," said the Queen of the Tie-Snakes, for it was she, "What a long time we've waited to have you here."

"You have?" said Alice. She edged around the fire and stood just out of reach of the Queen's whiptail. "How did you know it was me?"

"And because you have been brave," said the Queen of the Tie-Snakes, who was not listening, "and we reward bravery, but also because you have sometimes been cruel, and we reward honesty; because you have said the right incantations and sang the right songs, eaten the right fruits and drank the right waters; because, in short, you have done all the things a girl should do if she wants to survive in an unexpected world, we reward you with your choice of one of our alters." The Queen bowed her head and gestured with a regal sweep of her tail to the edges of the room.

"I don't think I understand," said Alice, looking around her. The room was hemmed with a wide array of junk. There were pop-bead bracelets and telescoping camp cups, plastic spoons that changed color when dipped in cold water, x-ray spectacles, false moustaches, one jelly slipper snapped at the strap. There were decoder rings and rusted slinky coils, an etch-a-sketch blacked in a mad labyrinth of lines, a red whistle, a cantering pony with a frayed, tangled tail. A miniature car. A miniature barn. A miniature cock doodle-dooing from on top of the weather vane. All manner of things, all manner of trash; some it, if she squinted, she might even recognize as once belonging to her. A doll's head, a doll's hand, a doll's dress in yellowed pink sateen matted to the doll's soft body.

"I don't think that's what I came here for," she said.

"Yes," said the Queen of the Tie-Snakes. Her voice was dry and stealthy, the sound of something moving with economy beneath a season of dead leaves. "Anything you want, dear Alice." She thrust forward, uncoiling from her throne, and stretched to impossible tension so her head hovered right beside Alice's own. Her tongue flickered as if in approval of her generosity, her vast, incomparable wealth.

"Ok," said Alice, who saw nothing there she wanted, "I'll take him then," and she pointed to the man in his lover's wreath of snakes. As soon as she said it, Alice felt something within her settle. It was a fleshy weight, like a bullfrog squatting to fill its hole, and she wished for a moment she had chosen the doll's hand—so cunning with its half-moon nails and the hole in the ring finger into which one could insert a gem—or the disheveled pony caught in permanent flight.

"Yes?" said the Queen of the Tie-Snakes, turning to face Alice, her tongue playing unpleasantly about Alice's cheeks, "My newest husband is what you choose?" The Queen returned to her chair, propping her chin on her top coil in consternation. "He owes us a terrible debt, Alice dear. I'm afraid you can't have him for free."

But Alice had not come empty handed. First, she offered the ball of tinfoil—so faceted, so bright at its peaks—but the Queen gestured with great disdain to a drift of just such spheres rolling loose behind her throne. Next, she offered the yellow thermos, still damp with traces of coffee, but the Queen sighed as if bored and some of her husbands who had lifted their heads from the brood-nest to watch made a sound like laughter, high and strange. Finally, Alice pulled the book from her bag—she had almost forgotten it, the story so sharply told, its pictures so brief and unshaded—and laid it before the Queen with little hope. A small sorrow pricked within her for the man who was now only loosely wrapped by the Queen's curious husbands, but who lay so still, limp and exposed on the floor.

"Ah," said the Queen, whispering down to the floor to turn the pages with her chin. "Dear Alice, are you sure?"

"Sure," said Alice, "why not?"

And this offering the Queen accepted with great celebration and mounted at the top of her tallest pile. The book sat open to an illustration of the mountaineer bidding his Sherpa farewell, their hands almost meeting through the tangle of the yak's rank pelt, before turning to face his last fatal ascent. Around them the mountain's permanent clouds were sketched in childish puffs. Under their feet the mountain's rock mounted into a brute vanishing point at the page's far right corner.

'A Brave Parting' the picture was titled, and the Queen and her consorts hissed their delight.

So, Alice came to her prize and took him by the hand. Out they went from the Queen of the Tie-Snakes' castle. Down from the pyramid and over the lake, across the meadow, through the forest, up the passage and out again to the world they had come from whose sky they saw was now burnished gold with the coming evening In the softer shadows where the tree shade touched the viridian stems of clover and vetch the world was cool and deep, plush, inviting. They lay down.

"My name is Alice," said my mother to my father and my father told my mother, "My name is Dax."

What else they said there, I don't know. I imagine many questions were asked as my father, who was a beautiful man, saw my mother who had read about many things, whose eyes were weak behind her glasses, who chewed the side of her finger with small sharp teeth like the petulant teeth of a kitten or a mink. Or maybe there were none—my mother satisfied with her endings, my father satisfied with the feel of her corduroy skirt and the pull of her buttons against their strings. Instead my father gave my mother a ring of keys.

"These are yours," he might have said to her, "and they open all the doors in all my castles."

And what my mother said, his hand at her throat, pinching the ridge of her collarbone...

"You may use all of them, but this one," my father said, sliding a small key off the ring and holding it up so she could see it in the failing light. "This key is the only thing forbidden to you, and if you use it, I will..." my father said, and my mother said... her hand on the small of his back...his hand....his leg...the key

under her tongue, thick, a taste like blood...and then ...when
she swallowed it...the key down her throat, past her breasts and
her heart, the key past her belly and the place where my brother
was being made...lost for awhile...for a long while lost in my
mother...the key...little blue key...forbidden..."I will kill you,"
he said...until finally, one day, she found it again...lost so long
she had forgotten...and used it...a stain like blood unwashable
from her hands...and made me.

# The World Below The World

Yesterday, we all went up the mountain. Sitting at the dinner table two nights before, Daniel said, "I don't understand. Why can't we wait even just two more weeks? The baby's so young still. It's a long trip."

This is how he refers to you, Ingrid, 'the baby.' Not your name, but your condition. I suspect this is how Daniel refers to all people: the lover, the suspect, the witch. It is to say the not-me, or in your case a distancing that means the not-mine. Though of course you are his, as you are mine and Jacob's. That is to say: none of ours.

I wonder if this will change as you get older and begin

to resemble one of your mothers. Then Daniel may say, "my daughter," a different sort of condition. I will always call you by your name.

In any event, we were eating a rabbit Jacob had snared in the forest, the meat comforted by a nest of halved potatoes and soft, steaming carrots, a bowl of barley, a salad, a loaf of seeded bread.

Jacob leaned forward to spear a haunch. This is how he argues: stripping the meat from the bone, cutting it into dark morsels and slipping each bite deliberately into his mouth. Jacob is not a large man, but he is tidily packaged. He moves as if he has considered each grouping of his body—the muscles of his arm, those of his back, the relationship of his ribcage to his spine, of his abdomen to his cock. He knows his impact as he hooks an arm behind the ladder back of his chair, takes a long drink, works the muscles of his jaw.

"It's not as if I'm belying the importance of your traditions," Daniel said. He turned to look at me. The two men sit at the heads of our table, which in its former life used to be the front door of the Feed Store. Despite Jacob's sanding, it is visibly charred at the base where he sits. On wet days, it emits a lingering smoky scent. I sit facing the window. Through it I can see the hen yard and past that to the path we have beaten to the creek, over the creek to the first of our hives. Thingy used to sit across from me facing the mirror that hung there. Through it she could see: the hives, the path, hens, her own self—pale hair darkened to hay, and pressed heavy against her cheeks—the table spread before her and myself. First my face with her own eyes, then the back of my head with the mirror's eyes. In her last few weeks, Thingy had become terribly swollen. In the evenings, when the swelling was worst, she would work off the rings she wore studded about her fingers and set them in a careful line before her plate. There they caught the candlelight and refashioned it. Five gold rings making the light run like boiling honey pouring from a fire-cracked hive...

Daniel said, "What do you think, Alice? You're with the baby more than we are." Both men were looking at me. Jacob chewed. His eyes are so thickly lashed that when he sleeps the lashes curl against his cheeks. His eyes themselves are large, a hazel so high that in some lights they appear yellow, and are set perfectly straight along their axis. If it weren't for the lashes, his eyes would be too impersonal. When I first met Jacob, the lashes made his eyes seem mournful or nostalgic. Later, I realized they are just hidden, like something moving in the fringes of the forest, a shape I can't really see.

Daniel, on the other hand, has very crooked eyes. They reflect himself so well it is as if in each eye there is a smaller version of Daniel, and in each of these Daniels another, even smaller, and so on. There are as many Daniels as there is room beneath each one's skin for another exact, slightly more compressed copy. Perhaps infinite Daniels. A Daniel at the subatomic level staring out at the incomprehensibly vast universe and asking it the same question.

Jacob chewed and I disappeared. This is how I argue; by osmosis, bowing my head and considering the barley which has been scooped hollow on one side by the serving spoon. Next to the bowl was a pot of honey, the first of the spring season's, and next to the honey, a candle rolled from dead wax and pressed in a mold with the same hexagonal pattern as the comb. Then Daniel's hand, covered as is his body with a nimbus of hair so fine he seems to refract the light around him. And then his fork, two pronged; his plate, nearly empty; his wine glass, the red wine pricked with light.... You see how this could go, Ingrid? And I haven't even gotten to the meat...

"Okay, okay," said Daniel, holding up his hands and laughing (the smaller Daniel raising his hands and laughing, and the next beyond that, the next). "You're right. Plus it's been so beautiful lately." He turned to you, propped in your basket where Thingy's plate would have been, and rubbed one fingertip along the bottom of your archless foot. "What do you think about that?" Daniel asked you. "What do you think about going on a trip?"

You answered him, but he didn't hear you. Instead, he lifted his wine glass as he forked his last bite into his mouth. "To Ingrid," Daniel toasted, shifting the rabbit from cheek to cheek.

"Ingrid," I said, lifting my own glass. Jacob swallowed. He rinsed his mouth with wine and laid his fork across his plate, considering me now as in the window behind you the tin roof of the henhouse caught the moonlight and held it there. A silver spark brightening in contrast to the mummifying candlelight. Sharp, but easily subsumed.

And so, the next day we went.

Let me tell you about the journey, which we make twice a year. First, we prepare. The men fill the packs and I get ready to leave the house. Outside the front and back doors, I make a mark in the dirt. Outside the hen house and their yard, I make a ring of crushed eggshells and draw another mark with a length of charred wood from our fire as the chickens cackle and strut for my attention. Outside the spavined tool shed, which in a previous life was used as a sty, I make a mark and many marks around the borders of the vegetable plot—at the corn which comes to my chest and rustles silkily; at the tomato vines sprung tall this year but not well fruited; at the pepper plants, the eggplants, the beds of herbs, the cucumber vines clinging prickly to their trellis of twine; at the gourds; at the tight budded heads of lettuce. In the mud of the creek bed, I mark against flood and at the hives, at Jacob's insistence, I mark and ask contritely—you at my hip, you remember—for them to stay a while longer, to grace us in the meadow we have made for them.

I carry you everywhere on my hip, Ingrid, so you will see the markings in the dirt and remember their shape if not their meaning, but you are restless, I understand, almost giddy in what for you is a new air every morning. You kick and arch away from my body. I put you down and you sit plump and stunned for a moment before reaching to slap at the dust, the garden soil, the scummed pie tins we use to water the hens, the spattered constellations of their shit.

It takes a long time. When we are finished the sun has already gone mean above the tree line, and the birds settled from their dawn cacophony into more practical matters—warning shrieks at the forest line, the catbird whose mate nests in our eves hawing rustily from the peak of the house to the cemetery gate and back again. Jacob is impatient. He sits at the bottom of the porch steps melting the frayed ends of his bootlaces with a lighter.

"All set?" asks Daniel. He is fondling the ears of one of the cats, the male who is sleek as a snake and looks at us suspiciously. I do not make a mark for the cats. They won't let me near them, though they follow Daniel as he works. This one narrows his eyes when he sees us and arches his back slightly for show. He doesn't move from the swath of sunlight where he is squatting and when Daniel gives his head a final rub with the ball of his thumb he rumbles hoarsely with pleasure. Jacob has already shouldered his pack and set off. As we watch, he slashes the head from a Queen Anne's lace with his stick and disappears behind the black locust that marks the head of the trail. Daniel smiles at me and shrugs. He scrubs his hands on the back of his jeans as he rises though here is nothing on his hands he needs to scrub away. Cat hair perhaps, which the cat himself leaves behind in a little gray drift as he slips over the porch railing to keep tabs on us from under the house.

We, on the other hand, are filthy. You in particular, wrapped in the cloth I use to bind you to me when I need my hands so only your head shows, but that smeared with dirt, your fine white hair darkened and matted above your right ear with something I can't identify. I imagine how we look together. The insect drone, which I hear so constantly I don't really hear, brightens and shifts to a higher register. You crow and fling your head forward into my breastbone. I am sweating and the places on my face where I have run my hand as I work feel stiff with salt and grime. I envision my face as I sometimes catch it in passing, reflected in the dining room mirror or blear in the thick glass of our windows: nose beaking out of increasingly exhausted cheeks, the chin too sharp, lines beginning to arc around my mouth like parenthesis.

These are bitter moments for me, before the start of any journey, but Daniel doesn't seem to notice as he shrugs the pack higher onto his shoulders and latches the straps carefully across his chest. Jacob is out of sight, not even a blue patch of his shirt bobbing through the green and gold forest, and you, little beast, jerk, surprised by something I can't see which you mark as it travels in the lee of the henhouse, which makes you jerk again as you follow its progress across the yard until you finally lose it behind the cemetery fence.

"Right-o," says Daniel. He licks his thumb and rubs it on your forehead with the same absentminded gesture he used on the cat. "Alright?" he says to me, but he doesn't touch me and I wish for the few moments I allow myself to wish such things, that I could pull my hair over my face and leave it there.

He goes then, burrowing his fingers into his beard which is new, blonde, beginning to curl. His other arm pumps awkwardly as he mounts the slight slope. We go. Across the loud yard—hens arguing, catbird hawing, insects remarking with tireless scandal, 'she did! she did! she did!'—out of the sun and into the cool crowning of the forest. You pipe thin notes like a song and Daniel calls out ahead of us for Jacob to wait. Just before we crest the ridge and pass out of sight of the house entirely, I turn to look over my shoulder. The yard has begun to settle with us gone. Even the hens are holing up under their hut to escape the direct sun. Golden motes glimmer above the path where we have kicked up dust in our passing and the house itself—grand but spare, porch strutted with simple columns and rising into gables once trimmed green like a living canopy, but now peeling down to the sun-bleached wood—sits as it has always sat, seemingly backward at the head of the bald, facing the mountain.

The male cat has come out from under the porch and hunkers in the grass, scrubbing his face with one paw. As we watch he startles, springing tense to all four feet. He is alert to something only he has heard which he watches as it comes again from behind the house and crosses the yard. Something you greet, seemingly ecstatic, clapping your hands and calling your high song into the suddenly silent air.

~

I will tell it to you as it was told to me.

In the Hall of the Mountain King, there are many families. His peoples are called by many names and come in various forms. Some are well shaped and handsome with long fair hair curling almost to the ground. Some are weak and sandy and live in terror of the wild geese that persecute them relentlessly, killing many of their number. Some of the peoples are water-dwellers and they live in the world like our world but below it. They eat deer and squirrel and wild turkey, never fish, but sometimes a child who confuses them by playing, as children do, at being a deer or a squirrel or a bird. Those they will spit and roast on their fires deep under the river, and though they recognize the mistake as soon as they strip the paper feathers from the child's arms, they will feast on these children with great celebration as they are not a people inclined to waste.

Sometimes, when traveling, a person will come across small tracks in the mud of a creek bed, or in wintertime marked in the snow, as if from a group of children all lost together and merrily wandering. If he follows them, often enough the tracks will lead to an open cave in the cliff face, little more than a dugout slanting back into the sheer cliff wall. There the tracks will disappear as if the whole company—boys and girls, he can see here where they have skipped, here where one has veered off to snap the head from a wildflower, strip a length of birch bark from the tree—has walked straight into the mountain, not one of them missing a step.

Sometimes, people do not return from the mountains at all, or are found many years later wandering deranged through what were once familiar streets. These people never live long back among their neighbors, but while they are there they tell fantastical stories: whole towns hidden in the mountain's caverns, peoples whose bodies have become encrusted with gemstones—rubies winking at the corners of their eyes and amethyst glimmering like scales at the inside of their wrists—who dance around their cold blue fires and send up out of the mountain the eerie squeal of thousands of gemstones rubbing against each other. And the food! Rough rock chalices filled with wine, phosphorescent mushrooms, pale slabs of fish gleaming with butter and cakes so light and crumbly that though they spent all day eating (a single day that was months for those left behind in the foothills) they never once felt satisfied.

And the women! How soft they were under their armament, how pale and fragrant. How (and here their voices drop to whispers) when their legs were parted the tunnel there was shot with silver like a loaded vein of ore spiraling through the rock. How, when the women took them into their mouths, they afterwards spit into a little basin and what rolled there were opals, moonshot and fiery, which the women fashioned into pendants they wore around their necks and wove into their hair.

What could their poor wives do? Here were their husbands back and still in their prime, but after so many years they themselves had withered. These men seemed like strangers. Rough ghosts. They treated them like mothers and the babies they had left behind were now lank teenagers, bewildered and angry, leaning against the doorframes while their young fathers cuddled against the women's sides and confessed.

In the Halls of the Mountain King, the women had birdcages woven of spun gold wire and inside them kept all manner of pretty things: a toad with a muddy stone set into its forehead, a white rat with a man's wet eyes. Song birds fashioned of gold gears and silver wires with diamond-chip hearts twinkling in the machine-work of their chests. Their houses were carved directly into the living rock. Some were simple—a hearth, a low shelf for a bed, the woman sitting cross-legged on it whistling to her little bird who perched on her finger and whirred and tinkled back. Some were as elaborate as mansions with seemingly endless rooms opening back into the rock. Salt caverns and caverns of ice. Rooms hung all about with luxurious furs and a room whose walls were as thin as fascia stretched over a pulsing, purple organ. A room whose walls, when pierced with a knife, yielded a thick well of honey dripping amber to the floor, and in one crowded hall all manner of statuary: fawns and serpents, satyrs and goddesses with struck lapis eyes.

Once there was a young woman who married a man who was blind. This sparked all manner of cruel jokes in the village about the young woman's looks, which were poor, and her prospects, which were few. What the villagers did not know, and wouldn't truly have cared if they did, was that the woman, who had had all her life to live with her weak chin and hooked nose, her small eyes and fat, sagging cheeks, had married for love, not security. Her bridegroom, whose fingers were long and white and sensitive, knew exactly what she looked like and didn't care.

For one year, they were very happy together. They lived in a cottage the young woman's father had left her when he died and ate the vegetables from her garden, the animals she snared in the woods, and the bread her husband turned and oiled with his patient hands. In fall she chopped down trees and split them into firewood, and in the winter she built the fire up until it roared and they sat before it, her hand on her husband's knee while she described to him the ordinary sights of her day and he carved figures from spare stove-lengths, the knife a wicked extension of his thumb. Then, one day in early spring when the lower slopes of the mountains were hazed magenta with blooming redbud trees, she returned home from the forest to find the cottage empty.

"Husband," she called, slinging onto the table a rabbit she had snared and bled, its throat open in a second, wetter mouth, "wait until I tell you what I saw today."

She meant to tell him about the bear she had stumbled across, still drowsy and weak from hibernation. She watched it from behind the safe tangle of a deadfall as it foraged on the forest floor, pried apart a rotten log with great delight and plumped back on its rear like a child as it scooped pawfuls of termites into its mouth. She imagined how her husband would carve the bear as she described it, capture exactly its clownish simplicity and even her little hidden fear, her voyeur's thrill. She sifted through the woodbin for a suitable knot as she called again, "Husband?" into the empty house.

It was no use; her husband was gone.

Though she searched for him for many months, calling over the hills and valleys as they darkened into summer and then blazed with fall fires, calling, her voice thin and cracked, through the still blue winter, she never again saw him or heard his voice and lived her life alone in the cottage they had shared so briefly in what seemed to her another time.

She never remarried and took little notice as over the passing years her body hardened and curled. Her back bent under the weight of her solitary labors until, as she scramble up the rock falls and hopped nimbly over the mountain's streams, she often resembled a beetle, round and hard. Though she never forgot her lost husband, and never passed a day in which she did not take one of his figures down from the mantle and turn it over in her hands, she reached a happiness of sorts. In the evening she sat before her fire and smoked a long clay pipe, the bowl comfortable with use. In the morning she woke under her quilt and heard what noise there was in the world. Birdsong. Snow tamping its hush down the long cut of her valley.

One morning, she woke to a different noise, one she couldn't be sure she recognized. She tumbled from the bed so frantically she tangled the bedclothes about her waist and dragged them trailing behind her as she rushed out of the cottage, her gray hair wild. Often in the mountains, noises are deceptive. What seems near at hand fades into a murmur many ridges over; what seems impossibly distant turns out to be hidden inches away, tucked quietly under a leaf, or shrilling in the damp lee of a stone. But the source of this noise appeared precisely in the place it sounded. The woman stood on the slate doorstep her own grandfather had laid almost three lifetimes ago and stared at her husband, curled naked amongst the wild violets, pale and mewling as piteously as any newborn mammal who finds itself turned out into a world it didn't expect.

He wouldn't tell her exactly where he had been or how he had gotten there. He was very thin and his skin so sensitive that everywhere she touched a red weal came up in the shape of her hand. She sat him before the fire and fitted him with his own clothes which she had kept all these years at the bottom of a trunk. Blue breeches and a soft linen shirt. The green coat she had embroidered all over with knots of climbing roses because he liked the feel of their shape under his fingers. The clothes hung from him as if they had been made for a much larger man. When he moved too suddenly, flailing his hands as he told her his stories, the cloth split, purring along its seams with the exhaustion of its age. Try as she might, he could not be tempted to eat, and she couldn't convince him, though she ran his fingers over and over her face, that it was indeed she, his wife, he was addressing.

He said he was cold, his fingers particularly cold, but when she built the fire up he claimed to be even colder and thrust his hands dangerously close to the flames. When night fell she took him into the bed with her and piled all her quilts high over them. She held onto him, trying to warm his body with her own. He ran his fingers over her back and up her legs. When he seemed not to find what he was looking for, he gripped her harder, digging his nails into her buttocks, scratching her stomach, pinching her breasts. He thrust against her side and when he came his semen spilled across the folds of her stomach and glittered there so strangely that when she held it up into the moonlight coming through the cottage's rough window she was almost unsurprised to find herself holding a handful of diamonds, sharp and coldly shining.

The next day she sat her husband in front of the fire and watched for a long time as he carved strange, amorphous shapes out of a length of beech wood. Then she packed a small sack with some supplies, touched her husband's fingers one more time to her cheeks and set off into the forest. For many days, the old woman traveled. She passed through her familiar lands and she passed out of them. At night she camped on the sides of strange ridges, making her fire under a ledge and watching as its smoke sooted the rock in cryptic figures. In daylight she trudged down into strange valleys—dark fens dripping with hairy creeper—and up again, always climbing higher, her pack slowly lightening on her back as she went through her food and did not bother to gather more.

At last she came to a place where the mountain ended. It was a sheer, rocky clearing, treeless and frosted with short grass. There was no shelter, no food. The wind blew in bullying gusts across the rock face but she did not build a fire or even pull her cloak closer around her neck. The old woman sat and waited. For many days she waited. During the day the sky hung around her like a gray veil, but at night the air cleared and around her a vast canolpy of stars were sprayed like droplets of milk beaded on a bolt of cloth that was so black it was all different colors. Sometimes it seemed to the woman as if another mountain hung above her, an inverted mountain whose peak stretched to touch this cropped peak and which was well covered with trees rustling in a different weather. But this was impossible and when she focused her eyes she found the vision disappeared and around her was the world as it had always been, the sky far away and empty.

After a number of days, there was no way for her to keep count, the old woman opened her eyes to see a rocky spur rising up from the mountain where before had been only the sheer plate of the plain. The rock wall sloped upward until its rising edge disappeared from her sight. Water seeped over its face. The old woman rose unsteadily to her feet and ran her fingers over its rough wall. She followed the leading edge until she came to the mouth of a cave strewn with rubble. Up from the throat of the mountain came a warm breeze, the smell of sulfur, a whirring noise as if of many wings stirring in unsettled sleep.

The old woman paused, mindful of the stories she had heard about the world inside the world, but nothing changed, and as long as she stood there, rocking on her bent, exhausted legs, the breath of the mountain was warm, its smell foul, its sound a shifting flurry. She put her hands in her pockets and found they were empty, so she turned her pockets inside out and walked into the cave surrounded by their wagging tongues.

Down the old woman went, down and down. The walls of the tunnel fluctuated around her, sometimes soaring so far away she could hear her footsteps echoing, sometimes pressing so close she scraped her elbows and shoulders against the rock. Eventually, the walls of the cave opened and she found herself in a hot, round chamber lit with yellow light. All around the chamber were stacked looming heaps of paper, loose nests of paper, tumbling sheets, monoliths collapsing to drift over the floor. Through the air flew sheets of paper that dove and dodged and spun around each other, battened to the roof or walls, heaved off again, some as she watched rearing stricken and fluttering to the floor. From these came the whirring sound which had grown steadily louder as she traveled, and which was now a deafening racket. At the far end of the chamber sat a figure, naked and clearly well fed. Her blonde hair fell over her breasts like shoddy curtains whisked provisionally across the stage and the old woman realized that this was the Oracle she had set out to find.

"What do you say?" asked the Oracle, who had not once looked up. She batted at a flock of darting stationary, dug around in a heap of crumpled, lavender-scented notes. "I have almost no time to give."

"Say it now," the Oracle said, "if in fact you have a tongue to speak."

But the old woman was struck dumb and could not make a sound. When she reached up to her mouth to see what was the problem, she found her tongue *was* gone—whether from lack of use or some other reason—and her mouth itself seemed a rank black cave, her breath a warm fug and the only noise that came from her throat a sort of whirring so soft it faded to a buzz in the cacophony of the chamber. The old woman was chagrined and stood with her hand in her empty mouth. She had come all this way, endured so steadily the long years of her life, but did not really know what she would have asked: What's next? Perhaps, what now? What happens?

Soon the Oracle forgot her entirely, she was so busy, so far behind, and the old woman stood in a corner of the chamber for so long that the paper piled up against her legs and over her knees. Finally, the paper came up to her old, round head, which, in such poor light, looked as black and bare as a beetle, and there it threatened to bury her. All this time the Oracle sifted and heaved, muttered and scratched. The countless sheets of paper rose and blew around her in a loving funnel, smothering her yellow hair.

At the end of this story, the old woman had stood still so long, had been so quiet and so buried, that when she came to herself again she realized she had been transformed. She had become a beetle and a fine, big one at that. With no small wonder, the old woman who was now a beetle spread her new wings and buzzed heavily into the air. She circled the head of the Oracle three times and when she had done that, she bumbled back up the long cavern and into the light of day.

In no time at all, the old woman who was now a beetle flew the journey that had taken her so long on foot, and came again to the little cottage her grandfather had built in the bald on the side of her familiar mountain. There she found everything as she had left it. The shoots still poked their blind snouts from the soil; the violets still shivered in their bloom. Smoke rose from the cottage chimney in curls like skeins of unraveled wool and all the doors and windows were shuttered and locked, just as they were when she had gone.

"Zzzz" buzzed the old woman, "zzzz zz zzzz," by which she meant, "I have not come so far to be stopped by a lock."

Soon she found she was so small she could slip in between the door and its hasp and thus make her way back into her home. There she saw her little bed and her chair, the table at which she had eaten all her meals and the black pots and pans in which she had cooked them. She saw her winter boots slumping shiftless in the hall and the sprays of bittersweet hanging like tiny persimmons over the door. It was all just as it had always been and the old woman who was now a beetle flew around her rooms, her wings working furiously, and exclaimed in great delight at the simple beauty of her previous life.

Then, winging around the corner, she came upon her husband sitting before the fire. He was as gaunt and pale as when she had left, his fingers as callused and clumsy. He tweezed the wood as if he gripped it with pinchers, and the knife in his other hand skipped and stumbled. When the old woman saw this she was overcome with sorrow. She landed on her husband's shoulder and called to him in her new buzzing voice. She rubbed her clever legs together and trundled the dear ball of her body over his lapel and onto the cool shaft of his neck, but it was no use. She was too small and he was too lost in the shape he felt turning out of the knot, the sweep of the knife's awkward rhythm. Finally, the old woman who was now a beetle began to weep and in her distraction crawled up her husband's neck and into his ear where she lodged herself behind the sharp bone of his jaw. There she stayed, buzzing to him what she had read scrawled across the Oracle's papers—all of it out of order, fragmented, strange—and if you don't believe me that there was no resolution after such a long journey and so many miracles, that so much has happened to her, one person in a world of so many, all I can say is they are both still there, just as I have described them.

You can go and visit them. See for yourself.

# The Oracle

It is mid afternoon by the time our own journey ends. It is a crisp, clear day and we are high enough that the trees have thinned. The sky has moved far away, as light and clean as a sheet snapped high over the bed, drifting slowly down. We aren't on a ridge, but rather on a slope of the mountain and there is no view. We might as well be surrounded by more versions of this—identical, hexagonal scenes of these massy pines and mounting rock slopes, this moss greening a thick verge by the water's edge and that bare stone crumbling into the mountain like a toothless mouth. That Jacob hunched over a tent of pine needles, blowing the fire to life and that Daniel craning his neck to see sky between the shifting tops of the trees. Of course, this Alice putting bread and hunks of cold, greasy rabbit on our tin camp plates and that Ingrid, loosed finally from the confines of the sling, levering herself onto her side with one stiff leg.

It's a pretty picture, actually. It comforts me to believe there may not be only one of me responsible for all my actions, though I know better. This is a singular place. I found it alone, have come here mostly alone and sense it still knows me first. Its awareness is an old one, cold and suspicious. As far as this place is concerned, the others—minus you, dear Ingrid—may as well be stray dogs run up the mountain from the distant garbage-strewn fringes of the town and paused here to piss on the bushes and snap at their yellow mange before ranging on. Lean and vicious and temporary.

The clearing is made by two streams wending down the mountainside. The first is why Daniel believes we have come. For most of its length, it is a creek, cold and thin, but here, due to a little bevel in the granite of the slope, the water is thrown back on itself and has churned a deep channel where it masses before slipping over the edge and tumbling in a shining rope 100 feet or so to rejoin the course of its bed. The result is a pool where the water is so restless nothing that needs shelter can live. The water is sharp and clean and the bottom of the pool is visible at all its depths: the rock licked smooth, the water plants standing like a miniature forest drowned along with all its own streams and caves and dogs and men.

The second stream is poisoned. It is not really a stream at all, but seepage leaking from the ruin of a collapsed mine wall. Somewhere far above us is the original shaft, perhaps now relaxed into a half-healed scar. It's possible all that is left of the shaft is a slope of rubble and broken beams grown over with beech saplings and tangles of blackberry vine, but I don't think so.

A carpenter bee will bore a perfectly round circle into dead wood and from there will tunnel relentlessly, carting the sawdust out in pale jodhpurs on his back legs, until he has fashioned a straight hallway a foot or more long, at the end of which he installs his queen. I imagine the miner's tunnel is something like this at first. It goes straight into the mountain, the rock tapped back, the thready vein of gold or silver or iron ore patiently trammeled through all its whimsical halts and flushes. But then, I imagine, something happens and a kind of madness ensues. It isn't long before the miner is blasting—tamped explosions shuddering the mountain's flanks—and the tunnels branch off, craze wildly, turn in on themselves.

I have never seen the miner's camp, but I know it is like this because of what has been left behind. Carpenter bees form colonies, each black female armed with a painful sting. Eventually the males, who are single-minded and industrious, will tunnel their homes hollow and the whole structure—a log, a shed, a house—falls in on itself. It is like this with the mine, although the bees move on and I suspect were I to look at the end of one of the tunnels I would find the real bones of a real man jumbled dry under his rotting clothes.

Regardless, the mine tunnels collapsed. Downslope from the mine's original diggings, we see the result as the mountain leans into itself and finds only still, black air. Here also are the poisons that were bound in the rock: acids and hard mineral leeching, natural toxins loosed and mixed with the chemicals the miner used to smelt the ore. They have seeped into the ground water that streams down the mountain's sides and formed their own little gully where they leak from the lip of the cave and collect in a second pool downhill from the one Daniel bathed his wrists in and used to wet his pretty beard. Here the water is sick, a mineral green that is almost luscious, and it leaves an orange stain on the rock. It smells and nothing will grow around its edges.

The cave is foul, soft and rotting. It is unnatural, an embarrassment. If we think of the place the old woman visited as the home of the Oracle—a round little chamber carved at the end of progress—then this is more like an Orifice, but not a tidy one that could speak or blink, excrete or lengthen and quiver. This cave is an interruption. A wound left open to weep and suck.

I came upon this place as a girl and was so leveled by it I squatted on the loamy ground and peed, my urine soaking into the heavy fabric of my jeans. Even now, my instinct is the same, but I am much older and have mastered those parts of myself that were once strange and wild. Now, I listen, edging closer to the cave's mouth as the wind picks up and sweeps across it. What I hear is broken, senseless, a mad jumble as all the voices of the mountain cross each other, a blatting as of gasses channeled the wrong way through the body. A hideous release. It is the Orifice and I write down every sound, hoping for some recognizable truth.

Sad to say, Ingrid, you are a prop in this scene. I have left you by the fire where Daniel wedges you in the crook of his arm as he sucks the lasts of the rabbit's juices from his fingers. Jacob, squatting between Daniel and the fire pit, shifts his weight to protect you from the heat, but also to shield me from Daniel should he look up. To hide what I am doing which is taking sheets of paper from the manuscript I have stashed in my pack and dipping them one by one in the Orifice's waters.

"Okay," says Daniel, passing you to Jacob who has motioned for you. "Keep the fire up," he says to me, "will you?"

I will. I am good at this, at stoking, at coaxing something higher.

I clear away the luncheon things, scrub out the camp plates with pine straw and toss the last scraps of the rabbit into the fire where they blacken and shrivel. Jacob, with you in his arms, crosses the poisoned stream in one long stride and Daniel follows him, stumbling into a jog, lunging over the water. I can see your head bobbing over Jacob's shoulder. He holds you with a firm, practical air the way a man might hold a loaf of bread still wrapped in its white paper, or a round rock he was planning to transform into part of a wall. Though he's doing nothing wrong—you are calm, your chin resting on his shoulder, your mouth loose and wet—Jacob looks so little like a man holding a baby that he makes Daniel nervous. He trails behind Jacob, lifting his arms to you at each dip or hummock in the ground.

When Jacob reaches the water's edge, Daniel says, "I'll do it. Can I do it? Does it matter which one of us holds her?" and, for once, lifts you out of Jacob's arms without waiting for a reply. Daniel cradles you on your back, too low. This is a mistake: you're cramped, your lungs compressed and you can no longer see the view. You begin to greet and stretch your neck, thrusting your hands in fists out before you. Jacob stands back and looks at me. He nods; my husband, brown and sleek as a mink, just as solitary. It is time to begin.

I first found the manuscript in the bottom of the cedar trunk Thingy kept at the foot of her and Daniel's bed and used to house extra blankets and sweaters. I was clearing up. It was only a few days after she died, in that dark period when you were taken from me and kept in the hospital for observation while Mrs. Clawson perched in the waiting room like a blonde mantis, shocked temporarily sober and brittle with suspicion. Mrs. Clawson is many things, but she is not a fool. I'm sorry to say, Ingrid, she disliked you from the start.

Thingy was keeping the manuscript in a series of biscuit tins, three of them, different sizes and patterns. They were under everything else in the trunk: the pink sateen-trimmed blanket and white and pink jacquard bedspread her mother had chosen for one of her childhood beds, the cable-knit sweaters—in mulberry, goldenrod, chestnut—and the tumble of wool hats, some with poms, some with rainbow ear flaps, all marked by strands of hair that poked like golden wire through the loose weave. As I lifted the first of them, I thought I had found a memento box. I was breathless, you understand, overwhelmed. It had been a strange few days. I felt something was off in me: a lodestone stripped of its magnetism, needle wildly oscillating. The house was empty. Jacob was in town making funeral arrangements and Daniel was in the hospital with Mrs. Clawson who would not speak or look at him. You were there, too: blue as a spacewoman in your plexiglass pod, your eyes bandaged lest they be dazzled by this planet's strange light. I had opened a window and outside I could hear the sounds of summer coming to the mountain. Bird song and ambient rustle of new leaves spreading their palms toward the sky.

If a truck had gone by or someone shouted, a dog barked or a lawnmower chugged into reluctant life, I would have been transported to my own childhood lying on the floor of my bedroom with a book open on my chest, watching the green dapple of the tulip poplar across the ceiling. Waiting for Thingy to come home from her swimming lessons and let herself in the backdoor. Calling to me, "Alice! Alice! Come on. I haven't got all day," as she crossed our kitchen, flip-flops slapping her heels, a trail of water snaking behind her as if she were a selkie or one of those lost children come back from the world underneath our world to rummage in my father's refrigerator for something to eat.

I opened the first box—a winter scene, children skating on a frozen pond ringed by dark, precise firs while in the far distance a doe, exposed!, sprung across a clearing, her white tail lost in the dazzle of the drifts. Instead of treasure, the junk of memory (a resurrection) I found a manuscript; chapters twelve through twenty-one, to be precise. Eventually, I read the whole thing. It was typed (when had she done this? *where* had she done this? there was no typewriter in the house, not even in the clutter of Daniel's study which, you may be sure after this, Jacob thoroughly searched), neatly annotated and close to finished. Thingy, displaying a facility for both subterfuge and psychological theory I had never suspected, had compiled her research, analyzed her data sets, crafted charts and bar codes, carefully codified the experiences of a life I had thought she was merely living. All that remained was to draw her conclusions. She had left notes, hand written on graph paper in her loose cursive, but her final word on the subject had been a question.

*"Given the directly quantifiable development of the motherless child into the fanatical narcissist can Subject A's reaction to the introduction of a proxy-child (female: Subject X) be extrapolated within secure parameters? Does the cultural history of Subject A's titular hive rival (Self) render the data-set too specifically referential? Consult Ellis and Wilson,"* Thingy had written.

Underneath this, in a different pen and dated the day she died—her last word on this, and almost any, subject—she had written, *"If A is the worker who figures Self as the Queen, how will she perceive Subject X? Rival, sister, or child?"*

The other two tins—one red, one green and stamped with a worn, Nordic version of St. Nicholas—contained the rest of the manuscript. The middle and the beginning; I had started with the end.

I found the title page in the green box. *Narcissist Delusion in Collectivist Isolation*, she had called the thing; then a semicolon, *Broken Matrilineage as a Developmental Model for Gender Pathology;* then another semicolon, Thingy never did know when to stop, *Wicked Witches and How They Come to Be(e)*; long dash, *A Case Study.* Underneath all this she had typed: by Ingrid Isolte Clawson, and after her name, in letters that had been traced over many times, etched into the page, Thingy had written: PhD.

So. That is what I was burning, Ingrid, if you would like to know, on the day your father and Jacob introduced you to the mountain.

Thingy's manuscript burned quickly in spite of its dampness. By the time I stirred the last pages into ash—"…indicative of both malevolence and a contradictory desire to please…" I read as the page disintegrated into lacework, spiderweb—the men had already waded out into the pool and thrust you under the water once, twice, three times, the spray which fanned out behind you glittering like gems, or magic seeds, or scales. With my eyes closed, I listened. In my mind, I copied what I heard, what echoed back from the mouth of the cave as the words Thingy had labored over lifted up on the drafts of smoke, drifted unmoored from their meaning.

The water was very cold, the feel of it on skin like crunching an ice cube between one's molars. Understandably, you were screaming by the time the men waded back to shore. Your face, usually so placid, was drawn tight as a knot and your ears, the skin around your flared nostrils and howling mouth, your fingertips and toes and the bobbed plug of your navel were turning a delicate bluish-gray. But I was there, a conscientious minder. I stoked the fire high and bright and soon we had you warm again, swaddled in towels like a grub pinking inside its cocoon. You were calm and I was calm. A wind across the Orifice carried over to us an old lost song about a turkey in the autumn forest, looking for his meal, imagining the sweet gold of the acorn when he finally found what he sought. A knot popped in the fire and a drift of papery ash rode up the spire of the flames.

By the time we came back around the mountain to the house, it was night. The clearing was dark and unremarkable, the hens asleep, the house just a collection of boards and nails fastened together and bid to stay put. You were exhausted and made the transition from darkness to electric light without waking up. I took you upstairs, set you in the bassinet and lay down beside you in Jacob and my bed.

It is easy to imagine a romance in this. Two girls in white—I had changed into my nightgown—asleep under the eaves of the house like dolls filled with wadded cotton. Often Thingy and I would go to bed before the men, both exhausted by Thingy's pregnancy, and this is what I would imagine then, lying in the close dark that is the second floor of any wood-heated house, listening to the drift and pitch of Jacob and Daniel's voices as they crossed the floors below.

Two dolls, silly things, picked for their pretty faces and the engaging lilt of their limp necks. Two dolls, heads too large, bodies sexless blanks ready to be dressed. But then, with the house finally silent and the moon gone round the mountain peak, its crescent a soaring caliper measuring the sky, an eye might open, roll. A finger with a hole in the center just the right size for a stone might stir and lift.

Most nights I went downstairs first and Thingy joined me. We sat in the kitchen, the only light a conical spill from the battered overhead lamp, and ate the leavings of dinner, often the makings for the next night's meal, talking, remembering some things, mutually and silently agreeing to forget others. Being with each other as we had always been and you held between us in your hot chamber, waiting only for the word that would call to you and you alone: awake!

When I awoke, it was much later. Jacob had come to bed and was lying with one arm crossing my stomach, hand limp over my hip. The house was quiet. I was a little worried you would wake up when I got out of bed (you often do, imperious, I might add, as if I owe you some explanation of just what I am about), but you were heavy and still, your white sleeping singlet aglow in the faint light seeping through the window.

In the kitchen, I erased a sign. In the living room and before the front and back doors. At each of the windows, I erased a sign, and at the foot of the stairs, at the end of the long hallway where I paused for a moment to look over the yard, each object in it picked out by starlight against the black swale of the forest. I erased a sign over each of the bedroom lintels and at the bottom of the stair which lead to the attic. Finally, I cracked the door to Daniel's room, paused there to listen for his uninterrupted breath, and slipped inside.

I was almost finished, a sign wiped from under the bed, the door to the closet, the windowsill, when, from the tin roof of the woodshed which joined the wall just below the window, something hurled itself at the glass. It was one of the cats, the female: fat and white and fond of Thingy who used to leave the window open for her at night. She rubbed her wedge head against the glass followed by her body, the flirting tip of her tail. Then she came around again and spat, battered the pane with her paw. Her white face was sharp as a snake's, her eyes slitted. I stumbled backwards and Daniel caught me by the wrist.

"What are you doing?" he said, reasonably enough. He was turning his head back and forth on the pillow the way he might if he had a fever, trying to find a length of cool cloth with his cheek. "What time is it?" but even as he asked he was pulling me back into the bed with him, and even as I answered, something innocuous, some dull tale of drudgery, he was pulling my nightgown over my hips and I was helping him, arcing my back, sliding my haunches up as he moved on top of me and met me, as he looked down at me, his eyes navy blue in the bad light and inside them a smaller Daniel pressing into me, a smaller one inside that. Smaller and smaller until he was so minute he could stop inside that one long shuddering moment and look around.

Afterward, I slept in Daniel's bed. Sometime toward dawn, he surfaced long enough from sleep to ask, "What was at the window?"

"It was her again," I said, staring out into the graying corners of the room. The birds were waking up, starting all over as they did every morning, too brainless to remember where they left off.

"The cat?" he said.

"Yes," I said. "That's what I meant."

# The Daughter's Tale

Once there was a widower who had an only daughter. He was always admonishing her to marry a good hunter, someone who could provide for her and keep her into her old age. This was somewhat ironic because the widower himself, who had been renowned about the county in his younger years for his sharp eye and skill with a knife, had forsaken hunting all together in favor of building cairns out of river rocks in the backyard. He was building a cairn for every animal he had ever killed. As he had lived many long seasons alone with plenty of time on his hands and had all those years a daughter to feed, this meant the backyard was rapidly starting to fill with stones. All the grass had been smothered, the tomato vines crushed.

"But father," said the girl as she stood on the back porch and surveyed the ruin, "I'm too young to marry."

"Nonsense," said her father, taking off a work glove to wipe the sweat from his forehead with the back of his wrist. "Why, when I was your age, I had already outlived two wives and soon would have outlived a third. You're never too young to make a start in the world."

The cairns were often top heavy and had no mortar to hold the individual stones together. No matter where the father and daughter went in the house, at all times of the day or night they heard the sounds of rocks sliding off each other and clunking to the ground. "Goddamnit," the father would say, "there goes another one." Much of his mornings were spent repairing the existing record before he could go on to commemorate something new.

Well, they lived in this way for a long time: the father admonishing, surrounded by rocks; the daughter washing the dishes, swirling her rag around the face of each dish as if it were the face of a human man, a husband she would come to love. Her father's cairns grew more and more elaborate and pressed closer to the house until one day the daughter arose to discover that there were pebbles piled up against the glass at every window and boulders in a dusty jumble blocking the front and back door. Smooth river-stones filled the chimney so that their fireplace had become a rockslide, their foyer a cave-in, their house itself a cave pierced by rays of strange, golden light.

"Dad," said the girl, "what were you thinking?" But her father was building a monument to a flea out of sand and didn't reply.

~

That was the day a suitor finally came for her.

It was her father who answered the door and gave the man he found there a hand as he scrambled down the loose slope of a cairn dedicated to her father's childhood pet, a budgie named Mary. Her father helped him brush off the knees of his pants and retrieved his hat, knocked from his head by the doorframe during his entrance and rolled all the way to the living room where it had come to a rest under the couch.

"Shit," said her father, eyeing the damage to Mary's cairn ruefully. He pulled a pad of paper from his back pocket and added Mary's name to the list of cairns to repair which, while very long, still did not compare to the list of ones yet to be built. "What's your business?" he asked the visitor who was peering around him as if even the dim light of the house hurt his eyes. The man was tall and thin and in need of a haircut. He wore an entirely brown suit with a brown hat to match which he held up before him and turned in his hands as if studying it, darting glances at the father over the bridge of his short, hooked nose.

"Well, sir," said the suitor, for it was he, "I've come to ask for your young woman. Or not quite," he corrected himself, fluttering the hat in the air as if to erase what he had said. "I've come to ask if you would ask her for me. Your daughter, I mean. I want to make her my wife." He had a strange way of talking, winding down through his sentences so they ended on a wheeze. The daughter, who had been in the kitchen this whole time counting the cutlery, a task she assigned for herself once a week, rain or shine, popped her head around the doorframe to look at him. When he saw her he smiled and gave a little wave.

"Hmm," said the father, sizing him up. "You look pretty weedy to me. Only a good hunter can marry my daughter. It's kind of a sticking point."

"Oh, but I'm just that kind," said the suitor.

"Are you sure?" said the father, sounding doubtful.

"I am just that kind," the suitor repeated, bending his knees and bobbing a little as if for emphasis.

"I'll talk to her," the father said. "But don't hold your breath."

After the suitor had left, seeing himself out, the father came into the kitchen and sat down heavily across from his daughter who had reached seventy-five knives and was on to the spoons.

"I suppose you heard that," the father said, pushing his hair back from his forehead. The daughter had noticed recently that her father was starting to look older. While this called up in her unpleasant reminders of her own mortality—and what would she do with him when he was too old to care for himself, too tired to walk down the side of the mountain looking for rocks, too sore to haul them home and fit them into their piles?— it was not a bad look for her father. He was the sort of man who had settled into his features as he aged. He had olive skin, a mobile, soft mouth, deep lines curving on either side of it from the high bones of his cheeks. He had black hair which he wore closely cropped on the sides and longer on top so it hung in a rakish forelock over his forehead. Recently, it had become marked with the same flecks of white as his sparse chest hair which grew in an even T on his chest. He was fit, all that rock-carrying, and in general looked as if he were blazing with the last full light of day—harder and faster and stronger than the indeterminate hours of morning or mid afternoon—that bursts from the ridges of the mountain just before the long, gentle descent into night.

Though she did not often examine the thought, the daughter had always sort of hoped that her husband-to-be, good hunter or not, would resemble her father in some small way. This one did not. He was too thin and looked soft under his suit. His skin was too pale, almost luminous, and instead of her father's almond-shaped, brown eyes, the suitor's eyes were perfectly round and blue, an unnatural shade as if he had dipped his irises in dye and slipped them back into his head still wet. His hair, a tawny sort of yellow, floated up from his head and curled out over his ears like feathers. He was, all together, an unimpressive specimen…but he had seemed kind.

But no one else had called.

"I don't know," said the daughter, polishing a spoon with the hem of her cotton dress. "What do you think?"

Her father looked at her and then he smiled, reached across the table to put his slim, hard fingertips on the back of her hand. "You're a beautiful girl," he said, turning her hand over and tracing the cup of her palm in a way that had always made her shiver. "He said he was a good hunter. I think it's a match."

"Just as you say," said the daughter and so the matter was arranged.

The next day when the suitor came back, the father met him in the front yard between a soapstone cairn for a deer struck on the highway and a teetering slate one for a mouse in a trap, and gave the suitor his daughter's hand. That evening they were wed and went immediately away for a short honeymoon in the Catskills where the suitor had rented a cabin. They went skiing and snowshoeing, ate heavy meals and stayed up talking and drinking wine by the fire. One afternoon they went for a long walk in the forest and came upon a clearing where it was so quiet they could hear each breath as they took it, almost the blood as it whooshed around in their veins.

"This is beautiful," said the wife, taking her husband's gloved hand in hers. The pines were tall and still. Heavy snow drifted against their trunks, cut into ripples by the wind.

"Beautiful," said the husband and he kissed her in his nipping, hesitant way which—she closed her eyes and examined her reaction—she believed she was beginning to learn to like.

At the end of the honeymoon they returned home to her father's house where they were going to live temporarily until they got on their feet. In her absence, her father seemed to have been busier than ever. The gutters were filled with shifting piles of pebbles; the roof was lined with them. On one side of the house, her father had begun to build cairns on top of cairns and so brought the rocks up level to the roof, which they had spilled onto, which they were starting to consume.

"Can you live like this?" the wife asked her husband.

He shrugged, stroking his chin. "It's only for a little while," he said.

The very next morning, the husband said he would go out hunting. He began to gather all the necessary accoutrements: the different scents and whistles, the camouflaged jacket, the bullets, the gun, but before he could finish getting ready, he changed his mind and said he would go fishing instead. An hour or so later, in hip waders and a cap pierced with hooks, he kissed his wife at the door and left, pole slung over his shoulder, bait box dangling from his fist. He was gone the entire day which the wife spent in much the same fashion as she had when she was the daughter.

She did the laundry and then sat on the couch in the living room. She made her father a sandwich and then washed his plate and watched him through a chink she had cleared at the kitchen window as he strode around the backyard with a measuring tape, checking the cairns for unnoticed drift.

In the afternoon, she watched a television program about two elephants who had been sent to a rescue park to live out the last years of their lives and, though they had been separated all that time, recognized each other from their babyhood as the stars of a traveling circus show. In the end, one of the elephants died and the friend went back to the place they had last been together to do things like lean disconsolately against a tree and turn over rocks with the tip of her sensitive trunk. It made the daughter a little weepy, though she had known from the beginning this was how it would end. She turned off the television and read a couple of chapters of a book instead. Soon, she drifted off to sleep on the old plaid couch where she had slept many an afternoon away in her long time in that house, lulled by the sound of her father pounding two rocks together in rhythmic counterpoint to the ticking of the clock which hung above her head.

When she woke up, her husband was home. He had brought only three small fish which she cleaned and scaled and pan-fried in butter, keeping their bones for a soup.

"No luck?" said her father. He pushed his meager portion back and forth on the plate, knife scraping against the china.

"Not today," said her husband, bobbing his head up and down over his fork as if too nervous to take the bite into his mouth.

"Tomorrow will be better, I'm sure," she said.

~

The next day her husband went out again to a different fishing spot at which he claimed to have never had a bad day. "Brook trout as big as your arm!" he said, wheezing. "Their bellies fat and speckled, eyeballs good for soup. You'll see," he said, kissing her at the door. In his excitement he nipped her so sharply that afterwards she checked her lip for blood.

The day passed in much the same way: laundry and dishes, watching and reading. The clock in the living room—a wood block carved with figures of rabbits and a swooping owl her father had picked up somewhere before she was born—broke the hours into minutes, the minutes into seconds, the seconds into even smaller parts that were so quickly gone they had no names.

Finally, her husband came home, but she saw right away he had not been successful. He had a sheepish air about him, pausing in the hallway to bob in the door frame and look in on her where she lay reading on the couch, and he carried the creel slung from his fist as if his prey were very light. In fact, there was almost nothing in it at all: just two worthless spring lizards limp inside a folded dock leaf, their bodies pierced as if he had caught them with a spear.

"What am I supposed to do with these?" the wife asked her husband, holding one of the lizards up by its tail. "My father will never eat a lizard," she said, shaking her head.

"Does he have to know?" said her husband. "Couldn't you bake them into something?"

She was dubious, but she set about making individual pot-pies, rolling the dough out thick, covering the butchered lizards with a kitchen towel as her father came into the house and walked past her, went into the bathroom to wash up for the meal. "What happened, anyway," she asked her husband who was sitting at the kitchen table watching her work. "I thought this place was a sure bet. Brook trout as big as my arm, remember?"

"I know, I know," said her husband, hanging his head. "Everything was going really well, but then a bird came along and scared all the fish. I would have shot it, but I didn't bring my gun."

He looked so mournful, blinking his round eyes at her, his shoulders hunched, that she took pity on him and after the meal, which her father picked at and largely did not eat, the wife pulled her husband into their bedroom and locked the door. In the dim light that filtered through the rocks covering the window, she looked down at her husband's body, at his hand on her breast, at his bony chest rising up to her as he propped himself up on one elbow, and thought, just for a minute, she saw a wash of feathers fluttering at his throat. But this was wrong, of course, and in the middle of the night she looked over at her husband and saw only the face of a man, relaxed in sleep, his brow smooth and unlined.

The next morning, the husband announced he was going hunting today and fetched his gun out of the hall closet. She stood in the doorway and watched him weave around the cairns and walk down the road, his peculiar characteristic gait making him look as if he were edging sideways along a steep drop instead of walking down a perfectly level, freshly paved lane. She leaned against the doorframe, thinking, peeling thin strips of paint away from the wood and dropping them on the stoop.

"Where's he going?" her father said, appearing at her shoulder and making her jump.

"I don't know," the daughter answered. "He said it was a spot he knew about from when he used to go hunting with his dad. When he was a kid."

"Humph," said her father. "Around here? What was his father's name? I would have known him, and I don't think I remember anyone's kid that looked like that."

"I don't know," the wife answered as her husband crested a rise and disappeared from sight. "I've never asked him. He never said."

That day passed in the way of the others, marked only by a restless hunger that kept the father and the daughter on the move through the house, passing each other in the hallways, bumping into each other more than once in the kitchen which was small. Lunch was a sad affair: a wilted celery stick for them both, a handful of raisins, a hard-boiled egg. Her father's face was set, the jawline sharp. He was looking a little brutal, which made her uneasy but also, a little bit, excited. What would happen next? she wondered.

When her husband came home it was late. The sun had long since gone down and she turned on the porch light so he could see to navigate his way around the cairns in the front yard. Her father had gone out.

"Fuck this," he said, rising from the table where he had been sitting in front of an empty plate for an hour, his hands clenched around his silverware. "It's nine o'clock. I'm going out for a beer." He banged around in the hall closet for his coat and the daughter walked out into the yard with him, loitering between the rocks indecisively as her father, hands crammed into his pockets, walked down the road and disappeared over the ridge just as her husband had that morning.

She passed the evening in a dissolute fashion and, by the time she heard the front door open, had already gotten into her nightgown and was brushing out her hair in front of the vanity which had sat in her bedroom since she was a child. She could tell it was her husband and not her father by the sound of his footsteps as he walked down the hall.

"Well," she said as he leaned in the doorway. "What did you get?"

"You look beautiful," her husband said. He looked tired. There were dark circles under his eyes.

"Thanks," she said and, though she knew once again it was slim pickings, she turned out the light and brought him to the bed where the sheets were cool beneath them and the night very long.

The next day she was awakened by her father making a lot of noise in the kitchen. Her husband was already up, already out of the house, and her father had discovered in his absence that all he had brought home the day before were some scraps he had found in a place where another party of hunters had cleaned their kill.

"What is this?" her father shouted, waving a fistful of viscera in her face, loops of intestine dangling almost to the floor. "And this?" he held up the heart, its strange oval tough and impervious. "This is what I am supposed to eat?" he yelled, tossing the heart onto the table where it slid into a candlestick and knocked it over.

"Calm down," the daughter said. "I'll make a gravy." But it was clear something more had to be done.

That night her husband came home empty-handed and the next morning, at her father's urging, the daughter waited until her husband had disappeared over the rise and set off to follow him. He travelled a long way and then, at a spot where the stone wall that bordered the road lay broken, he looked around him and left the track for the forest. At first, the daughter thought she had lost him. She had to duck down behind the stone wall to keep from being seen and when she made it to the spot where he had entered the tree line there was no sign of him. Not a broken branch, not a bobbing leaf; it was as if he had vanished. But, as the daughter pushed her way into the dark, thick forest, she heard someone singing a little song.

It was her husband and he sang:

*Come dance with me and be my love*
*My light in darkness, turtledove*
*Oh come to me, my heart's desire*
*The clearing where I build my fire*

He had a beautiful voice, high and silver at the top of the register, vibrating like a brass bell when he dipped into the lower notes. From behind a tree, the wife caught a glimpse of her husband's blue shirt as he bent and picked a blade of grass, twirled it between his finger and thumb. He sang:

*Against my body slide your hips*
*Against my body move your lips*
*And when it's time for us to part*
*I'll leave you with my beating heart*

He used his fishing pole to hack a path in the forest and she followed it, trying to walk on the sides of her feet as her father had instructed her and so make little noise. The morning had been cool but, in the patches of sunlight that filtered into the forest, it was beginning to warm up. Sweat beaded on her upper lip. She could feel it dampening the hair at the nape of her neck where it rubbed against the collar of her father's coat which she had borrowed because it was warmer than her own. She paused as her husband paused and wiped her face on the shoulder of the jacket. It smelled like her father: a mixture of sweat and sunlight, a musk. Her husband sang:

*So dance with me, my life's embrace*
*And turn to me your lovely face*
*To love you always that I vow*
*If not forever, then for now*

In this fashion they came out of the forest and to the bank of a swift river. The wife ducked behind a blackberry tangle and watched as her husband carefully wedged the tackle box and pole into a niche made by a tree trunk and a mossy boulder and began to strip off his clothes. As he took off each article—jacket, shirt, pants, underwear, socks—he folded them neatly and stacked them in a pile on top of the rock. Finally, he stood naked, still humming to himself, stretched his arms over his head and windmilled them as if warming up for something. She could see his ribs as they descended his back and the archipelago of his vertebra. She felt a little feverish, as if her senses were overly sharp. She could see his skin pucker into gooseflesh as a breeze struck him, the fine golden hairs that downed his lower back and swept over his buttocks, the cracks in the tough skin of his heels. Then her husband turned into an owl and flew out over the river.

She supposed she should have been more surprised. Shocked, even. Instead, she found herself admiring the sweep of his wings as he downbeat to land on a snag of driftwood in the stream and the powerful flex of his claws as he drove them into the wood. He ruffled his feathers and looked around him.

"Uh-gu-ku! hu! hu! u! u!" her husband called.

She said to herself, "I thought I had married a man, but my husband is only an owl." She tried to feel angry. She had been lied to, she and her father both. Yet, as she watched the owl blink its round, blue eyes, she found herself focusing only on the second half of her thought. "My husband is an owl," she whispered and caught her breath.

For a long time her husband stared into the water and she watched him. At last, he swooped down and brought up in his claws a handful of sand from which he picked out a crawfish. He flew to the shore with the crawfish impaled on his talons, shuddering as it died, where he took the form of a man again, dressed carefully, one article at a time, and wrapped the craw-fish in a dock leaf he pulled from a plant near where his wife was hiding. He was still humming his little song as he packed the crawfish in his creel and started for home. The wife followed him.

"And when it's time for us to part," the owl who was her husband sang. They were almost out of the forest. She could see up ahead the place where the light changed as the trees thinned. The wife felt very close to her husband. Something tremendous had been shared between them.

She thought of how hard her husband had to work to hide his owl nature, of how lonely he must be in his lie. He really was a good hunter for an owl, she thought and impulsively she jogged a few steps to close the gap between them, reached out and took her husband's hand.

"I'll give to you my beating heart," the wife sang, finishing the line. Her husband turned to her, his eyes widening in shock. His face fluttered back and forth, shifting from a man's face with its soft lips and sensitive eyebrows to an owl's face: beak agape, eyes huge and gold and totemic.

"Uh-gu-ku! hu! hu! u! u!" her husband cried and she smiled and held out her arms to him.

Believe it or not, there are rules that govern such things. The husband knew them because he was an owl, but the wife had lived a more sheltered life in her father's house. Even as her husband reached out to fold her in his arms (wings) his arms, she felt something happening to her body. Her back bent and then elongated, her arms stiffened, the elbow popping and bending in the wrong direction. There was a wrenching sensation in her pelvis, a stretching sensation in her neck. All over her body she felt a wash of prickling heat and her tongue became thick and heavy in her mouth.

"What?" the wife tried to say, but it came out of her mouth like, "Maa? Maa?" because, to her surprise, she found she had been transformed into a doe.

Her husband flew to a low branch and perched there, bobbing at the new level of her head. She examined herself, lifting her neat, black hooves, turning her head to consider the flirting tip of her soft, white tail. She was a fine creature with a shining coat and strong legs. She could feel the power in her new chest and haunches as she strode up and down the thicket. She could smell the rich underscent of the forest like never before and could interpret it and read its subtle warnings.

"Maa, maa. Maa, maa," she said to her husband in great joy.

He nodded in agreement and sprung from the branch onto her back. And so they went off together deeper into the woods.

~

That evening her father waited in vain for his daughter and her husband to come home. He turned the porch light on to guide them and fell asleep fully clothed on the couch, his boots tightly laced in anticipation of whatever might be required of him. The next night passed in the same fashion and the next.

Finally, the father had to admit to himself that something had happened. He had searched the road and the fishing holes, all the deer and duck blinds and the ruddy meadows where the bucks came in the autumn to stamp. He had gone in and out of the caves in the hillside with a lantern and trod lightly through the underbrush looking for a trail, a stain, any sort of sign, but found nothing. No trace of his daughter. No trace of her husband. It was as if they had risen into the air and now walked in the world above this world where he could not follow them. He didn't know what to do next, and so, for a while, he did nothing.

The father was unused to preparing his own meals and was clumsy in the kitchen. He ate poorly: undercooked scraps, strange combinations of condiment and meat. The father was also unused to providing his own entertainment. In the evenings he sat alone at the kitchen table where, in the past, he had sat with his daughter playing cards or just listening to her sing as he whittled at a stove-length. When she was a child, he had sat there with her and cleaned his knives and sharpened them. When she was a woman, he had watched her bend over her task and admired the simple way her hair caught the light. Now, the father was lonely, and the father was angry. What right? What right did either of them have: to go away from him, not to say goodbye?

Eventually, the last of father's store of dried deer jerky ran out and the very same morning he fried and ate the last of his eggs with the last grainy pat of his butter. It was time to move on and so the father went to the hall closet and assembled his scents and whistles, his camouflaged jacket, his bullets, his gun. He set off into the forest to hunt.

Toward noon, after a frustrated early morning tromping through a land that seemed suddenly emptied of all of its animal denizens, the father took a break to eat a light meal he had packed: a heel of bread, a scrap of cheese, a little thermos filled with coffee. He was sitting in a lean-to he had built with his own two hands many years ago when the daughter's mother was alive and he was barely out of his boyhood. The lean-to faced onto a small meadow which was grown up in starflowers and the bobbing heads of mountain daisies. It was a beautiful day, warm and clear. The father was surprised the lean-to was still there and, as he ate, admired his work which had survived untended all these seasons as the world around it changed.

Suddenly, as the father swallowed his last bite of bread, a doe appeared in the tree line and stepped into the meadow. The father could not believe his luck. He eased his rifle up onto his knee and then to his shoulder as the doe dropped her head to browse in the grass. For a moment, the father watched her through his sights. She was young, graceful. He almost felt guilty for shooting her. But, he thought, he'd build her a fine tall cairn at the peak of the chimney and so, exhilarated, he pulled the trigger and dropped her just as an owl burst from the forest for some reason and flapped into the field. Disoriented, the father supposed, by the sound of the shot and the bright, spring light.

"Uh-gu-ku! hu! hu! u! u!" the owl cried, its voice harsh and wild and familiar, but the father beat it away with his hat as he knelt beside the doe to finish her and take her home.

It had been a good shot, just above the heart, and the doe's chest was rapidly filling with blood. She would die soon, but the father was not an uncompassionate man. He grabbed her by the muzzle and pulled her head back, exposing the long line of her throat which he cut with a business-like slash of his knife. She kicked once and his hands and wrists were bathed in her blood.

But what was this? Just as he cut her, the doe's face flickered for an instant and he seemed to see—hadn't he known all along?—the face of his daughter, her mouth agape, cheeks pale. He looked again, and it was only a deer there below him, but even as the light dwindled from them he recognized some slide of her eyes, some expression, and knew in an instant what he had done.

"Jesus Christ," said the father, the breath knocked out of him. He pressed his hands to the deer's ruptured throat, but it was too late. His daughter was dead.

For a long time, the father knelt in the meadow over her cooling body. The owl stayed too, clinging to a branch of a tree, crying out until his repeated call penetrated the father's concentration and so annoyed him he rose to his feet, raging and throwing rocks, forcing the owl to fly heavily away.

The father returned to the body of the doe that was his daughter and considered the situation. It was tragic to be sure— he pictured her face as a child, her sweet lips, her fat hand clutching his—but he was not a man who believed in waste. After all, life must be taken if another life is to be lived. This, he believed, was the way it had always been So, with his eyes hard and his mouth set, the father took out his sharpest knife and slit the doe who was his daughter as he would have any other deer.

In no time at all, he had gutted her and, hoisting her carcass onto his shoulders, the father carried his daughter out of the woods and back to his home. He dried her meat and lived off of it for a long time, honing his cooking skills to grill tender steaks and drying her flanks to a jerky he cured with his own special rub. For awhile the father kept his daughter's heart in a jar of formaldehyde, for sentimental reasons he supposed. But the seal was imperfect and when the muscle started to rot, fraying in gauzy tendrils that floated to the surface of the jar, the father dumped it out in a creek behind the house and watched as his daughter's heart was washed away.

What happened next hardly matters. The father lived a long life, mostly alone, and died one fine summer morning when the weight of the cairns collapsed the roof and crushed him as he sat at the kitchen table salting his eggs. Where the daughter's viscera had been strewn a spring welled up, cold and fresh. The animals came out of the woods to drink there, often exposing themselves to other hunters who used the father's lean-to for many years to hide themselves as they waited for prey. The owl who had been her husband went deep into the forest where he pined away in grief and love until there was no flesh on any part of his body except for his head. He looked just like the owl he was for the rest of his days and when he called his wild call the young hunters all shivered and looked over their shoulders. They crossed themselves twice and performed other superstitions, but no harm ever came to them.

"Uh-gu-ku! hu! hu! u! u!" the owl called and mothers who were sick of their children crying for attention would say to hear an owl's cry was to hear the sound of your death. They were wrong, it turned out, but no matter. At a certain age, a child will believe anything it is told.

## Bitch And Dog

To the mother nine months can be a very long time. The body becomes gravid, its bloom withering and pulling back from the fruit. The woman's natural focus lowers. If she is a person who is drawn to gaze at the sky, she begins to scan the treetops. If she is the sort of woman who looks a man in the eye when she speaks, she considers his gut, his shins, his choice of shoes. Her perceptions sharpen. She draws new conclusions about the nature of his business with her and she is correct. For some women the nine months are spent in anticipation, for some (my mother) in ratcheting anxiety. I am saying, there are many ways to be pregnant, but there are not very many ways to be born.

~

If left to her own devices, everything around the mother will sing to her: Push Push Push. The teakettle sings it and the weave of the rug. The mother's own muscles and the baby of course, the baby-to-be not yet separate but already filled with volition.

Push Push Push sings the trestle table and the serving platter, the gardening magazine, the creamer cups cut for starter seeds. Push sings the clock, out of tune, and the egg timer, out of tempo.

oh push oh push
it is a tinkling aria spraying out of the faucet.

Puuuush Puuuuush
a dirge gargled by the eggplants which are drowning in the sink.

a PUSH even spared for the mother in the siren song of the ambulance which is wailing up Top Road, though not to her address, and carries in its dutiful belly a jangling array of vials and tinctures, hypodermics and gleaming silver tools which too are humming the little tune. It also carries the EMTs who are singing something different. *Break For Lunch*, perhaps, or *Bright Clean Morning*, or *Acceptable Risk*.

When all goes well the birth song is a tight melody, absorbing and tinged with just the right amount of melancholy. It is the sort of thing the Ladies Rotary would have driven en masse to Atlanta to see and come back secretly abashed by the intellectualism of it all, the lack of whimsy or costume changes.

"But why couldn't the mother have *dressed* a little better?" one of the Ladies might say after a meeting where, let's face it, they've had some wine. "Why couldn't she have worn some makeup, or a hat to give her a little *shade*."

But when left to her own devices, the mother does not wear a hat. She does not wear anything at all. She twists out of her elastic-waisted maternity pants as she feels them soak through, unbuttons her husband's flannel shirt over her breasts and rippling belly because she is hot, unbearably hot, the animal she has always known herself to be writhing on the floor, looking for a little more air, a little more room.

This is how my father found her when he came home that afternoon. He was working construction at the time and had spent the day driving nails at cross-angles into the framework of a house in the foothills that, when finished, would have the same outlandish foyer and faux French-rustic hutch kitchen as the other twenty-seven houses into whose framework he would drive cross-angled nails at more or less even intervals day in and day out until the development was finished. That is to say, off and on at different identical dug-outs in the mountainside for the rest of his life. That is to say, my father was a young man, not long married, who had already become suicidal with boredom.

His only defense was to develop the dubious skill of switching himself off at will. Thus, at work my father was a hammer or a post-hole digger or a line of fuse or a pair of scarred leather gloves. He was a vessel, an emptied one, whose condition depended not on being filled, but on preserving the perfect counterbalance between the weight of his body and the blank, humming static of his mind.

I have always thought of my father at work as something akin to the flipbooks Thingy and I drew as children. My father: 100 tiny pictures of a man driving nails into a board. When the pages were riffled the man would work. Rill them forward and he would drive the nails, rill them backward and he would conjure them free. But when they came to rest as they must eventually do, the illusion was revealed to be nothing more than those 100 tiny, repeated pictures. A man holding a hammer. A man holding a hammer. A man holding a hammer.

This meant when my father was at home, or at least not at work, and turned the humming synapses of his mind back on, he was often all but overwhelmed by the electrical backup, the sheer voltage of the release. When I was born, there was already evidence of my father's double life scattered about the house and property. The basement was littered with abandoned cathodes and stripped wires from his radio period; the ceiling of Luke's room was crowded with hive-like, papier-mâché bundles from his Mardi Gras phase; all the sinks in the house were stained with rings of elderberry, poke and toadflax from his short-lived, home-dying period. I still have a pair of socks my father dyed with the poke.

He gave Thingy a pair of toadflax mittens. These were by far his most successful project. They were wool and could be folded back at the tip and fastened either open or shut by two jolly, oversized buttons stitched to the wristband. My father bought them from the Feed Store at the Spring Discount Sale and let them soak and dry and soak again several times in the dye he prepared from the bushel of fresh flowers he somehow convinced the Pinta to pick for him. The result was a sunny, cheerful color that reminded me of a chick's fluff—mittens that fairly cheeped with optimism—and a yellow stain that ringed the metal lip of the kitchen drain like runnels of undercooked yolk and fooled the Nina, the only one of the girls who could be motivated to do house work, into extra scrubbing every time.

Thingy wore the mittens the next winter, but said they itched, and quickly they became too small. When I cleaned out her drawers in the house—thinking to save them for your future winters, Ingrid—they were nowhere to be found, but I can't believe she would have just thrown them away. Thingy felt about my father the way all women do. I could tell by the way she came across him in the house: he bent over some project at the kitchen table, or coming in the backdoor with welder's goggles pushing his hair into a silky crest above his forehead, and she always seeming to turn the corner, just happening into the room. Sliding out of a shadow and into the shared light while she called some non sequitur over her shoulder to me and laughed as if, no matter what we had just been doing, we were nothing more than simple girls, merry ones, the type who spilled over.

My father started most of these projects in the years after my mother died, but it would be a mistake to think of this tendency in him as a result of his grief. It was more like restlessness. The kind of tense, muscular pacing one sometimes sees in big cats at the circus or zoo—like a panther I saw on a filmstrip at school pacing in the background. While the narrator explained the fragility of her ecosystem, she brushed against the bars of her cage with her side and reached up to swipe at the same steel joist at every pass. Before, after, and most probably during his time with my mother, my father satisfied this urge toward motion with a variety of women he met in bars, on handyman visits, up on the cliffs overlooking the town's quarry where they had gone with their boyfriends to drink and sun. I don't think he meant to be cruel. It was just that they didn't last, or at least the parts of them he needed didn't last: glistening summer hip, raw winter mouth, the abandon in the throat and shoulders that showed him the risk they were taking together.

Once he said to me, "The sooner you figure out what a woman is like, the better off you'll be." We were in the backyard at the time. He was surveying the stone wall, picking up loose stones and either piling them back on top or flipping them over into Mr. Clawson's yard based on a sorting principle clear only to him. He had a half-drunk beer in his hand and another bottle crammed into the back pocket of his jeans which was stretched thin by just such use the way another man's pocket might have been worn by the pressure of his wallet or car keys. I was ambling along after him. It was a sunny day, early autumn. The mountains smelled like burning leaves and cold weather coming and something richer, darker, more subtle. The old trees in Mr. Clawson's orchard bowed under the weight of their hard, green fruit. I loved my father. I was very young.

"What is a woman like?" I said when he didn't continue on his own.

He hitched the bottle out of his pocket and sat down on the wall facing our house. My father was handsome in an exponential way. As a younger man, his face had been hard with the sort of brutal muscularity that only served to make his babyish lips and wide, dark eyes all the more striking. Hallmarks of the invisible wound on his soul, I imagine women like my mother thought. As he had gotten older, however, his face had thinned. His cheeks hollowed, showing off his high cheekbones, and deep, mobile lines had been etched around his lips. His hair, which he wore long and tied in a ponytail at his neck, was flecked with grey at the temples, and his skin was as smooth and soft as chamois with the same supple porelessness. It was hard not to be affected by my father. He expected it. He took it for granted.

Without looking at me, he stretched out an arm and beckoned me into the space at his side. Made just for me, is what he was implying, and as I nestled there, his hard, brown hand cupping my shoulder, I realized that other smell was the scent of him: a spice wafting up from his armpit that smelled like gold and leaf-meal, sun-warmed soil and, somehow, the sea.

"A woman is like a lot of things," said my father. "But mostly she is like the first picture she ever saw of herself where she really thought she looked damn good." He took a swallow of his beer and propped the empty in a chink in the wall. "If you can find that picture and study it, see what she's wearing and how her eyes look and if her mouth is open or closed, you can learn a lot about the kind of person she thinks she is going to be."

He wasn't really talking to me, but I was there and I was listening. "Pass me that bottle, will you, darling?" my father said, and I bent down and got it for him. For a moment, while he twisted it open, my father held me tightly in the circle of his arms, my face pressed against his chest where I could hear his breath and the beat of his heart. I thought about my own picture. Had it been taken yet? Would I recognize it when I saw it?

I was filled with a terrible fear that I would not, that I would go through life with no image of myself—my head tipped at some characteristic angle, light falling across my cheek and my neck—and so I would be lost. And so there would be no marker of my passing.

In the years before Rosellen, my father sometimes brought women over to the house. It was always the more encumbered ones, the married or engaged, and always at odd times of the day. Sometimes in the early morning before school, while the Pinta bided her time before her replacement arrived by dozing at the kitchen window and scraping the char off my breakfast toast into the sink, my father, who I hadn't realized was even up much less gone from the house, would come in the infrequently used front door and lean through the passway into the kitchen. Then he would extend an arm back to the dawn-lit living room—our battered sofa, recliner, fireside knickknacks all looking somber and portentous in the new light—and usher her in, whichever her it was.

"My family," my father might say and the Pinta, who found my father overwhelming, would mottle like an overripe strawberry and sidle into action: toast on the plate, knife in the jam jar, spoon loaded with oatmeal hoisted to my brother's slack, wet lips.

What must we have looked like to her, to whichever her, who had found this man stranded up against some hard place—the hard work, the deep glass. Now here was this whole other romance to be dealt with. The stupid or very young ones cooed at us and tried to pitch in. "What a smart looking girl," they might say about me, or they would sit next to Luke and enunciate their names very clearly to him—Bev-er-LY, a-MAN-da, CAIT-lin— or even pick up the spoon and take over his feeding. This was generally all right with the Pinta who by this point would be all but overcome by my father's presence. She would shuffle down the hall to Luke's bedroom, a sad, soft specter, and return divested of her bashful flannel nightgown to loiter about the brightening living room in varying shades of denim, a red plastic heart or cherry dangling from her ponytail to catch my father's eye.

If the Nina were there that day, however, the ground of the kitchen would not be ceded. Where the woman might lift the spoon, the Nina would brandish a damp kitchen rag to scrub over my brother's lips and chin. Where the woman might look over my shoulder to see what I was reading—I always reading, what else could I do?, a girl child, an ugly one, no mother and a father so lovely he could spin women out of the air like clouds wrapped around a woman-shaped spindle—the Nina would remove a half-loaded plate, clatter a handful of sticky silverware and generally lean, her bony shadow like a bouquet of thistles cast across the table.

Sometimes Thingy spent the night, even on school nights, more and more frequently as her father traveled and no second child came to disrupt her mother's precise domestic management, and was there in the morning cordoning off her breakfast foods: a tablespoon of cottage cheese, a isosceles triangle of dry toast, five dusky blueberries savored individually from the tines of her fork. If my father was taken aback by her presences, he gave no notice of it. It was unclear if he even recognized that Thingy was not, or should not have been, a regular member of his household. When the woman said, "What a beautiful daughter," my father did not correct her. Instead he would nod and smile sorrowfully, absent even as his gaze passed over us and lifted up to the hanging kitchen light and past that to the ivy border my mother had painted in lieu of crown molding at the top of the walls while his big, pop-knuckled hand stroked absently up and down the woman's thigh.

My father's most successful projects were ones in which he could use some of the same skills his body performed so mechanically at his jobs during the day. In our steep back yard, for example, my father had envisioned some kind of mechanical petting zoo. Using scraps from an array of construction sites, he had welded together a junk-heap donkey, a pig, two over-sized chickens and an ambitious and terrifying dragon whose serpentine body, made of oil drums and partially unsprung steel mattress springs, still dives in and out of the slope. Its tail tip is a garden trowel pointing a rusty arrow at Thingy's back door, and its battered coffee-can head—the eyes bicycle reflectors half lidded by snuff tins, the fangs saw blades that jut over the upper lip—rests on the ledge of the kitchen window where it oversaw my dinner for the entire length of my childhood.

"I tell you what," my father would say on the evenings he was home with us. "If you don't want to eat your dinner, you can offer it to the dragon." My father loved this proposition and, despite no evidence for it, never stopped imagining my delight at the prospect. He would prop both elbows on the table, his hands cupped around his mouth as if this were a secret we shared between us. To be kept from Rosellen was the implication, though clearly she could hear us and did not care.

"Give the green beans to the dragon," my father would whisper. "Give him the tater tots, the pot roast, the peas."

There was some talk at this stage of a feeding tube for Luke whose presence was now required at neither family dinner nor the monthly family meeting where Rosellen encouraged us to air our thoughts and express our grievances. "A family is like a business," said Rosellen who had opened and closed a number of small businesses in Elevation and was running a few more out of my father's house. "And a business is like a litter of pups. Every one of those little bastards is going to fetch a price, that's a given. The question is how much are you going to get versus how much are you going to have to put in."

Rosellen delivered these sorts of pronouncements from the back porch, the kitchen door open to air out the grease and cooking heat of dinner and a cigarette burning between her fingers. She did not talk to me, though it was always only me still at the table, but rather to the air around me as if her words were a part of a contiguous landscape, like a waterfall, which I had just happened to stumble across. Rosellen smoked a generic brand of a slender woman's cigarette. Today Ultra Slims they were called, each with a long white filter banded at the top by a pastel lemon stripe.

"Are you saying that a family is like a puppy?" I asked, my battle of wills with the baked chicken breast and crinkle-cut carrots momentarily forgotten. I really did want to know. This was shortly after Rosellen had moved in with us, vacating the studio apartment above the video-rental/tanning-salon which was her latest business venture, but before she and my father were married. A condition of her move was the dog run and heated shelter she had my father build out back and into which she promptly installed the breeding pair of pugs she purchased in anticipation of our yard. She bought the dogs from a breeder in Charleston and they were scrupulously pedigreed. While I'm sure they had elaborate, official names in some registry, with us they were just called Bitch and Dog and they looked almost identical—trim tan bodies at odds with their sloppy faces, glassy black eyes and foul rasping breath.

Bitch was pregnant, very close to whelping. They were not allowed inside, so at least once a day I went out to see them, sticking my fingers through the chicken wire enticingly. When that had no effect, I threw clods of dirt over the fence to wake them from their perpetual wheezing naps in the hollow they dug beneath the little peak-roofed house my father knocked together out of plywood and salvaged asbestos shingles. I wanted to see Bitch's belly, which by now was stretched so taut I imagined I could see the press of individual pups against its surface. I wanted to see Dog mount her which, even with the deed so clearly done, he sometimes did, albeit with a perfunctory distracted air, often pausing to rest his short forelegs on her shoulders and gaze about the yard, past the silted creek and over the stone wall as if the main purpose of this position was to appreciate the altered view.

Bitch did not seem to mind, or even to particularly notice. She was cumbersome and always hungry. She ate clods of dirt, blades of grass down to the ground and then dug up the roots and ate those too. She ate the worms she scratched out of the side of the slope, and, when she could catch them, the dragonflies that whirred through the chicken wire and perched too long on the mesmerizing lip of her metal watering bowl. Bitch also ate my dinners which Rosellen, after some unspecified time, would lift away from me in silence and scrape into a battered mixing bowl with the rest of the table scraps. Thus, in the final weeks of her pregnancy, Bitch ate sesame chicken and meatloaf, ketchup, hardboiled eggs, macaroni and butter, cheddar cheese, egg shells, watermelon rind and tomato soup, carrot and orange peels, celery leaves, meatballs, hamburger buns, hot-dog ends, rice…It was no wonder she wheezed so terribly; no wonder she dragged herself around.

"Because everyone waits for it for so long," I tried again, "or because it makes the dog so uncomfortable?"

Rosellen was still fairly new to me. She was a deviation from Dax's usual routine. For one thing, he didn't bring her to the house before the day she moved in. Rather, he brought Luke and I and for some reason—probably because she happened to be around, probably because she got in the van without asking—Thingy to meet Rosellen for the first time. He also chose to go on a day that the Sainte Maria was on duty.

Most of the businesses Rosellen owned, managed or worked for were located in the Elevation Business Park at the low end of Top Road, just on the other side of the high school. This was in December, a couple of weeks before Christmas, and someone had decorated the light poles in the parking lot as if they were candy canes, their hooked tips already emitting an unwholesome yellow glow in the early dusk. It had snowed the previous week, thawed and then frozen hard. Dirty ridges of snow were packed between the noses of the cars as if each car were a blind baby animal nuzzled up at the teat. Thingy and my boots tamped the snow down into crenulations like the tower of a castle. The Sainte Maria pushed Luke's chair over patches of frozen grit and I helped her lever it up onto the curb and through the door of the pizza parlor where Rosellen was waiting, fresh from her managerial shift at Bounce!, the woman's gym on the other side of the complex, wearing a purple leotard over shiny pink tights and looking at my brother, Thingy and I as if we were a trio of crows that had hopped in from the parking lot. Troublesome, sinister, but not too much bother to push back out with a broom.

Originally, Rosellen came from Florida, a sun-cracked town near the coast that I always imagined in shades of teal and peach as if someone had pressed tape to all of its surfaces and lifted the darker, truer colors away. I don't know what brought her to Elevation. She probably never intended to stay, but then she met my father and certain compromises were settled for on both of their parts. When I met her, Rosellen was in her early forties, five years older than my father, and was beginning to look slightly preserved. Her face was not attractive, and probably never had been—the eyes too close set, cheeks too thin, chin long and square at once which made her head look like a sickle moon—but her body was phenomenal, a showstopper, all of which she displayed to her best advantage even when seated on a wobbly bench at Stromboli's holding a limp wedge of cheese pizza up to her thin, frosted lips. She was already on her second slice, mincing it out of the platter with little mouse-like cries as the cheese burned her fingers, while Thingy and I stared and my father tried to fill the silence.

"So what's new with you, Ingrid," he finally said to Thingy after several conversational gambits had failed. "Is your father back in town?"

He was not. In fact, only the week before Thingy had told me that her father was renting an apartment in Atlanta to be closer to the office where his company organized most of his out-of-country travel. From now on, he would only be home on the weekends, though this was a weekend and I hadn't seen his car in the driveway or heard the pop of gravel under its wheels as he edged it around their mailbox and onto the blind curve of the road. This was a sore subject with Thingy, something my father probably knew. She slatted her eyes dangerously and took an overly large bite of her pizza, filled her mouth with cheese and shrugged as sauce spilled from her lips and pattered onto her paper placemat.

"Jesus," my father said. He hooked his arm over the back of the bench so we could see the torque of his biceps inside his tight, thermal shirt. "Fuck this," he said.

Rosellen chewed and scratched the back of his hand lightly with her long nails. She was still wearing the leotard, but had thrown a short, leopard-print trench coat over it, belted tightly at the waist. The jacket had an architectural neckline that framed her breasts as they strained against the leotard. She wasn't wearing a bra and I could see the outline of her nipples, puckered from the chill coming off the window behind her and my father. As she reached across the table for the shaker of red pepper flakes, I found I could also see down the freckled chasm of her cleavage to a pale little triangle of her sternum. When she caught me looking she actually winked; a slow deliberate shuttering that reminded me of the way alligators I had seen on the nature shows slid a clear lens over their eyes before they submerged into the murky waters of the swamp.

"Nice coat," Rosellen said to the Sainte Maria who, as usual, had worn the faux-fur leopard-print with the matted collar and unraveling hemline as if it were armor, hugging it close over her stomach and breasts all the way to the table where she had shrugged it off and slung it over the back of Luke's chair. Now, she looked up from Luke's plate where she was cutting his pizza into tiny morsels with the attitude of a person who has heard a loud noise and is trying to figure out if it is a misfiring engine or a shot.

"It's cute that we're wearing the same pattern," Rosellen said. She dabbed a spot of red sauce from the corner of her mouth with her napkin, then wet it in her water glass and dabbed the spot again. "I wonder what else we have in common."

There was something wrong with the Sainte Maria's face. It seemed puffy, swollen as if she'd had a tooth removed. Lately too her eyes seemed darker. If it were possible I would have said she had bruised only her eyes and that they were healing very slowly. Perhaps she had a cold, I thought.

"I got it at St. Francis," the Sainte Maria finally said. Her voice was low and husky and she took a sip of her soda. "They always have something like that there," she said. "It's nothing special. It's old."

A truck pulled into the parking spot just outside the window and idled for a moment with its headlights on. The beams spilled around Rosellen and my father's heads and shoulders, falling on the rest of us with a colder light. I felt caught, frozen like an animal in the field when the machine it's been dreaming of suddenly chugs to bright, belching life. But it was just a pizza parlor and we were just some people, loosely affiliated, crowding around a table for our chance at the meal. The guy in the truck turned off the engine and sat a little longer in the dark cab. Rosellen nodded her head, as if to say, 'yes, yes, it is nothing after all'; and the Sainte Maria, her cheeks flushed red, bent over my brother's plate and continued to furiously cut.

From there things developed very quickly. It wasn't long before I was used to watching Rosellen's scythe-like face in profile from my kitchen chair. She exhaled: a thin vapor of smoke appearing between her lips at the last moment, only to be drawn back into her lungs with her next breath. It was almost seven, the light thickening, my dinner cold. Soon, Thingy would trudge up the hill from her house and balance on the stone wall yelling my name until I came out to her. I would ask her what she wanted to do tonight and she would feign indifference, force me to suggest a number of lame alternatives before she would tell me what it was she had planned all along.

When Bitch had her puppies, Rosellen made sure I was there in the garage. She handed me one of my father's old handkerchiefs to rub the blood and amniotic slick off of each of them as they slid out of Bitch's birth canal and showed me how to clear the mucous plugs from their noses and tiny squawling mouths. A few days later when Bitch turned on her litter and devoured every one of them, Rosellen buried them by herself in a corner of the yard and would not let me over to see the glistening tangle of their remains. Thingy and I dug them up—a long enough time later that the pups were largely skeletons, the evidence of their suffering reduced to the slivers of tooth-marked bone—but what I am trying to say is that while Rosellen had no children, and did not ever think of me as a child, she was capable of kindnesses. Subterfuge was something Rosellen understood and respected. As was ambition. As was taking sides.

"No. You know what a family is like?" Rosellen said. She turned to me as if she had reached some new conclusion, but I never did find out because just then my father came in to rummage in the refrigerator for an after dinner snack and slapped Rosellen on the behind in passing.

"Dax," she said, her face breaking open the way it always did when my father touched her. "Alice is here."

"So she is," said my father, and then, as if he had never seen me before, he stood for a moment staring at me. He held the refrigerator door open, chill air pluming out of its lemon light while his eyes traveled over my face and up and down my hunched, spindly body. "I guess that's her, all right," he said. "Old Alice."

"Didn't you get enough to eat?" Rosellen asked. She fetched the ashtray she used in the house out from a cabinet and balanced her cigarette carefully in a notch on its rim. "You can have Alice's dinner if you're still hungry. She's not eating it."

My father ambled over to me and lifted the chicken breast from my plate. He held it up and turned it around, examining it as if trying to decide where to take the first bite, but then just held it pinched between his thumb and forefinger. "You know what, Alice," my father said, pointing at me with the chicken breast which dripped soy sauce on the table. "You're looking a little pale. You should go outside or something. Get a little sun."

I wanted to go outside. I had heard Thingy's back door slam and the sound of her voice as she shouted something to her mother, but sometimes when my father looked at me it was like he was doing a math equation, some kind of cold calculation being rapidly toted as he smiled or tugged on my ear. So, "I want to be pale," I said. "Suntans cause cancer."

"Well feed the dog then," said my father. He tossed the chicken breast back down on my plate where it caromed into the carrots, knocking some of them to the floor, and ushered me across the kitchen, carrying my plate for me and putting it in my hands as I stepped out onto the back porch. Then he shut the door and I heard the snick of the latch as he locked it. It was a dark, heavy, golden evening. Grasshoppers whirred up from the long brown grass and floated down again, not far from where they'd begun. Dog barked at me, short steady yaps that sounded metallic.

I put the plate down and climbed up onto the opposite stair railing where, if I leaned out over the open stairwell, resting my head next to the dragon's, I could see into the kitchen through the window over the sink. My father had caught Rosellen by the wrist and pulled her to him. He said something in her ear and she laughed. Then, he turned her, pressing her against him as if they were dancing and rubbed her back, sliding in small circles down to her buttocks which were still high and firm in the tight black workout pants she wore around the house. She laughed again, a giggle that trailed off into breath as my father suddenly slid his hand in between her legs and dug into her, his thumb strutted against her tailbone, his fingers working into her flesh.

His lips were still moving, but I had no idea what he was saying to her. If he looked up, he would have seen me and the dragon watching him, our faces drained into the same expressions of dumb, featureless greed.

"Alice!" said Thingy, standing on the stone wall, and I went down to her. "What do you want to do tonight?" she said. But I had no suggestions, not even bad ones.

Eventually, Thingy grew tired of waiting. She took the plate out of my hands and flipped the whole thing high over the fence of the dog pen. We watched as the plate separated from its contents: chicken, carrots and china spiraling out like components of an unmoored satellite, each turning with its own specific orbital weight. When the chicken hit the ground Bitch and Dog rushed out from under the doghouse and charged it. Bitch got there first and we watched as she devoured the breast, snuffling the dirt long after she'd finished the last shreds. When she realized there was nothing left, she looked up at us accusingly, her muzzle red with clay.

# Dolores The Duck

If this were a story it would be easier to tell. I am not an inventive woman, Ingrid, just as I was not an inventive child. I like to work with the world as it arrives to me, but I've found that involves a lot of repetitions. In your own life there will be just as many patterns. Some of them I can already identify: the bees, of course, and the color blue, a chicory shade like your and Daniel's eyes, running water, conjoined pairs.

But take, for example, a stranger's life. A perfectly ordinary life lived at some undistinguished point along the timeline. Unanalyzed. Unrecorded. My mother's life. She was born and grew up on the side of a mountain. She climbed the mountain up and down on her way from the school to her home; her home to her father's store or the movie theatre or the park; her home to some other place known only to her where she went to be alone. Her life was understood in a series of more or less cone-shaped journeys. My mother got married and had two children. My mother died, but all the while she must have thought to herself: "I have seen this before, haven't I? This shape, this pattern? Hasn't there been something before this about a dragon or a beetle, about a hole or a little snake uncoiling, testing the air with its tongue?"

Take another stranger. The Sainte-Maria, for example, who appeared and disappeared, appeared again like a needle diving in and out of the cloth. Who knows what she thought to herself as she loped around the town? She came from a large family, many children and many fathers. She was one of the younger ones, one of the only girls, and when she met Dax for the first time— she couldn't have been more than fifteen—I wonder what she recognized in him. Surely not another father. She didn't need one.

I imagine when she met my father, the Sainte Maria felt a stretching like the terrible rending that takes place in a seed as the shoot unfurls, breaks upward. She had felt that before, no doubt, but with my father it must have seemed a better bet. Some vegetative energy she had always suspected she contained—root energy, seed energy, the energy of stasis and dark, compressed places—that now seemed just on the verge of release.

Because the Sainte Maria loved my father. You understand that by now, don't you, Ingrid? And my father, as susceptible as any one of us to patterns, saw a young girl just stepping into the dappled parts of the world: the complicated geometry of a rock fall or a streambed, something that cannot be comprehended by a quick glance, or even solely by the eye. My father saw the Sainte Maria falter and he reached out a hand and he helped her along.

Well. If this were only a story, I could say some things. I could say: The baby is ready to be born and so the baby was born.

I could say: The mother was in pain and so the mother died.

The creek that runs by this house has high, overhanging banks and a sandy bottom where flat river rocks are washed smooth like paving stones. The water is clean, but a hazy goose-green color flecked with mica washed down from the peaks so when I stand in it and look down at my feet I appear to be gilded—a woman caught by a terrible spell and slowly turning to gold.

Of course, no such thing has happened. Our creek is the unremarkable outcome of the water cycle, gravity, geological shifts that channel water in and out of erodible beds. It is a good habitat for newt and minnows, colorful darters and the spring peepers which come down from the forest to leave their eggs bobbing in the lee of stones and snagged flotsam. Deer drink from the creek's banks and once, rising early in the winter to bring in wood for the morning fire, I saw a bobcat squatting in the snow. It froze when it saw me, but when neither of us moved it continued to lap at the water with its broad tongue and when finished sauntered back to the tree line without even a backward glance.

More recently, a flock of mallards have begun to use our creek to mate, nest and raise their young. They are noisy, companionable. Each year when they return, I think I recognize my individual favorites—the male with the crooked neck, the female with the darker beak and shabby tail.

The ducks are wary and, mindful of how far they have to travel and how many different sorts of predators they will meet on the way, I don't try to befriend them. Mallard separate off into breeding pairs and there are almost always more males than females in a mating flock. Frequently, a gang of these unmated males will band together and isolate a female from her partner. They will rape her, taking turns driving her under the water with such tenacity that she seems in danger of drowning, while others of their number beat off her furious mate. Afterwards, she will paddle in circles, preening her breast feathers and shaking her tail while her mate thrusts ahead of her expecting her to follow.

What can I say to that? If this were a story (the father is restless and so the father builds; the stepmother is powerful and so the stepmother waits) it would be very easy to make her a statement, a parallel to a larger, human condition. But she is a duck, Ingrid, and this is what I want you to understand. It's when we forget our bodies that we get into trouble.

This is the attraction. See what I could do to her if I gave her a name: Delores the Duck.

And a family: daughter of David and Marsha, sister to Ellen and Thad.

And some dreams: She was the littlest duck of the flock and wanted, more than anything, to be trusted some day with a leadership roll at the point of the V. She was a quiet girl, given to day dreaming, who loved to dabble in the shallows at the verge of the stream, splashing the clear water over her head and preening in it as it fell in sheets around her. One day, as she sang to herself about the bite of the cold wind in her face and the sound behind her of her family straining their wings to keep up, she was set upon by a gang of strangers, little more than boys, who brutalized her, taking turns driving her under the water over and over, shouting as they did so in wild glee. Afterward, she drifted aimless on the stream and could no longer see herself in its clear waters. She was a puzzle to her family, who knew nothing of what had happened, and they grew tired of her new sullenness and left her at the back of the V, no longer asked her opinion of where they should stop to bathe or eat or dabble in simple circles on the deep lakes. Eventually, one of the gods, who happened to look down, took such pity on her that he transformed her into a pebble which instantly sank to the bottom of the stream and rolled there, rocked by the gentle currents. Overhead, her family paddled back and forth calling her name.

Just like that, now she is Delores who must become a stone, rather than a female duck, one of many, who can settle her feathers and lead her clutch of ducklings in a ragged line along the banks. Stories do not heal, Ingrid; they expose. Like picking at a scab to see if underneath our bodies have transformed the miracle of blood into yet more, blank pink skin. Perhaps this is why we tell them.

Rosellen kept the notebook with her record of our family meetings in an easily accessible drawer in the secretary by the backdoor which had become a catchall for loose buttons, bits of string, half-dead pens, keys with no locks, pocket change, bank statements, loose playing cards (King of Hearts, Queen of Spades) and other comfortable detritus. Part of the point was the openness of the record. There were no secrets, Rosellen implied; no manipulations. Here we were just as we were—and weren't we a sorry bunch.

**April 26, 1992**

Dax Small: I don't know what to say. I guess I wish someone would take the trash out when it's full instead of waiting for me to do it every time.

Alice Small: [...]

Ingrid Clawson: At my house, we have a trash compactor that smashes everything together so we only have to take the trash out once a week. Sometimes not even once a week if we don't have any parties. Why don't you get something like that?

Alice Small: Why don't we get something like that?

(interruption from the cleaning girl—break to settle a problem with Lucas Small)

Ingrid Clawson: Now, where were we?

Dax Small: I'm done doing this. It's nine o'clock at night. I'm going out for a beer.

**June 3, 1995**

Rosellen Small: Where should we start?

Dax Small: [....]

Alice Small: [....]

Rosellen Small: Someone has to say something. The situation isn't getting any better.

Ingrid Clawson: He seems the same to me. He's always been like that, hasn't he? Did someone think the situation was supposed to get better?

Dax Small: Why are you here, Ingrid? Does your mother know you're here?

Alice Small: I told her to come. We're supposed to be doing a geology project.

Dax Small: Oh, yeah? What about? I didn't know you were interesting in geography, Ingrid.

Ingrid Clawson: I'm not. That's all Alice's stuff. I'm interested in the theatre. I'm going to be an actress.

Dax Small: You are, are you? What kind of actress?

Ingrid Clawson: Burlesque.

(major interruption by Lucas Small who has been brought in by cleaning girl—damage done to: 2 plates, 1 glass, curtains, cleaning girl's mouth, Dax Small's hand)

Dax Small: All right. I know. Don't look at me like that. I know.

**February 18, 1997**

Ingrid Clawson: Honestly, what's the big deal? It's not like this is Victorian, England. Right?

Dax Small: [....]

Alice Small: [....]

Ingrid Clawson: Dax, come on. It's not like, "What will the neighbors think?" because there aren't any neighbors but me and mom and you know what I think and my mom doesn't think anything about anything. All she wants to do is sit in the living room with a bottle of wine and listen to Chuck Mangioni. Who cares what she thinks?

Dax Small: It's time for you to go home, Ingrid.

Alice Small:[. ...]

Ingrid Clawson: There's a clinic in Ridley Township. It doesn't cost much and—

Dax Small: Go *home*, Ingrid.

Alice Small: [....]

Ingrid Clawson: Why did you tell him, anyway, Alice? That was pretty fucking stupid of you, if you ask me.

Dax Small (standing): [....]

Ingrid Clawson: All right! I'm going. I can see myself out.

The house is empty and so the house is filled. The children are lonely and so the children wander. There are so many ways to tell a story, Ingrid, that, in spite of our best intentions, we begin one almost every time we open our mouths.

# King Of Hearts, Queen Of Spades

I will tell it to you as I told it to my father:

"When I was young, I went into the forest. I didn't have an errand or anyone to see on the other side, but I could not be dissuaded, so my stepmother packed a basket with bread and cheese, half of a wild apple and a little bird she had cooked the night before with honey and the herbs that grow wild on the hill. I still remember how my father looked as he stood on the doorstep to wave me goodbye. I still remember the smoke that rose from the chimney and the rose bush which bloomed beside the front door.

After many days of travel, I had eaten all my food and came to a place I could not remember ever having come to before. It was a clearing where the trees suddenly ended and before me was a lake whose waters were gray and still and filled the valley in all directions like a bead of mercury, self-contained. I realized how it was, that, quite by accident, I had come to Gall Place and I set my basket down on a stone and began to cry. I was afraid because Gall Place is enchanted and only the animals can go there. Now something would happen to me for sure, I believed. And I was right.

After awhile, I don't know how long, I had cried with such great feeling that my tears formed a little stream, like the ones that bloom from the rocks after a storm. When my tears touched the water of the lake, there was a great shaking. The air around me seemed to shake like a blanket someone was snapping to clear it of crumbs, and then there were two men who stepped from the lake onto the shore. One of the men was very dark: his skin was as blue as a plum, his eyes like charred nuts, his hair black as a black goat's wool and clung to his head just as closely. The other man was very pale. His hair and eyes and skin were smooth and faultless.

"He would taste like biting into a wedge of snow," I thought, and imagined the rind of ice against my lips. Other than that, the two men were identical and I knew they were the Thunder Brothers who live very far to the west on the other side of the mountains and do not come home though their father has forgiven them for their crimes. Their shoes were wet from standing in the water. They sat down beside me to wring out their socks and lay them on the rocks to dry.

"Why are you crying?" the dark brother asked me. His name was Fet, which means A Terrible Noise.

"I'm afraid," I answered him. "I've come to a place where I am not supposed to be."

"You've got that right," said the pale brother; Taw was his name which means A Terrible Light. "How did you get here, anyway? Didn't you see the No Trespassing signs?"

I had not and I told them as much. Then, as no one seemed to be in a particular hurry, I told them the rest of my story: my long journey, my many challenges, what I had seen and how I had been during my time in the forest.

"That's nothing," said Taw when I was done, but Fet seemed appreciative, keeping his gaze on my face as I talked and slapping the rock with the palm of his hand at moments of particular wit or peril. All in all, we passed a pleasant afternoon and when the sun began to go down, balancing on the points of the firs like a halved peach pierced by the tines of a fork, Fet invited me to come with him and his brother to their home under the lake and have some dinner.

"Our sisters are already there," he said, helping me to my feet and pulling a twig from my hair. "They're pretty good cooks. Nothing fancy, but filling and fresh."

"What are their names?" I asked.

Taw rolled up the cuffs of his pants and shoved his socks into his back pocket. "They don't have any," he said and Fet looked regretful, but said it was true.

At first I was afraid to walk into the lake, but Fet assured me it was not water but the main trail that went past their house. "It's not far now," he said, and I found that it was not water but tall, waving grasses that closed over my head as I followed them. After a short walk, the grasses began to thin and we came onto a wide road on one side of which was a field and on the other a low, stone wall enclosing a peach orchard.

The sky was a dusky violet and all around us birds opened their throats and sang.

Taw climbed the wall and walked into the orchard. "This is a shortcut," he called over his shoulder, but Fet and I were enjoying the mild evening and went the long way around. We followed the road as it mounted a gentle hill and came in this way to a house in the center of a neat dirt yard with a well and a coop and a round fire pit in which a great blaze had been kindled. Taw was already there and so were the sisters who were tall and slim and both wearing orange dresses that belted high under their breasts and flowed all the way down to their feet, hiding them from sight.

The sisters were happy to see their brother and happy to meet me as well. They came to us and touched me all over, their hands dry and light as they stroked my face and forearms, touched my lips and eyelids and turned my hands back and forth to look at my knuckles and nails. While they did this, they smiled and nodded to me and each other, conversing with their hands and eyes. I saw that each sister had two snakes tattooed on her lips, one on the upper and one below. They were fashioned in such a way that when the woman opened her mouth, the snakes opened their mouths. I also found it was true the sisters had no tongues. Their mouths were pink and smooth and empty and so they made no sound but showed me in other ways that they were happy to see me and give me comfort after the dangers of my journey.

For dinner that night, Taw killed one of the hens and we ate her with beans and corn, wild ramps and a pat of sweet butter the sisters churned from the milk given by their old, brown cow. We drank a clear liquor Fet made from the peaches and after din-ner we sat around the fire and listened to Taw play a bone flute he pulled out of his pocket which was so straight and white it looked as if he were playing another one of his fingers snapped from his hand and held bloodless between his lips. Then, as I saw no reason not to, I stayed with them for many years and passed a happy time in this fashion.

Over the seasons, a few things became clear. For one, the sisters' feet were short and round, almost like a dog's paws, but this seemed to embarrass them and when they saw me looking they would sit down and readjust their skirts so I could no longer see. For another, what at first I had thought were chairs were actually turtles. They raised themselves up and stretched out their claws when we came to sit, but as soon as they saw who we were and their curiosity was satisfied, they settled back down around the table and went to sleep.

There were other things besides. The brothers had two horses which they rode fast over the valley. But then I knew they were really two horned serpents: a white one and a red one with a stone in its forehead the size and shape of a cartridge bullet. The saddles they used were also turtles and the bracelets they wore were other snakes which rustled around the brothers' forearms carrying the tips of their tails in their mouths. At night, before they went to bed, the sisters would take off their long black hair and hang it on pegs by the door. Their heads were round and smooth as pumpkins. Though I saw it every day, each night I would think, "Why, it is not hair at all," and feel the same surprise.

One afternoon, Taw rode his great red serpent out over the valley and was gone for a long time. When he came back he was agitated and drove the snake almost into the yard, leapt from the saddle and ran into the house without tending his mount or lifting the turtle from its back; unusual for him as he liked to keep things neat. It was a sunny day after a spell of rain. I was sitting in the yard idly braiding a new belt from corn silk given to me by the sisters. The hens, which had been sleeping by my feet, were startled by the commotion and beat heavily around me, showering me with dust. Inside the house, I heard Taw shouting and when I followed him I found Fet and the sisters were already there, all three seated around the table, all three looking anxious and the sisters very pale.

"I told you this would happen," said Taw, pacing in front of the door and running his hands through his hair until it stood up like a crane's crest. "There's no way there's enough time to clean it all up before he gets here," he said.

"Clean up what?" I asked. "Who's coming?"

When no one answered me, I set about tidying the kitchen, trying to be helpful, but Taw said, "She'll have to go. Tonight. Right away."

Fet shook his head and said, "Tomorrow morning. Let her stay one more night."

"Tomorrow then, but first thing," Taw said. "No dawdling." The sisters looked at me sadly, lips pressed together so tightly the snakes appeared to be starving. "What's going on?" I said, but by then I thought I knew.

Fet got up and put his arms around me. He smelled like pepper and some other sharp spice. "I'm sorry, Alice," he said and squeezed me. "But our father sent a message. He's coming to visit and he wouldn't like to find you here."

"There are rules," said Taw. "We broke them."

That night, as they had very many nights over the years, the brothers came to me in my little bed by the door. I knew them so well by then I could tell without looking which one's hand, which one's mouth. If I had suddenly lost all my senses, I would still have known from the way that they filled me which brother was above me, which brother was below. Afterwards we lay together for a long time, Taw with his hand on my breast and Fet petting the inside of my thigh with long, light strokes as he would the sisters' cat when she slept by the fire.

"What happens next?" I said, but I did not expect an answer. Taw stirred against me, hardening again as he rolled my nipple between his fingers and pressed his cold mouth into my neck.

"You know it won't live," he said to his brother.

"I know," said Fet. He lifted himself on one elbow and kissed my mouth, my ear, the corners of my eyes. Inside me I felt a rising flutter as if a small bird were battering its wings against the window glass.

The next morning was painful. All of us cried. The sisters said goodbye to me at the house, kissing me all over my face, pressing every inch of my body from tip to toe. They gave me back my basket which they had been using to store onions under the sink, and wrapped my head in a long orange scarf in case I had need of it on my journey. The brothers walked me back to the lake shore and said goodbye to me there. They stood ankle deep in the water and waved. Every time I turned back, they were still there waving until finally I turned and could see nothing behind me but trees. I knew I would never see them again— one so black he swallowed himself, one so white he burned very cold—and I sat down at the base of a pine tree and wept. I considered myself very sorry, alone now in the world and, I realized, lost in a woods through which I could not remember traveling, in which I had left no marker to guide me home.

"Hello?" I called out, but to whom? The forest was dark and unwilling. There is a story that says the pine is of the same nature as the stars and holds within itself the same bright light, but that is just a story and the tree I was leaning against did not bend to comfort me or brighten to beam me the way home. I was alone, alone. I was alone. And then something in my basket gave a little jump and began tapping at the lid to be let out.

Cautiously, you may be sure, I lifted the lid. I didn't know what to expect. Perhaps some present from the sisters—a magic bean, enchanted spindle. Perhaps one of the brothers' bracelets which had crawled in there the night before to get some sleep. What I saw was none of these things; it went beyond my talent for prophecy. It was the little bird my stepmother had cooked for me so long ago and whose bones I had sucked clean and wrapped in a twist of paper!

The bird beat the bones of its wings and hopped up onto the edge of the basket. It looked about, tipping one empty socket toward the ground and one toward my face, and sidled around the basket rim to step onto my finger where it nibbled at my knuckle with its sharp, black beak. I stroked the bird's skull with the tip of my finger. Its bones were cool and smooth, burnished brown with age. When it moved, it made a faint grinding noise. It opened its beak as if it was singing, but no sound came out. Its ribcage was empty; its brainpan was dry.

So, there were two of us: me and the bird I had eaten so long ago, whose flesh was so sweet, whose bones I had used to pick my teeth. We made an unlikely couple, but the forest is full of such strange friendships, and as we travelled I soon learned that the bird was better than I at direction. It preferred to ride perched on my wrist, but if I strayed from the right path it would hop up my sleeve to my shoulder and tug on my ear until I corrected myself. At night, it settled down beside my head and seemed to sleep as I did, though it was hard to tell: the bird's empty eyes were always open. Even when it tucked its head beneath its wing I could see their caverns through the screen of its bones.

In this way we went, day after day, through the unchanging forest. I ate mushrooms and roots I dug under the lichen. I scraped the inside of oak bark and brewed small, dark teas. Every day as we went, the bird opened its beak as if to sing me encouraging songs, and every day as we went my stomach grew rounder, harder, hot to the touch.

It was clear something was happening, but when the bird and I came to the edge of the meadow I had once called my home, I was unprepared for how shy I felt. There was my father's house: smoke rising from the chimney, rose bush tightly budded by the front door. There was my stepmother's bicycle leaned up against the porch railings and in the garage my father's tools, each on a peg inside the outline of their shape. Someone whistled as they walked past the screen door, their song composed of the same notes I thought my bird had been trying to sing.

All was just as I had left it, but though the bird hopped up and down my arm, I could not bring myself to step out of the forest shadow and into the sun. Instead, I stood there with my hand resting on my belly which was now so hot and tight it was like resting my hand on the side of a kettle. The little dead bird hopped up my arm and down again and I stood and the light began to change. Then, I was overwhelmed by a terrible pain."

My father stared at me. You can imagine: his hands on either side of his plate, his chop growing gray as it leaked into the peas.

We sat that way. Then my father lifted his fork and knife and cut a bite out of his meat. He chewed it, never taking his eyes from my face, and took a long, deliberate swallow out of his cup. "Now, let me tell *you* a story," he said. And this is what it was:

"Once there was a King who had need of a Queen. Never mind why; it was something political. His advisors proposed they search far and wide for the most beautiful or virtuous or well-read maiden in that or any other land, but the King was a practical kind of guy who liked to get things done.

"Just find someone in the village," he said. The advisors weren't pleased with it, but what were they going to do? They all went down to the village.

Once they got there, they were struck by a problem. The village didn't have the best reputation in the world. It was a pretty dirty place, littered with swine and turnips and other villagey things. The people were naturally suspicious of governmental authority, and usually so grimy and bent up in their sack clothes as they hauled around their heavy loads that it was really hard for the advisors to tell who was a fair maiden and who wasn't which was a criteria they thought was kind of important even though the King had said he didn't care.

One of the advisors was of a scientific bent, and he proposed that they find the new Queen through a process of systematic interrogation involving calipers and precisely weighted scales and reams and reams of graph paper. That sounded okay to the other two advisors in theory, but, as one of them pointed out, they hadn't brought any of those materials with them and they sure weren't going to get something like that in the village where the only things for sale seemed to be swine tonics and economy sized boxes of powdered cheese.

Another one of the advisors was a man of faith who had played around with the idea of going into the seminary for awhile when he was in his twenties, but then he had met his wife and one thing lead to another. Now he had ten kids, all daughters, and he felt a little pissed off at God, but also scared at being pissed off at God, so he walked around all the time with a tension headache.

"Why don't we just round up a bunch of them," this guy suggested, "and take them to the river. We'll strip them and scrub them down and go along the line making them recite something, maybe the alphabet or the Lord's Prayer, just to make sure no one's a retard. If we had them all in a group like that, one of them would probably stand out."

The other two advisors thought this was actually a really great idea, particularly the part about stripping the women and scrubbing them down, but then the science-minded advisor pointed out that most of the women on the street were in town with their husbands. While that wouldn't matter to the King— he was the King!; there wasn't anything too complicated about making a husband disappear—it was statistically very probable that it would matter to one or more of the village men who, guided by their genetic predisposition toward rash physicality, might make things kind of sticky.

The third advisor was named Beemis and he was new on the job. Originally he had thought of this gig as a stepping stone to bigger and better things, but the longer he stayed at court hanging out with the King's advisors and cooks and pageboys and stewards of the crown, the more he began to think that he'd made a tactical error.

"Just stick it out," his mother had told him. "Keep your head down. Suck it up. Put your shoulder in." But Beemis was ambitious. By thirty he wanted to be his own boss, and by forty-five he wanted to retire and buy a condo on this roving, twenty-story ocean liner he had read about where you did your grocery shopping port by port (wine in Marseille, bread in Gibraltar) and every night smartly dressed couples played pinochle on the aft-deck under the light of a gibbous moon.

If he couldn't figure out how to get the King's attention soon, he was going to try to move into a lateral position in the court of one of the country's neighboring allies, but this would mean buying a whole new wardrobe in that kingdom's colors and having to learn a new language. No country stayed allied with the King for too long, so potentially he'd have to do military service fighting against a lot of guys who he'd gone to college with and played with now on a softball league, none of which he particularly wanted to do. What Beemis wanted most in the world, the secret desire of his heart, was for the King to notice him and call him by his name. While the other two advisors stood in the street and argued, Beemis was mindful of the time and getting jumpy.

Finally, after they had gone round and round on the cost effectiveness of going all the way back to the castle for calipers versus the relative likelihood that their insurance plan would cover injury by mob violence, Beemis said, "I'll be right back," and took off trotting down the street and into a dog-leg alley where he was lost from sight.

"Jesus, *that* guy," said the second advisor, but nevertheless he and his colleague sat down on the side of a watering trough to wait.

Before too much time passed—they took in a Punch and Judy show and bought fried pies from a vendor who was selling them out of a tray he wore round his neck—Beemis returned and with him he had a woman.

"Who's that?" asked the scientific advisor, but the man of faith rose to his feet and exhaled, "The Queen…"

He was right, that's who it was. Or at least that's who she was going to be. She was wearing a brown dress of some scratchy material and sturdy blue shoes; not much to look at, but she seemed tidy and under the plain exterior it was clear that she had potential. Put her in a dress with an embroidered bodice, powder her face and slap a coronet on her head, and they would have the bonafide article. So what if she couldn't tell her oyster knife from her sorbet spoon or discourse on classical sculpture? She had clean eyes and a pretty good smile which she showed them from behind Beemis's shoulder where she was standing as if she were shy.

"Hi," she said, and that was that.

The next morning the advisors introduced the girl to the King and he said that was fine and the whole court started making preparations for the royal wedding. Even though the King was in a hurry—his political situation had gotten more urgent—a royal wedding has to be done a specific way so it would be a least a week before the girl became the Queen. Meanwhile, she was free to roam about the castle as, once the seamstresses got her measurements, no one really needed her for much. She spent a lot of her time in the royal library. She couldn't read, but there were big tapestries there which showed pictures of lords and ladies riding horses through the forest. All around them were animals they hadn't yet noticed peeking out of the leaves or hiding in the undergrowth. Also, the King kept a lot of atlases on hand and the girl like to open them at random and trace the strange rivers and shorelines with the tip of her finger. She hadn't had much opportunity for schooling in the village, and she thought it was really great how, no matter where it started, every one of those rivers eventually ended up at the sea.

Soon enough, the week had passed and the day of the wedding came. The girl was gotten out of bed very early by a team of hairdressers and dress fitters and makeup artists and aromatherapists who powdered and pinched and puffed and pried her into her wedding array. It was elaborate, to say that least: her hair so high it jangled the crystal of the chandeliers as she walked, her skirts so wide she wedged in the door and had to be pushed through like a cork being rammed down the neck of a bottle. She looked great, really swell, they all assured her, but she couldn't know for sure because there weren't any mirrors in the castle big enough to reflect the whole display at once.

When she was all ready, her team of dressers melted away and an elderly footman named Harold took her down the hall to the throne room and then, to her surprise, past the big empty thrones, through a curtain, down another hall and into a part of the castle where she had never been. There he opened a door and, after another little issue with her skirts, ushered her into a hot, close room with purple velvet curtains pulled tight over the windows, floor to ceiling mirrors on the walls and smack in the middle a huge, canopied bed. There weren't as many people there as she had expected. Beemis, for one, and the other advisors. Then some lords and ladies who were standing around the room in the finest wigs and hose, rustling and talking to each other, though they straightened up when she walked in.

"Great," said the King, holding out a hand to her. "Tell Mrs. Zuckerman good work," he said to Harold, leading the girl to the center of the room where there was an end table sitting next to a short stepladder and turning her to face the court.

The rest of the ceremony passed in kind of a blur. The King officiated his own wedding and there was a whole file folder full of official documents to read. The courtesans tried to seem interested, but there was a lot of shifting weight and stifled yawning, and for most of the wedding there wasn't anything for her to do but stand there and smile and every now and then, at the King's cue, repeat something he had read.

Then, the King said, "Now for the proofs." He told her to get up on the stepladder, which she did, and prop her left foot on the top step, which, balancing a little awkwardly in her silver heels, she also did. When she was steady in this position, the King knelt down before her and lifted a velvet sac she hadn't previously noticed from its place on the end table. He began to peel up her skirts, layer by layer, passing them up to her to hold so that soon she could no longer see what he was doing directly because there was so much fabric pressed under her chin and had to watch instead in the mirror. When the King finally got down to her bare legs, there was a different kind of stirring among the courtesans. She hadn't expected any of this and felt ashamed. Her legs were so white and skinny in the mirror they looked like some other kind of thing entirely!

The King opened the velvet sac with a flourish and pulled out a pair of silver shears. He opened and shut them twice for the benefit of the courtesans and then used them to snip the two sides of her white lace panties and pull the fabric away from her crotch like a magician pulling a scarf from the top of an empty hat. The bath attendants had done their job well so everything down there was trimmed tight and blonde, and the King, for the first time paying a little attention to the fact that it was a body there under all those clothes, stroked her thatch admiringly. Then, with the index and ring finger of his left hand, her pulled her lips apart and held them open while he dumped the remained contents of the sac onto the carpet. She gasped in shock. Five rough-cut rubies fell out of the sac and rolled around on the floor.

One by one, with a little flourish each time, the King inserted the rubies inside of her, pushing the first one up as far as he could with his middle finger, then using each stone to push its neighbor higher up the line. This was a little painful, but there was no blood and the King was fast. The whole thing was hard on Beemis since, it turns out, this was his sister, the only girl he knew who could be reached on short notice, but in the end he got what he wanted (the King had even patted him on the back a few times and called him Blemis, which was close) and his sister didn't seem too much the worse for the wear. She even looked a little proud up there surrounded by so much floating fabric and hair, chin raised, eyes locked on the mirror. Soon enough the ordeal was over and she was married. She was the Queen.

For a while, everything went well. As the Queen, she had a lot more free time than she had as a villager and she took up landscape painting and learned how to make lanterns out of rice paper and paste. The King got along with her well enough, and he liked the feel of the stones rubbing the tip of his cock as he fucked her, which he did pretty regularly despite his busy schedule. But then one day, as she washed up in her marble and platinum bathroom after a particularly vigorous session with the King, the Queen felt a sharp pain in her stomach and one of the rubies fell out of her vagina onto the tile. She was upset, but she guessed it probably wasn't that big a deal. It wasn't like she'd ever had rubies up there before, and the whole thing had seemed like more of a symbolic gesture anyway. Nevertheless, she took the stone into the King's drawing room where he was relaxing on the sofa reading the paper and told him what had happened. He shook his head and put the stone away in the velvet sack which, even though it was empty, he kept on his person at all times.

Over the course of the next few weeks, the stones fell out of her one by one. Without the stones, the King didn't find her as satisfying. She was loose down there, flaccid feeling, and even though he tried lots of different positions—her on top, backwards on top, from behind and squeezing her creamy white ass cheeks together for a little extra traction—he couldn't finish inside her anymore and had to get her to take him in her mouth or do it with her hand. "C'est la vie," said the King, who had lots of other options. After that, he left her alone. She was still the Queen, but word must have gotten around somehow because people looked at her a little differently. It made her paranoid and she took to wearing her hair down over her face and skulking in the corridors. She got involved with a number of irritating causes and became a major supporter of community theatre. Whenever she ran into Beemis, she pressed him into serving as her escort to the dog show or the ballet and, as she wouldn't allow him to either quit or transfer and the King had long since forgotten his name, she generally made life miserable for him out of a spirit of revenge but also pity because she knew some things he did not about the nature of the world.

Sometimes, she would go into the room where her wedding had been held and lift the velvet sack from the end table where the King kept it now that the rubies were back inside. She would spill the stones out on the coverlet and sort them, holding them up to the light and peering through them, piling them in her palm and testing their weight. But, no matter how old she got, nothing ever changed with those rubies. That's all they were, just rubies, though she could never accept it and so lived a long and tedious life."

This is what my father said to me. And with that, my life in his house had come to an end.

It was February when I left, a cold winter. The snow was fresh and my father, who was out of work, had not shoveled. I remember seeing my tracks behind me as I left the house. I remember expecting something more dramatic; droplets of blood steaming in the snow perhaps, but that was all—just the shape of my feet, the closed door, a patter of blue light from the television shifting silently behind the curtains.

I hitched my backpack higher on my shoulders. I had packed a couple of changes of clothes, some books. I hadn't been to school for four months, which was how old the fetus was, though I thought the two things were unrelated. Rather, at that point, I felt like I knew everything I was ever going to know. As if I had reached my limit and anything new would spill over the edge of my brimming head and sluice across my features like groundwater leaking down a ruined face of the mountain. I didn't want to make a mess, I remember thinking.

I stood for a long time in my father's front yard as my shoes soaked through and my toes began to burn, then freeze. Behind the curtains, I could see people walking: my father or Rosellen moving from room to room, but the curtains didn't twitch, no new light came on and none went out. Then, someone hoisted the venetian blinds in what had once been my brother's bedroom and sat at the window. It was Rosellen, but she gave no sign that she wanted to communicate with me; no wave, no finger tap on the glass.

She sat in the window and stared as if I were an image on the television screen, a subplot to a story she had invested too much time into following to turn off now. I stared back and for a long time we were like that: each of us expressionless, each of us gray. Then I turned and began to inch my way down the slick hill. I was going to the Feed Store whose lights came in and out of view behind the trees as I walked, and from there I would go to Thalia's house high on a bald on the south side of Newfound Mountain. I was like an animal then—my mind a gray buzz, my body a bloody socket into which an uneasy life had been plugged. My only thoughts were not to slip and how cold my feet were. I had no idea my real life had begun.

Oh, Push sings the kettle.
Please Push begs the chair.

The mother hears the siren coming up the hill, but it is going to her neighbor's house who is also expecting a baby, who was also supposed to travel in orderly fashion to the hospital with her husband, but who has panicked at the early pains and called the ambulance instead, waits now in the foyer with her bag in her hand as they pull into her drive.

It is a month too early for the mother and she knows something is wrong. "Wait," she says and says it louder, "Wait," trying to call over the birth song which is rising all around her, drowning her in euphony.

But the baby is anxious; it is filled with fear. Something has changed—a light gone out, a dazzle fading—and its absence threatens the baby with a loss that quickens her, makes her rough. Darkness Brilliance Darkness Brilliance. Where is it? She can't see over this red pounding. She can't hear over the rush of waters. It is gone. It is lost. The baby feels, for the first time, emptiness and she is enraged. She screams and the world becomes high and thin. It rushes away from her. She is lost in it, her will almost extinguished, and then she feels a thready tug, a fleet little pull from far away as the Other, the baby can sense it, also screams; as the Other, the baby can feel it, also spreads her new hands against a bright light.

It is the first time the baby has been comforted. It is the first time the baby has been. She lies very still, marveling at the fact of herself, feeling for the Other who is with her, who mirrors her. Who speaks down their shared current: I am I I I…I am I.

And this is how my father found me, many hours later, when he came into the house with a hammer in his hand to see his wife lying dead on the floor, his daughter beside her, and there at the window, unmoved by either pity or awe, the dragon, of course.

Who else would it have been?

# The Orifice

So you can never claim to have been misled, Ingrid, here is what the Orifice said:

"—indicative of both malevolence and a contradictory desire to please. Furthermore, Subject A's delusions—classic instances of magical thinking on a gradated scale from the superstitious to the frankly paranoid—adhere to a surprisingly sophisticated symbolic lexicon that she employs with evidence of nascent awareness of their primogenitors in both myth and popular culture. Some of these reoccurring icons, to be elaborated on in Chapter Seven, are: snakes and certain birds, the moon, a stone which Subject A varyingly describes as gem-like, rough or water-rounded, fire and ash, lost or hindered children, a dominant female figure in many guises, and bees, wasps and other hive-building insects. Though Subject A is highly skilled at oral storytelling, she displays little to no awareness of narrative goals; i.e. the nature of a story as a transformative tool *applied* to an existent reality with the intended outcome of either reinvention or manipulation of the audience's perception. Rather, she operates as if her highly iconographic personal mythology is a *continuation* of a contiguous narrative line, integrated into the quotidian domestic reality of her life in a sup*ra*natural fashion which overwhelms the "natural," obliterating rather than rewriting. Thus, the dualism between her bodily self and her consciousness is not Cartesian, but rather mythic: the god (or gods) who have influenced her life are irrational and unapproachable, but she must have done something to deserve their attention. From a diagnostic standpoint, it is clear how this paradoxical self image, at once both at the mercy and in control of larger forces, creates the opportunity for a dangerous abdication of personal responsibility, and furthermore—

—plant produces a stout, blackish rhizome (creeping, underground stem), cylindrical, hard and knotty. It is collected in the autumn after the fruit has formed. It has only a faint, disagreeable odor, but a bitter and acrid taste. The root is an antidote against poison and the bite of the rattlesnake. The fresh root, dug in October, is used to make a tincture. Also known as: Black Snake Root, Rattle Root, Squaw Root, Bugbane—

—The world is suspended at its corners. We have come after a terrible flood. The boy has a wild brother formed from blood washed in the river. They murder their mother and by dragging her body around the camp they grow the first corn. The bears do not demand of us; the deer give rheumatism; the reptiles make us dream; the birds and insects and smaller animals give disease and make menstruation sometimes fatal to women. The little men transform us and set us to kill the sun—

—which leaves or roots when eaten produce maniacal delirium, if nothing worse. Necklaces of root, when hung about a child's neck, prevent fits and cause easy teething. Also known as: Henna-bell, Henbell, Hebenon—

—overworn green color; clasping tendrils. Thready strings snipt about the edges. Spokie rundles. Bloody flux—

—running the risk of oversimplification, it is useful to figure the household within the context of a hive mentality. The arbiter of collectivist control (Subject B) is male and asserts a model of behavior whose clear goals are to not only control the necessary health, safety and comfort of what I term here as his "hive," but also to assert a system of emotional/psychic hegemony through which he believes his essential principles will be replicated in a fractal expansion with the addition of each new hive member; much in the way bees craft additional, identical cells to accommodate the expansion of the colony. Subject A appears to submit to Subject B's dominance. Indeed, she appears to do so happily which underscores my speculative theory of her causal infantilization outlined in Chapter Two. However, a subconscious conflict has emerged between Subject B's patrilineal approach and the ardently literal symbolist Subject A's strong identification with both matriarchal authority and her perception of collectivist identity as a female construct. Subject B views himself in the hive role of the Queen. In his mindset of almost pathological gender narcissism, there is no conflict between the feminine model and his overt masculine identification. In other words, he has subverted the cyclic, holistic nature inherent in a fractal model of community building in favor of an entropic mode which borrows from traditional Judeo-Christian iconography. He begins the timeline of the community, is able to reinsert himself at will along its continuity, is replicated in all other members of the community, and is the sole hive member capable of causing the termination of the community. Subject A, on the other hand, is unable to blend these two models. Thus, while she submits to Subject B's dominant will, she seeks another, female member of the hive to stand in as the Queen; albeit a Queen stripped of her decisive powers. This, as a clear result of our long-standing relationship, has come to be myself. Since the introduction of Self and Subject C into the hive community a year prior to this writing, Subject A has bifurcated her subservience to both fulfill the rules surrounding Subject B's hive expansion and serve the material and emotional needs of Self, her proxy hive Queen. As she figures this psychic schism through her usual narrative escapism, Subject A has become a most unusual sort of narcissist: a hive member that is *aware* of its lack of motility. The only person in all the world, she believes, who is able to know she is not in any way unique—

—untoiled places, overmuch flowing. Kind hereof. Leaves hereof. Untilled places: whitish-green color. Root hereof, roots hereof. Diverse other places. Thready root, mean bigness—

—There was a tribe of root-eaters and a tribe of acorn-eaters with great piles of shells near their houses. In one tribe, they found a sick man dying and were told it was the custom there when a man died to bury his wife in the same grave with him. The sky is an arch or a vault of solid rock. It was always swinging up and down. The moon is a ball that was thrown up against the sky a long time ago. Some say the stars are balls of light, others say they are human, but most people say they are living creatures covered with luminous fur or feathers with small heads which stick out like the head of a turtle. Some stars are called Where the Dog Ran. A dog warned us of the Great Deluge and showed us the place on his neck where the skin had worn off so the bones showed through—

—a solitary, stout, pale stem with tough, strong fibers enclosing a white pith arises from the midst of the felted leaves. Its rigid uprightness accounts for some of the plant's local names: Aaron's Rod, Jupiter or Jacob's Staff—

—"I become a real wolf," we say. When a rabbit was stuck in a hollow tree, he sang to the children: "Cut a door and look at me; I'm the prettiest thing you ever did see." The rabbit we know now is only a little thing that came after. The man could not even see the heart in his hands, but he swallowed it and when the girl awoke she compelled herself to go to him and be his wife. "I have sewed myself together. I have sewed myself together"—

—Shoot hereof. Fruit hereof. Washed therewith: other hot regions. Great broad leaves. Decoction thereof. Blue color. Sundry branches, raw humors. Seed hereof. Germ hereof—

—remains to be seen what effect the disintegration of the hive community will have on Subject A. While the study is by no means completed, external factors (including the looming arrival of Subject X) along with Subject A's increasing destabilization render the situation far too volatile for continuing study—

—She rose and brought half a cake of bread, half a wild apple and half a pigeon. She heard running and the door was flung open and the sun came in. Finally, he stopped and pulled the arrows out of his side. "And now surely we and the good black things, the best of all, shall see each other," they sang. "A bullfrog will marry you; a bullfrog will marry you," they sang.

# The Green Knight's Tale

Every summer for one month, Thingy would leave me and go to the beach house her mother and father owned on an island off the coast. She came back from these trips tanned very brown, her hair, eyebrows and eyelashes bleached an impossible color, like spider's thread which can only be seen in the early morning when it catches the dew. She also returned very salty.

"Lick my wrist," Thingy said for weeks afterwards, and then, "Eww," when I pressed the tip of my tongue against her pulse. She pulled her arm away and wiped it on her skirt. But then a few minutes later she said, "But you could taste it, right? That's the ocean. I brought it all the way back here just for you."

One year, when Thingy and I were thirteen, her parents agreed to take me along.

The trip took four hours. Mr. Clawson drove and Thingy and I played the cow counting game with him as her mother slept in the passenger seat. The car was new, sleek and black with round silver headlights. It was a car that didn't have anything to prove. The hood ornament was a cat which slunk down toward the grill as if stalking the road.

"Ten cows," said Thingy. "I have ten on this side."

"Pretty good," said Mr. Clawson, "but look up ahead." He sped the car up, smoothly muscling around a sedan filled to the brim with a pudding-faced family who all turned almost as one to gawk at us. "It's a grain silo, Ingrid. All your cows have been lost in a terrible flood."

We had never played this game before. I think Mr. Clawson was making up the rules as he went along. Every time one or the other of us got up above a ten or fifteen cows he would announce another common highway feature which, depending on what side of the road it was on, would cause either Thingy or my cows to be massacred by some sort of natural disaster. So far our cattle had been blown away by a tornado, burnt alive in a forest fire, dropped into a gaping chasm opened up by an earthquake and now, it appeared, they were drowning in a flash flood. I imagined Thingy's cows paddling across a wide, quick-moving river, stretching their necks above the brown waters, mooing to each other as they rolled their eyes.

We stopped at a truck stop a couple of hours into the drive for what Mrs. Clawson instructed Thingy to refer to as a 'potty-break,' after she had announced to her father that she needed to piss like a racehorse.

"I need to potty-break like a racehorse, then," said Thingy, making a face at me. The trunk of the car was crammed full of collapsible lawn chairs and folded beach umbrellas, deflated rafts in a delirium of colors (jewel-pink, mint-green, azure, maize), rainbow-striped beach towels, oversized hats, pails and shovels, nets and masks. Already the car smelled like coconut lotion and, increasingly, salt. I had never seen the ocean. For weeks, ever since I found out I was coming along, I had been walking around feeling as if I were carrying my heart in my mouth. As if, should I open my mouth too suddenly, my heart would fall out onto the table and beat there, bouncing up and down on the gingham-checked plastic tablecloth making a mess.

To Thingy and my delight, the bathroom stalls were heavily graffitied and there was a scale that would also tell your fortune for only a quarter.

"You go first," Thingy said, and I stood on the scale while she put my quarter in the slot.

My fortune said: Your Happiness is Next to You. It also told me my lucky numbers were two and seventeen and gave me the Mandarin characters for pony and water park.

"Your happiness is in a bathroom!" said Thingy, hooting with laughter as she elbowed me off the scale and climbed on.

Her fortune read: You Will Set Off on a Journey, and she was disappointed.

"I already know that," she said. "I'm already on one. What a gyp."

"At least your words are cool," I said. Thingy could now read the Mandarin characters for wizard and Mexico, but she was unimpressed. I offered to trade and she said not to bother.

"It doesn't mean anything," she said, but she was wrong.

~

A couple of hours later we arrived.

The Clawson's beach house was a part of a private community of near identical houses, tall and flat-faced with tiered porches and ceiling fans whose blades were more often than not shaped like the leaves of giant palms. The houses were painted shades of peach and apricot, turquoise and sea-foam green. They had sandy yards plugged with saw-grass and crossed by creeping tendrils of railroad vine, their moony blooms nodding in the breeze. The Clawson's house was orange as sherbet and sat right at the end of the cul-de-sac, nearest to the beach.

"Okay," said Mr. Clawson, getting out of the car and stretching, his hands on the small of his back. "Bring out your dead."

"Don't be fatuous," said Mrs. Clawson, fanning herself with her hat. "It's too hot."

After the house had been opened and the car unpacked; after Mr. Clawson had gone from window to window pulling up shades and throwing open sashes and Mrs. Clawson checked every kitchen cupboard and pantry shelf for tracks and trails, nits and eggs; after Thingy and I had dragged our suitcases up the stairs (white carpet with a deep pile, white banisters and white lathes, a white hall and at the top a mirror so it seemed we had beaten ourselves to the bedroom) and stowed our clothes, bathing suits, towels and toiletries in their proper receptacles; after Mrs. Clawson had made a list for the grocery store and Mr. Clawson had dragged the gas grill out of storage; after Thingy had shown me the special spots in the house (where she slid into the kitchen as a toddler and gashed her forehead on the corner of the counter top, where she had sliced her heel on the crushed oyster shell that lined the front walk and, not realizing she claimed, stamped one red foot behind her all through the house) and taken me into the backyard to shout over the fence at the neighbor's dog; after Mrs. Clawson had pulled the car back out of the drive, her sunglasses hiding half her face like the mantic eyes of a wasp and Mr. Clawson had dragged the hose out from under the porch and begun to spray rainbow arcs of water into the butterfly bushes, Thingy and I went down to the beach.

How can I say this?

We cut through the front yard to the road, shoeless, stepping carefully around flat pads of cactus. The asphalt was fresh, bubbling in the heat. Thingy bent down and popped a line of tar-bubbles. One, two, three. There was wind coming in from the ocean, lifting the tasseled grasses that grew along the top of the dune and fanning them out toward us. Sand was sifting onto the road from the dune, from the sandy slopes of the yards. The line between the road and the yard and the dune was shifting, fluid. Everything wavered in the sun.

"Come on," said Thingy, "It's hot." She ran ahead of me, mincing on the hot road.

There was a boardwalk: weathered boards, rusty nails which pierced the dune and rose with it so as I walked both the earth and I seemed to rise together, keeping pace with each other. There were flowers on the dunes: yellow daisies, a tough succulent whose red and orange blooms burst like bristles out of its plump green pads. A little mouse ran from the shadow of a dune to shelter under the boardwalk. It was an unusual color. Tawny, almost gold.

I was stalling.

"Come on!" said Thingy, out of sight, her voice catching on the wind and tearing to shreds.

The wind beat my face. Salt. Stinging. I realized my eyes were shut and so I opened them. I saw.

The sea.

It was flat. It was heaving. It swept gray and green and blue out of my sight. The light jumped off its surface as if flung back, repulsed. It came toward me. Was coming toward me. It flung itself toward me, hissing on the sand. Thingy was already down in the surf, running into the waves without even bothering to strip to the bathing suit she wore under her clothes.

"Wait," I shouted. I was terrified. She was leaving me, diving into a wave that closed like a hand over her silver head. I shouted her name. A sea gull wheeling in the air over the beach and was joined by another, a third. They called like cats. I couldn't see where the water ended and the sky began. I couldn't see the end of anything. There was a glare, heat. The gulls came to rest on the sand and sprung up again, back beating their wings to hover near my head. I could see the sheen in their eyes as they cocked their heads to examine me.

"Thingy," I yelled. I couldn't see her.

Then she popped up from the trough of a wave and raised one tiny arm to beckon me. She was drifting further out, kicking to the top of a wave and bobbing behind it. Rising again to cup her hands on either side of her mouth and shout.

"Come in," Thingy said: a speck, my heart's shadow. "Come on, Alice. The water feels fine."

Later in the month, Thingy's parents threw a party. All the neighbors were invited, plus people Thingy's parents knew who summered on other near-by islands, plus a contingent from

Charleston, plus some of Mr. Clawson's business partners who were in the country from Germany and needed to be shown a good time. This was how Mr. Clawson put it. It was very important that a good time be had by all, he told us. That meant Thingy and I too, he said. He tried to be funny about it, but we understood that this was a kind of an order.

On the morning of the party, a cleaning crew swept into the house and vacuumed the sand out of every corner, polished every surface and generally scrubbed away any evidence that four people had eaten and slept there for the past two weeks. By the time they swept out again at noon, the house was a gleaming artifact, almost hostile in its intensity. Thingy and I had been banished.

"Go to the beach, or go out back to the pool," Mrs. Clawson had said to Thingy. "It doesn't matter to me where you go, darling. I just need you out of the way."

When we returned for lunch we were just in time to see the maids leave and the catering crew pull up in their refrigerated van. Inside, the house was cool and quiet. Ocean light lay in white slats across the carpet and every object looked as if it had been considered in relationship to every other object, arranged to form sympathetic angles and soothing blocks of negative space. The lacquered clock over the mantle—abstract, made of interposed coral-colored triangles, lacking numbers—had been polished to a high shine and ticked as smoothly as a latch falling into place. The turquoise throw pillows that Thingy and I often stacked on the floor to support our heads as we read or looked at magazines, were placed at precise intervals along Mrs. Clawson's sweeping white suede sofa, each pillow plumped and then dented as if a casual lounger had just risen to his feet.

Thingy's mother was sitting in a white wicker basket-chair, her legs crossed neatly at the knee. She gazed out over the room with a blank, unwritten expression as she twirled a swallow of red wine around the bottom of a glass. Mrs. Clawson was wearing her usual beach gear: linen clam diggers that slide up over her knees as she sat, a melon-orange tank top. Her hair rose in a high wave from her forehead and tumbled over her shoulders, pinned here and there for shape by tiny gold bobby pins. She had not yet put on lipstick and her lips looked exposed, as if they were glimpsed for just a second between shifting screens of fabric. Happenstance, a prurient luck. Overall, she looked exhausted.

"The caterer's are here," said Thingy. Mrs. Clawson nodded, but didn't look up at us.

"So are the florists," said Thingy, sticking her head back out the door and waving it open and shut as she watched them unpack the van.

Mrs. Clawson sighed and stood up. "Shut the door, Ingrid," she said to Thingy, "You're letting in the heat." She wandered into the kitchen, leaving her glass to sweat a ring onto the end table. We heard the faucet turn on.

"Also we're hungry," Thingy yelled after her mother as the first of the caterers pushed past her into the house. They were closely followed by the florists and soon the room was full of busy, shifting bodies, everyone talking at once and all proffering before them foil-covered chafing dishes or buckets of hot-house flowers like offerings they meant to lay on an alter at the feet of a statue of some minor god, bare-breasted, already a little drunk.

At seven-thirty the guests began to arrive, and by eight o'clock the house was full. Thingy and I watched from the top of the stairs. I hadn't brought anything suitable for a party, so Thingy leant me something from her closet: a rose-pink dress with a belted waist and short, full skirt overlaid with silver netting. On Thingy it came to mid thigh and showed off the muscular stretch of her legs. On me it was much too big, hanging almost to my knees, the bodice loose and folding in awkward ways as I fidgeted on the stairs. Our feet weren't the same size, so I had to settle for my old, white sandals with the torn strap my father had mended using kitchen twine and a leather awl.

Thingy looked much older than she was. Her dress was strapless with a deep sapphire bodice and a black velvet skirt which bloomed from her hips like a black tulip. The dress made her seem serene, even chilly, nodding indulgently to the catering staff as she lifted another handful of miniature crab puffs from a silver tray. As for me, I remember thinking I looked okay. Certainly I didn't look as if I belonged there, but I didn't look terrible either. I stood in front of the mirror in Thingy's parent's bathroom for a long time after Mrs. Clawson had finished our makeup and gone to supervise the last minute bar setup. The mirror was large and oval with an ornate frame featuring an old-fashioned cornucopia motif replete with tumbling grapes and thieving sparrows perched as if to take flight. Someone had spray painted it silver and in places the paint was beginning to chip away. The effect was as if the frame had contracted a skin disorder or as if it were an enchanted garden, frozen in time, slowly remerging beneath a film of melting snow.

In the center of the garden was my face. Thingy's mother had chosen a very pale green shadow, shimmering like the wings of a moth, and outlined my eyes with slightly darker green liner. She had swiped my eyelashes with a single coating of brown mascara and left my cheeks alone. "Let's not overdo it," she said.

It was still me in the mirror: my sallow cheeks and slightly off kilter eyes, but there was something else beside. It was as if

I was wearing a thin mask that moved as my muscles moved, came down over my eyelids when I blinked. The mask did not obscure my features, so much as it redefined them. Underneath was my nose, but the mask's nose was for something other than smelling. Underneath were my lips, but the mask's lips felt no compulsion to open or smile. I put my fingers to my cheeks and pinched them, watching as the blood rushed momentarily to the surface. I understood, maybe for the first time, that this was how people went about in the world, how it was possible.

In the cold garden, when the prince bent over the sleeping princess and commanded her, "arise!" what happened next was not a gradual return to consciousness, not a surfacing. Rather, the princess sat up and shielded her face from him, groped all around her bier until she found her mask and slid it on.

By eleven o'clock the party was in full swing. We had been sneaking drinks for an hour and we were both loose on our feet.

"Let's go," Thingy said. "This is boring."

The party wasn't boring and I didn't believe she was bored. The house was filled with noise. The rumble of conversation, a high hysterical laugh from a woman in a tuxedo jacket who was watching a man in a white linen suit as he rolled his eye wildly and ate the carnation he had been carrying in his buttonhole. A joke, I realized, when he laughed too. He bent and lifted the hem of her skirt as if he were going to eat that next and she shrieked, delighted, her dark mouth like a tear in her face.

Elsewhere, a man and a woman were sitting on the couch pressing their foreheads together and an elderly woman with a face like a frozen waterfall was smoking a long cigarette and tipping the ash into her husband's drink. Thingy's mother was standing in the center of the room, inclining her head to listen to a short, bald man whose his head was as brown and peaked as an egg. Thingy's father was sitting at the piano picking out a jangling little tune with a woman who was jabbing at a single low note and staring very intently at the side of his head.

On the far side of the room from us, a woman was weeping, her face buried in her hands, and the man who was sitting at her feet patted her knee with absentminded regularity. Next to them, another woman was not paying enough attention to her dress. When she bent to set her glass on the end table, or stooped to pick it up, one breast, tanned as a glove, would slip out and hang framed in the deep V of her halter, swinging slightly as she shifted her hips in time to the music. Her nipple was fleshy and brown, like a fig.

The bar tender winked at me when I accidentally caught his eye and pushed a full glass of wine someone had abandoned there to the edge of the counter as he turned away. Thingy drank half and gave the rest to me. She crossed her arms over her bodice as she scanned the room, biting her lip. The room was full and the people in it so intent on each other and themselves that there was no room for her. No Thingy shaped space in which she could stand and be seen. My dear Thing had many qualities, but none of them were modesty, none patience.

"Come on," she said again. "Let's go for a walk."

We slipped out a side door that opened almost directly onto the dune. It was a still night, the moon full and the face in it clearly that of a woman, her mouth open in decorous shock. I was still carrying the wine glass, taking tiny sips of the warm, musty wine and trying not to gag. We left our shoes behind us in the sand and dragged our feet so our tracks looked as if they had been made by someone crawling on all fours along the hissing edge of the surf.

"Where are we going?" I asked Thingy. I was suddenly tired and feeling more and more drained the further we went from the lights of her house.

"Look," Thingy said. "There's someone standing under the pier."

Once there were two girls and one of them was me. That is the part I keep forgetting.

Sometimes, in stories, a girl will look into a mirror and realize the face she has been seeing all along is not herself but a girl from the other world who looks very much like her. When she realizes this she generally has to make one of two choices. She can trap the other girl by tricking her into exposing herself for what she really is. She can enter the mirror after her and hunt her down. In stories, girls are often predators, if carefully disguised ones.

To put it another way: an eastern newt, such as the one we turned up today in the shallows, Ingrid, spends most of its life as an unremarkable olive creature in the bottom of a murky pond. But there is a time of two or three years when this newt is actually a red eft. During this period, the newt-to-be races across the forest floor, rappelling between rocks and burrowing under the leaf mulch, in a brilliant flame-red skin that ripple over its ribs as it breathes. A red eft is poisonous and attention getting. It is looking for a safe home, but this is not how it appears to an outside observer such as a crow or a black tie-snake. Rather, the eft seems to be bragging.

Look at me, how fast and trim, is what the crow hears. Look at me, my dainty foot, is how it sounds to the snake.

~

This is not to say that we weren't also perfectly ordinary girls. Children of our time, not so unlike children of any other time, who were encouraged to believe our world would soon end. As children grow, they begin the life-long process of mythologizing their younger selves. "I put my pudgy little hand in my daddy's big brown one," a young woman will say. "I gave my mommy a kiss and ran into the woods as fast as my little legs would take me."

Thingy was no exception to this rule—witness her interminable collections: buttons and plastic rings, lockets bristling with locks of her own hair, pamphlets and mysterious shards of glass—but, to her credit, her own red eft stage came early and lasted an inordinately long time. Oh, she was wild and fair. It seemed to me, following behind her, as if she skimmed across the surface of the earth incandescent with disdain. She was never caught, no one even came close, and she left no trace of her passing: no footprint, no turned stone. There was no way to track Thingy's progress but, I suppose, myself.

When Thingy saw the other face in the mirror, she murdered it. Every time. It never seemed to occur to her that sometimes that face was mine.

To whit: under the pier. It was a bright night, the moon high and demanding. The sea lathered the sides of the pylons into a froth of sea haze and salt which glimmered in the barnacles' fans. On our way down the beach, Thingy and I had been flanked by ghost crabs sidling in and out of their dark holes, but here there seemed to be no animate life. Just the concrete and the barnacle encrustations. The creosote stained wood and the tightly shuttered winkles.

As we got closer, the immaterial forms under the pier so-lidified into three boys, a little older than us, who were leaning against the side of the concrete abutment and watching us ap-proach. Two of them were smoking cigarettes and there was a bottle in a brown paper bag screwed into the sand at their feet. Thingy walked right up to them.

"Hi," she said, fluffing the skirt of her dress. "Do any of you have a cigarette I could bum?" Of course, they did.

Up close, the boys were much older, closer to being men than we had first expected. Two were tall and very alike, clearly brothers with widely spaced eyes and dark eyelashes, sharp nos-es and thin mouths that seemed to draw their faces forward into a point. The other boy was the outsider, the instigator. He was shorter, but more muscular. His skin, even in the weird glamour of moonlight, was assiduously browned against his white T-shirt and his face had the homely, dangerous aspect of a mule: all nose and teeth, no humility, no forgiveness.

"My name is Ingrid," Thingy said, despite the fact that they hadn't asked. Their only response was a collective shrug, a lin-gering gaze from the short one that spent as much time on her bare feet as it did her frank, sea-dewed cleavage. There was a sense that we'd walked into the middle of something which had to be suspended due to our presence, a sense of biding time.

"I don't live here normally," Thingy said, as if responding to a further questions. "My family owns a summer home, down the beach." Thingy waited for their reaction and when none came she exhaled an thin line of smoke and lifted the wine glass out of my hand without looking at me as if I were some sort of retainer.

"I think I need a drink," she said, tilting the glass until the wine pattered a little hollow at her feet. "I've finished this one."

As the boys finally turned their attention on her, really looked, she smiled a smile thin as the crest on a wave and stepped forward, closing the circle, leaving me out.

(The eft was sprinting across the loam, her hide bright, her eye sure. The crow was dazzled; the snake was lulled. And what was I, then? A clutch of eggs? The mud-green mother? When you learn to say thank you, Ingrid, you might say it to me that you will never have to experience that sense of padding I was muffled in for so long. It was as if I was wrapped in layers and layers of gauze. My breath stale in my lungs, my heart slow and sluggish in my chest. I had to wait a long time for my life, but you, my dear, will get to live yours stripped and lean—a bright and furious instant, each of your many instants also your only one. This is a fact of which I would be jealous if I weren't the one, through whatever circuitous fashion, to bring it about.)

"Ingrid, huh," said the mule-faced boy, pouring a long shot into Thingy's wine glass. The smell was both caramel and antiseptic. He passed the bottle to the brother on his right who fitted the neck into his mouth in a way that seemed needlessly convoluted. Once it had made its way around the circle, Thingy passed the bottle back to me, yet, even as I drank, the circle did not bloom open. The liquor clotted in the back of my throat, almost choking me, and I sat in the sand, my back to the concrete abutment, headless of the prick of empty barnacles which I would later find had caught the fine material of Thingy's borrowed dress and torn it in a hundred tiny places.

"That's kind of an old fashioned name," one of the brothers said. He lit a cigarette of his own and I drank from the bottle. This time the liquor went down more smoothly. Something numbing was rising from my stomach up my throat and to the back of my tongue like a frigid tide. All three boys were wearing khaki shorts and one of the brothers wore a T-shirt with *End-Time Harvest* printed across the chest in squat block letters and underneath that a phone number. I drank again from the bottle. There was sand on the rim, sand in between my teeth. Maybe I had more than one drink, maybe another.

The brothers both wore their hair gelled into a plump swoop that rose from their foreheads like the crest of a water-going bird. A merganser, I thought, and I pictured the bird's lean hooked beak, its round eyes rimmed in black.

The water, far out but turning with the tide, dashed and foamed under the pier like a dog racing to strangle itself on the end of its line.

"Were you named after your grandmother or something?" the mule-faced boy asked.

"I was named after myself," Thingy said. She giggled and sipped from her glass.

How could we be so many things? Newts and efts. Fish-eating ducks and coarse-coated mules. Snakes and crows and girls and boys and the sea, which subsumed, and the mountains which marked where we were birthed into these forms and where we would be turned out of them.

Suddenly, as I now know it sometimes happens, I was drunk.

Belly drunk. Bone drunk. Drunk so I felt if I opened my mouth the pulpy mess of my being would push out of me and land in the sand at my feet with a wet thud. With my eyes open or closed I saw the same lurid slur: Thing, smoke, fire point, arrow pier, dark water, dark sand. Somewhere far away, but getting closer, a raging white light as thin as a wire.

~

"Your friend ok?" said a merganser.

"Is she going to puke?" said the mule.

Oh, Thing—oh mermaid splitting her fishtail, uncoiling her dark length in the surf. Oh, sharp-toothed snout, wall-eye.

No, it was only my dear as she had always been. Only the velvet bodice, her own knees, nicked with razor marks, thudding into the sand on either side of my feet and her hand on my jaw turning my face from side to side.

"Alice," Thingy hissed. "What are you doing?"

We are well past that, I wanted to say, but there were no words in me. I might have made a sound. I might have made a noise like a howl, but very quiet, very low. The mule and the mergansers clustered behind Thingy and looked down at me from over her shoulder. I could tell I was embarrassing them, though not Thingy who was made of sterner stuff. After all, she had known me when our world was only blood and the gummy slide of fluids. I had felt with her the plug of mucus in her throat and her rage as a slick gloved finger slide into her mouth to scoop it out. She had felt with me the vernix drying in my creases, the amniotic fluid stiffening on me like a second tighter skin. After that, Thingy told me with her stern gaze, we could neither repel nor charm each other. After that, Thingy did not say, but said, there was nothing in this world that could keep us apart.

"Why don't you go to sleep," Thingy said and, for the benefit of the mule, helped me by pushing on my shoulder until I tipped, the dress catching and pulling against the concrete as I slid. I landed in the wet sand, my mouth open, my arm caught awkwardly beneath me.

Then, I suppose, I slept.

This is what I remember from a summer night when I was thirteen:

Where Thingy stands is a bowl of light.

The mergansers preen. One dabbles his bill in the feathers of his chest; one rears back and beats his wings.

"It isn't that late."

The water comes hissing to Thingy's feet, laps her ankles.

Ha ha ha. Ha ha ha.

"My mother can tell time by the moon."

The mule bends and presses his snout to Thingy's belly. Something dark is in the surf.

Ha ha ha. Ha ha ha.

My Thing has a head made of light that floats above her shoulders. There is a song about this. A song I remember.

Something dark is struggling in the breakers.

"Give me another cigarette. Please."

~

No, that is the moon.

The mule takes the hem of Thingy's dress in his teeth and nibbles.

"You're friend's going to drown. She's getting sand in her mouth."

If I could hear someone hum it… If I could hear the first line…

"Look! Look!"

The mergansers have beaks like twin needles. Fire-point. Twin lights.

A song about a girl who has the wrong love. A song about what happens next.

When Thingy turns the mule presses his face in the small of her back, mergansers encircle her shoulders with their wings.

"Oh, look! Look!"

A turtle. It swims out of water, swims up the beach. So painful. Leaking water from its shell.

Ha ha ha.

"Give me the bottle."

~

The mule brays; his mane bristles.

The bottoms of Thingy's feet are white and kick up sand.

After the chorus, a mother travels a long way but cannot save her children.

In the end, someone cracks the eggs to bake a cake.

In my mouth, the ocean coils a finger.

My Thing glows inside her black dress and on the turtle's back she lays her hands.

# A Song About What Happens Next

When I came back into a better understanding of myself, I was alone under the pier. The tide hissed up the beach toward my face and fell just short. I watched the water recede, bubbles of foam bursting in its wake.

The tide hissed up the beach toward my face and slapped me. Seawater rushed up my nose and into my mouth and I sat up coughing, dizzy. I looked around.

Further in the direction we had been traveling, the beach was a long, clean sweep of gray sand. The dunes massed blackly behind it as if herding the sand toward the sea. In the far distance, the mainland blazed with the lights of hotels and restaurants, banks and stores that sold clever beach blankets and tins of sex wax. At the tip of the spit, the lights winked out leaving only an abandoned lighthouse to sulk at the mouth of the bay.

The other direction was mostly dark. The night had clouded up, the moon high now and small. There was no sign of Thingy or any of the boys. I got to my feet unsteadily, gripping the concrete abutment for support and scraping my palms on the barnacles.

"Thingy?" I said. And then, "Thingy?" I said again.

But she was gone, that was clear, and I was here surrounded by nothing more prophetic than an empty bottle in a soft paper bag, many cigarette butts stubbed into the sand like tiny, haphazard pylons and a fork, the shaft pitted, the tines bent willy-nilly.

I stood for a while running my hand through the wet, gritty tangle of my hair. I was still drunk and I remember thinking that the dress, which was clearly ruined, was not so much the issue as my face with which Mrs. Clawson had taken such pains.

I bent from the waist and vomited a brown stream into the churning surf at my feet. I did it again. And then again. There was sand in my eyelashes and sand on my lips. One side of my throat was stiff with sand and my legs inside the wet flop of the skirt pricked with salt and sand. I stayed bent, heaving like a donkey, the dress heavy as canvass against my shins, but nothing else came out of me. Eventually I straightened and turned back in the direction from which Thingy and I had come.

After a long struggle up the side of the dune, I found myself back in the road, the summerhouses presenting on either side of me their austere, flat faces. Most of these buildings were uninhabited. Their owners lived in Charleston or New York or Labrador or Bavaria, for all I knew, but they were not here and the road itself was dark and still. In some houses though, the lights were on and as I made my way up the road I saw through some of the windows and into the depressing grandeur within. A man was sitting at the kitchen table reading a magazine. A woman wearing a blue bathing suit was cutting the heads off a cluster of peony buds and cramming the tight, sour balls into a range of small vases arrayed before her on the table. In one house, a dog had fallen asleep in the bay window, its fur pressed up against the glass in brown and white whorls. Beyond it, in the bright sofa-adorned living room, people walked back and forth carrying things.

I took the turns at random until I came to a road that seemed slightly more familiar and heard, blown toward me over the constant groan of the ocean a babble of voices and music and a woman's rising laugh. It was Thingy's road and, at the end of it, Thingy's house: all the lights lit, the windows ablaze against the dark pit of the sky, people strewn about the upper balconies and the veranda while the small fires of their cigarettes rose and fell like lovelorn fireflies strobing their asses off in the sterile salt air.

Let's imagine for a moment, dear Ingrid, the scene. You haven't yet attended any parties—though if Thingy had had her way, this would not be the case. Well before your birth, you were scheduled to attend, indeed to be the guest of honor at countless mother's teas and luncheons, a Mother's Day brunch and a formal introduction to the Rotary, in which Mrs. Clawson was a member.

Thingy even bought outfits for the still imagined you to wear to these events. Little frocks in butter yellow with overskirts of white organdy polka-dot, miniature blush-rose gowns and long, flowing shifts in picked white lace—all of which I've kept as a memory of her. I've put them away in the attic, enough to fill six shoeboxes. You can unearth them later in your life, if you're so inclined, Ingrid. If you become the sort of girl who is charmed by the mysteries of the past.

Regardless, try to imagine the scene from a distance. The party has become a looser, messier event than it was even when Thingy and I first left it. There are fewer people in the house, fewer cars parked along the sides of the road, but those who remain seem to have swelled to take the place of their wiser or soberer compatriots. On the balcony and veranda there is a sense that all bordering lines have been eradicated. The provisional shapes of people's bodies merge into each other, merge into the wrought-iron railings and cunningly replicated Doric columns that distinguish the wall on either side of the front door.

A man is talking too loudly. He says, "Damn it, Cynthia," or maybe, "Damn you, Cynthia," and a woman laughs a teetering laugh like a gull caught in an updraft, soaring helplessly higher above the sheer, rocky shore. Inside the house there is a sense of many bodies moving very quickly. It is almost as if people are running back and forth in front of the windows; tearing back and forth with their arms over their heads and their dresses floating out behind them as if giving chase. Someone tosses a full drink into the oleander. Someone on the balcony tips the dregs of their glass onto the head of another someone standing in the yard, then runs into the house and slams the door.

Now, from the same critical distance, Ingrid, imagine me. Stiff-kneed, soaked, small as a rat inside my pink dress. Imagine my hair matted to my cheek and neck. The sand gritting in between my toes and the burn from a cut on my foot I didn't remember getting as I shifted my weight on the black, absorbing road. Is it any wonder, even at the end of such a difficult journey, that I took the long way around? Is it any wonder that I slunk?

I picked my way through the narrow side yard catching glimpses as I went of partygoers in all manner of disarray. At the foot of a bed of day lilies, I clambered over the low iron fence that ringed the Clawson's backyard pool. Despite the discarded glasses, puddles of melting ice cubes and an open tube of dark lipstick bobbing enticingly in the drain—all of which gave clear evidence that the party had indeed swept through the pool area with its scouring winds—I seemed to be alone. At the back of the house, a large plateglass window stretched the length of the wall. I perched on the side of a beach chair, adjusting the plastic so it cradled my haunches, and looked through the window, down the length of the brilliant, white living room where I found myself unsurprised to see Thingy with the three boys from the pier clustered at her side. She was holding a group of adults in disheveled formal clothing enthralled as she waved her arms in the air in front of her.

"They found a turtle on the beach," Mr. Clawson said.

I jumped and jerked around. In my haste I slipped out of my cradle of plastic slats and was dumped unceremoniously onto the ground, my legs braced like a marionettes over the chair's metal frame. To his great credit, Mr. Clawson didn't laugh. He actually didn't seem to fully notice, his eyes locked on his daughter as she hitched up her skirt and preformed a curious waddle across the living room.

"They watched her lay her eggs," Mr. Clawson said as he maneuvered around the chair. The branch of a struggling camellia snagged his pant leg and he pushed it away as one might the snout of a friendly, but impolite dog. He drank out of his glass and sung the ice cubes around its belly, the picture of a man at ease, a man preoccupied with ease. He stared a moment longer through the window, then, as I pulled myself upright, eased himself down onto the concrete by my side.

Thingy's father had dull, straw-colored hair which he wore very short on the sides and back and cut in the front in a straight fringe across his forehead as if to mark with its line the definitive place where his face came to an end. He had a round face, a snub nose and a thick, heavy jaw that had settled as he aged so it appeared to weigh down his thin neck. It gave him a contemplative look, the look of a deep thinker who was willing to dive ever deeper into his thoughts like an inexperienced tourist scubaing just a little further into the cave. He was wearing white trousers through the seat of which the denser white of his pockets could be clearly seen. As he braced his arms and leaned back against them, the sleeve of his polo shirt brushed against my thigh. He looked rumpled and distracted. He looked as if, at any moment, he might burst into some prodigiously mournful song, but he only sighed and sat with me in more or less companionable silence as we watched his daughter tell the tale.

For a time we sat quite still together, not talking, the sleeve of his shirt shifting minutely against my thigh as he breathed. It seemed possible we would spend the rest of the night sitting like this—drowsing under the silky spell of the pool, its toothless blue murmuring, its completely fathomed deeps. The entire night wrapped in stillness as the moon wore to a thin nacreous wafer and the ocean, it seemed just possible, faded too with the coming dawn until, pale as a cloud, it drew itself back and disappeared.

Where would we sleep? I was beginning to wonder. What would Mr. Clawson offer me in lieu of his missing sport's coat to make into a pillow for my head?

"How could anyone be expected to believe it?" Mr. Clawson finally said.

"I think it's true," I said. I was dry now and thought how it was that dryness was a condition noticed only by the lack of damp whereas to be wet was sudden and appalling. The sand showered from my skin in plates like calving glaciers. "I think I saw it come out of the water."

"I was there, of course," Mr. Clawson forged on, "but in the waiting room. That was the way things still were. The waiting room for fathers with its plastic chairs and even ashtrays." He plucked something off his lower lip and wiped it precisely on the knee of his trousers. "It was a terrible hospital, not the one we had chosen."

I had heard this story before. The story of Thingy's birth, but only in whispers that subsided into silence when I or my Aunt Thalia or my father was seen entering the room. Thalia, who had never whispered once in her life, was inclined to shout whatever last breathy word she had caught dying on the lips of the Pinta who believed death and romance were different words for the same story. "Went to the wrong house?" Thalia would roar, without breaking stride or even looking at the Pinta turned suddenly pale and sweaty as a wedge of cheese. "Well go on," Thalia would shout as she strode out the door, "The baby screaming on the floor, you were saying. Mrs. Clawson snug as a tick, you were saying. Don't mind me. I'd hate to interrupt."

From this, and from our own shared memory, Thingy and I had pieced together a plausible narrative: Thingy's mother's untimely panic, her father's absence, an ambulance called twice to houses on the same road and the sort of careless, take-it-for-granted accident that happens in a place where everyone knows the details of everyone else's lives. Including their due dates. Including, as my father would insist, how much they put in the bank on Friday afternoon.

In the end, the dispatcher assumed that the two calls, for side-by-side houses high on the same generally under-populated street, was a mistake, some kind of foul-up on the part of the operator, DeeDee Smitz who was fat and had bad skin, read novels about dragons and the societies that attended them while on duty, and was generally considered to be not all that bright. After all, what were the odds? After all, when considered from a purely objective, mathematical perspective, what was the likelihood? As a result, only one ambulance was sent. Mrs. Clawson rode to St. Francis Sans Souci in a froth of peach-colored maternity wear, accompanied by a halo of sirens and bleating horns, where she was dismayed to labor in a shared maternity ward. My mother bled to death on her kitchen floor.

"I think a woman can't quite understand the mystery of her parts," Mr. Clawson said. He was still gazing through the window where his daughter seemed to be telling the story all over again to a smaller, but no less enthusiastic audience. The two brothers had faded away into the far reaches of the house, but the mule-faced boy was still with Thingy, still stuck tight to her side and following her every move with his cruel, melancholy eyes. Mrs. Clawson was nowhere to be found. Not a trace of her. As if she had lifted through the ceiling, toes dangling pale and pointed beneath the hem of her dress.

"Perhaps it is because a woman is afforded both the exterior and the interior sensation of her parts—or the posterior and anterior?—" Mr. Clawson mused. He was leaning back more frankly now, his forearm pressed up against my calf which for some reason I didn't move.

"No matter. No matter," he went on, passing a shaky hand before his eyes to banish his confusion, "either way it's sure: she knows what goes into her and she knows what comes out. Any woman does. It's a matter of instinct, natural primal instinct—nothing wrong with that—but while she's busy bearing down, while she's busy expanding and contracting, think of the man. Think of her clueless mate, boozling around in the waiting room, buying her flowers, a teddy bear."

Mr. Clawson laughed and looked up at me. He had very white teeth, very straight. They caught the moonlight with an unapologetic frankness and I suddenly wanted to reach across the space between us and press the tip of my finger against one of his square, smooth, wet, white teeth.

"Can you imagine?" Mr. Clawson said. "A teddy bear. Well, I did—I bought a blue teddy bear and a bouquet of Gerber daisies, it was all they had, and I went down a long hall, through swinging doors, past all kinds of carts and other detritus, to her room."

Mr. Clawson paused, remembering. I could feel the thick wiry hairs of his forearm against my calf and worried that he could feel the prickle of my own hair growing back in from that morning's shower. Mr. Clawson had thin lips, almost non-existent. It was as if the flesh of his jaw and cheeks rushed right up to the hole of his mouth where it plunged out of sight. I imagined his lips would feel rubbery. They might even prick-le with stubble. He smelled of some sort of thin, clean spice. Something blue. We were sitting very close together, watching the busy house, listening to the busy ocean, apart from those things in the tidy isolation of the little, square yard.

"And there," Mr. Clawson said, spreading his hands before him like a magician setting up a miraculous substitution; a dove for an orange, a rabbit for a girl, "and there, laid out before me…Can you imagine the mess? The noise? Her cunt split right in half, it looked to me. My own wife's cunt which I had dabbled in so happily, so innocently up until this point. I had thought of it as a still, clear pond. A little resting place. When I thought of my wife's cunt, I now realized, I had imagined a sandy bottom, languorous water weeds…" Mr. Clawson laughed again. He looked up at me and gripped the back of my calf, laughing.

"Oh, I was forced into a reckoning," Mr. Clawson said. "I was forced to come to terms with what was weak within my own nature, and I have done that every day ever since. It's like a mantra with me." He pulled away for a moment to fetch his drink, but then came right back, resting his chin on my knee, passing his arm under my thigh to sip from the glass on the other side. I made a noise, some noncommittal noise that I hoped sounded casual and encouraging. Mr. Clawson seemed to take it that way.

"That's what I like about you," he said, gazing pensively over my thigh and into the camilla. "You're not so squeamish, so finely tuned. If we don't have language in common then what do we have?" He was getting worked up again, lifting his chin from my knee, raising his voice. "If we can't say what we have experienced in plain language and thus expunge it, then we must admit the thing into the secret chambers of our soul," Mr. Clawson shouted into the shrubbery. Behind us something plopped into the pool which made a slurping sound.

"Do you know what the soul is?" Mr. Clawson asked.

"No," I said.

"A blob of glup. Do you know what the soul needs?"

"No," I said. My legs were falling asleep, the circulation cut off by the edge of the lawn chair, but I was too precariously balanced to move. I felt proud of myself for not being the camilla, blighted by the strictures of its life, visibly withering. I also felt vaguely like we were playing a game, some call and response which would spell out an unexpected word I wouldn't be able to guess until the very end.

"No," I repeated, a whisper.

"Me neither," said Mr. Clawson and suddenly deflated. He rested his chin on my knee again like a good dog. He laughed. "What else could it possibly need?" he said, but not to me.

I wasn't sure what I was supposed to do in response. He seemed so friendly; he was almost panting. The hair on the top of his head swirled in an unexpected cowlick that made me feel very sorry for him. I think I did something like pat him on the head. If I am to be my most honest, as I hope I am always able to be with you, Ingrid, I will admit I buried my fingers in Thingy's father's hair and scratched his scalp the way I did for fat, little Dog whose legs were too short to reach between his shoulder blades.

Mr. Clawson took another sip of his drink and, still laughing softly, turned his head and laid his cheek against my knee. Against my expectation, I found his skin smooth and soft, with a resilient toughness where the muscles of his jaw bunched and stretched. I moved my scratching to behind his ears but became confused and shy. I let my fingers still at the nape of his neck but then thought it too much of a statement to pull away entirely. We sat there for a little while: his breath warm against my knee, my palm resting on his back and fingertips just barely touching the skin above his collar. I watched a plane wink across the sky, so far away its incredible speed was slowed to a crawl in my vision. Inside, the party had moved elsewhere and Thingy, left alone in the living room, leaned forward and accepted the mule-faced boy's hungry embrace.

"Oh, look," Mr. Clawson said. He reached out and grabbed my opposite ankle, tugged gently until I let him draw my foot up near his face. "Look, Alice," he said. "You're bleeding. You have a cut." And, even though the cut itself was shallow and had long since scabbed in a thin crust, Thingy's father passed his fingers over my skin as if pressing back rills of pumping blood, bent his neck and kissed the arch of my foot as if stemming a tide.

He pressed there for a long time, lingering, moving his lips in a speech I could feel but not hear. His lips were warm and dry. They brushed over my skin, but I swear to this day, Ingrid, I swear on my mother's burst body which I sent to the grave, I have no idea what it was Mr. Clawson asked me. All I know for sure is what I said in return. And what came after, of course. Which is where you come in.

# The Horse's Tale

Once, through a confluence of events and no fault of his own, a horse fell in love with a baby.

This happened at a busy crossroad where two well traveled paths met and mingled before going their separate ways. At first the crossroad was a naked x, pressured on all sides by trees. The roads that stretched away from that place were cold and thin, insufficient lines drawn between the mountain and the valley. Over the years many trees had been cut for lumber and the forest pushed back to widen the thoroughfare. Then someone had built a gibbet. Then someone had built a stable behind the gibbet and soon enough an inn next to the stable, a feed store on the other side of the road, an apothecary's shop snug at its side. Soon there were enough buildings and goods to consider the place a small town.

The crossroad was busy day and night but it was not named as a town would be. It was an in-between place. Often travelers were seen standing in the middle of the x, turning from road to road in a state of bewilderment. From each road came the same cool wind. Down each was afforded the same looming view of spruce and hemlock, rock, frosted blooms of lichen, hard dark earth.

One day, to the crossroads came a white horse ridden by a young and weary rider. They were on their way back down to the valley after a trip to a mountain town to secure the hand of a lovely mountain bride who had been promised but, souring over the months of postal courtship, now refused her betrothed on her father's very hearth. "That cunt," the young and weary man said over and over as they came down the steep road. He murmured it into the white horse's mane as he sank exhausted over the pommel and every time the horse flicked back one soft, sensitive ear as if to agree.

It is impossible to say what the horse thought of all this. At this point he was only a horse, though a handsome one with round knees, strong haunches, a lustrous tail and yellow hairs bristling from his pink, speckled muzzle. He had been born in a barn not so many years ago. He remembered everything that had happened to him since that point: sliding from his mother's quivering vagina and laddering himself upright on his own quivering legs, a whisk of straw scrubbed over his face and in his nostrils, a cold breeze as the barn door opened and someone else came in. After that came many, many days that were largely the same.

Immediately after birth, the white horse had been given to the young and weary man as a present and this man had formed the basis for almost everything the white horse knew about himself. For example, he knew he was an animal and that to be an animal was to stand when someone told him stand and go when someone told him go. He knew the sun, which was like his curry brush, and the grass, which was like the bit in his mouth. He knew a sly kind of joke which had to do with his eyes and lips and a quick, sideways shuffle and, if the man were in a different mood, he knew a stupid, towering fear of brown leaves and blowing paper down from which his master could disdainfully calm him.

The young and weary man was mostly patient, but sometimes used the lash. He mostly remembered the horse's soft mouth, but sometimes sawed the reins until the corners of the horse's lips split and bled. In this way the white horse learned what was expected of him and, because he knew nothing but this expectation, came to understand his most intimate self as a figure of what he would do next. Not what he currently was; not what he desired to become.

This is not so strange. Who expects a mule or an ox to have a spiritual life? Who suffers a crisis of self alongside a flea? The world is full of dawning. The sun comes up. If a man or a woman or a horse is awake to see it, they might mark the very moment when the sun appears to pull itself free of the horizon: shivering like a yolk, bouncing into its shape.

The horse brought his rider to the crossroad at noon. It was early spring and the sun was small and silver as a coin. They had traveled together all night. At first, spurred by the rider's spleen, they had pelted down the winding, treacherous road, blood in the white horse's nostrils, stones turning under his hooves. Then, when the moon rose, the rider relaxed and they traveled more slowly. There was time to watch shadows slide across the path in front of them. Time to smell the high, thin scent of the pines and listen once and then again as, close by their side, something heavy struck and something small shrieked and fell silent.

When the sun comes up in the mountains the world is very far away. The mountain is black and at first the sun is announced by a deeper blackness, a pooling in the valley. Then the world inches forward in slow shades of violet. Distance is uncovered and every creature knows a specific unease—to see the world unchanged when I have been so changed! to see the world cold and still when I am hot and pounding!

The horse tossed his head and flicked his ears as the sun came up over the side of the mountain. Below them the valley was filled with fog which boiled like the surface of an uneasy lake. Behind them rose the mountain, its face streaming with green water. The horse was small, his great heart beat. The rider leant against his neck and said, "That cunt. That cunt," in a voice as soft and thready as the new wind kicking up in the leaves. Then the path turned and they wound down again into darkness, quiet under the spreading branches of the pines.

So. When the horse and his rider came to the crossroads, at noon, weary from their journey, heart-sore and ill-at-ease, their minds were set on vengeance and on dinner, on pain and on a warm, snug place to sleep. This is to say, neither one of them was thinking of love. This is to say, they both nurtured within them a hard dark spot, like a black rock worn smooth by the river, which they turned and turned as if by turning it they would better be able to see....

The crossroad was busy and loud. A man in a red jerkin sold live chickens strung up by their feet. A woman wearing a silver mask was standing on a box waving her arms. Someone was selling meat pies; someone was selling pots. A man tugged on a woman's bodice and her breast popped out. A man sharpened knives on a stone he held between his knees.

The rider dismounted and looped the reins around the pommel. He gripped the white horse's bridle at his cheek and pulled as he used it to balance, standing on one leg and then the next, arching his back like a bow.

"Ten pots. Ten pots," said the man who was selling pots.

"I was buried in the meadow, but I arose," said the woman in the mask. "I was buried on the mountain, but I washed into the stream."

The horse whickered. His hooves felt sore and splayed. He urinated on the ground in a great, steaming arc and turned his head to watch the stream runnel through the dirt.

"Ten pots. Ten pots," said the man who was selling pots. He was walking away from them, a pack on his back hung all about with pots and he clanked as he moved. All in all, he was a funny sort of man, easily dismissible. His hair was black and stood up around his head as if he were wearing a crown. "Buy pots," said the pot selling man, and no one turned to mark him pass. He was like a slow, clanking shadow, unmoored from the sun, but in between all the pots was a sort of a hollow space and wedged in that hollow space was a kind of a pouch and in that pouch, her face purpling above the drawstring like a furious ornamental cabbage, was a baby girl.

The man turned his stone; he fingered it greedily.

The horse raised his head and pulled against the bridle. He opened wide a protesting eye and, for the very first time, he could see.

~

Of course, it didn't last. Even as the white horse strained his thick neck forward, the woman in the mask stepped off her box to buy a meat pie from the vendor and blocked the horse's view. When she moved again and he could see past her, the man selling pots had melted away into the crowd.

So it was that the white horse felt joy (her fat cheek! her furrowed brow!), and so it was the white horse also knew despair and a hunger that came not because something had been taken from him, as his oats must eventually be, as the comfort of his stall sometimes was in the early morning hours, but because something could not be taken from him. Something—this baby! this baby! the wide, clear eye that pierced his own as it looked back at him—was his to seek out, to possess.

"Where else was I buried?" said the woman. She slid the mask back on her head and nibbled at the edges of the pie. Some grease dribbled on her chin and splashed against her white collar where it soaked in. With her free hand she caressed the features of the mask—flat eyes, sharp nose, broad, clashing cheeks. She looked around her dimly. She kept asking questions.

The young and weary man had a terrible time getting his horse into its rented stable. It pulled against the bridle. It locked its knees and braced against him, its neck as long and obstinate as a goose. All he wanted was a meat pie from the vendor. All he wanted was to strike his lovely betrothed in the mouth and then sink to his knees at her feet as the blood flowed over her lips. This would take place in an orchard—early autumn with the leaves on the ground and fruit heavy on the branches, assaulted by wasps and bees. A sweet smell. Her little cries and her fingers in the hair at the back of his bent neck.

He struck the horse on the nose instead and was surprised when it reared up against the sides of the stall and lashed out with its hooves. But all this is temporary. There is something satisfying in turning one's back on a dangerous animal. There is something soothing about being very tired in the middle of the day, the sun on one's skin, people moving about with noise and purpose. If he left the horse screaming in the stable, it was just one more noise among many. What did it matter which way he turned when all the roads leading from this place looked the same?

"It couldn't have been the ocean," said the woman in the mask. "Where did I leave off?"

The young man bought a meat pie and ate it. Nothing was ever the same again.

For the rest of his life the white horse carried his joy and his rage on his back like a second rider. He grew sullen and would disrupt his master's journeying by trying to thrust his head over hedgerows and into open windows as they went. He began to gulp air, to fight the bit. He shied at bits of paper in the road, rustling leaves, the sudden heavy flight of crows and could neither be calmed nor jollied. His master put him in blinders. He employed spurs and rods, other more inventive encouragements, but the horse was driven, distracted by the weight on his back which was alternately as hard and cold as a ruby, sparking from all its facets, and as soft and dark as an organ engorged with blood, feebly trying to pulse.

In short, the white horse was ruined. His master—who had passed out of his youth but regained none of his vivacity and so was a stout and weary man, dark as a pudding, fairly steaming— used him to service the mares, but even at this the horse was fractious and unreliable. Eventually, his master put him out to pasture on a deserted, wilding side of the property, bound on three sides by thorn hedges and on one by the rustling forest. He forgot about him all together. There the white horse languished.

It is impossible to say how much time passed. What did it mean to the horse? Each day followed the next and it was the same sun, the same sky. The grass came up around his fetlocks and he bit it back down. A fox slunk out of the forest and trotted down the hedgerow, its black legs quick as shears. Later it came back with a rabbit slung from its jaws. The horse's knees grew swollen and boxy. His back swayed under the weight of his burden and his coat grew dull and dry. How many foxes? How many suns? The grass came up around his fetlocks and he bit it back down. On his back was a ruby, an organ, a ruby, a great, wet weight. One day, the horse went into the forest.

When a certain kind of girl walks she leaves behind her both the place she has just been and the person she was there. She breaks the new air with her new self and greets around her, with a shining face, all the possible versions of herself to come. Of course, she is caught up quickly. When she stops, even just for a moment to unsnag a thorn from her stocking, adjust the heel of her shoe, all the black weight of her self slams into her back and settles there. Her greed, her fear! Her nervous hands and the dark circles that press below her eyes like thumbprints. She must go on. Quickly, quickly. She must never look back.

A horse is a different sort of animal. The white horse left nothing behind him. He removed himself from the picture and the picture filled in. Simple as a soap bubble: iridescent, then pop.

~

The forest was not a natural place for a horse to be. The ground under his hooves was spongy and hummocked. Roots arced out of the leaf mold and zipped along a few feet before diving back in like trout choking a stream, the stream boiling with their bodies, he like a horse plashing witless in the shallows.

Was he thirsty? There was nothing to drink, though the forest had the lowering feel of a damp place and around him, at varying distances, he could hear the sound of water plinking against stone. Was he hungry? The horse lowered his head to graze as he went, a domesticate and thus accustomed to meeting many needs at once, but the ground was barren, soft and yet unyielding. Below him were vast hollow spaces. The roots pierced them and traveled on in darkness and in damp. The white horse could not see very well. The forest pressed around him like blinders, at once too close and too far: the dancing motes of light, gold and green; the suggestion past each trunk of a space opening out; the older trees shot like jackstraws, collapsed against each other's shoulders; a bird which called and fell still, called and fell still to listen. Was he thirsty? Was he hungry? The horse went on and on. His back hurt under its weight; his knees swelled and popped. A bird called. Water fell against stone. There was a great, rearranging flurry and then nothing. Silence. The forest drew itself up.

Eventually, as he must, the horse came out of the forest and into a clearing. Here the grass was long and thick. Through the center of the clearing someone had beaten a road; at the head of the clearing someone had built a house. What a pretty sight. A chimney. Rose bushes. There was a vegetable garden sprung with stands of rhubarb and clouded about the edges with pennyroyal and phlox. There was a shape at the window twitching the curtains and two crows perched meditatively on the garden fence. The roses were furled like champagne flutes. A curl of smoke lifted from the chimney and hovered in the still air like the shadow of something larger and further away.

And yes! the horse was hungry. Yes, thirsty, he was thirsty and stretched out his neck and called, his lips ruffling over his long teeth, for the pail fresh with water to be brought to him at once. Someone was asleep on the job, but he was forgiving. Dimly, the white horse remembered his best loved joke. Dimly, he bridled and danced beside the path, herky-jerky, all akimbo. The white horse was nothing to see, just another apparition pawing the turf at the forest's edge, and yet, here was someone who had seen him. Here was someone, opening the door, coming cautiously down the cottage path, who had heard and heeded his call. "Cush, cush" said the girl, wiping her hands on her pants and holding one out to him. "Cush" she said, sidling toward him through the tall, damp grass.

(The sun pulls itself whole from the horizon line. Egg from a hat. Bird from an egg. A burst of doves battering around the ceiling which here is the sky. And the rest of the room? The forest, of course. Oh please, can a horse not lay down his burden? Oh please, can't he just rest it here, here at your feet?)

Because this was she: the baby who had become this girl. Unmistakable, though her look was entirely altered, and had the white horse the capacity to imagine, he never would have dreamt her so shrunken and ill-favored. He remembered the sour bud of her lip, her imperious eye, clouded as marble, her soft round cheek, her corona of hair...Still, there was no mistake. It was she, she!, who braided her rough fingers in his mane, she who wrinkled her sharp, monkey face and said, "Poor thing," as she ran her palm over his ribs. It was she and she was his. He pressed forward to take her. The thick grass. The trembling roses. What a pretty sight at the edge of such a forest. He loved her, he loved her. He reared up to put his forelegs on her shoulders and show her his love.

But she said, "Whoa." She said, "Stop!" She stumbled back a few paces, her feet white in the grass, and as he came after her, she brought up a hand to block the sight of him. She ran back down the path and bolted her front door.

So, there they were. She inside and he without.

The white horse was puzzled, but it was not a condition of his being to question. The cottage path wound up to a little concrete stoop, three pretty steps with pots of red geraniums set at their edges, and a wrought iron railing swooping down both sides like extended wings.

At the top of the steps was a green door.

What was behind the green door was his.

This seemed simple enough to the horse; and yet the door was closed; and yet the steps, so foreign to his nature, were un-navigable. The curtains twitched. The sun went behind a cloud, then out it came.

For awhile the horse grazed in the cottage meadow. When she did not come, he went to the windows and stripped the leaves from the tops of the azaleas. Sometimes, he sensed she was just on the other side of the curtain. Sometimes, he thought he could even see the outline of her body, a shape perhaps like the shape of her eye framed in a miniscule gap in the fabric. At those times he pressed his muzzle to the glass and nipped at it eagerly, but she did not come. She gave him no sign. After the third day the smoke stopped coming up the chimney. After the fourth, as he strolled in the warm dirt of the garden and ate the ferny tops of the carrots, he saw her clearly in a dormer window, fiddling with the sash as if she were about the throw the window open. But when he whinnied with excitement and craned his neck to see her better, she stepped back, a mannequin shape in the dark room, and then just a shadow, then gone.

Had the horse the capacity to speculate, he might have suspected she was out of firewood and probably food. Had he the ability to calculate, he might have realized he had almost won. The house seemed still and cold, though in the meadow the sun was warm on his back and the new apples broke like hard, sour eggs between his teeth. Had the horse been his master, or even had his master been there to guide the horse's perceptions, he might have seen how he had trampled the garden, worn ruts from window to window, stripped the flowers from their stems, fouled the waters of the little creek as he slid down its bank to drink, scrambled up its opposite bank to see if it was not so that, while his back was turned, his beloved had come out again to welcome him with open arms.

Had he been a man, the white horse might have recognized all these things as signs of his eventual triumph. He might even have rejoiced, though with regret for all the necessary waste; with annoyance, perhaps, at the silly goose who had caused him to go to such lengths in the first place. But he was a horse, and so lacked subtlety. He fed on roses and carried his burden. He waited patiently for something to change.

On the sixth day, her father came home.

~

Imagine, for a moment, the scene from afar. Here is the familiar road, one hewn by your own hand. You can remember the trees that once stood there, the squeak of their wood as your axe bit. You can remember your body as it was then—like a machine, each motion foreshortened for greatest efficiency, each muscle in easy relation to the next. To lift and swing. To lift and swing. And then all those years of walking this very same road. Moss and berries in the verges, flowers thrusting up their doddering heads in the spring and in the winter the snow thick and crisp, patterned with the crosses of bird's feet and the hush of their downbeat wings.

For a strange man hung about with clamor, perhaps for any man at all, there is nothing in the world that feels so much like himself as this road and, at the end of it, the clearing he razed, the house he built, the girl who is his, who he made. She bears no expectation but that he return, and he has!, bearing pots! The rattle he makes is another way the road and the clearing break the forest. His bronze clangor, his clinking tin. He has come, bang a drum, he has come! In this way, the father strode from the forest and into the sun.

For all his oddities, the father was an astute man and not without imagination. He took in the scene before him: the garden ruined, the meadow deranged, the horse, slat-ribbed and broken, stretching the terrible crane of his neck to lip a peachy rose from its vine. Inside the house his daughter pulled back the curtain and stood there framed by eyelet white. She looked like the head of a water parsley. The curtains were the frothy bloom, and she herself the black pip in the center that either says, 'eat me', or 'beware', he couldn't remember which. In short, she did not seem herself, but a hardened seed of that self. She did not lift a hand to him but merely stood and stared and, as the white horse saw her and rushed toward the glass—his lips coated in slaver, his tail arched and trembling—she slid backward as if on a track and disappeared from view.

It is worth noting, that the white horse noticed none of this. Not even when the father, his pack and pots set down at the head of the road, edged around him, up the steps and in the front door. Not even when the sound of voices came from inside, rising and falling, shrill and sharp, or when that sound was replaced by the sound of something heavy sliding and many small doors being opened and shut. The horse was absorbed, blinded more surely than by any blinker, because he had seen her, at last it was her, there in the window, so close at hand. Though he had come too late and again the glass was in his way, at least now he could see. The curtains were pulled back, the room behind a sitting room: a couch plaid in broad bands of green and gold, a strange clock, shelves of books, a braided rug. Nothing to see, but something she had seen. Nothing to touch, the glass cold and slick against his nose, but something she had touched, where her arm had lain, her foot had tread. A book she had been reading was slung on the table, a hawk's feather tucked between the pages to hold her place. A pillow she had used to prop herself up was still wadded against the arm of the couch, dented with the shape of her elbow or head.

Without realizing it the white horse began to keen, his voice juttering in his rusty throat. He reared up and struck the side of the house, his hooves denting the clapboard, his back legs uprooting one bush and then another. Red and white azalea petals floated in the air like red mites in a burst of feather ticking. Meanwhile, the father had gotten his gun.

~

This seems a simple story. Why has it taken so long to tell? The gun was in the hall closet, a stubborn shape in the corner, behind rubber boots and oilskins. The bullets were in a kitchen drawer. In any story, the pieces are easy enough to assemble but hard to make move. Here is a woman who must enter a cavern; a man who must move a stone; a monkey who must climb to the top of the tree where the last green coconut bobs just out of reach. And yet they hunker down, stolid and stone-faced. They refuse. The gun was well oiled, the bullets slid home. From where he stood on the doorstep, the father could see both the white horse, still straining at the window, and his daughter who stood in the hall: barefoot, grey, wearing a grey sack dress she had tied at the waist with a dishtowel, her hair on her face like a veil.

Everyone has assembled. Pretty soon, the story will end. But the father balks. A decision must be made. Here is the horse: a pathetic thing, so lonely. He cannot live, but cannot help the way he has lived. He cannot learn from his mistakes. Here is the daughter, grown so long ago out of the shape he made for her on his pack and then kept growing. If he is honest with himself, this is not the first homecoming at which he has found her irreversibly changed. Indeed, every time he sees her—coming into the kitchen in the morning, walking down the hall to find her sprawled on the couch, one foot one the armrest, her face in her book—he finds he has to blink a few times before it is her that he sees and not just some vague and restless woman-shape dusting his house with flour.

The father stands on the doorstep he himself laid and looks from one to the other. He has a decision to make—here is a man who *must* fire a gun—and after a while he lifts the stock to his shoulder and takes aim.

~

When I finished talking, Thingy was quiet. We were in her room, sitting cross-legged across from each other on the silvery-green comforter her mother had bought to go along with the room's new color scheme. Thingy's mother redecorated the house on a regular basis and didn't consider Thingy's room an exception to this rule. Though it could hardly have been this sudden, it seemed to me as if these transformations took place overnight. One day, the living room wallpaper was patterned in cabbage roses and pomegranates, the next it was a severe, pin stripe blue. One day, the kitchen was country plaid, the next all sleek granite and chrome fixtures.

It was as if the house were actually a dollhouse, the food molded from the same plastic as its bowls, the people clothespins to which different skirts and jackets, trousers and dragon-stitched dressing gowns could be velcroed or clipped. Except Thingy. If Thingy was a pin at all, she was a hat pin: her visible features a cheery simulacrum of a cluster of cherries or a bunch of grapes, the rest of her lean and sharp and made to pierce through and through.

This time, Mrs. Clawson had chosen a spring motif for Thingy's room, perhaps as a wistful nod to Thingy's new status as a woman, though a very young one. Tender, tremulous, able to be romanticized, is what the pale green wallpaper with its motif of climbing ivy seemed to say. The year before Thingy had had a coming-out party at the VFW Hall. This month she had been accepted on early admission to a university in Atlanta and in the summer she would pack up all her things and go. Mrs. Clawson was preparing for this eventuality with a new desk set and vanity, an oval maple-framed mirror on a claw-foot stand, Queen Anne's chairs upholstered in striped mint sateen, a canopy bed overflowing with pillows in dreamy shades of yellow and faint, whispering green.

It was early December. Outside the first snow had already fallen, melted to a hard crust of ice and been covered by a second, deeper fall which tamped the world down to a still, hard place. Icicles rimed the eaves of the houses and ice sheathed the limbs of the trees, so when a wind did blow, the trees gave off a faint clinking, like spoons rattling together in the back of a drawer. Occasionally, a limb would snap below the weight of the ice and the sound echoed between the mountains like a rifle shot. It was a cold time, dark.

Inside, however, in Thingy's room, I felt like I had been buried in a chest deep under the loam of the forest floor. Eventually, after years of humid darkness, the wood of the chest had rotted away and roots and new sprouting shoots had tugged and turned me up and up until there was only the thinnest scrim of dirt between me and the gold and the green and the rustling and the damp, expectant air. Mrs. Clawson was forcing paper whites on Thingy's sill, but the bulbs were old and the faint, oniony smell of their decay only heightened this impression. I loved Thingy's room—any one of her rooms—and I would be sad when this was no longer a place where I could come. Not so long now. In the summer all would be lost.

"Give me your hand," said Thingy. While I spoke, she had sat and looked down at her lap. She drew one finger around and around the dome of her ankle where it rose between the cuff of her jean and the top of her white, cotton sock. If I hadn't known her better, I would have thought she wasn't listening, but I knew that the slant of her shoulders, the furrow that deepened between her eyes indicated deep concentration, all her attention focused on me. Not that there was too much I could tell her:

how far along, that the father didn't know and wouldn't. But not who he was—I never told her this, though who's to say she didn't guess—and not what might happen next because that I didn't know.

"I'll tell your fortune," Thingy said, and when I didn't respond at first, she laughed and shifted toward me until our knees were touching, pulled my hand out of my lap and unfurled it into her own. Thingy smoothed her fingers over my palm and stroked my wrist where the veins stood blue and branching in my thin, winter skin. She stretched each of my fingers and then bent over my hand until all I could see was her wild, zig-zagging part as she squinted at my lines and creases like a watch-maker intent on the tinkering gears, the tiny jewels and threads of gold that make the clock tick and lurch.

"Ok," Thingy said, straightening up and looking me in the eye. "See, it's not so bad after all. Here's your life line and your love line." She traced her finger down the center of my palm and back up, flattening my hand again as if to see more clearly. "And here's your marriage line, which means you'll have one, and if you make a fist and look here, you'll see how many children, and look, only one. So that means you're getting it out of the way." She smiled at me and pulled my hand even closer to her face. I could feel the puff of her breath when she spoke, almost her lips there on my rough, red palm.

"If you look close enough, Alice, you can tell just about anything from a person's palm," Thingy said. "See, look here, I can see your future house and oooh, it's a pretty big one." She looked up again, serious, her eyes so wide and intent it seemed as if she might cry at any moment.

"See Alice," Thingy said, tracing shapes on my palm with one light finger, "here's your garden and your greenhouse, here's the garage and two, no three stories, and here, right here…" She pressed and dug in a nail. "If you look really closely right here you can even see your pool, regulation length, a diving board and everything." She kept her finger in the center of my palm, as if saving her place and looked up again, willing me to play along.

"Don't you see it, Alice?" Thingy asked and, even though I knew what came next, I said, "No, I guess I don't."

"Well, let me show you then," she said, triumphant, but instead of spitting in my palm, which was how this game was supposed to end, she laughed, brought my hand up to her cheek and scooted around so she was lying on her side with my hand pressed under her head, pulling me after her until we both lay on the bed with the pillows heaped around us, laughing and looking out the window.

We lay like that for a long time. Eventually, we were quiet. The room was quiet and the house quiet around us save for a muted ticking as the wooden beams of the roof shifted and popped, and the faint rustle of Mrs. Clawson moving rapidly from room to room, bent to her own purpose. At any moment, I thought, Thingy would start asking questions and I didn't know what I would tell her. How could I not tell her the most central fact—who? says the owl though the forest will not answer, who? who? who?—when every other part of my life had been her story as much as mine? But she was still, her hair filling my nose with its bright, eucalyptus scent, perhaps even asleep with her body pressed into mine as if she were the one who needed comfort.

I didn't begrudge her that. Even then, as it would for the rest of our lives together, there was something growing between us. "The size of a beetle," said the book I had read in snatches in a seldom used corridor of the library. I was too afraid to check it out because the librarian, Miss Fawcett, went to the nail salon Rosellen was currently running, and because she was a soft, bleary-eyed woman who told me when I was nine that if I ever needed a place to stay I could always come and live with her for awhile. No questions asked, she said and laid a finger directly in the center of her pale, chapped lips.

I don't know what she imagined she was rescuing me from. Poverty, perhaps, or beauty in the form of my father who, when he came to the library to pick me up, seemed incapable of seeing her at all. As if Miss Fawcett were rendered invisible to him by her kindness and her instinct toward self-sacrifice, the soft, flinching way she took the books from my hands as he stood behind me and stamped each one carefully in the allotted space.

So, a beetle then. Membranes over the eyeballs, paddles instead of hands. "Congratulations!" said the book. "Soon your uterus will be the size of a softball. Some things you might be feeling this week: fatigue, a sense of unease."

Outside, a shelf of snow fell hissing from the branches. The wind caught it and it pattered against Thingy's window as if asking admission, politely tapping with white gloves against the glass. No, Thingy would have said, then and now. No, she would have sternly said, leveling the intruder with her cool gaze, casting him out.

Oh Thing, come back! Come back to me!

We were facing the back yard, the slope, the stone wall, the empty dog pen and the rusty, snow-heaped dragon. My house, my own window, curtainless and occluded by the stickers Thingy and I had saved over the years, but from where we lay I could only see the sky crossed by a craze of glittering twigs as it deepened from pearly white, to violet, to slate. The room grew dark and Thingy sighed and pressed closer against me.

She was looking for warmth as all animals do, for comfort in a world where the wind blows and the ice cracks. Every year it does and there's no using hoping this time it will be different, no use at all forbidding entry to what would like to visit or stay. Between us there was something else and for the first time we couldn't get close enough to each other to share a skin.

That wasn't you, Ingrid, not exactly, but given time, years from that day, it would be. It was, at least, the possibility of you, the will of you, something of your stubborn heart, the size of a poppy seed and already beating. What happens next is complicated, but right then it was simple. Thingy and I were asleep, snug in our burrow while outside the wind blew and the ice cracked, the mountain held still and the night came down.

## "I," Said The Sparrow, "With My Bow And Arrow. I Shot Cock Robin."

Sometimes I treat you as if you were blind, Ingrid. As if I were your eyes rather than just a memory you don't happen to possess. You must understand, I've been put in a difficult position. I am not in your mind, but I imagine it a cool place, supremely architected. How can I know this? I assume it because of Thalia and what she taught me, but if I didn't know by now that Thalia was not an honest tutor—untrustworthy, loyal only to her own essentially reptilian concerns—then I would be more of a fool than anyone could have thought.

So really, though Thalia is responsible for the root of my ideas, what I think of you, dear Ingrid, is no different from what any animal might think of an element of the world it has lived in so well and inhabited so thoroughly. A world it has both observed and remembered from season to season, storm to storm.

I assume your interior because I knew Thingy and Dax, Rosellen and Luke, the Sainte Maria, the Nina, the luckless Pinta who just last week I saw at Abbot's, finally fat in a purple dress, filling her cart with broasted chicken and stacks of firewood. I knew Thalia and the Clawsons, Jacob and Daniel, others even than them who came into my essentially solitary life and swirled it around. Others who laid a mark on me that I, in turn, lay on you, writing and writing as I do through all these sudden mornings and late, weeping evenings. Scribbling through a whole season—so much time! last year's acorns have rooted and sprung, the touch-me-not is bobbing in its bower and the lobes of the mayapples are thick and green between the trees, their flower already swollen into fruit—to record the events of an entire life. The one life that is mine and Thingy's. The one life that is also yours, at least so far.

But none of this is to say I really know you, Ingrid. That is becoming more and more apparent as you grow.

For example, today, when I gave you your morning bottle, I realized your eyes have changed. I don't know when it could have happened. It must have been sudden, perhaps even overnight. I admit to a moment of foolish panic. I stripped you out of your cotton singlet and turned you over in my hands, held you at arm's length as you kicked convulsively, the seams of your joints raw from the heat even that early in the day, and examined you. I went so far as to lay you on your back in the middle of the table and stand in the doorway peering in, as if from a distance, lulled into security by the still shortened reach of your senses, you would slip up and give yourself away.

But, after all that, it was still you. There is a mark on the sole of your foot, as if you had trodden on a thorn, that is unmistakable. There is a certain scent about you, milky and yeasty like a sweet roll baking; an undertone of citrus as if someone had grated rind into the dough. So you, now with green eyes—more challenging, less lucent. Showy, like the underside of a young leaf or, in certain lights, the band of feathers at a mallard's neck. You now, who blinks more often, lowers her brow.

A few nights ago, as I crept about the house, I came into your room to check on you, or simply to stand in your presence while you were away, traveling through the intricate corridors of your mind. I often do this. It soothes me to have a destination and there is nowhere else in this house I do not either associate with the past or the enduring present. The bedroom which looks out into the forest I share with Jacob who snuffles in his sleep as if he is tracking something over rocky terrain. The bedroom which looks out over the clearing, over the henhouse, cemetery and creek, is Daniel's alone now, but Thingy is there too—in the spread of the floorboards, in the rumpled valleys of the sheets. Every movement toward order is countered by one toward chaos. This is at the heart of everything Thalia taught me. In a way, it is all that Thalia taught me: how to see the invisible world in all its fixed certitude and whirling bedlam. How to stick a finger in there, stir things up.

The rest of the house is made of rooms of work or rooms of echoes. The kitchen, the parlor, the dining room, and cellar. On the third floor, the low room under the eaves. It will be yours when you are older, Ingrid, but today the door has swollen in its frame from lack of use and, snug against each window, is a little bed draped in a soft white sheet. Dust has settled on the sheets' hummocks like the fur of trees on the mountain's flank. The last time I was up there, I saw a pane in the window was broken. The star come at last? Hurtling through the glass no bigger after its long journey that a dry fall pea? A bird had hopped in through the jagged gap and been unable afterwards to find it again for an exit. It lay dead at the foot of the one of the beds, head cocked, wings spread around it like the skirts of an actress dying on the stage.

No matter. I was telling you a story.

Before you were born, some nights I would leave the house and go into the forest. I always did this with great secrecy and haste, no telling who could be watching, but once I had eased the back door shut behind me and skirted the exposed meadow, I was in the pitch-black shadow of the trees and could not be seen.

There is no exit like the final one, Ingrid. I know that. When the doors of the mind slam shut one by one, when the draft they make stirs up the dust and fallen leaves, the sheets of notebook paper (yellow, with their endearing red margin line) and piano tablature, the candy wrappers, scraps of fabric, neon wristbands still curled in the empty shape of the wrist; when the self is driven before them, bothered, her hair a fright, and every time she turns to rally, regroup, another door—since when have there been so many? and all different sizes and shapes: one silver, one oak, one pierced with vents like a pie safe, one thick as a vault, twice as dull—another door slammed in her face as if it were she who has intruded and not this wind, this raw blustery thing whisking and whisking her onward, harried, out of breath, until there's nowhere left to go and still another door slammed shut behind her, a key in the latch.

Out the nose, Ingrid. That's where the soul exits. A last hot exasperation and she's forever gone.

Even when I was very young, when the moon was full and I was full and we seemed to have a kinship in heaviness I knew my exits were nothing like this final one. For one thing, I could go back. For another, I could take something with me to eat along the way. There is a story necessary to tell any story. It is a chain that way, only loosely linked, but binding. I went into the forest many times, and one time I saw something I should not have. One time, I left something there behind me. When I was seventeen, there was a sheep on the news every night. My father, who had broken his thighbone sliding off the steep pitch of a roof he was patching after a mid-winter storm, sat with his leg propped on the coffee table and made dire pronouncements.

"But what is it *good* for," he finally asked, gesturing toward the news video of what looked to be a perfectly normal animal chewing hay in a perfectly normal pen while a crowd of beaming scientists surrounded her as if she were a plaque or an oversized check. One of the scientists, a woman, kept reaching over the stall partition to stroke the sheep's ear, rubbing its velvet nap between her fingers The sheep's eyes were yellow and blank. A blue tattoo was inked inside one of her ear's grey folds. This animal was the future, I understood, but I wasn't sure what that meant about the future itself, or, more specifically, what that meant about me, a denizen of the future as surely as I was of the past. Which is to say not surely at all. Which is to say not all borders are permeable. Some stop you short.

"I guess think of all the lamb chops," Rosellen said from the doorway, her breath pluming with cold and smoke. "Think of all the wool sweaters."

Later that year, a princess died and, against expectations, did not arise refreshed from her centuries long slumber. In fact, she never got up again. When her face came up on the television screen, Thalia would snort and change the channel.

Later that year, some people in America shot a rocket filled with the remains of other people in America into space. When Thalia saw this, she sat up and leaned forward in her chair.

"The fools," she said, perhaps to me, perhaps to something else that was still in the house, though it should not have been. It was hard to tell with Thalia which world she addressed. Often, it didn't matter.

"Out of reach," Thalia said, "but not forever." And, in fact, she was right. Eventually every rocket stops its blue whirling and falls back home. They come back as rain then, as haze or scouring particles in the wind. "What a mess," she said, her cold eye scanning a future that was getting hotter and louder with every passing year. She was right about that, too.

This is to say that nothing ever passes that doesn't come around again, but at seventeen I couldn't know that. Even now, thirteen years later, I don't quite know that. I only think I do, and I speak the words I believe will fix it all in place—the hot, loud mess that heaves and pulses all around us—as if to say if I could only *see* it, get just a second of silence to focus on a few of its individual parts, I could divine the right pattern, prepare myself. But that was Thalia's talent, never really mine. I can tell you the past, Ingrid, and after that I am all but blind.

~

When I first came to Thalia's house, it was winter and night. I rode up the mountain in the passenger seat of the old green truck Thalia seemed to drive through force of will rather than by an application of pedals and gears. The woods to either side of us glittered with ice, reflecting the moonlight and our headlights with such dedication that, though the night was very bright, it was also very hard to see. There was no heat in the truck. My breath rose before me in a thin, anemic thread, but Thalia's breath as she hunched over the wheel smoked and rolled until it washed up against the windshield like a wave roiling up the side of a concrete damn. Then it subsided. She didn't talk to me. Some kind of animal slipped darkly below our wheels and flowed to the other side of the road, our wind in its tail were a passing fancy, of no account.

"Where are we going?" I asked her.

"Up the mountain," Thalia said, rolling her eyes at me as if surprised to hear me speak. I had a thin coat on, no gloves. The beds of my fingernails were so blue they looked like cornflowers nodding in the ditch in summer time.

"I know, but, to the house?" I asked.

"To the house," she said.

"The house where my mother grew up?" This was the point, the only real question.

"The house where your mother grew up," Thalia said and leaned further forward over the wheel in a way that made it clear she was done talking. At least to me.

The road curved black before us. On Thalia's side of the truck, the mountain had been blasted away, the funnels where the dynamite had been rammed home still visible as grooves in the graded cliff face. Water was squeezed by the winter cold through the rock and gushed here and there in frozen plumes like dragons' beards flowing under stone snouts. On my side, the earth dropped away and the mountain plummeted into the valley. Far across it a little steam or smoke was rising against the black hulk of the next ridge. Steam from a hot spring, smoke from a house fire; it was impossible to tell. From this distance, it didn't matter. The trees closed in on the road again, their green-black trunks a screen, their ice-sheathed twigs finite and precise.

We drove up and up and up. Eventually, we turned off the main road onto a rutted path and followed that through thick woods until we got to a clearing. A henhouse, a creek, a cemetery. The skeleton of a vegetable garden, dead tomato vines iced into loops of silver wire around their poles. The slink of a cat slipping along the sagging peak of the pig sty, another following close behind, their bodies long and flowing in the weird light. At the head of that clearing was the house on Newfound Mountain. Backwards it seemed, crowded up to the mute face of the mountain while behind it the chickens shifted in their sleep, the sow sighed to the shoats who crowded her and the hives packed still and cold, dead wax all the way to the center where the sisters crowded into a ball humming a simple winter song.

"It is cold. We are here. It is cold. We are here," they sang.

The house: simple but austere, many gabled, in need of paint.
The house: all its windows dark, but far from empty.

The place where my mother grew up.
The place where she was buried.

"Well, get out," Thalia said, and reached across me to unlock my door.

~

When I showed up at the Feed Store earlier that evening the dinner rush was over and only a last few stragglers were still nibbling strands of meat from their chicken thighs, spearing English peas one by one on the tines of their fork. The Sainte Maria, on a break from the kitchen, was eating a bowl of soup by the dining room door. There was someone new on dish duty, a man who had his sleeves rolled to his elbows and was wearing the Pinta's old, rubberized apron. This was Jacob, come at last. Are you surprised to hear it this way, with so little fanfare? He was wearing a blue shirt, jeans in the same shade. The yellow apron tied at his waist was the only thing marking the shape of his body in all that blue and I remember thinking his head was too round, unnerving, as if it could roll off his neck at any moment and fall heavily to the floor. I remember thinking he was doing a poor job of it—splashing too much water out of the sink, leaving a rind of soup crusted on the lip of the pot—but that is all I thought. Jacob never turned around and Thalia ignored him. I had one life then, a life that had closed around me like a fist; I wasn't looking for another.

While I was telling Thalia what had happened—the baby, my father pointing to the door with his fork, Rosellen standing in the window—the Sainte Maria came in and slipped her bowl into the soapy dishwater. As far as anyone knew, we hadn't seen each other in years. The summer I was thirteen (while I was at the beach with Thingy, in fact) Dax and Rosellen had moved my brother to a long-term care facility in Ridley Township.

"For his own good," said my father. I hadn't even unpacked. My battered suitcase was still sitting on my bed, gritty with sand and the tiny, white shells Thingy and I had sifted out of the dunes and kept both for their severity and their cuteness. I was wearing one of Thingy's halter tops and a pair of her shorts. I felt browned and drum-tight, like a bird that has been slowly turned over the flame until every part of it is slick and full and juicy. My toenails were painted alternating shades of pink and green. I was a new girl, a whole new creature. I hadn't noticed my brother was gone or anything else about the house except for the new me in it.

What was there to see? The same couch and armchair, the same television set topped with the same ceramic shepherdess and her blushing, blue-britched shepherd. The same pass-through, shedding rabbit-foot fern, wire basket filled with sprouting onions. The same kitchen sink, which dripped, refrigerator, which knocked, yellow, strawberry-patterned half-curtains which my mother had sewn when she and my father were first married.

Down the hall, the beige carpet peeling back from the wall in a frieze of loose pilings...

In the bathroom, the shell-shaped soap holders jutting from the wall to cradle shell-shaped soaps, the towels monogrammed, but mismatched...

In my room, set like an extra tooth at the end of the house, the bed with its peach corduroy bedspread, the child's bookshelf, the window open to the long, familiar view...

There was nothing to see and so I didn't look. I slung my suitcase on the bed and unzipped it.

"For his protection," Rosellen amended. She stood across the hall in the doorway of Luke's room with her arms crossed over her chest as if she were cold, though the house was muggy, all the doors and windows open to catch the cross breeze.

Summer on the beach had been hot but lean, a clanging kind of heat like two metal garbage can lids being banged together. In the mountains, the summer was green, yes, but each tree its own particular green, each shrub and sprung weed, each spear of onion grass, each lifting leaf. It was hot, yes, but one kind of hot on the road, mincing across the bubbling asphalt, and another in the clearing where all around the forest whispered of cooling. One kind of hot in the town square where the sod crisped and browned, another in the lumber yard where the dusty, yellow smell of mangled trees coated the inside of one's nostrils and throat. One kind of hot in the house where the wind died on the sills and another in the body where heat came up and up.

I felt dizzy, short of breath. Behind Rosellen, in Luke's bedroom, the bed was gone and the cot the girls had used on night shifts. His chest of drawers was gone, his mirror, the misshapen masks my father had hung from his ceiling, the miniature disco ball the Nina had hung by his window so it would catch and refract the sun. In their place was a desk and a green metal file cabinet. An armchair and a wicker wastebasket already overflowing with balls of crumpled paper. An office, in other words. A place of business.

"He was getting bedsores," Rosellen said. "He was too heavy for the girls to lift anymore and not all of them were to be trusted." She said the last darkly, cinching her arms still tighter around her rib cage so her breasts were lifted into the scoop neck of her T-shirt. In truth, Rosellen's body was starting to go. Her breasts had fallen into a long line of cleavage down the front of her plunging shirts. Her butt too had lost its dome-like bubble and, no matter how many sit-ups she performed, grunting on the living room floor in pre-dawn light, her belly had fallen into a little pouch above her pubis like a muff she was carrying around with her in case her hands needed to be warmed.

"Not that I'm accusing anyone of anything," she said, which meant she was.

With no more ceremony than that, my brother was gone.

In simpler days, the Pinta told me that before a baby was born it lived in God's pocket. I pictured a mass of squirming pink bodies with huge eyes sealed behind translucent membranes, like the nest of infant rats Thingy and I had turned out of a rotten stump at the meeting edge of our yards. When a baby was ready to be born, the Pinta said, God would pluck it out of his pocket—fumbling his way around bits of knotted string and lint, sprung paper clips and match books, rose hips and tortoiseshell buttons…He would pluck it out, the ready baby, by the scruff of its neck and pincher it all the way down down down to earth where he would put it in the mother's body.

"How does he do that?" I asked. We were in the bathroom. The Pinta was propping my brother up in a few inches of tepid water and lathering his back with the soft side of a kitchen sponge. I remember the smell of the soap in particular, a milky, lingering scent that wafted up from my skin for hours after the bath was over as if, instead of scrubbed clean, I had been dipped in a powdery wax and sealed off. My brother's penis was rocking gently back and forth on the ripples the Pinta made with her sponge. I wasn't supposed to look at it. "Give him his dignity," the Nina always said, but the Pinta didn't seem to notice what I did. She was singing to herself, a long, rambling song which she repeated over and over beneath her breath so the only words I understood was the phrase, "'I' said the fish, 'with my little dish, I caught his blood,'" to which she gave a particular emphasis.

I thought my brother's penis looked like a turtle's head pulled back in its shell, only pinker and less skeptical. I stared at it as I sat on the lid of the toilet and watched.

The Pinta thought for a moment. She made a shelf over Luke's eyes with the side of her palm and squeezed the sponge over his forehead. She ran it over his cheeks, down his neck, over his thin chest and down each of his arms. My brother had a black, perfectly round mole on his chest that the Pinta always rubbed a little harder, as if shining it. He had a strong chin and beautiful skin that seemed to flow over his muscles and bones as if it had been poured. His eyes were very dark.

"He does it with his thumb," the Pinta finally said and she held out her own thumb to demonstrate.

I imagined first my brother and then myself lifted by the scruff of our necks and swung through the air. We were uniformly pink, our skin tight and shiny, our eyes huge and black and wet beneath our lids. We were smooth and identical—identical bald heads, the place between our legs a smooth cap of skin—and we hung from God's fingers, curled like shrimp, spit bubbles forming between our lips. We were the ready ones, but we weren't yet anybody. Just babies. Just one out of the rubbery, blind, indistinguishable mass wriggling in his pocket, rubbing up against each other. And then there was God's thumb, square like the Pinta's but broader, the nail flat and yellow and well polished. And then there was our mother and somehow…first one and then the other…

All that, it seemed to me at the time, in order to lead up to this moment in the bathroom where my brother, who liked the water, stirred his hands just below its surface and I, who had already had my bath and was naked and damp inside my terry-cloth robe, stared at his penis. "Who killed Cock Robin?" the

Pinta sang, but the answer was lost under the rhythmic splashing of her sponge.

But that is not the truth. God and his thumb, our willing helplessness, these are figures of the truth and the truth itself an unshaped thing, ravenous, void. The truth is that at the heart of every something, at its rigid, concentric core, is the nothing from whence it came. When a something is created—any old lentil or bird's egg, baby or igneous batholith—it does not supplant the nothing that was there before it, but merely takes its place in conjunction with that continuing void. A child is something that does not replace nothing. When Luke was born, the nothing that was there before him was also born. As it was when I was born, when Thingy was born, when you yourself, Ingrid, were expelled screaming into our shared world.

"Tell me the truth," Mrs. Clawson said to me. We were in the hospital waiting room again, downgraded from the cushy, rose patterned privacy afforded to the families of the dire and ushered instead into a crowded mint-green room with blue plastic bucket seats, tattered magazines on the kidney-shaped tables and an electric carafe in the corner merrily burbling its coffee down to a thick sludge. We were there because you were fine, Ingrid, and always had been. Because Thingy was dead and Mrs. Clawson, wearing a light camel coat and the shimmering lip gloss of mourning, was constitutionally incapable of imagining either formlessness or unappeasable hunger.

"Tell me the truth, Alice," she said, but when I did she couldn't hear me. Then Daniel came back with another sheaf of papers to add to the bundles he was amassing in his study— overflowing manila folders, avalanches of green and pink forms:

your footprints, a count of your heartbeats, a chart that detailed the exact lucidity of your skin, other charts that ranked your eliminations, your respirations and reactions to heat and cold, pin pricks and pinches, in spidery lines tending valiantly upwards.

("To reach the top!" said that long ago explorer to his Sherpa, his yak. "And then what?" the Sherpa might have said had he been asked. "And to what purpose the earth?" might have opined the yak.)

The truth! The truth! The truth! It all depends on how you deal with it. Thingy took her nothingness and stitched it to the bottom of her foot. I took mine and sent it spinning into the forest where I pretended it perished—eaten by a bear, felled by the forester's axe. Daniel and Jacob have made formulas of theirs, albeit very different ones, and my father pressed his to him as he would the body of a woman, reveling in the way it defined his form.

But Luke was an altogether different sort. Luke looked into his abyss and what he found there satisfied him so fully he couldn't be tempted to look away. That's why when anybody asked me what exactly was wrong with my brother, I answered them truthfully.

"Who killed Cock Robin?" the Pinta asked and asked. The answer was everyone, from sparrow to bull.

"What's wrong with your brother?" asked Thingy and Mrs. Clawson, asked Rosellen and the other children at school, old women in the grocery store, young men plugging quarters into machines at the arcade, new mothers plugging them into machines at the Laundromat. What's wrong with your brother? and I answered, nothing. It's nothing that's wrong with him.

~

The truth! The truth! The truth!

If you hold a mirror to my brother's face you will see his skin but not his self. If you put your fingers in his mouth you can feel his pulse at the base of his tongue and the square monuments of his teeth, but no lingering speech, no hot breath of desire. If you lie next to him on his narrow bed, as I have done so often to whisper in his ear, you might feel deep within him the stirring pip of his being, but it is not you he is interested in. My brother might as well have been a wax doll—his body rigid, his features set and even as if carved in great curling swoops with the little bone knife—but there is no one else alive with such an uncompromising knowledge of himself.

"We are the children of a black snake," I told him, or of the dragon, of the mountain, of a mermaid who split her tail just long enough for the snow white bull to force himself inside, but Luke knew all this already, and anyway, he wasn't listening. When I was thirteen and my brother was taken away from me, I mourned, but I realize now it was for myself, for the stories that would no longer have an audience, and not for him at all.

But when I was thirty and Thingy died…ah, then from the forest came that thing I had thought so long ago banished. It took me between its jaws and it shook me the way any animal will when it has at last what it has hungered for so dearly. It is shaking me still.

# The Weeping Woman

My grandfather Mick had died only a few weeks before I moved into the house on Newfound Mountain. There were still traces of him lying about: an armchair pulled closer to the fire-place than Thalia would sit, a pair of man's loafers, broken at the heels, laid just inside the door to the bathroom as if they had served as slippers. I slept in Mick's old room, where Daniel sleeps now, the one with the window overlooking the tin roof of the tool shed which Thingy would leave propped open for the cats. Though Thalia did the wash the day after my arrival, that first night I listened to the sounds of the house settling and breathed in the papery musk of my grandfather's smell. Bitter cloves and thin skin. Powder and black soil. Then she erased him: the chair moved back to a corner near the window, the shoes tossed into a bin on the porch where they swelled with the spring rains and eventually grew a lush crop of yellow horsehair mushrooms.

Mick was not buried on the family land, but in a plot behind the First Presbyterian in the center of town. He lay between his father Clell and his only sibling, Baby Boy Luttrell, whose gravestone is ornate, flecked with pink granite and topped by a curly-headed lamb as if to make up for the practical decision not to give him a name.

"Your great-grandmother was hard minded," Thalia said. We were in the kitchen scrubbing canning jars in the deep belly of the sink. It was spring, too early for tomatoes, but Thalia planned ahead, setting the gleaming jars on the kitchen shelves alongside others already stuffed with brining peach halves and the ruby duck eggs of last season's beets. I was six months pregnant and Thalia had begun to address herself largely to my stomach. She never touched me, not even so much as taking my elbow to steer me out of the way, but she talked a constant mumbling stream. Correction, instruction, Thalia's voice not so much like water as the rocks at the bottom of the creek bed, grinding against each other, wearing down.

"What would you do?" Thalia said, handing me the lids and rings which must each be meticulously dried. "Before you get so high and mighty, ask that. Someone hands you two eggs and one is whole and speckled and one gives off a stench. Are you going to waste your time feeling sorry for the chicken? Are you going to beat it into the batter and hope for the best?"

She rubbed her hands dry on a dish towel and watched me as I ran a kitchen rag around the lip of a ring and around again for good measure. Thalia had blue eyes, blue irises and blue-tinged whites. Her eyes watered and she kept a red paisley hand-kerchief tucked in her back pocket with which to wipe them. Thalia already knew what sort of choices I was likely to make—my heart wrung out every morning as I collected eggs still hot from the hen's wrinkled, pink brood patch—but she remained curious to watch me decide.

"What would *you* do, little mama," Thalia said, but she wasn't talking to me. Inside, something pedaled its legs and took a firmer grip.

The cemetery on Thalia's land, my land now, is bounded by a stone wall made of stacked slate. The ground within is raw, kept assiduously scraped clean of grass and other opportunistic sprouters by yours truly. A little iron gate, topped with a series of diminishing, hand-hammered scrolls, swings from a pole that does not quite meld with the wall to the one side and latches on the other by means of a twist of chicken wire snipped from the coop.

All together, the cemetery is an amateur affair. The stones of the wall are untidy and precarious. Some section of it is for-ever eroding, the stones sliding past each other to fan out across the little slope the cemetery tops like a wave collapsing across the shore. No matter the weather, the slate doesn't seem to retain heat and I imagine they were pulled this way—cold and sharp—out of the side of the mountain by my great-grandmother, per-haps her mother, and stacked on a sledge to be trundled through the forest.

Inside the gate, which often comes loose to swing and clang against its moorings, are the graves. Four of them are marked by tidy stone mounds, their neatness striking when compared to the wall. Someone, many someones over the years, has taken the time to build these solid and then to maintain them, but why? It's all just rock after all, and what lies beneath another kind of rock: the hollows of the skull just like the pocks in a boulder when a pebble has been caught and rattled around by centuries of water and ice; the teeth, loose by now, I assume, scattered like chips flaked from the spearhead being turned and turned in someone's hand.

Yet, there is a difference between a wall and a grave. An even bigger difference between the four graves that were here before me—each marked by a stone that says Mother and above that stern pronouncement, as time passed and children were born, shallower etchings that proclaim one Great-great-grand, one Great-grand, one Grand, and the last still simply and starkly alone—and the fifth that I laid with my own hands and marked with only a wavering, poorly carved, T.

All this to tell you who is not here, Ingrid: the menfolk. Which should tell you all you need to know about who is still hanging around, about the whistling in the eves when there isn't any wind, about the handprints on the banisters and the flour laid in mounded lines at the tops of all the stairs.

Thingy and I used to entertain each other at night by re-counting the long, grim tale of Emily Murten (Poor Emily, Maid Murten, The Weeping Woman, as she was called among other things) who was said to have died of sorrow after being spurned by her handsome young lover to whom, oh folly of youth!, she had given herself on the chilly and austere plank floor behind the raised pulpit of the First Presbyterian, one of the oldest churches in town and, conveniently, the only one with its original bell in its original white clapboard steeple which Emily now assiduously haunted.

"Spread out before man and god," Thingy said, pinching me under the sheet. "And all because she couldn't keep her legs shut, just couldn't wait for a little taste."

Thingy loved Emily, loved the whole story: the creak of the floorboards beneath her lover's knees, his breath on her neck, in her ear, the blood she had to mop up behind her. ("You can still see the stain," Thingy said. "Indelible.") Then the way the boy refused to see her, how stiff his face was as he looked past her, and how frail she became, how thin, almost transparent. Finally, she died and her bewildered parents buried her on the very same ground that had harbored her venial sin ("In the *church*," Thingy said, "Can you imagine? All those empty seats.") only to find she would not rest easy but came back the next full moon—white and gauzy in her winding shroud—to batter herself against the bell like a giant moth and lean out from the steeple's cupola, weeping a warm rainstorm on whoever happened to be beneath her.

"They say if you if you get any of her tears on your skin it will stain you forever," Thingy said. "Spots as red as blood." She held up her slender hands for us to consider, turning them back and forth in the dim yellow light from my own kitchen that was leaking down the slope and through her bedroom window. It was a warm night but we still piled together in the center of her bed under both a sheet and the pillowy comforter. When one or the other of us shifted our weight or fluffed the sheets to stir up a little breeze, I could smell the stale exhalations of our bodies, but still there were no ghosts in Thingy's room. And none haunting the steeple, though Thingy swore she had seen her once, Poor Emily, and had even, she showed me a strawberry birthmark on the back of her calf, been marked by her tears as she turned to run.

"What I don't get," Thingy said, "is why she just didn't give the guy a blow job. Surely, you don't have to hang around in a church for all eternity for sucking a little dick."

But what Thingy really didn't understand is that there's no such thing as punishment. Only eternity, only the wind and the rain, the rock face and the burrowing root. Once we are made into a form we cannot unmake it and to be buried, even to be scattered through the forest, rendered by the harrowing teeth of dogs, is nothing but a blink in the body's long, unwavering gaze.

"I see…I see…." says the body, ruminative, long abandoned. And all the women that whisk through this house—for all their rustling footsteps and clenched fists pale among their skirts, for all their jangling keys and drifts of hair floating in the dust-light behind them—all these women are cyclic as breath. Rushing in crisp and biting, soughing out warm and wilted and damp.

So, there are these little artifacts: a moldy shoe, five gold rings that seem to retain the warmth of their wearer's hand. And there is you of course, Ingrid, an inhalation finally come around again. And Jacob, myself, your father Daniel who I am watching right now as he splits stove-lengths next to the hen house. He has taken off his shirt, but sweat is still running in rivulets down the channels of his spine to darken the waistband of his jeans. His back is to me and when he stands with the axe hoisted above his head, poised in the moment before the swing, I resist the urge to tap on the window and call his attention. To stop him before he does something he can't take back.

When I first came to the house I knew very little, certainly not how to recognize what was right in front of me. Along with my room and board, and, I naively assumed, the eventual room and board of the child I was carrying, Thalia took in hand my educational needs as she saw them. This bore no resemblance to the dutiful memorization I had preformed in school—information scented even now with the slick, plastic tack of textbook illustrations and the whining bite of the ammonia the custodians sprayed on our desks after hours—and nothing, really, to do with any kind of recognizable teaching principle. Instead, Thalia showed me what was there and then what was also there all around it. A typical lesson would go something like this:

Thalia: [pointing to the base of a tree] What is that?
Alice: [tired, hungry, deep in the forest] A flower.
Thalia: [snorting] It's a redring milkweed. Good for snakebites and bee stings. Poisonous to fleas. Make a broom from its leaves and sweep the floors in case of infestation.

"What shape is it?" Thalia would then ask and I, looking at the woody stalk and top heavy circle of blooms would say something like umbrella shaped, or pincushion shaped, to which Thalia would shake her head and instruct me to close my eyes and look again. After standing this way for some time, I would come to see, guided by Thalia despite the fact that she stood silent and very still, that the plant was actually shaped like a series of overlapping, blade-edged ovals. That this shape extended from the plant itself all the way through the clearing, fading only at the bulwark of a silver, splintering hickory which had fallen a little way up the hill. This shape intersected many other shapes—loose spirals, regimented hexagons, boxes and circles and blooming cones—which echoed from other plants and hidden animals (a newt with a shape like tongues of flame; a cicada deep in its pupate burrow with a shape like stylized cresting waves). And, though these intersecting lines seemed at first like a hopeless tangle they were actually quite distinct and resistant to change.

If one knew how to look they could be manipulated, plucked almost, though the music that made was unruly and often discordant. If one had the right sort of touch, they could be braided, made into signs of calling or signs of warning, portents wholly other than the ones they had first exclaimed. There were words that could be spoken, bits of songs. If this seems fanciful to you, Ingrid, think of the birds. What are they doing if not casting spells? Every morning perched on the lip of the gutters, in the black locust, at the peak of the henhouse roof; sex spells and safety spells, dangerous wardings.

This is what Thalia taught me: how to never again be alone. Which is also pretty well how she cursed me and, if you think of it a certain way, how I am now cursing you. History is a crowd. Story is a mob. There's no place on the mountain you can hide from that sort of company, Ingrid. Maybe you should stop listening right now. Plug your ears. Go to sleep.

Thalia taught me other things, of course. How to stock the wood stove so its flame burned low for cooking. How to skin a rabbit and butcher it so as to make the most of its meat. Meanwhile, the winter passed into a damp, mild spring and that itself burned off into the hay-strewn summer. Far away down the mountain side—between us acres of forest and untrustworthy roads, so many vibrating, intersecting lines that a girl who didn't know how to lay her own thread behind her would surely be snagged and left to dangle—Thingy took her own lessons and learned what she would from them.

~

In June (blooming June, buzzing June, the swollen buboe of summer), Thingy graduated third in our class and I was seven months pregnant. I could see the outline of the baby press against my stomach as it turned inside me and further could see its shape—a pulsing, hammer-struck line—as it radiated out around me. I could see the wind coming down the mountain and what exactly was within the storms it brought. I could see who walked down the stairs when no one walked down the stairs and what stayed at the edge of the forest, curious, lamp-lit eyes huge and round and yellow. I tamped the fire lower for Thalia's eggs, which she liked soft and almost whole, sliding them one by one down her gullet, and felt the pullet's pebbled skin for the joint where her bones would separate from her sockets and open her bloody and bare. I swept the floor with a lavender broom and a fescue broom and one made of foxtail. I walked to the hives with a bucket of embers and thrust my arm deep into their cracked, golden cores. I braided a sign at the door and one at the window, a sign on the bedpost and one webbed like cat's cradle between my own red palms. It was a hot summer, the water steaming up from the earth like breath. At night, though Thalia forbid it, I often went into the forest alone. One day, Thingy drove up the mountain to say goodbye.

When Thingy was pregnant she bloomed like a peony. A big, dozy top, all ruffles, layers and layers of cream and then the shocking pink that was supposed to be internal—for no one's eyes but yours, Ingrid—but was pushed by the sheer force of her swelling right to the surface. It's not that she wasn't beautiful, she was born with beauty between her teeth like a bit, but she was dreadfully exposed. Even in those first few months after she and Daniel moved in, even before she knew herself, it was clear to anyone who really looked that Thingy was flushed with the thin-veined flush of a flower right before it goes to seed.

In contrast, I was pregnant like the hard, horny burl a tree grows around a cleft where some burrowing worm has laid its egg. The tree does this to protect itself, though inadvertently it also protects the insect's larvae as it twitches and grows. I was pregnant symbiotically, all interiors. But this isn't really a fair comparison. They were such different times in our lives, after all. I remember that summer so well: the grass high and wet against my shins in the morning; the phoebes skimming the creek for gnats and catbirds tenting their wings to cast a shadow across the crickets and armored pill bugs; a smell like water and crushed greenery hanging in a fog over the meadow; Thalia standing in the side yard, two chickens whose heads bobbled loose at the ends of their snapped necks in her hand, eyes closed and face turned up toward the sun.

I don't know what Thingy remembered. I never asked her. I was tight as a drum and felt whenever I opened my mouth as if a spotlight would beam out of me. I was preoccupied, I guess I would say. Suddenly, I was a source instead of just a reflection.

Nevertheless, time passed. Many years later I washed the baseboards of the house with a rag and a pail of soapy water.

Here the dust gathers like ash. There's no explanation for this and yet, without vigilance on my part, the tabletops mist over with grit and the pages of all the books in Daniel's library are seamed with it as if they are webbed with mold. I wash the baseboards once a week and the dust turns my rag and bucket water black. It gathers along the fine hairs of my arms as I dunk and wring until, by the time I am done, my forearms look lightly furred as if I were stuck in midtransformation: caught forever in the body of a woman that is also the body of some shy black creature with not enough fur to keep it warm. Daniel compares our dust to the ash that falls from the sky along the Ganges, where he traveled when he was in graduate school and writing his dissertation.

"It coats everything, all of your exposed skin, in the creases of your clothes," he said. "It gets in your eyes, your mouth. Later, you go back to your hotel room—white sheets on the bed and billowing white, gauzy curtains, they were big on that, to denote luxury, I guess—but you'd blow your nose and in the tissue it was black. Coming out of your own body, the ashes of other people's bodies." He told me this as we sat together on the porch and watched the forest darkening. Inside, Thingy was listening to one of Thalia's old records. Something with clarinets that swooped and moaned. I don't know where Jacob was. He had taken the truck. He had left us.

I can't remember exactly when this was in the timeline. Was Thingy heavy or slim? Was she roaming through the house in frayed jeans, barefoot on the cool boards, or in the hideous yellow peignoir she adopted during the last months of her pregnancy? Was she inside because she was digging happily through something (Thalia's records, quart jars full of unassigned buttons she found under the cellar stairs) or because we were outside, her husband and her best friend sitting together at the end of a day?

Night comes quickly into the forest and soon, though a lozenge of light still oozed across the porch railings, the scene before us was pitched into a jumble of silhouettes. Black trunks darker than the black tangle of brush behind them, black leaves shifting black shadow onto the black turf. Something moved quickly through the grass and then held still. The fireflies winked up one by one and drifted around us as if they were all jockeying for a better view.

Daniel's dissertation was titled *Death Rituals Among Tribal Peoples Newly Settled in Developing Mega-Cities*. It had been published by a small university press who had spent a disproportionate amount of their annual budget on a glossy black cover stamped with the outline of a black skull which lurked just behind the embossed letters of the title. Daniel was somewhat embarrassed by this and had stripped the dust jackets off the four or five copies he kept on a shelf in his study (previously the house's formal front parlor) and folded them in a drawer in his desk. A shaft of light crossed his ear and creased the side of his soft, pink cheek. A firefly dipped close to his head and he held up a finger as he talked as if he expected it to land there.

"In Mali," said Daniel, "the Dogon tribe will perform elaborate funeral rites for a man who has gone missing, who they presume dead, and if he shows back up again even just a moment after they are finished they will refuse to recognize him, as if he is invisible." The breeze shifted and the heady odor of the Chinese privet, which had escaped from someone's garden and grimly colonized the roadside ditches all the way up the mountain, washed over us like a thicker, slower form of air.

"The Merina in Madagascar take bodies out of their tombs and dance and talk with them, show them the recent changes in the area," Daniel said. "A fallen tree or a flood marker. A new house. A new carburetor in the car."

Inside, the clarinets came to a more somber understanding of themselves. They mourned like owls. Thingy switched on a lamp in the window and its light, neatly sectioned by the panes of glass, spilled out around me. When I lifted my arm, Daniel was lit up, his arm resting on his knee, his empty hands—neat and clean, the nails trimmed—dangling into the darkness.

"Lotus blossoms," Daniel said. "Spider tattoos. The crackle of burning grasses. The thwack of a stick breaking the skull."

When I lowered my arm he was hidden again, the shape of any man surrounded by hovering, attendant lights.

Then Jacob came home, I suppose. I seem to remember a wash of headlights spilling across the porch and the sound of a door slamming. Then we went inside to eat whatever it was I made from whatever it was Jacob brought me and sat around the table at our accustomed places: I facing a window, Thingy facing a mirror; Jacob and Daniel facing each other and between us all the long, uneven table that had once been a door.

On some other day, at some other point in time I washed the baseboards on my hands and knees and so crawled down the hallway until I came to Thingy's door. It was open and directly across from the doorway the brass bed that had once been Thalia's creaked under its heaped weight of bodies, pillows and rumpled sheets. For someone who had always been slim, Thingy had begun to gain weight very early in her pregnancy and put it on steadily all throughout. At this point, she was close to full term, perhaps at the beginning of her eighth month, and was top heavy and plagued by back aches and varicose veins. She spent much of her time in bed where she had made a kind of nest for herself: the fitted undersheet stripped from the striped mattress and mounded around her, pillows plumped behind her back, trapped between her knees and dimpling under the weight of her plump, flushed arms. Thingy filched sheets from the linen closet on wash day with no regard for their size or pattern which meant all those months Jacob and I slept beneath a shifting array of checks and stripes, faded roses clashing with blue plaid pillowcases, sheets which were often too big and billowed to the floor on either side of our small bed as if we were dolls put carelessly to sleep under an oven mitt or a larger doll's discarded smock.

Thingy had propped the window open. A spring breeze, damp with exertion, puffed in and out of the room. It was afternoon, the sun slanting down toward the valley, and a panel of bright, white light was flung across the foot of the bed as crisp as paper. I straightened up in the door frame, putting my hands to the small of my own back to work out the kinks, and looked in on her. She was lying on her side, the sheer yellow fabric of that hateful peignoir taut against her belly, and had fallen asleep reading. I remember thinking this was the danger time, when she was asleep, when she couldn't be misdirected. She had changed so drastically during her pregnancy that she didn't look like my Thing at all—less the beautiful scullery maid with lentils in her hair and more the head chef cutting lattice for the pie; less the pert sister forcing her way down the throats of the flowers and more the heaving queen, moribund and carefully fed. If she were to sit up and speak to me, for the first time in our lives I didn't have a clue what she might say.

I shifted my weight and a board creaked under my foot. The cats, who had slunk in through the window, lifted their heads in unison from the hollows where they had nested. I don't know how long I stood there, arms black to the elbow, rag dampening my jeans where I had forgotten it and pressed it to my hip, before I realized that Thingy too was awake and watching me. Six eyes then: green, gold, blue. Six silent, six scanning for signs that they should spring, as they were all poised to do, up out of comfort and into the chill afternoon where they would balance on the tin roof and from there escape. I pictured Thingy with the sheets streaming from her arms and legs plugging the window like a hysterical gosling. I pictured her stretching her neck and greeting for help. I laughed then, and I'm sure it was laughter, but who knows what Thingy heard in the noise I made. Regardless, she didn't sit up or speak, but only watched me and in the end I was the one who slunk away. Rather, shall I say it?, I fled.

Out the nose, Ingrid. Banished from my last home.

*'Pity me at seventeen.'* Isn't that what the song says? Something about brown-eyed girls, ugly girls. Something about the men who call them at night and murmur obscenities.

*'Love was meant for beauty queens.'* I am sure of that. Equally sure there is nothing in the lyrics about how the brown-eyed girls might have felt to hear the voice catch and rasp on the other end of the line, how private and thrilling its greed must have been and how they too might yearn for words to perform their long promised transubstantiation.

For the tongue to become a tongue, I'm saying. For it to lick her hot, sweet…for the fingers to slip into her tight, pink…for the nose—plugged it sounded, did he have a cold?—to snuffle against her moist, hairy….for the teeth, oh the teeth, to gnash between them, grind between them, to nip and nip her rosy, swollen, tender, dripping, pearly, quivering, juicy, wet, wet, wet…

Another kind of essentially empty line, a one-sided conversation, is the one on which the birds chatter. "Oh baby baby baby," says the goldfinch and the phoebe responds with a sound like a telephone ringing in its cradle. "Pity pity pity," requests the cardinal—though of whom? Though for what?—to which the crow, cutting to the chase, responds with the sound of a tolling bell. At seventeen, Thingy pulled up to Thalia's house in a red jeep her father had bought her as a graduation present. Almost before the engine had stopped rumbling, she flung herself out of the car and up the porch steps, tripping on the last one, bowling into me and nearly knocking me to the ground. "You look like a weeble-wobble," Thingy said, smacking me on the stomach as if it were a watermelon she was testing for ripeness. "Seriously, you're huge."

Thingy and I hadn't seen too much of each other since February when I went to live with Thalia. We talked on the phone—the conversations colorless and watery as if coming to me thinned by altitude—but I didn't know how physically I missed her until I saw her again. She was a shock, almost literally like touching a faulty switch. I realized then, standing on the porch with Thingy's hands all over my stomach, rubbing my ridiculous belly hard enough to make the skin flush and then turn red, that I had been thinking of her all this time as a child. The Thing who I missed, who I pictured in my mind's eye while I listened to her hum and fold her laundry on the other end of the phone line, was no older than eight, silver-haired, wearing the galoshes she had favored then (white with the toes painted yellow like a duck's beak, black eyes bright as seeds painted on either side of her arch). On her hands yellow mittens with a jolly, oversized button that could fasten them open or fasten them closed. Clutched in her fist, a long, wooden spoon.

But it wasn't my own eight-year-old self—perpetually runny nose, hair plaited in a braid like a raccoon's tail down my back— who talked to Thingy. It was my self as I understood it now. My self which contained another self and in that self (a girl, of course, I didn't need a machine to look inside me and tell me that) the seeds of other selves. Millions upon millions of them, though even now, even as Thingy stood before me with long legs and full breasts, sweat beading in the hollow of her collar and her hands, studded with rings, chiming across the surface of my stomach, four million potential selves had become two and would be reduced even further before my baby was born. Lost in the slosh.

Still, "Pity pity pity," I had said to Thingy in those conversations, and she had responded with a sound like a bell and a sound like a bottle breaking. Pip-pip-pip, she had said. Tur-a-lee-lee-lee. Coo-coo-ra-koo.

We took a tour of the place. Thingy was particularly interested in the hives which we watched from the other side of the creek so as not to get in the way of the thrumming lines the bees were laying to and from their secret, jealously-tended feeding grounds. She was less interested in the chickens who strutted for her approval, tilting their heads and pecking at nothing at all just to show her the busy dart of their beaks. Eventually we ended up in the meadow, lying together on the little rise just above the creek. The clover was blooming white and purple. Thingy pinched them off low to the ground with her fingernail and braided them into a chain.

"So, tell me," I said and Thingy did. About graduation; about Atlanta; about her new roommate who had already written her a letter ("She's hideous," Thingy said. "Fat and wears nothing but rose pink and Laura Ashley. You can tell from her handwriting."); about her father who had unexpectedly offered her a room in his apartment if dorm life didn't work out and said he was thinking of spending more time at home; about a boy from our school who had crashed his car into a creek bed and slept there all night with the water flowing over his lap; about the Sainte Maria who she had seen stocking shelves at Abbot's, an ugly orange smock hanging off her hips, her hair cut short and the bangs dyed purple and green.

It was a beautiful day, the sun booming in the sky, no wind at all to stir the trees. The sow had birthed a new litter—her last it turned out—who were now squealing at her teat and in the hives row upon row of ladies swathed in white were waiting their turn to be brought to life. A touch on the crown of their heads like a wand perhaps, or only the busy brush of their sisters' mandibles as they tamped a cap in place, packed them in. A bird called; a bird answered. Thalia got in the green truck and drove away.

*Goodbye,* said Thingy, but only to me. To the rest of the world she gave a enthusiastic greeting and inside me the baby, asleep until now, woke with a start and pushed up against my skin as if suddenly lonely, desperate for warmth.

I didn't know what to say to Thingy, so I seized on the story of the Sainte Maria and we talked about her instead. Since Luke's exile the summer I turned thirteen the Sainte Maria and I had barely seen each other. Or at least not at more than at a distance. Not more than in parts: her bare ankle flashing below the bat wing of a car door, the sleeve of her coat—the same tattered leopard—caught up for just a moment on the doorknob before she tugged it free.

This was mostly true. On that day four months before when I had walked down the slope from my house to the Feed Store, the Sainte Maria, standing in the restaurant's kitchen and sliding her dirty bowl into the dishwater, looked at me with the same lack of interest a well-fed cat lying in a square of sunlight would regard a small rodent or bird. As if to say *Tut Tut*, as if to say *Well, look at you....*

The Sainte Maria was wearing black jeans and a cropped black T-shirt. She had a bruise on her hip, just a small one as if she had been poked with a small, bony finger. She looked, standing there among the steam and damp and huffing impatience of cookery, like a seed pod that had been blow in out of season. Not insubstantial, you understand, but thorny. Not waifish or childlike, but densely concentric, liable at any moment to begin expanding rapidly outward.

She looked like a stranger, which is perhaps why I treated her like one—like the real stranger, Jacob, who turned from his work, didn't he? Who turned from the mounds of dishes that must forever be scrubbed but would never be cleaned and looked at me with his eyes like something else's eyes, weren't they? As if he had lived a long time in darkness—

In reality, I had seen her only the week before, sitting at my father's table, drinking a glass of milk.

# The Egg's Tale

I shouldn't have been home at all. It was a Wednesday morning, a snowfall the night before tamping the world to a murmur as if just beyond the range of my hearing a great, calamitous noise was going on and on. I had stopped going to school the month before, when I could no longer deny what I had known from the first.

(The door to the motel room snicking shut behind me, the parking lot adrift with brown leaves. It was mid afternoon, a weekday. His was the only car in the lot but we'd taken a room on the side of the building facing away from the highway, and it was a company car, identical to any number of glossy, black others. I left first, before he had gotten out of the shower. I liked imagining him coming back into the room, sleek and pink, rubbing the coarse motel towel into his ears and under his armpits. His moment of confusion when he realized I was gone; perhaps even a few words he might say to the empty room. "Alice, did you know…" or "Alice, have you heard…" before he trailed off into the lack of me: a neatly made bed, the rickety chairs drawn back up to the round table, the curtains pulled, but in between them a zip of clean, white light. Behind the motel was an empty lot grown over with fescue and great bouquets of goldenrod. There were signs all over the lot proclaiming it *For Sale! Reduced!* but these too were weathered and overgrown. A wind was blowing. Some scrubby trees that had grown up along the fence line tossed and shook, but not a single one of their brilliant red leaves broke free.)

I had refused to acknowledge my pregnancy because isn't that what one did? Girls like me in my particularly predictable situation. I admit it had occurred to me to will this nonknowing to its farthest flung conclusion. To be one of those girls like me who give birth in the bathroom of the hamburger joint or on the floor of the laundry room at a friend's house, sneaking away from the party, still holding my drink. The music thumping out my little sounds and the baby—born dead of course, was there another way?—bundled into the washing machine with the guest bathroom towels where, even as small as it was, it would unbalance the load. Small as a mouse, I imagined. Covered in fur but with a human face peeking out between its soft, oval ears…

That was impossible, I knew, a fantasy. I was always very small and began to show almost immediately. By February, when

I came home unexpectedly in the middle of the day, it was still possible to wear loose clothes and pretend I was merely gaining weight, but I couldn't keep it up for much longer.

"Looks like your metabolism's finally catching up to you," Rosellen had said only the week before, eyeing me overtop a coupon circular which advertised discounts on tanning, gym memberships, mulch and ground chuck among other things. We were eating breakfast, my father long gone for a morning of plowing roads or clambering around on the roofs of houses he himself had built and which were so shoddily constructed that the shingles were already peeling beneath the ice sheets like scales sloughing from an ill-tended hide.

Pretty soon he would slip off one of those roofs and land with his right leg folded beneath him, the sound of the bone snapping, he said, prolonged and somehow chewy. He came home from the hospital in a blinding white cast that encased his leg from foot to hip. Rosellen took it upon herself to tend the cast by spritzing it with bathroom cleaner; the bleach, she reasoned, serving both the kill germs and keep the thing from growing dingy. Instead it was my father who grew dingy, his skin graying in comparison to the plaster, a smell about him like a damp cellar in which someone had foolishly been storing a side of meat.

During his recovery, Rosellen put my father up in the same way someone would swaddle and store the good china, knowing all along it would never again see the light of day. She heated blankets in the dryer and tucked them around him while he sat on the couch. She fed him soups and lit his cigarettes in her own mouth, propping them in between his lips as if everything below the level of his neck had been struck off—snicker-snack!—with one blow of the axe. My father resented this, as one might imagine, but Rosellen sailed through the house impervious and serene, happier than she had been in a long time. When my father walked the crutch and the metal bar attached to the bottom of the cast to keep his weight from spiraling up the bone conspired together to echo through the house. Thump and drag, thump and drag. "Fie Fi Foe Fum," yelled Rosellen from her study. My father broke a dish in the sink.

All this was on the horizon, though coming closer. Perhaps even as we spoke my father was climbing the pitch of the very roof. Perhaps he was taking a little break, catching his breath; straddling the house like a horse as he looked out over the cowed, white valley, wreathed as it must have been with plumes of his own breath. It would have been very quiet up there, the tacking hammer blows and shouts from the rest of the crew as they worked on other houses in the development coming to him as if from far away, as inconsequential as the cawing of crows lifting up from some tree or other, clustering in a tiny, distant hubbub in the ice gray sky. Who knew what they were saying? He might have thought of both crew and crows. Who cared?

"And then bam, I was falling," my father narrated from his position on the couch. "Just like that. One minute I'm a man sitting down and the next a man spinning through the air." I imagined his shape, arms spread like a snowflake, spinning airily downward. In reality, he surely fell more heavily—crumpled even, like a bird folding around the sudden hole in its breast— but I like to imagine him drifting, give him some leisure to look around. My father blew from the roof of the house to the ground, see-sawing as he fell. First he saw the sky, then the bristle of pine tops; the sky, then a window in which a woman looked out at him, shocked, amazed.

~

He landed on his back, that much I do know. "Knocked the wind right out of me," he said. "Rolled my eyes back in my head. Tim Pruitt got there first and he said my eyes looked just like hard-boiled eggs. He said you almost wanted to touch them they were so white and so round."

(We are not often together. Six times in four years. This is the seventh. We do not talk about our bodies, or our minds, the spaces behind our eyes. "Alright?" he says and I say, "Yes. Yes, okay." The next time we see each other, he will ask how my father is doing and nod, not quite looking at me, reading the paper and stirring his coffee so the spoon hits the side of the mug. Ting-ting, ting-ting, ting-ting. When I think about him, I think about two people. They are both essentially strangers, but one muscles the car around curves, adjusts his wife's umbrella in the sand, bows his head when I answer, "My father is fine," as if I am much younger than I actually am. As if he has to decipher the slurred honey of baby-speak coming out of my mouth. The other would like me to hop up on the dresser, just like that, back to the mirror, back against the mirror, he would like to see my teeth. *Good, all right? yes good...just like...is it good?...oh, it is just like that, like that, it is....*

Not a single leaf blew off the tree, though I stood for a moment too long watching them shake and tremble. I am supposed to make my way across the lot and up the hill. There is a brief fringe of forest, the underbrush dotted with flotsam—socks and straws, small bones and plastic bags, beer cans, hanks of fur, pyramids of perfectly spherical dung—and then the tree line breaks again on the outskirts of Elevation, on the alley alongside the TreeTop Diner, to be precise, where I will enter and sit and order myself something to eat.

The woman who owns the diner is named Marta. She brings my plate and doesn't ask why I'm not in school. In a moment he will drive into the lot, parking his car at an angle to the road in between a white utilities truck and a hatchback with a spidered windshield where something has struck and bounced heavily away. He is just stopping in, getting a quick bite on his way back to the city. I am a surprise and when he slides in across from me in the booth, he is only being polite. How is my father? Marta brings him a plate of country ham, a cup of coffee. My father is fine. Ting-ting, ting-ting. My body blinks and when it opens its eyes again there are three of us and it has started to rain.)

Everyone thinks my father is dead. Tim Pruitt says it first and then dead echoes through the crowd that has gathered. He isn't breathing after all, the wind knocked out of him, though he can hear perfectly well. He hasn't moved.

"It wasn't exactly peaceful," my father said, "but it wasn't too bad either. I couldn't see anything, but at the same time I could see the sky and it was bigger than before, flatter. Like if I punched my fist up I could tear through it and feel around on the other side, but I couldn't move and that was okay too. I just watched the sky come closer and closer. Big, flat, gray sky."

"And then what happened?" I asked. Rosellen clucked and re-adjusted his blanket. Outside, Dog, geriatric now and unsteady on his legs—Bitch long dead and buried under the dragon's belly—began to wheezily bark.

"Then Tim Pruitt stuck his damn finger in my eye," my father said and opened his mouth for a spoonful of soup.

~

*(Oh oh oh. Is this okay? Is this…yes…Is this…*He will give me a ride back to town, because it is raining, after all, because he is concerned for my well-being. "Why aren't you in school?" he says when Marta bends over the table to refill his coffee. He cuts all his ham into little bites and then picks them up one by one to put in his mouth. Marta jingles the coins in her apron and would like to not hear us. She has been here for a long time watching people cut their ham into little bites, offering them pie. "Would you like some pie?" she says to me. "Isn't it a school day?" he says to me. Marta jingles her coins and moves on. *Oh oh oh. Is this okay? Yes, it is. It is good.*)

Instead of school, I had been going to the library and spending my days with Miss Fawcett. The building is an old one and used to be the train station when the train still came through town. The ceilings are high and vaulted, painted a deep blue and the vaulting a jungly green as if the passenger waiting for her train was taking shelter beneath a bower made of vine, tendrils uncoiling even as she pressed her lips against a tissue and snapped her compact shut.

Now, however, everything is falling apart. The building was then and I assume remains damp, the books closest to the wall swollen between their covers. Miss Fawcett too seemed damp, like a handkerchief soaked and then wrung dry. After a few early attempts to find out what I was doing there, she largely left me alone to browse the stacks. Sometimes as I read a patter of green paint chips would sift down from the ceiling and drift across the pages of the book. Sometimes, Miss Fawcett would sit down across from me and offer me half of her sandwich, watch me as I ate it with an avidness that made me feel as if any second I would find my mouth filled with soil, a vine shooting out of my nose and curling up toward the decaying net of the ceiling.

"You might as well have this, too," Rosellen said, tapping her toast on the napkin in a shower of crumbs and sliding it onto my plate. "Or do you want another egg? I could boil one."

"Tuna salad," Miss Fawcett said. She wrinkled her nose as if she weren't the one to make the sandwich just that morning, pulling a leaf of lettuce from the head as she stood at the kitchen counter, trimming the crusts. A sheet of snow slid off the roof and rippled past the window. We were all buried alive, it was true. Nothing to sustain any of us but dry toast and tuna salad, a mildewed copy of *Watership Down*, an egg timer, a gust of wind that somehow made its way inside and then racketed around.

"Hard or soft?" Rosellen said.

Miss Fawcett tapped the book's cover, her blunt nail striking the air just above the rabbit's head. The book showed a beautiful place: a long slope of waving grains, a golden wood receding into umber shadows beneath a pale golden sky. The rabbit, too, was gold and wary; his ears skewed to listen, a ring of white around his liquid eye. "It's hard to believe someone could find so much to say about a rabbit," she said. Then she coughed. Then she sighed and looked out the window where the white world deadened itself, no shadows.

One Monday Miss Fawcett was ill, blowing her nose into tissues she then left wadded up on the countertops or in the shelves like stiff, white chrysanthemums. The next day she was sicker still and Wednesday, when I came down the hill from the school and tried the library doors, I found them locked and a handwritten sign in the front window that read *Closed, Due to Illness* There was no one to replace her, which is not to say she was irreplaceable, but it did leave me in a quandary. The steps were icy. A path had been scraped straight up the center by the man who ran the auto parts store across the street but had been left to glaze slick and narrow between wind-carved banks of snow. There was nowhere to sit. Nowhere to enter. It was very cold.

A car came down the hill and spun on the ice, its rump swaying gracefully back and forth over the lane marker. The driver looked right through me, her face a pale oval filled with other ovals. Then the tires caught. She inched past and disappeared around the bend.

I rattled the door again, but the lock held. Up the street two old woman were walking with their arms latched at the elbow, puffy pink heads bent down toward their feet. A bell rang at the school. The wind whirled up a funnel of salt and sand which blustered around the street and then subsided.

There was nothing to do but go home and so I went: up the hill and around the bend, past the Laundromat, past the saw mill, past Thingy's house where the porch light was still on, its yellow stain swallowed by the snow, through the side yard and up the stairs, ducking under the dragon's neck. I had warmed my key in my pocket, but it was still stiff in the lock and had to be coaxed and jiggled. Even with all that extra warning the Sainte Maria didn't see fit to rise from the kitchen table or pull her shirt all the way closed.

(An egg pushes the golden wall. Pressure from below, darkness. There is a tide that pushes past, something that drifts and clings. Feathers in the wall which push, push. A quavering, a shivering. The egg bounces into shape and floats free. Then comes the long journey down the mountain.)

"I could hear them all," my father said. "He's dead, he's dead, they were saying, but how could they have thought that when I was still right there? I mean, there I was. Lying in front of them, listening to them yammer on and on."

But that was later. Or earlier. Time was strange for me. I was inside a parenthesis.

The Sainte Maria sat at our kitchen table smoking a cigarette. Her mouth looked raw, as if she had erased the edges and then left all the pink rubbings lying around. She was wearing a button-down shirt—my father's shirt, red and blue, the pocket frayed—and black panties. Nothing else. Thump and drag, thump and drag. My father stood in the door in his walking cast. They both looked at me and the shape we made in the room was a triangle. Against the snow-light coming in the window, the cheery curtain, the ivy border; against the space on the floor where my mother had lain and the space in the door where my father had stood; against the sprouting onions, the dishes in the sink, the beautiful, furred plume of smoke the Sainte Maria unfurled above her head; against the violet pucker of her nipple we overlaid a wedge-shaped core of darkness, but it was true that anyone could have stood at any of its points and created the same effect. There are times when geometry unsettles the world and times when it fits right in. Then the moment passed and my father said, "What are you doing home?"

~

Thingy shook her head. She had plucked all the clover within arm's reach and crawled to a fresh patch so she could continue her chain. "I guess it's not a surprise," she said. "But still a shock."

She snipped the stem of a clover with her nails and twirled it under her chin so its purple crown just brushed her skin. Her profile as she gazed out over the bee meadow was very sharp and straight. Not so much like a statue as a pair of shears; golden ones for sure, but still capable of clashing.

"She was always so weird," Thingy said. A bee, attracted by the clover, swooped down to the level of her mouth and hovered there, buffeted by her breath. "So intense. You know my mother always called her The Fox. In a really nasty tone. 'I went to Abbots and saw The Fox,' she'd say and do you know what else?"

"What?" I said, watching the bee as it darted to the left and right as if to outflank her, lifted finally and settled near us on the head of a flower which it began to comb. Thingy braided her clover into the chain and held up the length to examine it. She tied the ends together and passed the loop flower by flower through her hands.

"She said if the Sainte Maria were any kind of object she'd be a paper plate with a stain on it. Mustard or something, smeared right across its face. Isn't that mean?" Thingy said, brushing another bee away with the back of her hand.

This seemed unusually invested for Thingy's mother, but I remembered a day when I was very young and the Sainte Maria had taken Luke and I out into the backyard to get some sun. Thingy came up the hill with her father behind her and, while we played a game where we found important stones and heaped them in a pile in Luke's lap, Mr. Clawson fidgeted on the other side of the wall where the Sainte Maria sat and ran his hand from the crown of his head to his eyebrows until his hair laid flat and straight across his forehead like a curtain.

Where was Mrs. Clawson? Was there such a thing as the blinds twitching? Her knuckles battering the glass? It seemed much more likely she was on the side porch with a book and a glass of wine. Mrs. Clawson doomed by my memory to drink and finger the page, wear white pants and seethe.

The sun was shining that day, too. I put a green stone in Luke's lap and he inclined his head toward me. "My liege," Thingy said and danced away.

(I dreamed I was sewing together a white shirt. Up one side I stitched tiny white xes, a hole for the arm, a hole for the neck. On the smock I stitched a white peacock, a white bear, a white horse and white owl. When I was done, I turned the shirt against the darkness and saw I had made a mistake. The animals could not agree. They tore at each other, claws piercing fur, hooves splintering bone. Soon there was nothing left of them but raveled ends which I picked apart and set aside. I unstitched the shirt and laid it out in pieces. I gathered my needle and thread.)

One night, at the beach, there was a terrible storm. It was far away, but anyone could tell it was only the ocean that held it back. At any moment the tide could turn and the storm would rush to our doorstep. Meanwhile, it made a beautiful show.

We all watched from a different place in the house. Mr. Clawson was on the veranda, a drink in his hand. Mrs. Clawson had last been seen pacing the hallway looking for flashlights. Thingy and I were side by side, each in our own window in the little white sandy room that was ours. The thunder rolled across the ocean like a carpet being flung out. The lightening struck and struck and struck.

"A fistful of stingers," Thingy said.

I wondered about the fish below. The whales and sharks and sea turtles flashing into x-ray, their eyes flat and impassive in their heads.

"Relax, Alice," Thingy said. "It happens all the time."

(I dreamed the needle was a bone and the thread was a bone. I dreamed the cloth below them was bone and, as the needle punched in and punched out, flakes of bone pattered onto my skirt. I dreamed the shirt itself was finished and it clinked and clattered as I folded it into a box. Much later, I dreamed I guided a little arm through the arm hole, a little head through the neck. The shirt was stiff and unyielding. When I set it out into the water, I saw that it would float.)

When Thingy finally came home, Mrs. Clawson threw her a party. Everyone we had gone to school with who was still in town had been invited, the house lit inside and out—paper lanterns hung from the porch roof, the pagoda strung with fairy lights—so from the tip of the mountain all the way down Jacob and I could see the house nestled on the ridge like a softly glowing egg. When we went around a curve the house was gone, had never been. When we went around another there it was again. We had been invited; I had the invitation in my lap where I could dig my thumbnail into the thick cardstock and scallop the edges. Jacob drove. His hands were dark shapes on the wheel. We went around a curve and the house disappeared. It was like we were a river instead of two people in a car: winding down, going wherever we had carved a path.

~

"It wasn't an accident," my father said.

"What did he mean?" Thingy asked. She strung the clover without particular order, but still a pattern had formed. Purple and white, two whites and another purple. A bee settled on the chain and Thingy blew it away. Another took its place.

"Was he trying to kill himself? Wracked with guilt?" She laughed to think of my father affected by anything so conventional. Once, when we were seven, he had dug a pit in the backyard and run the hose into it for five hours. This was in the early morning. By noon we had a mud spa in which to perfect our complexions and he sat in there with us all afternoon. Two girls in polka-dot bathing suits with skirts, my father in his boxers, drinking a beer, stretching one long, hairy leg across the pit to prop his foot up in the sun.

Once, when we were a little older, he took us out for Chinese food and detoured on the way home to stop at a green house on the far outskirts of town. He was gone for an hour and we sat in the car. When he came back he was humming under his breath and didn't say a word though we called and called to him as if he had gone deaf or were sweating deep in a fever. When Thingy pounded on his shoulders from the back seat, he reached back and caught her wrist, held it straining over his headrest as he steered one-handed around the curves, and smiled, and hummed.

"We met at a dance hall," Rosellen said, giggling, lightly scratching the back of my father's hand. "I was there with someone else."

My father had black hair and tan, hollow cheeks. My father made Thingy yellow mittens and pushed his welder's goggles back on his head so his hair stood up behind them as if he had always just come in from a high wind. When he walked women bowed before him like waving grasses, but because he never looked back he didn't know that when he passed they rose up again, their edges sharp as razors.

"Fie Fi Foe Fum," Rosellen said. When she fed him, she pushed the spoon a little too far into his mouth. When she wiped his cast, she let it drop back onto the table with a thud.

"Seriously, what did he mean?" Thingy said.

"I was thrown," my father said, his leg encased before him, slowly turning to stone. "I was flicked out of the universe. I was tossed. How else do you want me to say it? I was expelled."

(The egg settles in a valley, but in the very first battle it is pierced. So much for fortresses; so much for rose-twined mullion. It grows a golden web—latticework, hatch stitching—and never, it will never again…But no use, no matter: the enemy is in the gates and already asserting his preference. Gone are the great, green tapestries where the hart and the hind panted in the thicket. Where the lord blew a horn and the lady pricked her finger on a spindle. Gone is the lacquered screen, inlaid with pearl; the gilded chairs covered in some gay tapestry revealing a woman lifting her dress…The enemy will not poison the well, but he will move in a day crate for his dog. He will not pillage the spoils—a chest full of gold and one full of ashes, a chest full of gems and one of white moths' wings—but he will insist on track lighting and regular meals. "Put some meat on your bones," he will say as he takes off his shoes. "Come watch the end of this show with me.")

~

Much later, I woke up and the storm was over. It was raining, the water buffeted regularly against the window as if an extension of the waves, but no flash, no bang. In the bed across from me, Thingy slept tangled in the sheets. One of her legs was flung out across the mattress and I could see the luminous swell of her buttocks where her nightgown had rucked up. Her hair was in her face, a curl slipping in between her lips as she breathed. Otherwise, the house was still.

Too-ra-loo-loo-loo, sang the birds in the mountains. They were idiots, I thought, hardly worth the attention. Here the birds shrieked and mewled, got to the point. "Give me," said the seagull as he sidled toward me on the fleshy petals of his feet.

Toward the end of the night the crowd had thinned. Gone was Missy Howard, voted Most Good Natured; gone was Ronald Tolliver, who, in the fifth grade, Thingy had kissed in the science annex while Mrs. Dory's captive spring peepers looked on. In the years since I had seen her last, Thingy had graduated and graduated again. Sometimes we wrote letters. She wanted to do something about the world; she wanted to take it apart and see if there was a different way it could be put together. I wanted a mild winter, an early spring. Then, out of the blue, she had written with a different sort of proposition. She was coming home and she was bringing someone with her. I had been up on the mountain in that old house for so long, hadn't I?, just Jacob and I, and she knew there was plenty of room.

"We won't disrupt your routines at all," Thingy wrote. She used a blue pen which bled through the page when she let it rest to think. "In fact, we want to become a part of your routines.

We strive for seamlessness. Daniel needs a quiet place to write."

Tomorrow would be the first night. I had spent the day making up beds and sweeping out corners. It was spring. The garden was in, but not yet growing; the chickens were molting their winter down which blew across the yard in dingy drifts. Jacob had agreed but he had conditions. Now he was standing beside the Clawson's back stoop in the dark. Once in awhile I could see the wet glimmer of his eyes as they caught the dimming lights. The lanterns out, candles smoking, someone using a flashlight to write their name on the lawn. Thingy wore a long white dress that covered her feet. She kept pressing my elbow as she passed, saying my name: Alice Alice Alice. Up the hill, my father's house was dark. It was only a shape, like a rock or a massive deadfall. It could hardly be seen.

Finally, the Sainte Maria said, "It's good to see you again, Alice." Her breasts were small and sat high on her chest, the nipples dark and complex in their folds. She had one foot propped on a kitchen chair, but she moved it and nudged the chair toward me so I could sit. In front of her was a big, white, clunky glass of milk which she finished in one gulp. Behind her, the passthrough which could connect us to anything: the living room or a long tunnel leading downward...plaid couch and china figurines or a cross section of the river...green weed, gold drift, silver needles of fish darning the current.

There was something very wrong in the room, but it is too easy to say it was the Sainte Maria. The top of the Sainte Maria's panties were black lace and some wiry, surprisingly red strands of pubic hair poked through their weave. She had a birthmark in the hollow of her sternum, just between her breasts, as if someone had pressed their thumb there and twisted it around. There was snow on my boots, so I unlaced them and left them by the door. I came over to the table and sat.

"Jesus Christ," said my father. He was melting away in the doorway, slowly fading back into the shadow of the living room. Soon, all I could see of him was the beacon of his cast and then that too was gone and the Sainte Maria and I listened to him stump across the house to his bedroom where he slammed the door.

"I'm sorry about your father," she said, but that could have meant anything. What was wrong was that we were all too close, had lived overlapping each other so that our shapes became confused, our colors muddled, our lines tangled. Though I didn't know it yet, the Sainte Maria made a shape like a spiny sweet gumball; the Nina one like a lasso; the Pinta one like a flat, smooth shell. My father had one shape, Thingy another and I another still, but all atop each other we had become monstrous, many-headed. All atop each other, there was no room to breathe.

"Would you like a cigarette?" the Sainte Maria said, pushing her pack across the table.

"I can't," I said. "I'm pregnant."

The Sainte Maria had fed me dinner and given my brother baths. The Sainte Maria had pinched me when I whined and shown me the place in the stone wall where the chipmunks stored the sunflower seeds they stole from Mrs. Clawson's garden. Somewhere in the house was her leopard print jacket and somewhere in the pocket, worked all the way down by now into the lining, was a little wax ball with something unspeakable inside.

"I think her father was a gypsy," Thingy had said, both of us banished to my room for washing Dog in the kitchen sink and plugging its drain with his hair. "He came in some kind of caravan, selling pots or something, and stuck it in her mother and was gone the next day."

"The Nina told me her father is in jail," I said. I was a girl who was fond of the facts. "He robbed a liquor store."

"That's what I said, Alice." Thingy rapped me on the forehead with her knuckles. "Weren't you listening to me?"

Though the sky was flat and white, the clouds indistinguishable from one another, they still moved across the sun which threw patterns of shadow and light. Everything on the mountain fell under them, but sometimes a trick of the slopes would make the effect seem less arbitrary than it actually was. One house would be engulfed in shadow while right next door another blazed with light. One face was dark and hazy while another was bright as bone.

"Good for you," the Sainte Maria said as shadow and light swept through the kitchen. She put her hand over the back of mine and squeezed.

(Already the sex is determined, the whole genetic code. A fish that dreamed of being a bird. A bear who dreamed it was a man and woke up blinking. It was spring! If you fall asleep on a feather bed and rise in the morning from a mound of straw…If you eat a little oat cake and find your mouth filled with dung…If a man gives you a raspberry and it grows in your stomach until it is a pie's worth, a bushel basket, a whole bush's crop…. If the crows come down and snip you open…. If they eat you clean…. These are things a mother should tell you, but already there are eggs inside the egg, a habitual gesture, a film receding from the wide, black eyes. At a certain moment, the heart begins to beat which it will do forever after. Forever and ever, until it stops.)

~

Some nights I would leave the house and go into the forest. I always did this with great secrecy and haste, no telling who could be watching, but once I had eased the back door shut behind me and skirted the exposed meadow, I was in the pitch-black shadow of the trees and could not be seen.

Then, as I walked between the trees I felt a great lightening. Coming out on the edge of a ridge, I watched from the comfort of the treeline as the tops of other trees rustled and tossed in a wind I was above, removed from. The moon was full and heavy. The face within it—eyes and mouth, twin pits for a nose—pulled down as if gravity were wiping it from the moon's skull. Soon it would slide off to flutter into the forest and be picked apart for nests, dragged into dens to cozy the young.

I walked all over the mountain this way, my belly thrust before me. I was very young.

"I made you a soft one," Rosellen said and slid the egg cup in front of me. She tapped around the crown of the egg with a spoon and lifted the shell free so I could pierce the floating yolk, slurp it up

*...I live in a golden house with no doors or windows...Scarcely was my father in the world before I could be found sitting on the roof...*

When I didn't dip my spoon in right away, Rosellen said, "A lot of people eat an egg like this and think they're eating the chick, but let me assure you there was never anyone in that thing. It's an also-ran, a never-was."

"Sterile as a stick," she said, losing interest in me and moving away to the window. "Barren as a box of rocks."

"Are you looking for trouble?" Thalia said. "You'll find it."

From the top of the stairs I could see out across the living room where Mrs. Clawson was standing by the window. I sat down behind the railing and resisted the urge to thrust my legs through the slats. They would fit, I was sure, only a little trouble about the knees, but I was still that small, still that unformed. To kick my legs like a child above the dim, pulsing air of the room. The white couch and carpet, chairs and piano, the white sheer of Mrs. Clawson's pajamas, a silk pantsuit with amorphous buttons made of pearl. My legs could be like beaters, stirring everything to grey. I could be a little girl and not understand what I saw.

The rain came down, pocking the dune, bending the grass. Mrs. Clawson looked rumpled. She stood without touching anything, not even herself.

"Alice, Alice, Alice," Thingy said. "I want you to meet someone."

Her dress flowed over her breasts and then descended like a pleated column from the high, banded waist. She looked like a candle and her face flickered and shifted like flame stretched upward by a draft. I wanted to touch her—my friend! my friend!—but she had her hand on a man's arm and was pulling him toward me.

"It's nice to meet you," Daniel said. "I've heard so much about you I feel like I already have."

Of course, I recognized him right away. Hadn't there been something before this about a dragon, or a beetle, about a hole or a little snake uncoiling, testing the air with its tongue? But I couldn't think of the right story—after all, where was his brother? Where was the lake from which he should ascend?

He wore a brown corduroy jacket and khaki pants. His hair was darker than Thingy's, heavier, but he was still very pale, very gold and blue. Suddenly, there was almost no one there: Mrs. Clawson by the refreshment table talking to a man with a cane, a girl our age, very drunk, laughing as her boyfriend pulled her again to her feet. And Jacob who came up next to me then as silently as if he had swum across the yard. Jacob, who didn't touch me, but still laid his hand.

"When I was your age we would bake cakes and bring them over to each other's houses," Miss Fawcett said. She twitched her nose, red from blowing, her eyes pink and rheumy as a white rabbit, overbred, allergic to straw. "We would try to outdo each other: Lady Baltimore cakes bursting with daffodils, King cakes with plastic babies baked into the rings."

All the books in the library were fat with decay. The explorers and pirates, velvet rabbits and talking fish, the finches and cinders and centaurs and genies, sloe-eyed maidens and dead kings floating just beneath the waters of the lake: all laced with nets of algae, their eyes gelid and blind. The slightest ripple and they bobbed away from me: pages purring from their binding, covers slicking my palms with mold.

"Such disgusting cakes," Miss Fawcett said. "Too sweet, improperly set. And we didn't bake them for each other, oh no, but we were who ate them. Imagine five or six girls standing around the table. The squeak of sugar on our teeth, choking on batter. Imagine how we forced ourselves and still no one noticed us. Not one person said to me, 'You look like a girl who can really *bake*.'"

(Immediately, the process of division begins. It bubbles up like froth in the eddy, like frogspawn riding the rill. Soon the eyelashes form and the pads of the thumbs. Soon enough the pattern of the hair—falling straight across the brow—and the joints and the bones and the teeth and the brain. Lights flicker— is it spring?—a blue pulse at the belly and one at the heart. The story is almost over now. No more roles to play. I dreamed the edge of the world: a rock upthrust, chill tooth, and the water lapping. The white sky and gray water. A boat that came closer and closer until it washed up at my feet little more than a tiny white shirt, complete with smocking. Peacock and bear, horse, and owl. They turn and see each other. They rear to strike.)

One night I walked further than usual; too far, in fact, and I knew I would have trouble making it home before dawn. Still I pushed on, through the thickets, around the stones. The moon was always out those days. It had abandoned its cycle and when we came into a sudden clearing it gaped with me at the two streams—one sharp and tingling, one so sick it almost moaned—at the rock face and the crumbling cave, at the giant serpent, white as a grub but banded with red, horns on its head, a great blazing crest on its forehead like a diamond. The worm was the size of a well-grown man and rolled in the sick stream. It splashed the fetid water over its scales and rubbed its blunt, soft face against the ground. There was a terrible smell and the crest, as it swung its head from side to side, blinded me with refracted light, but still, there was something familiar about it. Still, I sank to my knees in the dirt and stared, only dimly aware as my bladder let go, my pants soaked through, liquid pattered on the leaves below.

"The Kerewe invite a stranger from another village to sleep with the widow three times before she can free herself from the pollution of death," Daniel said. "The Baganda believe the placenta is the child's twin and if the child dies at birth both are buried separately and separately mourned."

"There," Thingy said, and settled the clover chain around my stomach. She lay back in the sun and the bees rose and fell around us. One bee, ten bees. How many bees is too many? What an impossible question I could hear her laughing, though I hadn't asked it, and we lay together in the green and blue world, under the bees which rose and fell, under the sun which turned away.

"Goodbye, goodbye," Thingy said, but then she came back to me, many years later, and stood before me like a candle I had only to reach out my hand to take.

"I know you're there," said Mrs. Clawson. She didn't turn from the window. The storm was passing; the storm was past. From where she stood she could see darkness and a slow drip from the roof.

"Don't think I didn't hear you," Mrs. Clawson said, "Sneaking around. Breathing through your mouth." Her voice was rising, though she hadn't turned, hadn't looked. I stood up and backed away. Behind me was the long, white hallway, the little sandy room, my Thing who slept so soundly she had once slept through an entire firework display curled in the back of my father's truck. "I can't have a moment to myself, can I? You ingrate. You thief. From the day you were born, I couldn't have—"

But I was gone, down the hall, into the room. I shut the door behind me a little too hard and the change in air pressure sucked the blinds into the open mouths of the windows and spat them out again like rattling tongues. Still, Thingy slept, her breath heavy and sure, and it wasn't until later, back in my own bed and wrestling with the damp, salty sheets, that I realized her eyes were open.

"What's the matter, Alice," Thingy said when she saw me looking. "Did you see a ghost?"

Born dead. Is there any other way?

But in the dark I couldn't see the stain, and with the scent of the worm in my nose, its heat flowing over my skin, I was nothing more than a beetle lifted from one leaf and set down on another, stunned by the immensity of the void in between.

The worm swung its head toward me and I saw its snout, its fangs. Its eyes were blue and though I wanted to run I was afraid if I stood up I would walk right toward it, keep walking until I had delivered myself into its mouth.

"So that's the kind of girl you are," the worm said, its voice low and clotted. "I guess I can't say that I'm surprised."

And then I did run, stumbling as I went over a bundle some-one had wedged under a root—blue jeans and a man's leather belt, a thin red T-shirt emblazoned with white script—through the forest and across the ridge, over the meadow and the creek, up the stairs and to my own room where I locked the door and huddled in my bed, my hands clasped between my thighs, a pain in my belly that grew and grew.

(On the way back to town, we were quiet and he fiddled with the radio. "Ring-a-ding-ding," someone sang. He kept switching the stations. "She-bop-a-loo-bop" "Too-roo-ra-loo-ra-lay" The wipers smoothed the rain in arcs across the windshield, but when they retreated it bristled back up again. This time around I had noticed him aging. He had never been a hard man, not wiry like my father, but there was a new kind of softness to him, a smothering as if his chest and his stomach, his arms, thighs and the pink curl of his penis were all collapsing in toward some interior mouth, toothless, gumming in his midsection. But then we had moved further into the room, further into the mirror, and touched here and here, here and here...It was an old trick—the rabbit out of the hat, a burst of doves from the silk bouquet— but as soon as his penis rose to touch the top of his leg and then the top of mine, straining from its nest of white-blond hair as if it had caught a scent, my sense of his body disappeared and he was again himself, agelessly older than I, kind because he didn't care.

The road wound out of the forest and empty lots began to open up on either side. Soon we would be at the school and he would drive me right to the door, a concerned parent after all, and I a truant, well caught. Green light flashed in and out of the squalls of rain, a willow shimmied in the library's side-lot and a flock of sparrows darted into a gleaming chokecherry which would, in the spring, once again suffer under its weight of hairy, white blooms. It was a vain hope, that we could skip the winter, and yet it still felt worthwhile to observe that while the rain soaked the earth, it did not flood. "YEOW" said the radio. We pulled into the high school turn-around and parked behind a glossy yellow bus. After today he would return to the world he had imagined for himself, filled with entrances and egress points, directional markers, signs rattling in the wind. After today, I would never again be alone.

Some kids were standing under the school's front awning, their jackets tented up over their heads like broken wings, waiting to make a dash for the parking lot. They looked at us curiously and, never knowing what to do at this point, I reached over and shook his hand.

But the rain didn't stop. Isn't that the point? Soon enough all water joins the flood…)

It wasn't until the morning, I saw the sheets were filled with blood. A few days later, we had a little burial in the forest. Thalia made the box herself and gave me a length of cream chenille she said her mother had once intended to make into a dress with which to stitch the lining.

"Pity pity pity," says the cardinal, but no one answers and soon the bird moves on, secure in his bright coat, in his need to be pleased.

When we got to the clearing, Thalia didn't ask how I knew it was there. When we left the box in the cave, neither of us spoke any words. It was a summer day, the summer forest tossing all around us. I was seventeen, and that is the whole story, Ingrid. All you need to know.

Unless you're the sort of girl who is curious, the kind who won't take no for an answer, who sneaks down the hall in her bare feet to eat the last slice of cake in the dark, who doesn't clean up her crumbs.

In that case, I'll tell you her name, but nothing further.

It was Alice, of course. Alice Small.

# The Orifice

And the Orifice said:

Do You Love Horses? Are You Going to Heaven or Hell? Good News! Cockatiel Confessions—Everything You've Heard Is True! Plus, the Marvelous Cichlids of Lake Malawi. The Who, Why and How of Talking. Plus, Our Amazing Spaceship Earth. Care and Feeding Tips. Safe Branches for Perches. I Wasn't Sure Whether I'd Enjoy the Good News. Rush! Toxicity Info. Safe Moving Day. Baby Cories, Dojo Loaches. Essential Chemistry Needs for Popular Species. Rabbitfish. Puff Up or be Eaten. True Story: I'm a Junior Endurance Champ. Inside! The Vasa

Parrot Profile. Stressed Out? Plus, Territorial Aggression. 2 Tricks: Climb the Ladder, Ring the Bell. Too Hot? Too Cold? Why Does God Allow Disasters? Good News! Good News! Would a Compassionate, Merciful God Inflict Excruciating Pain and Torment on Human Beings in Terrifying Hellfire for all Eternity? Isn't it about Time You Discovered the Truth?

# The Black Knight's Tale

Today we went into town, all together. The men are foragers; they did the shopping. The women, myself and yourself, Ingrid, you were there, we went to the Laundromat.

Jacob is a man to whom it has never occurred he might lose his mind. He doesn't believe in losing his mind and so it will never happen to him. Daniel is a man who sees his mind all around him—in objects, in other people's expressions. I have seen Daniel cut a pear in half and sit there stunned by it. I have seen him reach out to touch something like a watering can or a silk flower, his finger trembling with anticipation, and then just stop. Not touch it at all. The object becoming a symbol to him of something far larger inside himself that he cannot see.

It makes for an uneasy pairing. It's a wonder they can get along at all. Yet, they are friends, Ingrid, and I think honest ones. Daniel walks slightly behind Jacob. He keeps his eyes on the back of Jacob's head. Jacob responds to Daniel the way he does to everything: with certainty, with uninhibited control. One is my husband and one is my lover. I thought about this as I put their shirts in the washing machine and smoothed their socks flat on the folding table.

Someone knocked on the window. I looked up and it was my father.

The Laundromat is like a terrarium. There is the same faint curve to the glass windows which trap the heat of machines and bodies, and a tendency toward obscuring mist. They both have the same iconography of arcane objects—carts and metal hangers, pirate chests, machines that dispense powder and ones that dispense colorful liquid, miniature motion-activated tiki gods— and the same general attitude of frozen display I observed in the frogs and green lizards kept in school to teach us the value of scientific detachment.

Today, the Laundromat was mostly empty: just you and I and an elderly couple who I didn't recognize. They were both overweight, both with the same creamy skin that stretched over their fatty bodies as if it were a glove they were pulling on. The man was having a problem with his breathing. His breath sounded as if it were being artificially forced in and out of his body and he couldn't seem to stand all the way up. He walked from the washer to the dryer and back again breathing in that fashion, curled into himself, as his wife murmured in the corner. She was folding his underwear. A pile of it sat fresh and airy and white in her lap.

My father crossed the room with the same impatient grace he has always had. He doesn't look much older. Astonishing. All these years have passed for him too and yet he looks to me just as he did when I was a child and could lean into his warm chest, smell his smell and listen to his thumping heart. And yet I am so different. And you, Ingrid, you hadn't even begun.

"Is this it?" he asked. It seemed he had not yet looked at me. He went right to your basket. He put his finger in your fist. "This is the baby," my father said.

When I was young my father took Thingy and I to a circus which had set up in the vacant lot across from Abbot's. We went early, an hour before the show and he walked with us between the brightly colored caravans and smaller tents where the circus performers and their animals lived. We saw a goat standing on a wooden spindle and two elephants, chained at the ankles, twining their trunks under and around each other while they gazed off in opposite directions. We saw a trio of trained dogs with wicked skulls and puffy blonde tails. The dogs were the only animals that responded to us. They were leashed to a wire that stretched between a blue caravan with an ornately curved red roof like a Chinese pagoda and a jumbo RV hung about with silver and orange bells. When we approached them, the dogs yipped and raced back and forth along their line. They weren't afraid of us, but rather rejecting us. They were too highly trained, too intelligent: dogs that could walk like a man and choose from a platter of thimbles which one concealed a pea. They knew who we were. The audience. The dumb marks. Thingy wanted to pet them anyway and chased after them, her hands outstretched, jelly slippers flashing in the last light as the day began to fail. It was time for the show to start.

The circus was a cruel place. I felt assaulted by it, as if my eyes were being pushed back into my head by a pair of massive thumbs, but also wildly excited. The show had not yet begun when we took our seats in the bleachers high on the side of the central tent. The lights were still bright and everyone was talking: mothers and fathers, so many children the air fluttered with their high thin voices as if their voices had transformed the air into a thousand pairs of wings. I suppose I was an unusual child. Highly strung. It must have been hard for my father to know what to do with me. I think I was often hard for my father to recognize. Sometimes when he came into a room in which I already was his eyes would slide over me as if I had unwittingly perfected some blend of camouflage and crypsis: my skin taking on the pattern of the couch cushion, my real eyes concealed beneath huge, flaring spots that whorled on my forehead. "Where's Alice?" he might ask the Nina or the Sainte Maria, but I would be right there, sitting beside him, my fingers in my mouth and skin as cold as a frog's.

My father settled Thingy and I in our seats and left to go buy us all sodas and popcorn. "Don't move," he said, leveling one square, brown finger in Thingy's face and slowly moving it over into mine. "Don't talk to anyone," he said to me. Oh, my father. I loved him. I wanted always to touch him. My hand on his knee or in the crook of his elbow. My hand on the back of his neck where it looked like a blob of Vaseline against the burnt brown creases of his skin.

"I want extra butter on mine," said Thingy and my father laughed as he left us and picked his way down the rickety bleacher stairs.

He wasn't back when the show began, the lights falling suddenly and pitching the tent into blackness wherein the adults gasped and the children, wild and unbidden, screamed. Thingy and I held each other's hands. A spotlight came on. It wavered across the bleachers, illuminating the audience as if it were a long, white finger searching for its place in a book. Sometimes the spotlight would pause or go back for a closer look and whoever was caught in its bleaching light would have a few moments to shift uneasily in their chair, some of them hiding their faces in their hands, some of them, the children, waving. I remember thinking as the children across the tent from me beamed and waved how few teeth everyone had. There were so many holes in the other children's faces. So many holes in mine which I worried with my tongue as the light dipped down to the packed sawdust floor of the central ring, failed to find what it was looking for and began to travel through the bottom rows on our side of the tent.

"I hope it doesn't land on us," said Thingy, squeezing my hand. The light swept up the rows just below us, so bright and obliterating it seemed to be erasing the people it cast upon rather than illuminating them. "It will be horrible," she said, turning to me, her eyes wide and very dark. "It will be so hot."

I had thought of the light as a cold thing—it looked cold to me, a concentrated spear of moonlight, well-oiled metal—but I saw in an instant that Thingy was right. It was a hot light, white hot. The whitest, hottest heart of the sun blooming outward, sweeping away everything in its path as it grew. There was nowhere to go. We gripped each other's hands and panted as the children in the row below us were swept into the light, screaming as it passed over them, raising their hands into the air.

But of course, when it did reach us, nothing happened. We squinted for a moment, blinked. Green roses bloomed in our

vision as the light moved away and left us again in the dark. We
had been wrong, but we didn't know it. We were children, right
on the edge of an adult reckoning, adult guilt, but still buoyant
in a world of hazy possibility. We were adrift, tied to the rocky
bottom only by one ankle with a mooring so thin at any moment
it could be snapped like a strand of brown kelp and we would
be swept into another world, the world below this world, or the
one below that.

We didn't feel foolish; we felt lucky. Thingy laughed with relief and pressed her lips against my cheek. The show began. In a
way, this is what it felt like when I first met Jacob, only that time
the light landed on its target. More like a thumb than a finger, it
turned out, moistened as if to turn a page.


Once, when Jacob was eight, his Uncle Robert brought his
father home stretched out in the back seat of his own car. This
wasn't an unusual occurrence: his father not returning to the
house, but being brought; Uncle Robert steering the car around
the road's hairpin turns with one hand, the other arm cocked
out the window as if he owned both the car and the afternoon;
the sun suspended in a long, leaking evening; the day panting
hot until a hot night came down like a cardboard box trapping
everyone inside; the stars airholes poked with a pin.

I know nothing about the house Jacob's father was brought
to. There are no photos and the only location I have is north, but
not too far north. Another state, but the same blue mountains.
Similarly, I know nothing about the mother who stood on the
porch or the child who ran halfway out into the yard and then
stopped, warned away by some rasp in his father's breathing or
by the flaccid nature of his father's thigh inside his jeans. Not
dead, but dead drunk. Not dead, because if so the child could

come and touch the body, could feel in the space just above the skin where the armor of the self had crumbled the way a cicada shell would crumble if stroked with too eager a finger tip.

Perhaps Jacob's house was one of many identical houses clustered in the hollow, each of them with a hall linking the front door directly to the back so looking through the screen was like looking through a telescope. Perhaps there was a clothesline in the front yard, an upturned wooden crate that was once used to transport lettuce. Perhaps the whole area was thick with pines and the ground carpeted with their needles and their amber scent in the air, twining through even the scent of garbage and motor oil, cooking grease and wafts of his mother's perfume.

I could imagine anything, because Jacob tells me nothing. Was he a pretty boy? Was he good? I think he was watchful, his yellow eyes unblinking from the first. I think he was an unnerving infant, but he was one of many—at least six sisters, another one who is only ever described as the baby. Perhaps at night, Jacob's mother stood over each of her children's beds and felt their features in the dark, her hands fumbling over their faces on the pillow. This one the eldest girl, right where she should be; this one the baby, a young teenager now, but still sucking the corner of his blanket into a nipple molded by the roof of his mouth. When she got to Jacob, I imagine she felt his forehead and then the bridge of his nose, his chin—weak like his Uncle Robert's—and then his eyelashes fluttering like moths against her palm, the eyes open though unseeing. The boy asleep, but refusing to be blind.

I come back again and again to the boy standing in the yard watching as his uncle drags his father out of the car and lets him fall into the dirt. Uncle Robert worked in the mines. So did Jacob's father. So did the neighbors on both sides and the ones next to them, and behind, and before. The mines radiated out around the boy like the threads of a web. On every strand someone is struggling, bouncing the web up and down. At eighteen, Jacob too went underground. It wouldn't have been much of a story except for that, at twenty-two, he came back up.

Underground, Jacob wore a reflective vest and a yellow hardhat whose lamp he could turn on and off by twisting the lens. He was a bucket man, part of a small, mobile crew-for-hire who moved up and down the mountains tunneling under the surface of used-up strip mines for the deeper seams that kinked through the rock. The crew was composed of: Harry, the foreman, Pete, who ran the big machines, Lotho, a wiry black man whose muscled arms gleamed as if, beneath the coal dust, were a denser, radiant stone, and Piro, the foreigner whose perpetually runny nose carved tidal channels through the black powder that clung to his luxuriant red moustache.

In every shaft the miners strung electric lights as they dug. These hung drooping at the roofline, suspended from a tough orange extension cord. The bulbs themselves were in cages like canaries which exuded yellow light instead of song. The lights were powered by an external generator, but the system was unreliable, often shaken out of service by the chunking and grinding of the continuous miner as Pete steered it into the rock face, the teeth of its rotating drum ripping the coal from the seam. When the generator went out, all the men were plunged into a momentary darkness. This was so total it seemed for just a moment as if the deafening sounds of the machine, their own breathing, the groan and shift of the rock above their heads were also extinguished though the Miner still dug, the conveyor still turned, the bucket suspended forgotten at the end of Jacob's arm—his arm itself forgotten, unnecessary to the beautiful, dark, beating self that was here, for just a moment, warm and spreading in a world that could not distinguish its borders—still filled and overfilled and spilled out broken rock over the toes of his boots. Then, one by one, the other men would twist on their headlamps and bob about in the shaft like jellyfish, their distance impossible to gauge. The silence would be revealed to be horrendous noise and Lotho, standing behind him with the bin, would say, "Woah! Wake up, Jakey. Where've you been?"

At night, when the machines finally came to rest but before retiring to the trailers they bunked in, the crew hunkered down in the slag heaps and lit bituminous clinkers on fire in the great metal claw of the backhoe. Then, as the coal exhaled its boggy gasses (peat and black water, the shimmering chitin of Jurassic dragonflies, the curled fronds of ferns) the men passed around a bottle. Some nights they told stories.

One night Piro told a story about twelve brothers who lived beside a lake somewhere near the village where he grew up. When the war came, as it does to all villages, the brothers were conscripted into service and when they returned many years later one of them was missing some vital part.

"One had blow off his legs," Piro said. "One his arm. One: no eyes, but scars only like a mask. And one, no penis." Piro paused to let this sink in. The other men laughed because surely with twelve brothers and not a whole man among them there was a punch line coming, but Piro said, "I know this one best. Bruno. He live to be an old man when I was little boy and he say, 'The only place the bomb strike. The only place," and pat his trouser here—pat, pat—but it was empty."

Piro patted the crotch of his filthy pants. His hands, which he scrubbed with lava soap at the end of each day, were star-tlingly white and looked small and furtive clasped between his legs. Everyone was quiet. Someone drank from the bottle and spit a jet of liquor into the fire where it hissed. Then, Lotho said, "Shit, I know that guy. He wasn't called Bruno, though. His name was Henry, ain't that right? Henry Smalt?"

He pointed across the circle at the foreman who held up his hands like he was surrendering or warding off a curse, then grabbed at his own crotch and shook it as if what were inside were unmanageable, coiled to strike. Then it was all right to laugh and they all did, even Piro who cleared his nose with his fingers and wiped the black snot to glisten in the dirt. Twelve brothers and not a whole man among them. A joke.

That night Jacob dreamed of twelve brothers standing at the edge of a gray lake. They had their backs to him, facing out over the water, yet in the manner of dreams he could still see their faces: the blasted hole where a nose should be, a web of scars cocooning the empty sockets of the eyes. The brothers were setting up a camp. One dragged logs up from the waterline with his remaining arm and stacked them inside a ring of stones. Another, an empty pant leg pinned neatly beneath him, sat on a rock and unpacked tins of potted meat, glass jars of jam, loafs of bread wrapped in tricolored paper from a large, green haver-sack. One brother held a tent stake in place between the stubs of his wrists while yet another, his legs gone below the knees, knelt on the ground to pound the stake home, the blows of his hammer echoing back from the lake like silver bells.

It was late in the day. The hike up to the site had taken lon-ger than the brothers had anticipated. The light was failing and yet no one seemed to hurry. Each brother went about his task as if this action his body was now performing were the inevitable outcome of all the other actions that had come before, another knot in a string that stretched backward in tidy square hitches, forward in a smooth, uncomplicated line. Aiming a gun leads to slicing a loaf of bread; thrusting a torch into a hay loft is now dipping a bucket into the still water of the lake. Running toward an earth ridge rimmed in fire is threading a pole through the peak of a tent. Lying in the dirt, the ground beneath spongy and red, is lifting the chiming bottles one by one from a basket, pulling the cork and tilting it to drink.

When their chores were done, the brothers gathered around the fire to share their meal. In the flickering light, they passed around bread and meats, hunks of soft cheese and little cakes wrapped in wax paper. They talked quietly to each other. Every now and then someone laughing or clinked a bottle against a stone. One brother began to hum and soon they were all singing, a song with many verses which they often interrupted to argue about wording or order but picked up again immediately, the tune low and mumbling and soft as fur. The youngest brother had blonde hair which shone in the firelight and all the other brothers went out of their way to touch him as they moved about the circle, as if to reassure themselves that he was still there.

After a time it was completely dark and the world that surrounded them all constricted itself to the circle of fire light and the sound of the lake water lapping against the shore. Jacob— always on the outside, still lurking in the darkness—noticed something it seemed only possible to see by the light of the campfire. The brother's bodies had begun to reconstruct themselves, but not out of pale flesh and coarse, wiry hair. Instead, where a brother was missing an ear a sheen of downy, black feathers, each as small and precise as a tiny clam shell, had grown back in its place. Where a brother was missing a leg a bundle of glossy, black quills bristled from the cuff of his pants, and where another's jaw had been ripped from his face a sheaf of wing feathers rustled in the black hollow of his mouth.

The youngest brother, who was by now quite drunk and resting his head on his nearest brother's shoulder, had lost his arm. He was wearing a green shirt from which the sleeve had been cut away to expose the gleaming knob of his amputation and earlier in the evening Jacob had noticed how the stump flexed and rolled in sympathy with the labors of his remaining arm as the boy tossed sticks onto the fire or dragged logs to serve as seats around the pit.

Now, when the youngest brother leaned back away from the fire all appeared as it had before. Clearly visible was the empty sleeve, the knob of bone, the delicate shading of his ribs sliding under the skin as if they were a cage under shallow water. But when the boy leaned forward again, catching a joke and shifting into the fire's circle to laugh, Jacob saw that where before there had been emptiness now was a black swan's wing with feathers long and glossy. The firmly muscled joint bent as the boy beat his wing with delight and his brothers laughed with him and leaned in, their hair brushed back from their faces by the wind he made.

"Of course," Jacob said. "They have a sister," and then he woke up in the silver, bullet-shaped trailer in which he slept. Across from him, Lotho snored and flung an arm out over the sheets.

The crew traveled up and down the mountains in a caravan of white trucks and a single semi driven by Pete which hauled the miner. The shafts they dug were poor, holdovers from more lucrative projects, and in this they were like a clean-up crew, hollowing the last of the coal from the thinning mountains, mitering the walls smooth and then leaving the pits to fill with green water, their runoff seeping into the towns below. Sometimes there would be people standing by the side of the road as they wound through a town on their way up to a mine site higher on the ridge. Mostly these were children, excited, running after the trucks and shouting.

"They act like we should throw something down," Lotho said. "Candy or something."

"Get out of the way, you little fucks," Henry said, laying on the horn as he steered around a curve.

One evening, on the last day of digging a particularly dissipated site, Jacob went back into the mine at the end of his shift to retrieve and coil the lights. The mine was an old one and had once been a big production. Its shafts radiated out around him, dug seemingly at random into the rock face, and the rooms carved out around the support pillars were long and ended in darkness. They had spent a month here already, the men walking the tunnels to scout for rooms that had been abbreviated or places where the possibility of a cross-shaft had been ignored. The results had been poor and in the end what they were really there to do was the work that would commence the next day: retreat mining when they would yank the support pillars with their loads of coal out from under the roof and let the rooms collapse behind them like a block ladder cascading down its hinge of string.

Their last act would be to dynamite the mouth of the primary tunnel and sink a metal sign officially leaving unwary explorers to their own devices at both the crumbled mouth of the mine and the head of the access road leading back to it. Then the site could sink back into whatever obscurity it chose. It was a pretty place, the rough embankments of the original cuts already overgrown with jessamine and mountain laurel, the clearing where they parked the trucks and set up the trailers rimmed by a stand of young junipers, still little more than shrubs, advancing from the forest's edge. Of course, that had all been cleared to make way for the new digging, but it would come back—the rank vines, the tremulous leaf—slowly at first and then in a dark rush, like a great paw sweeping out of the forest to clamp down on whatever still wriggled there. It made Jacob uncomfortable, particularly in the evening hours when the insects and birds would all pause at unexpected moments as if collectively listening. He had volunteered to go back down for clean up and no one protested.

Dear Ingrid, it strikes me now that you have never been inside the earth. Under water, yes; under dust and heat, under a summer fog wet as a tongue, but not yet under the indifferent weight of rock and soil and miles of roots. How could you know the way the ceiling arced over Jacob's head as convulsively smooth as a length of bowel? The way the standing pillars seemed to curve toward him and the stillness and the slick damp? The way, miles down the corridors, a light winked on then out, then on again, flirting around the bends in the tunnels as he reached the end of the electric lights' halo and, pausing only briefly, reached up to twist on his helmet lamp and kept walking?

When I imagine you grown, Ingrid, I imagine you in a blue dress, barefoot, dust streaking your calves. You move as if you are used to sliding around things: a sway of the hips, a quick shift from the ball of your foot to its tough, arched side. You are always moving away from me, your hair pulled together in a loose bush at the nape of your neck, and you are always carrying something tucked against your hip. A basket full of eggs. A wicker cage in which some animal quiescently shifts.

I see you this way because I have no power to predict you. I know you too well, have known you every moment of your breathing life and before that, I would add, when your lungs practiced on amniotic fluid alone. What I will know of you in the future will be based on my exhaustive experience of your past, but about Jacob I know next to nothing. Even after twelve years of marriage, of working and eating with him, sleeping next to him, shifting on top of him as his hands hold my hips, I am free to imagine almost anything about his life before I was in it. In a way, I think this means I know him better than I ever will you, Ingrid. Because I have made him. Because I can leave him to his own devices and return to find him still in that mineshaft, walking further than he meant to, his own footsteps echoing back to him as meaningless as the drip of water radiating back from the corridors that crook blackly all around.

Jacob walked in what seemed like a straight line, but it wasn't long before the shine of the last electric light was lost behind him. Before him the dancing will-o'-the-wisp too disappeared and he was left alone with only the yolky illumination of his headlamp. Jacob stood there for a moment and felt the mine stretch empty around him. It was a crooked place, a place that had been looted even as it was carved. If this were another land, Jacob may have kicked a shard of pottery away with his foot or traced crumbling ochre outlines across the walls—the head of a dog! the head of a snake!—as they unfurled a story deeper and deeper into the dark. As it was, these were our mountains, Ingrid, and they were bare, barren, scraped clean. Jacob turned over a rock with his foot and found below it another rock. After a moment or two, he reached up and switched off his headlamp, turned at random in the sudden pitch and entered one of the rooms.

I think, in the dark, with his lamp off, above him the weight of the mountain, and the sky, and the peak of the mountain in the world above this world grinding down like the tip of a worn tooth, Jacob stood and felt all the pieces of himself that were missing grow back in a rush of black feathers. He had sisters too and, even if they weren't given to weaving, there is an edge at everyone's making that unravels for the lack of the next stitch. So, there he was: feathered but flightless, watchful but blind. I don't know how long he stood there in darkness, listening to darkness radiate around him, listening to darkness inside him make its familiar noise. He must have turned his light back on. Or perhaps he simply turned and moved forward. Came to the next thing, and the next after that. Regardless, he must have come out of the mine eventually because the next time he had a weekend off, Jacob borrowed one of the work trucks and drove back to the telescope house in the piney hollow where his mother fried meat, his sisters dipped their sharp tongues in and out of pitchers of milk, the baby worked on an engine in the front yard and his father, waxy as a long-dead king, slept and slept and slept.

They all ate dinner together that first night and his eldest sister said, "There's something different about you, Jacob. I don't like it." The other sisters echoed this in a chorus and the baby, its mouth full of meat, paused in its chewing and nodded its head.

It went on like this: the next day at lunch as they all gathered around the table, that evening at dinner again. "There's something about you, Jacob," said the sisters. His mother slapped a chop on each plate and kept her own counsel. His father, joined to their meal by the open bedroom door, grunted in his sleep and rolled over.

Finally, on the last night he was home, his third oldest sister regarded him across the steaming kettle his mother had set in the middle of the table and said, "There's something about you Jacob…" and Jacob reached up over his head and pulled the cord dangling from the bulb, plunging them all into darkness. At first there was a clamor. The sisters hooted and moaned, the baby wha-wha-whaed its highest pitched cry. Then, slowly, the noise died down and there was silence broken only by a flurry of rustling and the drip of far water echoing as if down long, blind corridors of stone.

When Jacob pulled the light on again, it was clear everything had changed. They all looked around at each other, amazed. Where before a sister had a face like dish of butter, now she was revealed to have the broad mouth and round, golden eyes of a toad. Where before the mother had huffed and steamed, gusts of Shalimar wafting damply from the folds in her sack dress, now she whirred along, a perfect, chugging engine. The sisters cawed and croaked and rustled inside their suddenly ill-fitting clothes. One stretched her long neck and honked.

Oh, and the soup was made of stones: each bowl a dock leaf, dark and damp.

Oh, and the baby was a great sack of pillow stuffing; the chairs they sat on nothing but turtles who groaned and closed their heavy eyes. In the open doorway, from the bed piled high with quilts and linens, their long slumbering father sat up and stretched and looked around.

"I see," the father said gravely, surveying his family. "I've been gone a long time, too long perhaps, and yet I only have one question." He rose and drifted toward the door, his feet long and pale, the nails blue as flax, and leveled a finger across the room at Jacob, his only son. "What manner of creature is that?" he said and so, though his mother chugged and his sisters' bleated, there was nothing left for Jacob to do but fly out the window in a great, glossy rush. From there he circled the world three times—sometimes flapping noisily through the underbrush, sometimes running on four swift black legs—until finally he slammed, panting, against the side of a building and slumped to his knees and could not go on.

It turned out he wasn't all that far from where he began. In Elevation, in fact, where there was a job washing dishes for a woman who reminded him, in some ways, of the mother he had left chugging purposefully on the dining room table. And so he settled there. And so he stayed. Waiting, I suppose, though probably not for me.

But how curious that here too, in his new home where he was not known, no one could tell quite what he was. A swan or a mink? A man or only the skin stretched thin around what it has eaten?

When my father came back—a long line, he said, gesturing with the popcorn which was half eaten—there was a contortionist act in the center ring and two clowns in hobo garb miming stealing a pie from the fat lady off to the side. The trapeze artists had already gone on—"No net," Thingy said, "That'll make a mess,"—and the elephants who balanced on balls and picked up their trainer and passed her back and forth between them with their trunks. The little dogs had appeared wearing tuxedo vests complete with pert, black bow ties and stood on their hind legs to prance and bow as if they were at a cocktail party from another century.

A sequins spangled woman had come into the stands to drag children out into the ring where they served as unwitting straight men for the clowns, or nervously offered trays of champagne flutes to the dogs who took them in between their paws and gestured with them as they hopped about on their straining hind legs. Thingy had bounced up and down in her seat and waved her arms over her head when the woman came up our aisle, but to my great relief she ignored us both, passing on without another look.

"Ladies and Gentlemen," said the ringmaster. He was dressed all in black, his face gaunt and white beneath a black top hat which, even at that distance, I could clearly see was patched. But he had beautiful skin, smooth and cold as cream, and he stood very still in the middle of the ring and said no more as around him the contortionists writhed into hoops and rolled toward each other—four women, their ribcages flattened to the ground, toes splayed across the backs of their heads, mouths red and open, smiling.

"Ladies and Gentlemen," said the ringmaster again and my father said, "Now, *here* we go," as if everything that had come before had been nothing more than a twitch in the curtain. He tapped Thingy on the top of the head and said, "Pay attention."

Is it possible then that the ringmaster looked at us? Surely not; we were so far away, so nondescript in our expectation. The women rolled into each other, twined around each other until their bodies were a complicated knot, four red smiles twisting this way and that toward the crowd. The ringmaster bowed from the waist and dropped his head as if it pained him to see, but not before he looked up at us, looked right at us: at Thingy, surely. Perhaps at me.

"Imagine that," my father said and from the peak of the tent, lost in blackness, a rope came down, capped at the end with a cartoonishly large, black hook. When the hook reached the women the knot somehow opened and took it into their depths. Then, to the great wonderment of the crowd, they were all lifted into the air, a writhing bundle, vaguely oval shaped. The children in the audience screamed again and many of them laughed. It was funny to see so many things happen all at once. It was funny to stretch to the very end of the tether, to drift just above the black chasm and trust the current to shift and bring you back.

"Still no net," Thingy said and then, high above the packed dirt floor—the clowns whose faces were smeared with blueberry; the fat woman, brandishing a rolling pin, colossal breasts heaving beneath her prim, starched apron; the little dogs who had snuck back on stage in various stages of undress like late night revelers reemerging for the second stage of the party; the ringleader who did not move from his bow—the women split open (legs and arms pulling apart, waving toward each other as if with regret) and out of their midst a body plummeted toward the floor.

Oh and then we all screamed, of course. And, when she was brought up short by a rope so thin it was almost invisible just before she hit, unfolded herself over the ringmaster's head like a kerchief fluttering out of a lax, white hand, then we all gasped. She landed—a girl in a blue dress, a basket over her arm and in that basket a pie still steaming from its vents which she gave to the fat woman as if to say, "Nothing a little beauty won't fix. Nothing to take so seriously,"—and then we laughed and laughed.

Because it was a joke after all. Twelve brothers and not a whole one among them. A girl in a blue dress born from an egg in the sky.

The ringleader stood up and put his hat back on his head. Everyone involved took a bow.

At the end of the night, as we walked back to his truck, my father whistled a little big-top music and took us each by the hand. "What did you think?" he said, steering us around heaps of discarded rubbage and out of the glow of headlights. "Was it everything you'd imagined?" He was in a good mood, swinging our hands up and out as if he were directing the tempo of his own whistling, every now and then hauling us up off the ground when we didn't step quickly enough to avoid a rut or a puddle of standing oil.

"I wanted the girl to come back," Thingy said, "She was the prettiest. The one with the pie."

In fact, she had come back a number of times. She'd been one of the girls jumping from rump to rump as horses streamed around the ring. She'd been the magician's assistant, the knife-thrower's target, the damsel-in-distress menaced by a lion and rescued at the last moment by the lion-tamer's whip. But I knew what Thingy meant. When she'd fallen from the sky was the only time she'd been the prettiest one of all. When she'd offered the poor fat lady the pie was the only time she'd been the wisest, the funniest, the most beloved.

"And what did you think, Alice?" my father said. "What did you want to happen?"

I had wanted to the rope to break, but because I was in love, I couldn't say it. "I wanted the same as Thingy," I said. "For the girl to come back so I could see her again."

And again and again and again, I could have added. Walking toward me and then away. So small I could lift her with only one arm and then, as must always be, so large that even dwindling on the horizon she is taller than me, blocks more of the sun.

In the Laundromat, the old woman paused in her folding to watch my father lift you out of your basket and examine you. Her face was pleasant and empty as a sock. When my father did nothing more than raise your shirt to look at your tense, mottled belly, then turn your head from side to side to inspect your ears, she went back to her work as if whatever entered the room could be nothing but what she expected. If a horse were to come bursting through the door, wicked hooves gleaming as he charged the machines, I felt sure the old woman would say, "Well, of course. It is a *white* horse, after all"; if a hole were to open up under our feet, spiraling down into the gullet of the mountain, I'm sure the old woman would say as we fell, "But it isn't very deep, you know. Only long."

She held up a pair of her husband's underwear and shook it. There was a faint stain running in a line down the back which she pinched with her fingers as if to rub it clean and then used as the central line on which she folded the cloth.

"The likeness is really remarkable," my father said. He turned away from me and pumped you over his head as if you were a trophy he were holding up to an arena of cheering fans. I could see your face bobbing up and down over his head and you looked at me as you laughed, delighted, his hands snug in your armpits and brown, square thumbs crossed over your chest like an engraving. A pair of dates, perhaps. A beginning and an end.

"In this world you have work to do," Thalia said.

"And in the other world?" I asked. I had seen it: the world beneath this one, the one beneath the waters. Where do the children go who are mistaken for turkeys or fox kits or other wild things? When my child was born she weighed as much as a newborn bear cub, and, just like a bear, she was immediately sealed in a cave to protect against the continuing weather. Don't tell me I will never see her face again. Perhaps looking up from the underside of the creek, gold and green, dreamy with algae?

"There is no other world," Thalia said. "Don't be that sort of girl for the rest of your life."

"Get your hands dirty," Thalia said. "Then wash them clean."

# A Woman Married A Man Who
## Said He Was The Sun

But all that was a long time ago. Today we went into town and came back with folded laundry, sacks of dry goods, a plush toy Jacob, of all people, picked up in the grocery line and presented to you, Ingrid, as if he were giving you a chalice studded with gems.

"See," Daniel said when you didn't immediately crow with delight or grip it in your still fumbling fist. "See, Ingrid, it's a love bug," he said and smoothed a finger across the thing's broad, pink forehead as Jacob had done, squeezed its boldly striped torso to make it vibrate and tinkle out a little song.

When we came back up the mountain, I gave you to Jacob to hold while I unloaded the baskets of laundry from the bed of the truck and put them away in their various closets. I made our dinner—rice, last season's pole beans, ramp soup and the stringy breast of a hen who only that morning had trotted up to Jacob's hand knowing he had something special just for her, something denied to each of her sisters in turn hidden in his hard palm.

When the platters were full, I went to the porch to call the men to the table and found Jacob still there with you, the love bug discarded on the slatted wood where it occasionally jittered and ground out a few lost notes. You were sitting on his knee facing the forest. His palm was on your back to hold you upright and you swayed and lurched with the tiny corrective movements of someone riding an extravagant, but familiar mode of transport—a pasha aboard her elephant, perhaps. A mountain girl astride the moth-eaten back of her husband-to-be's old gray dray.

For all that, you were both very still and, for once, the forest was still. It was sunset, late for us to be eating dinner, everything delayed by a sense of thickness in the day as if I had to push through the air to reach the real objects on the other side of it. Soup tureen, carving knife, salt and pepper shakers fashioned into tiny pine trees, ceramic hen under whose breast nestled the butter as round and simple as her heart.

"Pling, pling, pling," said the love bug. It was a strange creature: pink and purple, its wings both veined and furred. Across its body stripes of black vinyl gave it the comical appearance of a jailbreaker bumbling toward freedom. Its eyes, great, dewy disks of plastic, were set forward on its head. Predator's eyes, like ours, single minded and designed to track. The better to gaze into your own, Ingrid, I suppose. The better to be beloved.

Around the edges of the world a lemon light seeped up. It was as if we were being submerged in batter—cool and thick and nothing for it but for the baker to pop us into her waiting oven. A breeze ruffled through the tree branches but didn't reach us three on the porch. In his study, Daniel switched on a light as someone must always switch on a light, and what reached us showed me again the whorl of hair that swirls from the back of your head like silt in an eddy, Jacob's broad hand on your back and his middle finger slipped down the collar of your tiny white shirt to hold you in place. It seemed to go on forever: the cool green forest, the lemon light, the taste in the back of my throat that is awaiting only sweetness to enliven it, the hollow on my tongue where sweetness must surely come to rest.

When Jacob and I first met, Thalia slid the paperwork across the table to him and said, "Don't think of this as a beginning. This is just another knot along the way." He signed and when he passed the sheaf of documents back over to me I imagined, young as I was, that I could decode something from his very lack of curiosity which would show me what he saw. A girl, still slack around the middle, clothed in a red gingham dress that had once belonged to her mother. A girl who had been given very little care and so was due a tremendous store of luck.

I signed my name below his own. Alice Small: the i topped by a bubble, the ls loose and wandering. Thalia was the witness and the next week Jacob and I were wed in the courthouse in Ridley Township, I in the same gingham dress and my mother's bell-sleeved coat, he in a black suit that didn't fit across the shoulders. It was Thalia's idea that we marry, of course. "You are both loose ends," she said, as if that finished it, as if the rest of our lives should be dedicated to the act of tidying away. Jacob got land out of the deal: the house, the grounds, the mountaintop. And I got a place to linger. My house, it would have been after all, my mountain top, but Thalia said, "What good is it to keep something if you have no one to give it to?" and along with the marriage license she signed away her rights to the land. And myself along with it, it seemed. To Jacob I bequeath both girl and mountain. To my dishwasher because he fits the story.

On the courthouse steps, Thalia gave me back my bouquet—white larkspur and cushion mums, all floating in a frost of stiff, baby's breath. "Throw them," she said, though there was no one there to catch, and so I did. They landed on a stiff berm of snow churned up from the street by the plows and when I passed them again on my way to the old green truck Jacob and I were borrowing to take us to our honeymoon cabin I was surprised to see they hadn't melted a hole in the snow bank—alive as they were, stubbornly green at the stem—but rather lay there as crisp and cold as the frill around the lip of a white china plate. Decoration, but one destined never to be stained or chipped. A cold, proud, useless beauty and one that faded as we pulled away from the curb.

When Thingy and Daniel moved into the house on Newfound Mountain, Jacob and I had been married for almost eleven years. Our life together, which had at first seemed so accidental, had assumed its own shape, independent from the shape our lives had taken apart. Thingy stood in the front hallway with her bags at her feet and craned her neck to see into the parlor where the book Jacob had been reading lay tented on a cushion, then into the dining room where I had laid the table with a white cloth that had belonged to my grandmother and lit five taper candles made with wax from my own bees. "Oh, Alice," she said and lifted her hair away from her neck to fan it. "It's just exactly like Thalia left it. You haven't changed a thing."

Jacob and I had spent a week honeymooning in one of a bank

of cabins just north of Elevation. The cabins were primitive but had lights in all the rooms, an electric range, even a rabbit-eared black and white television if we had wanted it. I found an oil lamp in a hinged bench at the door and Jacob trimmed and re-threaded the wick, lit it and trapped the blue flame under its scratched glass bell. We set the lamp in the window. It was the height of winter, snow deep on the ground, the forest silent but for the creak of ice-weighted limbs and sometimes their sudden snap. We were the only ones there.

Later, we took the lamp with us as we walked from cabin to cabin and stood on each of their porches like carolers. Our tracks in the snow behind us wavered in and out of each other: Jacob's sturdy and narrow, the rind of ice glittering where he had broken through. Mine were more like a bird's tracks skittish seeming, uncertain. In reality, I had been looking at Jacob: the way his neck strained above his padded plaid coat, the peculiar, tense curve of his back. Jacob against the ice-light of the river which chuckled and rilled. Jacob against the dark bulk of a cabin, peering in a window. He handed me the lantern as he cupped his hands over his eyes so I was suddenly alone in its halo, water seeping in at the sides of my shoes, a bird's nest—the plaintive, messy architecture—drooping from a pediment of the porch. Jacob lowering his shoulder to the door, thumped it once and popping the lock.

Each of the cabins had the same sofa, waterproof pillows patterned with oak leaves and acorns, and every cabin had a variation of the same story hanging above the bed. In one an angler stood in the river, the water swirling to the tops of his hip waders and his line lax. In another, trout—sleek and brown and attended by their own perfect, sleek brown shadows—hung at different levels in the dappled tea water, wreathed by weeds. In another the line was taut; in another there was a net. Sometimes there was a white bridge in the picture, its stones gleaming in the first spidering rays of dawn. In most the fisherman had brown hair, but in one, where the net bellied under the thrashing arc of the fish and the fisherman had started toward shore, his hair was a deep, clownish red. Hair like an afterthought or a poorly examined memory. "There was something here, wasn't there?" the artist might have said. "Something hovering just above his head…"

We broke into a different cabin every evening and woke every morning in a strange bed. Every morning we were confronted by each other's bodies—brown and pink and white and puckered—and by the cold world waiting outside the pocket of warmth we had made in the sheets. I got up and made breakfast. Jacob got up and put logs into the woodstove, naked. With his back to me, his torso was a tight, brown line that ended in the sudden white snarl of his buttocks. A spark flew out of the stove and landed on the white skin of his upper thigh. He swore and slapped at it, swung around and saw me watching him and we went back to bed as the eggs burned up on the stove. In this way, we wanted each other. In every other way—eating, sleeping, walking out into the white woods in the morning, building up each cabin's fire higher and higher—we were separate and didn't talk beyond our immediate needs. "Pass me that," we said to each other. "Please." It really is not so different today, although we say more without having to say it and know already what the other one wants.

At the end of the week, we drove Thalia's truck even further up the mountain and moved into the house with her, our room already set up on the side of the house that faced the forest, our linens turned and a list of chores she expected us to attend to sitting on the bedside table. The paper was held down by a weight shaped like a fish, back bowed against the rocks, gills gaping.

Four months later we saw the smoke punching up over the ridgeline, but didn't know what it meant until a trooper drove into the yard to deliver the news. The fire had started in the kitchen, hardly a surprise given how cheaply Thalia had built it, but how quickly the flames spread was a little unusual. The Feed Store was a short walk down from Elevation's fire department but nevertheless, by the time the pump truck got there and started spraying the roof, the fire had already spread down the hallway to the dining room, into the attic space, through the store and was licking up the front door.

"Shit," the trooper said, "it was punching holes in the roof before they even got the hose on the hydrant." He was Jacob and my age, which is to say very young, and I thought I might even recognize him from school, the outline of his bullet head highlighted against the pouring light of the frosted glass main doors.

Still, he called me ma'am as if I had been automatically aged by this tragedy, and tried very hard to look appropriately somber, but he was excited and who could blame him. He had seen the fire, after all; felt the pressure of it as it coiled just behind the door and then heard it roar as it sprung all at once through the roof and up the doorframe. I imagined the fire rushing through the crooked alleys I had spent so much time in as a child, fattening itself on bags of diatomaceous earth and novelty cricket cages, pot holders shaped like lobster claws and the dark, murderous bulbs of allium and daffodil, bearded iris and yellow tulip trapped dreaming in their net sacks.

"I'm sorry for your loss," the trooper said, fanning himself with his hat and turning, as if in spite of himself, back toward the ridge where smoke still rose. A thin, mean line now, straight as an arrow, pointing toward disaster.

In point of fact, they never did find Thalia's body, but, by the accounts of the customers who had paid up and left just before the fire started, there had been at least six people in the building when it burned. Four of these had been diners, a family from out of town and Mr. Tauft, a regular who enjoyed his chop well done with lots of gravy. The other two were Thalia herself and the Sainte Maria who was doing triple duty as a server, cashier and dishwasher as Jacob's place at the deep-bellied sink had not yet been reliably filled.

The family—a man and a woman, a teenage boy—and Mr. Tauft were identified easily enough by their dental records and some simple guess work on the police's part who tracked down the registration of the only car with out of town plates which also happened to be the only one on the street to which no one laid claim. Oddly enough, the Sainte Maria had never been to the dentist, and her body, charred beyond recognition and found huddled next to the melted cash register in the main room, was identified through a process of elimination. She was a small girl and this body was small. She wasn't anywhere else in the town or, as far as anyone could tell, outside of it. A scrap of her leopard print coat had wafted up the fire's draft and fluttered down with the rest of the embers of burlap and forget-me-not wallpaper, flaming receipt paper and tufts of molten insulation to land like a letter at the fire chief's feet.

Of Thalia, they never found a trace. Not a strand of hair; not a single fire-cracked tooth. That she was dead was as much wishful thinking on the town's part as it was inference and yet, at her funeral in which we buried an empty box, everyone who owed her money—a considerable portion of the town's people and the farmers who tilled the outlying ridges—showed up and each brought a flower to heap on her grave.

Jacob and I cut the heads off all her peonies which she grew in a sunny rectangle she had dug between the house and the cemetery, and whose buds she sprinkled with sugar every morning to encourage the ants to come help them bloom. If there had been a body in the casket, we would have fought harder to bury her on our land, but, as it was, we settled on bringing something of the land to her, though, by cutting them too soon, we damaged the young plants so badly they never fully came back. I have a bed of wildflowers there now: white yarrow and hyssop, pearly everlasting and pink fireweed. I leave them alone to seed themselves and some years they all froth up—a fountain of white pricked by lavender and sharp pink—and some years I have nothing there but onion grass and weeds. Still, I consider it one of my gardens, and, when the urge comes on me at night to walk out into the forest, that is where I go instead.

Because I am afraid of what I will find if I wander any further, I admit it. Because I know what Thalia would have had to become in order to leave nothing of herself behind.

And still in my dreams that scrap of fabric flutters down from the smoke-gray sky. Singed around its edges, but whole and, as it unfolds at the fire chief's feet, revealing in one of its many soft, bruised eyes, the single burning ember that would have caught and consumed it had not the chief brought down his sturdy boot and stamped it out against the curb.

Now it is night, very late. I have gotten up alone and come down to my own room to write. I brought you along, Ingrid, so that if you cried I wouldn't have to run up the stairs again to fetch you. Though you woke up the moment I slid my hands under your back, you are now lying in your basket at my feet looking at the sheen of my lamp reflected on the window glass in what seems like perfect contentment. I have spent all the months of your life—not so many, I could count them on one hand—wondering what it is you see and what it is you don't see. Now I am beginning to think it doesn't matter: that we all see some things meant only for our own eyes.

Today Daniel received some important correspondence from his publisher and when he told us about it at dinner he said, "This is finally the beginning for me." He said this as he chewed, his beard wagging below his jaw as if mimicking him. You were sitting in my lap, Ingrid, and across from us was a window framing the last creeping light of day as it slunk across the meadow, an empty chair, a burn mark etched indelibly in wood.

"This book is closer to home," Daniel said. "It had to be, given the circumstances." He was gesturing with his fork, pointing at you, Ingrid, at me, out the windows to the dark meadow which we nevertheless understood was green and white, a faint blue along the razor edges of the grass, yellow dusting the fat, glossy blades.

"I used the cemetery here as a starting point," Daniel said, twirling his fork to encompass us all. His cheeks were flushed above his beard and below, the glow fading down his neck where it broke up into a rashy red just above his shirt collar. At the far end of the table, Jacob stood up abruptly and poured himself more water from the blue enamel pitcher I had set just slightly out of reach of everyone. On purpose, Ingrid, on the principle that it is important to remind your lover of his desires, your husband of his need.

"A theoretical starting point, of course," Daniel continued.

"I hope you don't mind. My editor said the second book needed to contain more of myself and I thought, at the time, how? How, given my previous model for research, how can I be in this book in any way other than the great white sahib—the eye, you understand, the observer who can only see himself reflected in the quaint ritual around him? I tell you, it made my skin crawl. But then, well, then the accident happened and the baby was born." He stabs at you again, Ingrid, and in my lap I feel you stiffen in a way I believe means you are amused. "And suddenly I was already in the book, all the research I had done, all the theory…It was always me, I just had no perspective, no applicable counter tension to put pressure on the data set." He put his fork down carefully beside his plate. He considered the remains of the chicken splayed before him. "So then I sat," Daniel said, "and for a long time I thought about death."

Daniel thinks about death and his face blooms open, petal upon petal ringing each replication of its shape like a dandelion. A dozy weed, a sun nodder. Jacob snorted, but made no other comment and I, who always think this way, looked up at the window expecting to see something. There was nothing there, only the grid of the window screen sectioning all our reflections into manageable squares of color and smeared light. When something did come, it was only a small white moth attracted by the same bleary brightness. It pumped its body against the screen and stayed for a long time, crawling from sill to sill, battering its faint wings as if they themselves were curtains it was attempting to draw.

"What could it have been?" the artist might have mused and, though he settled on hair, I believe any number of more appropriate images might have flitted through his mind first. I, for example, might have painted a fork or a crown of bees. A peignoir blooming as if swollen with water, a cairn of loosely stacked stones, a rabbit that runs and runs, its legs on a hinge, its ears laid flat against its skull.

"I'm not criticizing," Thingy said. "It's beautiful. Like an homage," and she put her hands over my shoulders and pulled me into her, both of us leaning awkwardly over the barrier of her suitcase. I could smell her hair—a crisp, mobile scent that stood out to me even through the exotic garden layers of shampoo and perfume—and I felt her take my own hair and wrap the braid around her fist, tug gently like it was a steamboat pull as she had done when we were children and knew without thinking what was in each other's thoughts.

"I'm glad to be here," Thingy said and I, overcome at the foot of my own stairs, hearing my husband come up the porch and a man I didn't yet know behind him, talking already, kicking his boots against the sill, I said, "I love you."

"I love you, too," said my Thing. She pulled away and looked at me, her eyes water eyes, coruscate, opaque. "You silly goose," she said and kissed me on the cheek.

When Thingy and I were twelve and Luke sixteen, the Nina drove us down to Ridley Township to see a movie. It was a foreign film, a princess movie, which was only playing in the rickety art house theatre that sat in the center of the downtown. To save money, the Nina had brought snacks with us: dried apple rings she fished out of the bottom of an oversized freezer bag, a sack of hard candies Thingy and I split, Thingy only eating the purple ones until her tongue was slick and almost black with the dye. The Nina ended up being disappointed in the show. "Too much music and not enough songs," she said, "and why were the animals so unfriendly? Their eyes were drawn so beady you could hardly see them."

In the movie, the princess was spunky, but very very small. At one point she and her entire castle were lifted into the air by a girl with golden ringlets who mistook the thing for an elaborate, sugar-spun candy. She was a stupid girl, willful, but from the princess's point of view she had teeth like slabs of mountain rock and when they crunched down on the spires of the castles—not sugar-spun at all, but crumbling just the same— the danger was the princess's to bear alone. All the unfriendly animals had fled long ago; the rats from the pantry, the pigeons from the eves. She had no parents and there appeared to be no prince waiting in the wings to rescue her or awaken her or marvel at her technique with a spindle. In the end, the stupid, greedy girl was somehow thwarted, but the castle which wasn't candy was not saved. The princess, I assume, continued on spunkily in the ruins. Taking a turn in the garden. Tossing her little golden ball up into the air.

"I wish the girl had eaten her," Thingy said.

"Me too," said the Nina. "Then there could have been scene like in Pinocchio with the castle floating around in her belly."

We had gone to the morning show and when we got back to the house it was only early afternoon. The Sainte Maria had taken part of the Nina's shift, watching Luke so the Nina could take us with her, and her battered sedan was parked carelessly across the driveway, forcing us to park in the street. It was fall, the trees already drawing themselves up, moving away from us.

Instead of trudging into the house after the Nina, who was tired of us, happy to leave us behind, Thingy led the way around the side of the building and into the backyard. Though it wasn't

yet cold, the air around us was stiff and heavy with chill. Thingy
and I were both shivering, but I understood she didn't want the
trip to end—to return home, even if it is not your own home, is
always a small defeat—also, the Sainte Maria was there, the one
person who could make Thingy self conscious and whose company she tried to avoid. Thingy plucked a glossy pink strawberry
barrette out of her hair and turned it over between her fingers as
she perched on the bend in the dragon's tail. She touched it with
the tip of her tongue, as if she expected it to have turned into a
candy, and then tossed it over the fence into the dog run where it
sat in the dirt catching my eye no matter how I tried to ignore it.

"What is actually in our stomachs?" Thingy asked.

"Digestive juices," I answered. I was in the advanced biol-
ogy course at school and had memorized the diagram of a cat's
body, drawn splayed open with the animal's head turned coyly
to the side, the tips of her longest teeth just peeping out from
underneath her lip. We had studied what each of the organs
did, which filled with air and which with bile, and I understood
that the general principle was the same for us all. Here a sac to
store poisons, here one to distribute blood. A series of taut pink
purses to be filled and then emptied and somewhere under all
that fur the various holes through which this would be accomplished.

"I know that," Thingy said, annoyed with me. She flounced
up the back stairs and I followed, a few steps below her. "I
meant in addition to that. Like are there things we're too huge
to bother about? Little bits of things that just stay in there and
rattle around?"

She was thinking of Pinocchio, of course, and the giant
girl in the movie. What could there be inside myself that I don't
know about, Thingy was thinking. A raft? An oil lantern? The

remnants of a breakfast strewn across the table? But I was annoyed too, and cold now, ready to go inside.

"No," I said as Thingy scrambled up the railing to peer in the kitchen window. I climbed up next to her and rested my chin beside the dragon's head. "The only thing in your stomach is purple candy."

"Says you," Thingy said, but her heart wasn't in the argument anymore. In the kitchen we could see the Nina, the Sainte Maria and Luke all sitting around the table. The Sainte Maria and Luke were finishing lunch, a bowl of soup sitting in front of my brother, her plate empty and serving as an ashtray. The Nina sat with her head tipped in her hand and nodded as the Sainte Maria said something, smoke spilling out from between her lips. Luke was between them, his eyes not quite engaged but not so far away as for it to be impossible to imagine him listening, about to contribute his own opinion to whatever it was the girls were trying to decide.

"Look at Luke," Thingy said. His hands were on the table, on either side of the bowl, and he moved them restlessly. The Nina said something and he inclined his head toward her, as if conceding the point, a lock of his hair falling across his eye. The older Luke got the more he looked like my father. A face that was at once both sharp and wide, gaunt cheeks. His shoulders were square inside his T-shirt, and his hands broad and thick knuckled. They curled on either side of his bowl like plaster casts, white and somehow slightly dusty. The Nina said something else and the Sainte Maria laughed and brought a spoonful of soup up to Luke's lips. He turned his head to her and accepted it ruminatively, again as if he were just on the verge of saying something. A drop splashed out over his lips and landed on his chin. The Pinta, or even the Nina, would have scooped the soup up with the spoon, dabbing at Luke as if he were an infant, but the Sainte Maria folded the sleeve of her shirt over her thumb and brushed it away without looking at him, her fingers trailing across his cheek.

"What about him?" I said. He was my brother—my brother struck dumb at the moment of his birth—and I paid as much attention to him as I did to myself. Which is to say, we were bodies only, bulging and softening as bodies did. My favorite part of my own body was my breastbone which protruded from in between the new nubs of my breasts as hard and stubborn as a turtle's shell. My favorite part of Luke's was his ear, pink and white, whorling in tightening spirals: in, in, in.

The Nina laughed and leaned across the table. She gripped the Sainte Maria's wrist and shook it, resting her head on her forearm. The Sainte Maria laughed, too. She looked up across the kitchen and saw us at the window, but it meant nothing to her. She kept laughing. She stubbed her cigarette out on the plate.

"Fuck you," Thingy said and pulled away. Luke cocked his head as if he were listening and his lips parted, a smile? For a moment it seemed as if he were opening his mouth to say....

Later in the week, Thingy was over at my house after school to do homework. This meant we sat in front of the television with our books open before us and a bowl of chips at our side. Thingy liked to slick her fingers with their grease and draw translucent designs on the book's glossy pages. We were studying the economic output of our mountains and marking maps the teacher had given us with little drawings of apples and hogs, cairns of coal, reams of cloth, different colored triangles which were supposed to represent the spiteful wink of minerals and gems.

Thingy got up to go to the bathroom. As the final credits came up on the show, I realized she had been gone a long time. She didn't answer when I called to her, so I crept through the house—turtle-like, slow to everything—thinking perhaps we were playing a game.

I found her in Luke's room, lying on the bed with him. Clearly, she had spent some time arranging the tableau. She had rolled him over onto his side and tipped him so she bore the brunt of his weight on her hip. His hand was on her ribcage, just under her breast, and his right leg was cocked over her thigh. His face was buried in her hair and when she saw me in the doorway she put a finger to her lips and raised an eyebrow—as if he were telling her something, as if she were delighted to hear.

"He says he likes this game," Thingy whispered, and wasn't there, sleek in the rustle of Thingy's fine-spun hair, just the slightest of movements? As if he had nodded, his head sharp and black as a snake's...a whuffling as if he had chuffed between his pale, parted lips, blown into her ear...

Then Thingy jumped up, sliding out from under my brother's limbs as he shifted more deeply into the pillows, and said, "I was just kidding, Alice. You should have seen your face." She sat on the edge of the bed and motioned me to help her as she tugged Luke back into a more accustomed place: his impassive face propped at an angle, his long legs bent and his smooth feet crossed over each other on the coverlet. "Look though," Thingy said, pointing to the crotch of my brother's sweatpants where the outline of his penis was clearly visible, its bulge rising against his thigh. "He was telling the truth, after all."

Then we heard the Pinta cross the living room and we scuttled down the hall into my own room where I shut the door. "Don't be mad," Thingy said, holding my hands between her own and scanning my face, but I wasn't. I was too busy trying to figure out which of all the games was the one they were playing. Which had made my brother come so close to the surface, almost close enough to see.

"What did he say?" I asked in spite of myself, but Thingy only laughed and kissed me on the cheek. A pretty gesture she had copied from a movie or a television show or a story. The sort of thing a pretty girl does when she is beloved. More importantly, something she does when she has won.

Then, all of a sudden, we were adults, admonished never again to look back lest we turn into pillars of salt. Of course, we did look back. How could we help it when back was the only view? The past, filled with such enticing details: dancing dogs and sugar plums, purses stitched from a tasseled sow's ear, slippers that spun and twirled until your own blood ran freely over their soles. Really, there seemed no consequence. Why not live in the bright shadow, childhood a garter snake flashing its yellow racing stripe? And the future? Nothing but gauze and white strapping tape. Miles and miles of it, trussing things up.

It was our gravest mistake, Thingy's and mine, but how can you blame us for wanting always to be ourselves? When the rain came and we melted away, even then I can't say we were sorry. To this day, Ingrid, there is a spot on the creek bank where the butterflies cluster: fritillaries with their military precision, brilliant tiger swallowtails and tiny, West Virginia whites who pump their dusty cabbage white wings so slowly, with such exquisite languor.

What is it they want there? Are they sleeping, dreaming, dying? Sometimes there are as many as twenty of them, packed so tightly their fairy-haired bodies press against each other, their wings rippling orange and black, yellow and azure, a faint silver-green as if they were a very fine cloth, pinned at one corner but caught nonetheless in a persistent breeze. If you are a quiet girl, Ingrid, a natural observer of the world, it will be possible for you to get close enough to see them in detail. Their narrow heads, for example, on which their true eyes sit like tessellate soup cups. Their tongues uncoiling to flitter about the soil.

They are feeding, my darling girl, a salt slick there and only there which entrances them with delight. And who is to say if that is the *exact* spot where Thingy finally fell and could not rise? If that is the *exact* soil on which she battered at her throat as it swelled with trapped air? Where, in spite of our belief that our lives were uniquely the same, there came from between her legs first a rush of water, then one of blood…?

I am to say it, and I will.

Right there, on the edge of the creek, Thingy and I melted away in a wash of salt. Right there, slick with blood and earth, right there you were born.

There is another storm I remember, seven months after Thingy and Daniel moved to the mountain.

"What is your book about?" I asked Daniel at dinner.

"Well, it's difficult to break down into one idea," he said, eager even then to stab at us all with his fork as he talked. "I'd say, in general, it's about cloister. About ritual."

He seemed about to go on in more detail, the fork twirling in the air as is if trying to hone its focus, but Thingy, who was sitting at his left hand side, a black winter night ringing her head, laughed and said, "Daniel's all about opposites right now. He's doing the exact opposite of everything he's done before."

Later that evening, I was out in the yard checking on the hens. It was late. The moon had torn itself free of the trees and was wafting fat and proud across the sky. There had been a noise, an uproar in the hen house as if the hens all at once had sensed some terrible calamity, though when I shone the flashlight around their fence I could see no tracks, no signs of digging. An ephemeral calamity then, or something far in the future. Regardless, I picked up a stick and made a sign at the gate and one at each of the fence's corners. I wove a sign out of tufts of dead grass and threw it up on the roof. The hens were quiet again and the meadow quiet, the forest behind it all so quiet it was as if it were sneaking up on me, counting footsteps and freezing the moment I turned around. It was very cold.

When I turned around to go back to the house, I saw Thingy had come into the dining room and flicked on the light. She was wearing a white nightgown, not yet pregnant enough for the peignoir, and sat sideways across the chair, drinking a glass of water, looking around. It was all so clear. I in the cold with my breath frosting in my eyelashes; she in the house, alone and looking not to be, the veins in her legs where her nightgown had pulled up deep and blue and tangled. Then, I heard a noise behind me and when I turned again—always spinning in place, always looking over my shoulder—it was Daniel.

"Hello," he said.

"It's late," he said.

Surely, I said something back. He is a lion-headed man, even without the beard, Ingrid. Or a sheep-headed man, perhaps. Something that nods in the sun, dreamy-eyed, not particularly alert. Something with either the deep ease of a predator, or the power of prey. He hadn't zipped his coat and there was an exposed triangle of skin, bare and white at his throat. His eyes are blue, I have mentioned that, like Thingy's eyes. His hands were on my shoulders.

"What are you doing out here?" he said, and then one of his hands was on my neck, one at the back of my head.

I have never said Jacob's name, not once. He and I have always been very quiet, though when I look down at my husband I can see in his eyes a little figure of myself, breasts swinging, hair wild, mouth drawn open like a panting cat's.

But, "Alice, Alice, Alice," Daniel said, and I said, "Daniel."

We were nothing more than two people and all the best language for it (thick and tight, pink and wet, deep and hard) was lost in our unwieldy layers and the splinter of sycamore-green clapboard wedging its way into my buttocks where later Jacob would pass his fingers over it, a black seed in the center of a strawberry of blood.

Did I think about Thingy? Of course I did. But it was night and, thinking herself alone, all she could see in the gilt-framed mirror across from her was her own beautiful face, composed if somewhat puffy, and the cloud of her hair lifting across her shoulders as if filled with its own private breeze.

Until she stood up that is. Until she turned off the light.

We didn't notice when it began to snow, the flakes so light in our collars they were like nothing more than a shifting of cloth, but in the morning the drifts were deep and the whole yard covered with tracks. A hen had been taken after all, the only sign left of her two soft, gray feathers, three drops of blood that fell in a shape like an arrow pointing toward the woods.

~

At end of her doctoral thesis, in the margins of one of the very last chapters, Thingy had made some notes.

"Because we have known each other so long....?" says one.

"A lack of the Other resulting in hyper-awareness of the Self...?" says another.

"A woman married a man who said he was the sun," says a third, "but on their wedding night, when she pulled back the covers to get into bed, she discovered that from the waist down he had the body of a rooster. The woman was very angry and scolded her new husband. 'If we have any children, they will be nothing but eggs,' she said to him, but when it turned out that he could not help his nature she grew so furious she flew up the chimney and circled the world three times, blotting out the stars as she went. Eventually, because she was making so much noise, the real sun found her, but she had become old in her fury—no teeth and a face as wrinkled as a withered apple. He was disgusted by her and burned her to ashes on the spot thinking, perhaps, he was putting her out of her misery."

"Someone told me this story," Thingy wrote a little further down the page. "I can't remember who it was."

# The Brother's Tale

Once there was a boy who was born into a family of great wealth and political power, but who, as sometimes happens, were forced to leave him alone in the mountains for the wolves to eat. There was a wind stirring the dark pines, a dusting of snow on the ground. It was a servant who did the dirty work, though even as she bent to drop him, she wrapped his blankets more snugly about his chest.

At first he waves his arms and legs in the air, a lusty baby, furious if unusually small, but when no one comes he grows still. Eventually, he is quiet as a toad; then, quiet as a rock. His wrappings have fallen away. His skin is the color of lead. His breathing is so slow he cannot feel it in his chest...breath...a red squirrel chirring from a tree...breath...the seesaw of birds calling in the branches...And then a woodsman! Just that morning, he sharpened his axe. The boy can hear him coming from miles away: the sound of the forest splintering.

Though generally an unsentimental sort, the woodsman was charmed by the baby's tiny size—his fingers no bigger than grains of rice, his head as big around as a bobbin—and took him home where he was wrapped in the woodsman's wife's clean linens and popped in the oven to ward off death. Every part of the baby unfroze, except for a part deep inside, hardly bigger than a pea, which was always after cold, severe and leaden. The woodsman and his wife were busy people, but not unkind. A few years later, they had a daughter who had many needs and, because the boy they found in the forest was always silent, it became easier and easier to tuck him away and forget where he had been placed. Lost among the spoons; lost in the crockery. Because the boy never grew though now he had a sister.

Oh well, one May the mother died. Shortly after, the woodsman took to the road and left his daughter in charge of the house. "Don't let anyone in or out," he said and he slipped some coins into the bodice of her pinafore and he kissed her on the top of her head. He did not say, "Take care of your brother," who was tucked into an oven mitt hanging just above the stove, but the girl decided to hear this anyway and, as soon as her father had passed out of sight down the road, she fetched her brother down, put him in the pocket of her apron and gave him an acorn cap to wear for a hat. At first the girl fed herself and her brother from what was left of their mother's pantry. Heels of bread, stale oatcakes, porridge. Then, when this fairy-tale food was exhausted and real hunger set in, she began to make small excursions into the yard and the fringe of the surrounding forest, coming back with toadstools, song bird's eggs, berries and the slim, white bulbs of wild onion. At night, she sang to her brother of whom she was fond. She imagined he was comforted by her songs and even thought at times she could hear him humming back. Unbeknownst to her, however, her brother was an exiled duke and could neither understand her language nor unbend enough to press her pretty, plump hand between his own.

(There was a terrible darkness, a buzzing. In the forest a mother wolf had come from between the trees and said, "You will be fine fine fine. A fine fat morsel for my cubs." Then the trees splintered open and out of their golden hearts the woodsman appeared.)

One night, when the girl had found very little to eat in the woods, she and her brother made due with a soup made of grass and loaves of bread she patted out of dirt. A ring of green stained their mouths and she found herself exhausted. "You think you'd be a little more grateful," she said to her brother, pretending he'd complained. Though he was many years her elder and silent always in the way of something that has claimed its ground, she said, "You bad baby, all you ever do is cry," and she slapped him on the back of each of his hands with her thimble.

Immediately, the girl was filled with remorse and resolved to make up this lapse to him in any way she could. With the last of the coins her father had tucked into her bodice, the girl bought a ream of golden cloth from a traveling salesman who sometimes stopped at their front gate and a little spool of golden thread. In the evenings, after she had made the dinner and fed them both, tidied the house and filled each of the oil lanterns in turn to keep out the dark, the girl sat beside the fire with her brother in a basket at her feet and sang him her songs while she stitched together a beautiful robe. Into the weave of the cloth, the thread never seeming to empty from its spool, the girl stitched scenes of her brother. There he was in the womb—round as a pea, then round as a golden ball—and here he was in the forest, his pale face peering out of a jagged lacework of branches. Here he was as he might have been: tall and slim, slipping a dancing slipper over the arch of a dainty foot; and here as he was, tucked in next to the fire, surrounded by the sturdy lathwork of poverty and desperation, hunger and, of course, love. The robe was for her brother to wear, though every day it grew longer and longer, spilling out across the hearth and piling up against the door. "No little poppet for you," the girl said to her brother who was sleeping in the bowl of a spoon. "No little tuck. No little fancy."

(In the forest, there had been a bird that flew from tree to tree calling as if its heart would break. There had been a wind that blew everything silent and passed on while all behind it cowered and held close to the ground. Even so small, he had understood immensity. "If we are born for death..." he had thought, "If there is no land above this one and no land below...")

From the center of his silence the boy, who had in the meantime become a man though a very small one, watched his sister work. Often she pricked her fingers and cried as the blood soaked into the cloth because she had a horror of ruin, of no turning back. Perhaps he even felt grateful, perhaps even kind... But he was born very proud and it is more likely that he went on in that fashion. A dear girl, but beneath him, as was the doll's spoon she stuck in his mouth, the pine-straw teddy she tucked beneath his arm for comfort in the night. And the peasant songs she sung. And her peasant face—ill favored, withered as an apple in the deep leaves.

So it always is when the cold world meets the warm one. A struggle right along the edge of life and the worlds' two impulses (one for silence, one for raging noise) compressed together into a mean line—sharp as a razor, bright as the melting sun. "Oh my love, my love, in a sycamore tree," the girl sang. "Climb down, climb down, and marry me."

When she was finished with the robe it proved to truly be a splendid thing. It was the deepest part of winter, the snow heavy in the branches, and the cupboards were bare as bone. Still, the girl felt very proud of herself as she spread the robe out on the hearth and admired its scintillating ripples, the intricacy of its figures as they gamboled and piped, chased one another through the lindens or stirred a pot of soup on the stove. It was by far the most beautiful thing the girl had ever seen, but, because she had made it herself, it didn't belong to her and so, with a sigh of regret, she lifted her brother out of his basket and wrapped a corner of the golden robe around and around his still, leaden body so all that could be seen of him was the tip of his nose and the point of his sharp, gray chin. Immediately, there was a darkness, a terrible buzzing. In the way of one herself transformed, the girl opened her eyes and saw on the hearth not her tiny brother, but a tall, handsome man whose skin was the color of apricots and whose eyes were angry.

(And then the goose is strung up in the larder. Sometimes, a marriage; sometimes the well belches a heavenly river. There is a cake made of golden flour, a drink made of heart's own blood. A girl could dance until the bottoms of her feet are sheered to ribbons. A girl could be tricked into living underground, sitting forever beside her dark husband, remembering the sun. "Would you like a wish?" asks the fish in the bottom of the boat. A clever girl says no, but how many of them are there left in the world? I could count them all on the fingers of one of my hands and still have some left over to do the darning. I could wrap all of them up in a single long blanket, rub their cheeks to roses, comb their hair.)

What actually happened is the young man who had never really been her brother stood up on the hearth and said, "You fool, you have exposed me. Now they'll come for sure." Even if the girl had understood his language, even if she had been braver and more true, it wouldn't have mattered. They did come, sliding out of the fringe of the forest as if they had stood there for years and only now happened to turn their heads. It was a mob—the men in leather breeches, the women apt to pull their skirts up over their heads. They carried pitchforks and pine resin torches, rusty cleavers and lancer's spikes left over from the last war fought on their behalf. Their mouths were holes that led straight to their guts and they ringed the house in rows four deep. Set fire to the thatch. Drove an axe through the woods-man's own front door.

~

When the mob eventually forced their way inside they carried the exiled duke, still wrapped in his golden robe, to the doorstep and they cut off his head. Then they hoisted it on a pike to peer in each of the girl's windows as she cowered and cried. "This is not a joke," someone made the head say, though clearly they all thought it was very funny. "I didn't think it was," the girl replied to her brother's head which, despite the size and the ragged lacework they had made of his neck, looked very much the same as it always had: the eyes cold and gray, the mouth a thin, disapproving line. When they finally went away, they left her with a terrible mess to clean, but when she was done and her life restored to its regular patterns, the girl couldn't help but think that if she only had her brother back she would do things very differently. "I would beat him with a thimble all day long," she said to the fire, stroking the golden robe which she had laid across her lap. "My poor, dear brother. I would bash in his head."

And every day, though she was all alone, she sang:

"My love, my love in a sycamore tree.
Climb down, climb down, and marry me."

# Goodbye, Goodbye My One True Love

When Thingy and I were very young, my father and a friend of his discovered the body of man who had been shot. They were hunting turkey in the mountains, only slightly out of season, and had two toms already cleaned and trussed under a tarp in the back of the truck. It was a wet day, the afternoon an inhalation between showers.

The man had been shot in the ear with a small caliber gun, a neat black hole punched overtop his regular canal the only overt sign of trauma. "You could tell something had happened in there, though," my father told the Sainte Maria. They were sitting in the living room: my father with his arms spread over the back of the couch like wings, the Sainte Maria perched on the armrest of the recliner. "There was blood on his teeth and a look on his face like someone had gone in there and scrambled him all up."

The man was someone who lived in one of the hollows and that was enough for us to believe we knew something about him. How he had eschewed the companionable hostility of the town for a whistling kind of solitude. How he lived, I imagined, in little more than a raw place dug in the earth like a fox or a weasel.

"What did he look like?" the Sainte Maria asked. She was very young herself, probably not much more than fifteen, but recently my father had made the switch from calling her, 'little girl,' to calling her 'darling,' something he had not yet done with any of the other girls.

"He looked surprised," my father said. He shifted his weight on the couch so the old springs creaked beneath him and propped one boot up on the coffee table. "Not shocked, mind you, just surprised. Kind of like someone had played him a good joke."

Where was I while this conversation went on? In the room, because I can see them both in memory: my father, red clay in the ridges of his boots, his shirt rolled neatly up his ropy forearm; the Sainte Maria in jean cut-offs from which her pale legs crossed nervous and noodely and striking in the light. It must have been spring. It was spring light, a dappled, lily pond light that lapped across the carpet as they talked. I remember how it pooled in the lap of the little shepherd girl on top of the television. She was so certain of herself, her bisque cheek turned up to accept her shepherd boy's kiss, even as she admired the drape of her skirts across her knees. And, although there he was with his back turned, edging away, who could blame her? They had been made for each other, after all. Even their outfits matched.

I must have been in the corner by the door. There was a hatrack there which was often draped with coats, a marble basin in its pedestal that I liked to fill with stones and acorn caps. I could have been behind a coat, hidden. Or, more likely, just sitting with my back against the wall watching the light shift across the sandy carpet as if stirred by fishtails far above, watching my father pat the cushion beside him and then laugh, teasing, when the Sainte Maria, red to the roots of her hair, fidgeted on her seat and pretended not to see.

"It was probably someone he knew," my father said. "Someone he trusted enough to let him get real close. He had to have been close to put the barrel of the gun right inside his ear."

For many years afterward I dreamed about that man my father found dead in the scrub brush. Or rather, waking or sleeping, I flashed onto an image of him which lingered with meaningless precision. The body: dressed in a white undershirt and dungarees, the arms and legs splayed as if he were shot in mid lope like a four-legged animal. In my image of him, the man had reddish hair and a long, unpleasant face. His teeth were bared and, yes, bloody, a patter of blood on his chin where a bubble had been blown and burst. Every time the image flashed through my mind, I tried to concentrate on his eye—open or shut? brown or blue?—but every time I centered on his teeth instead, the blood on his chin, the hole on top of the hole, wider and deeper and black around the edges as if he had done something so simple as not wash very carefully that morning before he went out. As if he could have reversed his fate as easily as wrapping a washcloth around his index finger and twisting into his ear. "To dig out the potatoes," the Nina always said.

The man my father was hunting with that day was named Bo Hickett and according to Dax he had hunkered down behind a deadfall not ten feet from the body without noticing a thing other than a slight smell which turned like the other smells of the forest beneath the leaf mulch and the sweetness of rotting wood. They were hunting on logging land, an area that had been stripped years before and then replanted. The rows of young pine were so unnaturally straight they seemed to bend at the edge of their vision as if they were standing in the center of a pinwheel. Dax and Bo had parked the truck high above the turn-off from the main road and walked two or three miles back up the trace but, though it had been such a consistently wet spring that the standing pools in the dirt road were frothing with tiny, seed-like tadpoles, neither man noticed another human's foot-print or any trace of another truck.

"We saw a bear track," my father told the Sainte Maria. "A big fucker where it had turned and gone back into the woods." Even that was old enough to have filled with water itself and to contain in the depression of its main pad a single black tadpole, twitching mindlessly.

Whatever had happened, it had happened not long before the men arrived. They found him because Dax, backing up to get a better sight on the gravel pit they were luring a turkey into, stepped on the side of the man's boot and the turn it gave under his foot was so familiar, so much a part of the manufactured world, that he found himself apologizing even as he hopped away and realized what he was apologizing to.

The body was stiff, but not swollen. There was no smell. "So fresh the flies hadn't found him yet," Dax said, though there was one, a fat bluebottle, which was perched on the rim of his ear, scrubbing and scrubbing its forelegs. Dax loved that detail. "Like he just couldn't wait to dive in there," he said, and I imagined my father, transfixed by what he must have believed, if only for a moment, was not a man but a trick being played by his eyes. A chance arrangement of leaf and twig. The fleshy plush of a fungus perhaps, rotting at its core. Behind him, Bo Hickett blew a soft, rolling call meant to reassure the tom he saw parting the fescue on the other side of the clearing that he was welcome, wanted, long-sought, and motioned to my father to line up the shot.

Even now, I still sometimes dream of that man I never saw. I never even knew his name or if his killer was caught which seems odd to me because, after all, it was my father who found him and my father who waited with the body while Bo Hickett hurried back to the truck to call up the county patrol on his CB. (And to hide the illegally harvested turkeys in the underbrush, no doubt, to stow the guns and prepare the story of a nature walk, stretching their legs. "God's domain," he might have said, gesturing to the mountains behind him. And they so blue, so magisterial, they could be evoked to stand for almost anything: bounty and progress, splendor and grace. Really, however, they are old and cold and made primarily of stone. What Bo Hickett points to, standing in the road with mud on his knees as the two troopers take notes, around them the dripping pines, their needles heavy and dark, pierced by the teetering call of the siskins that dart about their upper branches, is actually the spaces between the mountains. "God's grandeur," he says, shrugging, spent shell casings clinking in his pocket, and he means the petal-blue wash behind the massed stone and the wispy clouds that drift to encircle their crowns. No one gives a thought to the black spaces within: the crooked tunnels and stale pockets of air, the ropes of water spilling down through the half-moon spouts they themselves have cut over the long centuries only to plunge into still, black lakes—deep and utterly silent—from which, eventually, the water seeps back into the rock and bursts forth in rills and freshets, little cataracts and spills, white with foam, that pool on the mountain face and cloud with algae and mosquito larvae where Bo Hickett, crashing through the underbrush, stops with the troopers for just a moment to point out a track—the bear again—and say, "Can you believe it? Right by the road.")

"Maybe it was a suicide," the Sainte Maria said, but my father snorted the suggestion away. Murder was a better story, after all, and what was one more murder in a place teeming with it? The fox of the mouse, the squirrel of the flea, the turkey of the nut which it splits in the autumn months to feast on the golden heart meant to become a tree.

"Time belongs to God," Thingy's mother once told her. For awhile, right after Mr. Clawson moved more permanently to Atlanta, she'd become heavily involved in the church and hosted frequent tea parties for the other ladies of the 1st Baptist. After they left, she would roam through the house lifting items and putting them down in slightly different arrangements: a tea cozy whimsically cocked over the ear of a china cat, a copy of Hillary's *High Adventure* peeking out over the edge of the silver ice bucket. Mrs. Clawson leaned in the doorway to Thingy's room and said, "Time is God's parlor, girls. Lest you forget." This was a bad year for her, I remember. She had ginger cookie crumbs on her chin, a comet of jam arcing across her stiff, poplin collar.

Some months she let her hair go until the roots were almost black, but scrubbed the increasingly empty refrigerator until it glowed sterile and blue, the yellow box of baking powder huddled in the back as if sheltering from an unappeasable weather. She was unpredictable to say the least. I had never been more lonely for her.

"I'll be sure to mention it to him when I get there," Thingy said, rolling her eyes, mistaking, as was always her way, time for heaven. But I was listening. I heard what she meant to say: about boxing up the years, about putting only those with high polish or an interesting filigree on display.

"In God's parlor the fire is always lit," Mrs. Clawson meant to say. "And God himself so wealthy than when he runs out of firewood he can bring to hand any sort of ornament or precious trinket to throw on in its stead."

What a despot God is! How Thingy would have admired him.

"He'd shat himself," my father said so long ago in our living room while light swam across the legs of a beautiful girl who didn't know it yet.

"Don't look so shocked." He laughed. "There's worse things in the world than a little smell."

To me, just a couple of days ago, he turned and held you out, cradling your bottom in his palm as if you were a sack of sugar he was considering buying at the market. The laundry machines hummed and clunked behind us. The elderly couple wheezed in peaceable witness. Sometimes, of all the other possible images, it is still that hole in a dead man's head I see when I look at my father. "How could you resist sticking a finger in?"

I want to ask him. It's what I would have done, although, since I've never asked, I don't know that it's not what he did as well. I can imagine it of him. We're not all that different, after all. Father and daughter. Doomed from the first genetic twining to be too much alike.

I took you from him and held you in the crook of my arm, Ingrid. Then, I hoisted the basket onto my other hip as if about to leave, but when we just stood there, the terrarium light smoothing all our edges into one another, I slid the basket back onto the counter and asked instead, "How's Rosellen?"

"Rosellen? She's fine. The same," my father said. His eyes were still on you, a beautiful baby falling asleep with her hands curled on her chest. Over his shoulder I saw Jacob open the door and stop to take in the scene. He said something to Daniel standing behind him and then turned and went back out, pushing Daniel along with him. They stood indecisively in front of the window for a minute and then went back up the street the way they had come. To the truck, no doubt. To the groceries souring in the open bed. It was time to go, but there was my father, who was looking at me now, tapping his wedding ring against his belt buckle with a rhythmic ting. He edged around the corner of the folding table and fidgeted, leaning forward to chuck you, Ingrid, under your milk-sweet chin.

"Listen," he said, moving closer. He took my arm, his hand almost meeting around my bicep as it always did no matter how many years passed or how long it had been since we saw each other last. "I was so sorry about what happened. With Ingrid, I mean. I never told you how sorry I was. I know it must have been hard for you."

Hesitantly, he brushed my hair away from my temple and kissed me there, his lips full and dry against my skin, the way he might have many many times when I was young and reminded him in some obscure way of my mother, always so far away with her books and her baubles, her sharp little teeth and her habit of sucking the tips of her hair. Or, perhaps, when I reminded him of himself and, in that fashion, he remembered both that he had made me and that he had meant to. That, from the very beginning, it was my face which had swum in the air between them as he sat at the kitchen table and my mother, belting a strawberry-patterned apron around her swollen abdomen, slid a knife from its block and began to chop.

"I'm sorry, Alice," my father said. And that, Ingrid, though I believe I will see him many more times after this day, is how my father said goodbye to me.

"I have to go," I said and hurried toward the door with the basket.

"Look, it's Alice," said the Sainte Maria, rising from the recliner all those years ago. She stooped over me and picked me up, balancing me on one hip though I was almost too big for her. My legs dangled past her waist, coltish and covered with blonde down. My father came over and pinched my chin, moving it back and forth as if his next step would be to examine my teeth.

"How long has she been there?" he said and he leaned down and kissed the top of my head. How warm his breath was, stirring my hair. How warm it must have been on the Sainte Maria's collarbone, and how close he was as he straightened up again, taller than her, his lips level with the top of her pink, flushed ear. She shifted me slightly so I was no longer between them and then, quite suddenly, stepped back and whisked me away into the dim kitchen where the curtains were drawn and the overhead light burst on like a flashbulb, overexposing the scene.

~

"You've dropped a sock, dear," the old woman called after me, but we didn't stop. We didn't look back, though afterward I wondered what my father looked like, standing with his hands empty for once. Or maybe raised to wave at us as if we were departing down a long avenue of flowering trees, dancing further and further away in the pollen-hazed light, instead of pushing open the Laundromat door and stepping out into the hot hum of the parking lot. Goodbye, Goodbye, my one true love. But no one gets to say that. Not in real life. A boy on a fat-tired bicycle swerved to miss us at the last minute and bumped off the sidewalk into traffic. Jacob honked the truck horn and motioned for us to hurry from up the block. The place where my father kissed me last was like any other stretch of skin on my body: a net designed to let some things out and keep others tucked inside forever.

Goodbye, goodbye, God says, propping his feet up in front of the fire. It is a cold night, the owls hooting far away then almost at the window. When the fire burns low, God tosses in a rosewood ring box, then, in quick succession, a silver cruet, a bronze-molded shoe, a dancing doll, a collection of stones all shaped like hearts, a little dish of Jordan almonds, a pat of butter, a loaf of bread.

What strange light the fire now gives. Almost like being underwater; almost as if, were he to look up right now, God might see another face peering down at him. A child's face, too young to be wary, and fringed for some reason with paper feathers; blowing, for some reason, a wooden reed in order to make a high, gobbling song.

# Subject X

One morning in April, Thingy rose from her bed and shooed the cats out the window. White cat, tabby cat; sister and brother. They paused at the edge of the roof to look back at her before leaping from the gable and swirling along the gutter like rain. It was a beautiful day, the first of many. This was what had been promised.

In the meadow the bees were also awake. For weeks now the workers had been busy turning cups of wax out of the comb. The Queen, so large, so humbling, had filled every one with an egg and some of her daughters had come behind and sealed them off. Pat, pat, pat—the little girls, still asleep, but growing. Pat, pat, pat—princesses all.

So too, in April the trees fur with new leaves and, in the lower elevations, redbud, then dogwood, burst open and shake their boughs as if weeping. Pink, white, red; how beautiful in the hollow where the trillium bloom. How beautiful the lady's slipper, swollen and yellow…rare and yellow…coming down the stairs now with her peignoir sweeping around her swollen white feet.

Thingy poured herself a glass of milk and pulled a chair up to the table. There was no one home: Jacob in the forest, Daniel tinkering with the truck's worn engine, Alice in the parlor eating bread and honey. No, of course not. But someone had baked a pie and left her a little dish of strawberries by the cutting board. They were sour in the early season, tiny and rough.

But no, she would not accept them. It was too little, too late: the little white bowl, the stained board. The morning was getting on and she, in an unusual place at the table, the wall to her back and before her the window, the meadow, the mountain… Inside her the baby with so little room she could see the elbow, the heel, the palm of the hand as it passed across her stomach. Thingy drank her milk. She pressed back, palm to palm. The morning was getting on and that little bowl…

Unconscionable! As if to say: little featherhead, little mummy. As if to say: bought and sold with nothing more than fifteen berries, fresh and wild, pulled from the forest edge. As if her favorites could blind her. As if the long years, the secret histories, could shut her up.

But she could see, could she not? Out the window, up the slope to the first of the trees. What was the difference between watching and waiting? Between now in the clear day and all those nights when what was growing grew? The bed was empty when she woke and the moon a cold spectator drifting past the window. In the morning, Daniel would be back again, his clothes in their accustomed pile by the door. He was always so sleepy these days. His eyes were always so clouded and far away. There was mud on his shoes. There was wet grass rubbed into the knees of his pants. "And you? How did you sleep?" he would say, one ear pressed against her stomach so it could have been her he was talking to or the baby inside her which spun and kicked in response to his voice.

And where was Alice, after all? There, across the meadow, hunkered in the grass with a basket, dressed in white. A strange shape for Alice, like a tent collapsed in the grass, fluttering at the edges, but Alice where she'd always been: in plain sight.

In April, a fingering wind blows, inspecting what has been sewn. Catch hold, little girls, fat on jelly! The nurse maids have all left to attend the Queen who has not been fed for a week. She's a strange shape now, stripped for flight, and all her daughters around her jostle to feel her touch. A stroke of the foreleg, a drape of the wing. By the time you are born, your mother will have already flown and left it up to you to decide who you will dance with and who you will sting. Who you will starve and who you will marry.

Thingy left her empty glass at the table. She went outside into the day.

And so it was that one last kindness (a bowl of berries, painstakingly picked) revealed us all for what we were. It was too much for Thingy: not what she knew, which only on that final morning, her belly resting across the tops of her thighs and light streaming around her from a window I had just washed, did she allow to become certain, but what I knew of her. That she liked these little berries and that she would be greedy for them. That she liked comfort and part of that comfort was to assume her power in our relationship without having to assert it. And yet, here in my house…And yet, now on my mountain…

I had never woven any signs for Thingy. She was too close to who I was, not a future that could be manipulated, but a constant present, and I was the same for her. That's why she chose to write about me. That's why, had I been any other woman, she might have risen to the occasion of my betrayal with a kind of towering, operatic glee—it was a story, after all, and a familiar one with recognizable characters (the temptress, the errant knight) and a common-place denouement. Because it was me, however, she rose confused and then, quite frankly, deranged. Had she seen herself in the mirror before she left the house, she might have given herself pause—self reference was always Thingy's stabilizing compass point—but she did not. By some quirk of habit she sat in the wrong place and so, when she made her final decision, all she saw was me.

Even as far away as I was, I heard the door slam and turned from the bees to see her as she started across the yard. The sun was wicking through the thin fabric of her gown so her legs glowed as they stretched, then snipped into shadow. She was coming too fast for her condition, her gait rolling, her face red. When she got to the creek, she waded across it without bothering to lift her skirt and, because she was already yelling, she couldn't hear me warn her back. It was the spring swarm, the old queen leaving her hive to her bloodthirsty daughters who, as soon as they awoke, would set about stinging each other to death. Thalia had shown me how to soothe them with smoke. How to follow the swarm and drop them gently from their first resting place onto a white sheet on top of which I had placed a new hive box, a convenient palace if not the one they might have imagined. Thalia taught me how to think like the bees— long live the Queen and all her retainers, her glittering retinue, her genius for organization and power won simply by the facts of birth; everyone a daughter: the nurses and the knights, the cooks and the thieves. But no one ever taught Thingy anything. I shouted, but on she came.

*Cinderella dressed in yella*
*Went upstairs to kiss a fella*

There were so many rhymes we used to sing. Songs about steamships and snakes, princesses woken and princesses dead.

The first of the bees settled on Thingy's hair, then, as she batted them away and pressed forward, they moved into Thingy's hair, burrowing without stinging as if they believed themselves caught in a cloud of filaments, promising pollen. As they burrowed they blended with the color of her hair and seemed to disappear making it seem as if her hair itself were heaving, roused as all of her was roused, standing on end. Still, she came forward, beating her arms against what must have seemed at first nothing more than the usual fringe of docile workers hovering around the hives. I, in my bee-keeper's nets, stood startled and clumsy in the middle of the field, mouthing incomprehensible gibberish.

The Throne Room. The Singer's Hall. The Grotto. White limestone for the fronts and sandstone for the portals and bay windows. The Knight's House, the Courtyard, the Bower. Dove marble imported to finish the arch ribs, the columns and capitals. Inside, every room a mural and every mural's coppice home to startled hinds picked out in gold. "Spare no expense," her Majesty said. A Rumford oven to turn the spits. A wishing table sinking through the floorboards in a clatter of bisque and bone. And in the Grotto: a waterfall, a rainbow machine. In the Queen's Quarter's: a blind alley, a panel of opaque screens. "Her Majesty wishes," her Majesty said, "for the ship to be placed further from the shore, that the knight's neck be less tilted, that the chain from the ship to the swan be not of roses, but gold…"

How disappointing then when the first scouts came back with no better news than a lightning-struck tree, a hollow log, the crumbling rim of an old tractor tire. How enraging when her materials turned out to be nothing more than spit and polish and her artisans the same feckless children she had left behind her. And so when a dragon stumbled into their midst? When it reared practically before her with its flashing eyes and floating hair? Well, what better dream of coursers could she hope for, even without the pomp and bugle blast? A war Queen after all, an old one. Stripped for flight atop a snow-white charger.

"Her Majesty wishes," her Majesty said, "to sting it to death."

"Go back," I yelled, or something like it.

Whatever Thingy said, her last words to me, were lost to the bees who settled on her hands, her face, her lips and, when she opened her mouth to scream, her tongue, her teeth, her cheeks, the back of her long, long throat.

*Cinderella dressed in pink*
*Went upstairs to strut and slink*

*Cinderella dressed in black*
*Went upstairs to take it back*

When Thingy finally turned and ran back toward the creek, it was too late. The bees were maddened, one wave wrenching their ruined bodies across her flesh even as the next landed and stung. When she fell and I finally reached her, they had made their way down her bodice and up her skirt, and when I ripped the peignoir off of her and flung it away to float downstream, I saw they had welted her breasts and her belly, her thighs and even up across the swell of her pudenda. There were bees squirming under the fold of her breasts, bees trapped under the mound of her belly. All across her body were strewn their stingers and the white run of their guts, the curled bodies of the dead and the furious thrust of the soon-to-die.

I rolled her in the creek, swatting bees out of her hair and away from her face. She was blind by then, almost surely, her eyes swollen to slits and her body's sense of itself so damaged she didn't squint or blink even as I sluiced creek water directly into them. What did I say, my last words to my friend? I can't recall. I know a bird called close at hand and then another and another, attracted by the feast of bees. I remember shouting and, from across the field, Daniel and then Jacob shouting back as they began to run. I remember dragging Thingy's body by the ankles downstream to a pool where I could submerge more of her, and the flapping of my nets around me, and the rasping noise she was making in the back of her throat.

Her hands rose in front of her face as if trying to break away from her body and then fluttered there, lost. I was too busy trying to save her life and I didn't grab them as I should have; I didn't hold them in my own as she died.

*By mistake she kissed a snake.*
*How many doctors did it take?*

The birds chipped and willowed, delighted at their bounty. The water flowed over the rocks and the bees fell back slowly at first, then faster as the Queen, left with only a few loyal guards, dropped down onto the white sheet I had spread for her and, with exquisite slowness, waddled through the dark arch of her new home.

And then Jacob and Daniel were there. Someone, perhaps even me, was making a low, moaning sound and Jacob hooked his hands under Thingy's arms and pulled her body from the water. "What happened? What happened?" Daniel said and Jacob made two fists and pressed them like a rolling pin against the top of Thingy's rippling belly.

No matter what reason Cinderella mounts the stairs, it is always only one snake that bites her but as many doctors as you can count to bring her back. In black, in pink, in red, in yellow; in gauzy skirts and cut-off jean shorts, polka-dots and a pattern of twining roses, she climbs, eager for her assignation. I would like to end the song here and let her climb forever, busy imagining whatever it is she thinks she will find in the chamber at the top, always just a riser away from the mistake that will kill her or, at the very least, send her into her ruinous sleep.

But there's always another verse. The rhyme demands it. And so it was with my Thing whose thighs I spread as far apart as I could and between whose legs I saw first a thatch of bloody hair, then, eyes already open, turning as if to examine me, your face, Ingrid, born at last and so familiar that, when I cried out, it was not in grief, but recognition.

# The Orifice

And the Orifice said:

There once was a woman who married the sun...

...married a rooster....

...married a china dish...

...a loaf of bread...

Her husband was a slant-eyed giant and, when he left her

alone, she threw her blood into the river where it first became a fish and then a child.

Another man came to visit her....

      ...her father came to visit her...

      ...her brother, in his hand a golden axe, around his neck a long, black feather...

When he came to a cave like a doorway in the side of the mountain, he heard the sound of a drum and voices, as if many people were dancing inside the mountain.

She came out to him, holding the hand of her child.

Long ago, while people still lived...

      "...What have you done with our child?" her husband asked, and, when she showed him the place in the river where she threw her blood, he reached in and pulled out a fish which changed in his arms to a daughter...

"But I can never leave this mountain," she said and so, though he came back many times, she never did.

Long ago...

      ...there was a woman who married...

Long ago...

....there was a woman and he saw what was in her hand was his own heart...

"How can I have made such a terrible mistake," she said.

Even to her final day, she did not know if she lived within the mountain or without it...

...if her husband was a god or a pile of rocks...

...if her hair were gold or a ravenous fire...

...if the child were hers or only a little thing which came after...

# The End

This morning the sun rose and cast the meadow in a wash of pink. It was a light from the inside of the world and I went out in it with a pan of feed for the chickens half expecting at any minute to come up against a soft barrier against which I could brace my hands but which I could never pierce. Of course, I found no such thing, although perhaps it was only that I didn't go far enough. The hens clustered at my feet, clucking approval and darting their sleek beaks into the dirt. Even as I stood for a moment with the pan on my hip to watch them, I saw them turn the real colors of the earth up under their feet. Dun and ochre, white roots and a blue-black beetle. Then the sun cleared the trees and green came back into the world.

I am at the end, the last page which I will turn and lay on the back of the manuscript before squaring the whole thing and sliding it into its drawer. I admit I have never looked forward to blankness quite so much, and, though I thought this was my only story, I find myself already imagining the next project. A chronicle, I think. An observation of the weather written in the form of letters, though not exclusively to you, Ingrid.

*Dear Jacob*, I might write, *a slow fog today, smoking along the ridges. Apple cake for breakfast, four eggs from the laying hen.*

*Dear Dad, It is very windy here, Love Alice.*

Right now, however, I am still on the last page, confronted by its final border, and beside me you are very still, a mist over your eyes as if what you see is a screen behind which other shapes cast and flicker. But this morning, when I lifted you out of your basinet, you reached out to me and to me alone. When I held you against my chest, I felt the tense curl of your body press against mine as both our hearts slowed and realigned.

When you are older, Ingrid, I will teach you how to look at a map. How to recognize the dun squares of the fields, the ripple of the forest. Where the waters flow and where they turn back on themselves. More importantly, I will teach you the compass rose and how, no matter where you stand, you are in the center of its flowering. Straight ahead of you is always north, Ingrid, the direction of mountains, and behind you, in the deep past, is the place where the waters empty out and lose themselves.

It was still very early and though dust from the chicken yard rimmed my ankles my nightgown, fresh from the laundry, was still bright and crisp in its creases. I unbuttoned its top few buttons and slipped you inside, between my breasts, where you hummed sleepily and scratched me with your sharp nails. The smell of you, orange and yeasty and rising, wafted up to me as if it were the smell of myself: a little sour with the night's sweat, a briny slick—Jacob or Daniel, it doesn't matter who—damp on my thighs as I walked. No one else was awake. No one else in the world but us two. I held you against my chest. You wrapped your fist in my hair. I laid a cake and a pitcher on the table for the morning meal and together we went up both sets of stairs to the little room at the top of the house where, despite all the stories we have been told, we opened the stiff door to find nothing more than two dusty beds and a dead bird, the spidery skeleton peeking through its drift of feathers. We stayed there for a long time watching the light change. Beneath us, the house unfolded. Its morning sounds heaved up and down—a crash of cutlery in the sink, men's voices; a bird singing close then far then close again, something scratching inside the walls—and the light thinned yellow then silver then a pure, hard white.

What happened, I feel I can tell you now, is that nothing happened. First there was a maelstrom in which all the things of the world whirled and collided. In that time, there was no difference between a rocking chair and a black bird's wing, a sock and a boulder laced with veins of quartz. For a long while, eons I suspect, all these things bashed into each other, causing a great commotion, terrible damage, until, their velocity finally unsustainable, they began to funnel down into a tighter and tighter point. Everything that was dark and spacious, ravenous and insurmountable was squeezed into an unbearable pip as fine as the hole punched by needle.

As we all know, what comes afterwards is the thread, orderly and tense. Time, in other words, which drags the great plates of the world together and binds them but ultimately can be shorn through with nothing more significant than a pair of sharp scissors, or, in extremity, your very own teeth.

*Dear Ingrid,* I will surely write to you, *a soft rain today, the new leaves flattened silver against the limbs.*

*Dear Ingrid,* I will say in another season, *the earth still turning, winter coming on. And apple cake for breakfast, of course. A little thermos full of coffee to warm you on your walk.*

This morning I laid you down on my mother's dusty quilt and watched you for a moment while you held your hands up over your face and opened and closed them. "Just now," Daniel said in response to something I couldn't hear. He sounded close, standing perhaps at the very foot of the stairs, but he turned and his voice trailed away. "Do you want me to wait?" I heard him ask, and then his heavy tread and the creak of the risers fading as he went down them, the pop of the screen door as he left the house.

I rose, went to the window and looked out over the yard and the henhouse, the meadow and the sturdy hives around which the bees rose and fell, their individual lives nothing more than blots against the green finery of the grass and the blank, white walls of their homes. My mother rose and went to her window. Before her were the mountains, behind her the long, disastrous slide to the sea. She was only a child and the fingerprints she left on the glass were child-sized smudges, portending nothing, and yet behind her Thalia, her fine, horsetail hair wrapped in papers and pinned about her head like a crown, watched her with a very specific sorrow.

When my mother turned around again, she saw her sister had settled herself, oversized and steaming, at the foot of her bed with a brush in her hand. "Come here," Thalia might have said, "I'll tell you a story," and, for 100 crackling strokes through my mother's hair, her sister gave them both a little more room.

"Let me tell you a story," I said to you, Ingrid, but I was looking out the window still and behind me your only response was to rustle against the quilt, grunting as you kicked your legs out in front of you like a frog. The End, I will write in only a few minutes. I won't be able to help myself.

I went to the window and saw Daniel, an axe slung over his shoulder, talking to Jacob who was carrying a gun. I turned and fetched you and held you so you could drum your feet against the windowsill as we watched them talk, the yard radiating out around their center. You panted and kicked, danced in my hands, and my nightgown caught in an obscure breeze that jetted through the broken pane and puffed out around my thighs. It was a cool wind, come from very far away. For just a moment it touched us both and then it was gone.

When it comes around again, we will not recognize it, Ingrid, and perhaps that is best. There are already so many distractions in the world, so many shadows that might keep us from seeing what is directly in front of us. Two friends, for example, moving away from each other as they bend toward separate tasks. One stands a log on its end on top of a deeply scarred

stump and raises the axe above his head. The other tracks diago-
nally up the rise and stops in the last band of sunlight just at the
lacy edge of the forest's shadow. He tents a hand over his eyes
and looks back, standing so still it is as if he and the nearest tree
and the gun are all the same long line canting backward. Finally,
the axe comes down and, as one friend straightens to wipe the
sweat out of his eyes, the other raises a hand and waves.

"Goodbye, goodbye," he seems to say and then he turns
and walks into the forest.

# Author's Note

This book is in part a pastiche of themes, images, icons and reoccurring oddities borrowed from sources that will be familiar to most readers, particularly those who had western childhoods. The unlucky girls as well as the terribly lucky ones, the dutiful sisters, transformed brothers, the itty bitty and the great big, the animals who talk or plot or watch or lend guidance, and always, always, the vast, impenetrable forest owe their origin in my private mythos to the work of the Brothers' Grimm, Hans Christian Anderson, Charles Perrault and Lewis Carrol in my distant past, and to Italo Calvino's collection *Italian Folktales*, the disquieting stories of Georges-Olivier Châteaureynaud and the unflappable stories of Lyudmila Petrushevskaya in my more recent readings. It is to these authors, among others, that this novel owes its sense of its symbols as echoing along a continuity of like images, echoes which crowd into the blanks.

Many of the particulars in the tales told here, however, owe their genesis to a much more specific source: the myths, cosmologies and cultural histories of the Eastern Band of the Cherokee. When I first began to conceive of Alice Small I started with an image—a woman, little more than a girl, looking through a window at another woman, dressed in white, with her back turned. Over and over, as I went about my humdrum, sometimes extraordinary, days this picture flashed in my mind, and, as I examined it, the image began to spin out themes: something about jealousy, about betrayal, about deep, abiding love, about wanting to be let in. When I started writing the book that would become *Hex*, the girl outside looking in became a person—Alice Small in the ferocious flesh—with both a history and a place to which she was tethered. Simultaneously, the fairy tales I grew up with began to seem insufficient to fully explore this woman who came from such a different geographic and psychological place from me. At that time, I discovered James Mooney's exhaustive ethnographic work *Myths and Sacred Formulas of the Cherokee*, primarily collected among the Eastern Cherokee living in the Qualla reservation in western North Carolina in successive field seasons between 1887 and 1890. Mooney's work was originally published by the US Bureau of American Ethnology in 1891 and 1900, then gathered into a single volume and reissued in 1982 by Charles and Randy Elder in collaboration with Cherokee Heritage Books, an educational program of the Museum of the Cherokee Indian and the Qualla Arts and Crafts Mutual in Cherokee, North Carolina. The stories I found within were ground shaking on a scope matched in my writing life only by the moment, in graduate school, when I stopped thinking of fairy tales as familiar, children's stories and opened new eyes on a language wild, fleet and strange.

The World Below the World is a Cherokee world and the figures that live there and topside in the mountains I share with them are: the owl husband, the rooster husband, the husband that is the sun, the woman who enters the mountain, the woman who flings her blood into the stream, the beautiful sisters with heads like pumpkins and the shy feet of dogs, the Thunder Brothers who ride horned serpents and sit on turtles only nominally disguised as chairs, and other peoples, themes and turns of language besides. Yet, even as I sifted through the wealth of what Mooney compiled, I was more and more troubled by the fact that what I was receiving had been filtered through a perception alien and necessarily revisionist, or even hostile, to the culture that produced these tales, in spite of what seems to have been Mooney's own best and most sympathetic intentions. By all accounts and evidence, James Mooney was a conscientious ethnographer, an exhaustive archivist and a meticulous collector of the names, tribal affiliations, myths, histories and cosmologies of the American Indian peoples at a time when they were suffering what was arguably the most organized, systemic, at once bloodthirsty and coldly bureaucratic program of genocide seen in the modern world right up until March 20, 1933, when the Dachau concentration camp opened its gates outside of Munich. He seems to have been a scientist perpetually drawn to the edge of disaster—a kind of triage ethnographer. Mooney documented the Ghost Dance movement after the death of the Hunkpapa Lakota holy man and tribal chief Sitting Bull in 1890; a few years earlier James Mooney went into the last Cherokee strongholds on their traditional lands within two generations of the peoples' forced removal and relocation to western reservations along the Trail of Tears following the Indian Removal Act of 1830 and gathered everything he could. The results, particularly in the case of *Myths of the Cherokee*, are collections of data, images, oral histories, tribal manuscripts and lore that conscientiously seek to document a culture as it faced eradication through assimilation or massacre.

In the introduction to his text, Mooney writes, "The enforced deportation, two generations ago, from accustomed scenes and surroundings did more at a single stroke to obliterate Indian ideas than could have been accomplished by fifty years of slow development," (*Myths of the Cherokee*, 12). Later, in the concise timeline he devotes to the Cherokee peoples' cultural and political development both precontact and then in conjunction with European settlers, Mooney describes the removal of 1838–39 as a "tragedy [that] may well exceed in weight of grief and pathos any other passage in American history." He even hints toward the culpability of the European aggressors in this matter, describing the mobs that looted and pillaged in the wake of the soldiers who had swept down on the Cherokee villages and farmsteads as a "lawless rabble," and "outlaws"(12).

However, at least in this text, Mooney constrains his implied criticism to individuals—the lawless rabble, a few bad seed soldiers—and does not go so far as to condemn the systems present behind these vicious expressions of institutionalized racism, the ultimate aim of which was to exert the force of the dominant culture's military might not in an act of defensive war, or even really as a means to territorial expansion, but as a theft, pure and simple, of lands, materials and resources. I cannot know what Mooney thought of the moral identity of a country that could commit such crimes. From my temporal and cultural remove, I cannot really know how he—a product, after all, of his times—came to rationalize his work among the people of the Eastern band of the Cherokee with his position as a paid employee of the government that had instigated their liquidation (was he regretful? Radicalized? Subversive or scholarly? Did he identify? Exculpate? Did he rage? Sigh?). I do not intend here to judge the motivations of someone who has, after all, left so much of value behind. But I do know what *I* think on these subjects and I record here a deep unease with my own appropriation of Cherokee texts sourced through the language of a translator who is, ultimately and in spite of what appear to have been his intentions, the oppressor. Consider this moment from *Myths* found in the section of Quadruped Myths: "The unpleasant smell of the Groundhog's head was given it by the other animals to punish an insulting remark made by him in council. *The story is a vulgar one, without wit enough to make it worth recording*" (279, italics mine). I am right to be uneasy, Reader; so too should you be.

And yet, as this book's themes began to develop and solidify, as Alice's own story became concrete and then dissolved again into the mists of the stories she herself was telling, it began to seem more and more appropriate to me that the main source text for this project was one plagued with broken lineage, corruption, manipulation, a subtext of power and abuse. Alice is a motherless child born of a motherless child, a girl given very little care and so due a tremendous store of luck. What Alice knows of the world and herself in it she has had to invent from the scraps of a history shredded before her insertion into the timeline. Though I am by no means conflating the suffering of a single fictional character with the very real, ongoing, struggles of the American Indian peoples to navigate and preserve their cultural identity in the face of its near eradication, I am saying there is a sympathy here; an echo, however faint, that reflects the damage done when the world we inhabit must be created forever anew because the people who should have been our forebears are gone. Carried away from us and with them a large portion of who we are, who we might have been believed to be.

And so, in spite of the violent subtext of history that haunts his work, I am still grateful to James Mooney. To his memory, and to all those who seek the hand behind the artifact, I say a heartfelt thank you. Yet, please know that these stories are not history, but rather a living thing, echoing with all the voices that have come before in the ongoing storytelling tradition that still exists among the Eastern and Oklahoma Bands of the Cherokee. Without the telling there is no tale.

# Acknowledgments

My grateful thanks to the editors whose magazines published individual stories from this novel:

"King of Hearts, Queen of Spades," *Black Warrior Review
Online*, ed. Kirby Johnson
   "King of Hearts, Queen of Spades," *Spolia*, ed. Jessa Crispin
   "The White Horse," *xo Orpheus, Fifty New Myths*, ed. Kate
Bernheimer

This book owes a creative debt to some specific authors
whose energy, indignation, sorrow and spirit of play I've been

uprooted by time and again. Without the work of Kathryn Davis, Noy Holland, A.S. Byatt, Rikki DuCornet, Barbara Comyns and Kate Bernheimer my own sentences would be chapped and paltry, creatures most miserable indeed. I also owe a great personal debt to Kate Bernheimer beyond the boundaries of her work. If she had not been my teacher at the University of Alabama, if she had not been my mentor and friend beyond that, if she had not said read this, then read this, then read this and this and this…so much would have gone unsaid, unthought.

Other sources consulted during the writing of this novel include: the works of the Brothers' Grimm, Charles Perrault, Hans Christian Anderson, Lewis Carrol, Italo Calvino, Georges-Olivier Châteaureynaud, Lyudmila Petrushevskaya, *A Modern Herbal* by Margaret Grieve, *Disability, Deformity and Disease in the Grimm's Fairy Tales* by Ann Schmiesing, *Individualism and Collectivism (New Directions in Social Psychology)* by Harry C. Triandis, *Narcissistic Wounds: A Clinical Perspective* by Judy Cooper and Nilda Maxwell, *The Hero With A Thousand Faces* by Joseph Campbell, *A Short History of Myth* by Karen Armstrong, *Impossible Exchange* by Jean Baudrillard, *To The Lighthouse* by Virginia Woolf, "In the Hall of the Mountain King," (*Peer Gynt*) composed by Edvard Grieg, "At Seventeen" written and performed by Janis Ian, *Lohengrin* by Richard Wagner and the architecture and frank madness of Neuschwanstein Castle in Bavaria, Germany.

In terms of practical support, I owe a great deal to the following institutions and individuals: Dr. Roy Fluhrer at the Fine Arts Center for fiscal support and public exclamations of triumph; the Metropolitan Arts Council of Greenville, South Carolina for sending me to read; Vermont Studio Center for giving me a room to write in and a river to write beside. I am deeply indebted to the readers through whom this book passed on its way to completion: John Pursley III, Melinda Zeder, Suzan Zeder, Claire Bateman, Mike Stutzman, Carl Petersen, Hilary Plum—thank you for getting past page fifty, and for your belief in what you found there. Thank you as well to the fellow authors at FC2 who have read with me over the past few years and welcomed me again into their company with this novel: Lance Olsen, Jeffrey DeShell, Noy Holland, Michael Mejia, Matt Roberson, Joanna Ruocco, Elisabeth Sheffield, Susan Steinberg, Michael Martone, Jessica Lee Richardson, Hilary Plum. And to Dan Waterman, Lou Robinson, and all the staff at the University of Alabama Press: many, many thanks for making the idea a thing.

Thank you to my mother and my father who, when I said I wanted to be a writer, said, "We know." Thank you to my grandmothers who took me to see dragons and asked that, when I did write a novel, it have some cats in it. Thank you to my sister who listened to a lot of stories in the dark and never once pretended to fall asleep.

Helen and Louisa: you are right in the middle of everything, looking out.

John Pursley III: without you I would never have become a human girl, but would still be a bit of fluff, a lost left shoe, a thistle at the edge of the forest. All the good things in my life come from you.